Heartbreak Hotel

Heartbreak Hotel

GABRIELLE BURTON

CHARLES SCRIBNER'S SONS
New York

This novel is a work of fiction. Any references to historical events; to real people, living or dead; or to real locales are intended only to give the fiction a setting in historical reality. Other names, characters, places, and incidents are either the product of the author's imagination or are used fictitiously, and their resemblance, if any, to real-life counterparts is entirely coincidental.

Library of Congress Cataloging-in-Publication Data

Burton, Gabrielle.
Heartbreak Hotel.

I. Title.
PS3552.U7728H4   1986   813'.54   86-13963
ISBN 0-684-18594-6

Copyright © 1986 Gabrielle Burton
All rights reserved
Published simultaneously in Canada by Collier Macmillan Canada, Inc.
Composition by Maryland Linotype Composition Co.
Baltimore, Maryland
Manufactured by Fairfield Graphics, Fairfield, Pennsylvania
Designed by Ruth Kolbert
First Edition

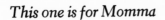

This one is for Momma

Without Eleanor Torrey West's Ossabaw Island Project, this book would not have been written. I am also grateful to the MacDowell Colony and to Yaddo for their support.

I am indebted to the following people who joined in the fight to save Heartbreak Hotel when the City Fathers were trying to close it down.

Roger Burton
&
Marilyn Abel
Peter Child
Paula Estey
Ray Federman
Lucy Ferriss
Leslie Fiedler
Sally Fiedler
Elaine Ford
Tony Gaenslen
Al Greenberg
Bruce Jackson
Norma Kassirer
Ward Mohrfeld
Betsy Rapoport
Ilene Raymond
Mary Richert
Jeff Simon
Liz Sonneborn
Miller Williams

ACKNOWLEDGMENTS

Portions of this work originally appeared in *Maenad* and *Pig Iron* magazines. Grateful acknowledgment is made to the following:

The passage on p. 192 from *The Bird of Night* by Susan Hill. Copyright © 1972. Reprinted by permission of Hamish Hamilton Limited and Richard Scott Simon, Ltd.

The passage on pp. 187–88 from *Women Who Kill* by Ann Jones. Copyright © 1980 by Ann Jones. Reprinted by permission of Holt, Rinehart, and Winston.

The passage on p. 192 from "The Evil Eye" in *The Awful Rowing Toward God* by Anne Sexton. Copyright © 1975 by Loring Conant, Jr., Executor of the Estate of Anne Sexton. Reprinted by permission of Houghton Mifflin Company and by the Sterling Lord Agency, Inc.

The passage on p. 82 from *From Time to Time* by Hannah Tillich. Copyright © 1973 by Hannah Tillich. Reprinted by permission of Stein and Day Publishers.

The passage on p. 193 from *A Vision* by William Butler Yeats. Copyright 1937 by W.B. Yeats, renewed 1965 by Bertha Georgie Yeats and Anne Butler Yeats. Reprinted by permission of The Macmillan Company, U.S., and by A.P. Watt Ltd. on behalf of Michael B. Yeats and Macmillan London Ltd.

The passage on p. 40 by Frank Reynolds as told to Michael McClure, *Free-Wheelin' Frank*. Copyright 1967.

The lyrics on p. 195 from "Heartbreak Hotel" by Mae Boren Axton, Tommy Durden, and Elvis Presley. Copyright © 1956 Tree Publishing Co., Inc. Copyright renewed. All rights reserved. International Copyright secured. Used by permission of the publisher.

The lyrics on p. 100 from "Daddy's Little Girl" by Bobby Burke and Horace Gerlach © 1949 Cherio Corporation. Copyright renewed 1977 Cherio Corporation. International Copyright secured. All rights reserved.

ix

Heartbreak Hotel

PROLOGUE

She heard the car edging toward her before she saw it in the rear-view mirror, it was the same blue Ford that had gunned motor behind her at the last light, nudging her, goosing her, there are always people like that around when you're on a motorcycle, you keep an eye on them, but if you really thought about all they meant, you'd never ride again, she automatically moved to the right but the sound stayed constant, she moved farther, on the shoulder now because the sound was louder, and just before the car in the mirror and the car on the bike became one sickening blue flash, she saw she was going to be gravely injured, "Oh Shit," she said, and then she was flying.

The Intensive Care Unit at Our Lady Of Victory Hospital is a white rotunda with a round desk in the center. Each room in the circular wall has a glass front which permits the nurses at the center desk to glance up at any time, swivel, and monitor the machines over the patients' beds. Ringing the inside of the round desk, small machines audibly and visibly signal any critical changes on the patients' machines, in case the nurses are not glancing up.

The staff changes every eight hours, but there's no ordinary hospital routine, because each patient is extraordinary. Time is different in the ICU: there are sometimes lulls when the staff grabs a bite, smokes a cigarette, or chews the fat, but never with any predictability; at any time and many times during the day and the night, lights flash, bells clang, and all hell breaks loose.

At the moment, a patient, vacating Room #7, is being wheeled out through the swinging doors down the hall to a new room: a promotion of sorts, this patient will still require round-the-clock nursing care, but of a little less intensity. The sheets are barely changed before the ICU has NO VACANCY again.

"It's Margaret Valentine," one of the Emergency Room nurses helping with the hookups tells an ICU nurse.

"The curator?"

"Yeah."

"Jesus. What happened?"

"Hit and run. She was on a motorcycle. Comatose, massive fractures, internal injuries. . ."

"Head?"

"No visible marks, but EEG's all over the place."

"Prognosis?"

"Not so hot."

"Family out there?"

"Still trying to reach them."

A little flurry of excitement zips up the usual ICU sky-high adrenaline: Margaret Valentine's kind of a celebrity, there'll probably be reporters. At the round desk, a nurse swivels her chair to face #7's glass wall, her eye on #7's EEG needle which skips to my Lou.

INTROIT

1

"I hear the Museum'll be closing up shop," the cabbie says. "I'll be sorry to see it, me and the family spent some nice Sundays up there."

"Where'd you hear that?" Daisy asks, she hands a fiver through the window.

"This fare, that fare," the cabbie shrugs, "I hear a lot in this business."

"Same with me," Daisy says, "no, keep the change."

"Good luck, lady," he calls.

She nods, swings open the wrought-iron gates, passes under the curved arch that says: HEARTBREAK HOTEL. She passes the large sign that says:

Houses bearing this symbol   are designated official havens for employees of the **Museum Of The Revolution, Buffalo, New York.**

She moves swiftly down the elm-lined driveway, unlocks the ornately carved door of the mansion, and passes through the vestibule into the cavernous hall.

High on a wooden beam above Daisy's head, the enormous tapestry made by her ex-Mother Superior moves disjointedly in the draft like a scarecrow, its woven Latin words spell out the *quasi modo* Introit for Low Sunday. The colors of the stained glass windows are flat, the ceiling skylight dull, Daisy's shoes tap and echo as she passes the gloomy bookcases filled with old registers containing the names of all former residents of Heartbreak Hotel. To the right of the closed French doors that lead into the living room, the current hotel register rests on an antique Bible stand, open to a page that says: At the moment, we are seven living in this house.

One is Daisy,
Two is Pearl,
Three is Rita,

Four is Meg,
Five is Gretchen,
Six is Maggie,
Seven's Quasi,
"Quasi's in a coma," Daisy says, she shuts the French doors behind her.

Pearl stops playing and looks up from the piano. "How can you tell?" Pearl asks.

Maggie, sitting on the windowseat, flicks her eyes from Pearl to Daisy.

"She's had a terrible accident," Daisy says, she crosses the room and sits at the library table.

Meg stands to the side of the fireplace and practices karate kicks. "She *is* a terrible accident," Meg says.

"You and Pearl aren't very nice," Gretchen says from her armchair, her legs are extended, five-pound weights Velcro-strapped to her ankles, she raises and lowers each leg alternately.

"Oh for Heaven's sake," Rita says, she stops filing her nails, "What happened?"

"She wiped out on Meg's motorcycle," Daisy says.

"*My* motorcycle, I'll kill her, I just sent in my insurance last week, I'll cut her heart out, I'll stomp her. . . ."

"She may never come out of it," Daisy says.

". . . hump like a beetle shell!" Meg shouts, but Daisy's voice turned inside out strikes core, echos, reverberates, strikes again until the room is filled with silent sound.

Rita bolts first.

The draft from the hall rolls in. Pearl sighs, gets up and shuts the French doors Rita left open, pokes up the fire, returns to the piano bench. This morning, we were seven living in this house, Pearl thinks, now one of us is in a coma. Gretchen raises her legs. Seven is an infinite number, Maggie thinks. None of us will get off scot-free, Meg thinks. Gretchen lowers her legs. There is a growth of stillness in this house, Daisy thinks.

In the bedroom directly above the living room, the vibrator starts.

"Rita's polishing her shoes again," Pearl says.

No one laughs.

Pearl shrugs.

Pearl is on health leave from the Museum Of The Revolution as they all are, except for Quasi whom Pearl says has been on health leave since birth. Two months on/two months off is the normal work schedule, but Pearl works one-month shifts. Pearl is a comic. Comics tire faster.

The Museum Of The Revolution is twenty city blocks long and ever expanding. Pearl works the 20th City Block. Four comics working the high teens have killed themselves this year. Not one died laughing.

Pearl hardly ever laughs. On her months off, she flies like a homing pigeon to Heartbreak Hotel, a renovated Victorian mansion that, like all the rest homes maintained by the Museum, is a house of shifting times and populations. Maybe there is a difference. While Pearl shrugs, Daisy narrows her eyes, cocks her ears, and thinks: A growth of stillness *hides* in this house, is it benign or malignant?

The vibrator whirs.

Gretchen the cheerleader gets up, does three perfect cartwheels within the borders of the Persian Sarouk, sits back down, and resumes her leg lifts.

Although one month into her health leave, Gretchen still wears one of her Museum Guide's uniforms: a crotch-high white pleated skirt, a nipple-busting royal blue sweater with a large **MR** logo on the front, white vinyl boots. She has fantastic legs. They are so smooth and shiny people have a hard time not touching them. Gretchen works the Museum's 1st City Block which is not as easy as it sounds. The 1st City Block has more exhibitions per square foot than anyplace in the world. The rooms are warehouse size and have wall-to-wall bleachers. A typical room contains the College of Cardinals, the Supreme Court, beauty contest promoters, male gynecologists, Sears and Roebuck servicemen, and Norman Mailer. Each room on the 1st Block is so predictable the guide has to hustle to keep attention from glazing over. 1st Block guides are generally cheerleaders, drum majorettes, geisha girls, and doctors' wives. Everyone rushes to get into Gretchen's group. She yeas and rahhs and sisboombahs, she cartwheels past the peepholes. Mini versions of her pompoms have sold so well in the souvenir shop a full-size version is in the works. "And people thought I'd be washed up after high school," Gretchen said on her thirty-second birthday.

All the Guides are living exhibits, Pearl says.

Gretchen chalks that remark and a good many others of Pearl's up to plain old green with envy. On her health leaves, Gretchen also always chooses to come to Heartbreak Hotel which she fell in love with at first sight. Pearl's concurrent presence three times a year is a cross that reminds Gretchen there is no Heaven on earth. If she holds on long enough, she figures Pearl will go to some other rest home. So what if Pearl came here first, Gretchen says, she can leave first.

Through the ceiling, the vibrator drones.

Pearl notes that her shoes need polishing.

Upstairs, someplace in the middle of her forty-third sequential orgasm, Rita begins to croak, "Nothing says loving like something in the oven," but the forty-fourth hits her, she can say no more.

"Hunchbacks are supposed to be good luck," Daisy says.
"Maybe I should get one for my key chain," Pearl says.
Gretchen clicks her tongue in disapproval.
Maggie sips her bourbon and doesn't say anything. Maggie Magpie, Rita calls her, because as Pearl hardly ever laughs off work, Maggie hardly ever talks. "Why talk shop?" she said once. Words are Maggie's trade: she is a simultaneous translator at the Museum. She has a remarkable talent for languages. Pearl said once that Maggie speaks tongues without an accent, and nobody knows if it's a joke. Scientists from the University of Buffalo have asked seven times in seven languages to study Maggie, but she has declined seven times in seven different languages. "I'm just happy to have a full-time job," she says. "They're not easy to get." Before Daisy hired her, she was employed as a Kelly girl with a reputation for discretion and neat work.
The only movement in the room is the raising and lowering of shiny limbs.
"What happened to my bike?" Meg asks.
"Totalled," Daisy says.
"Fuck her to death," Meg says.
Gretchen frowns.
"I really could kill her," Meg says.
Daisy frowns.
"It's not only my bike, the insurance'll cover my bike, it's the thought of that slime *touching* my bike," Meg says.
Gretchen thinks of swamps, of slugs, of that drooling oozing hairy thick white thing touching her the way it touched Meg's bike, she speeds up her leg lifts. "It's a blessing," she says.
"Goddam your bike and your blessings to Hell," Pearl says.
Gretchen bends down and adjusts the straps on her weights.
"What's your beef?" Meg says to Pearl. Meg doesn't move but Maggie the translator watches her back off. Meg is a cop by profession, a cop by nature, and her antennae know business when they hear it: why tangle with Pearl now?, Meg thinks, Pearl's a psycho and a dangerous one, there'll be a day Pearly'll be walking down a dark street. Meg can't tangle with anyone now, she's on a special health leave: Special Assignment For The Curator, Meg calls it; six months' parole in Daisy's custody, the judge calls it. Meg has done four months, one week, and three days of her time.

"How about something to eat?" Daisy asks, although she privately started a fast from solid foods when the news about Quasi came.

Daisy is an ex-nun. An ex-missionary. Just your run-of-the-mill recovering Catholic, Pearl says about Daisy, who is currently the atheist curator of the Museum Of The Revolution. The women generally would follow Daisy anywhere, but right now they all follow her to the kitchen because she's an excellent cook, and they don't have any other place to go.

As they pass through the main hall, the words on the Introit tapestry leap out at Maggie, "What does that mean?" she asks Meg. "How the Hell would I know what it means?" Meg says, "It's in Dutchy talk." But Maggie wasn't asking Meg what the words say, she has already silently speedread the Latin words, *"quasi modo geniti infantes . . . ,"* simultaneously translated them into English:

> *"Wherefore laying away all malice,*
> *and all guile, and dissimulations,*
> *and envies, and all detractions,*
> *As newborn babes,*
> *desire the rational milk without guile,*
> *that thereby you may grow unto salvation."*
> —PETER, Chapter 2, Verses 1 & 2

Maggie has passed under this tapestry before, but hasn't noticed until now that it has Quasi's name, doesn't understand what it means in Latin *or* in English, feels stupid, what's the good of knowing words if they don't tell you something, feels anxious, hurries on to catch up with the others.

Daisy turns around from the open fridge, "How about pigs' knuckles in beer?" she asks.

"An inspired choice for unexpected drop-ins," Pearl says.

Hold the pigs' knuckles on mine, Maggie gets ready to say.

But Daisy's just kidding, they're not going to have pigs' knuckles, she's almost a vegetarian, she puts everybody to work chopping vegetables, except Gretchen who says, "I don't want my hands to smell of garlic." Gretchen stands by a counter, leafing through a copy of *Time* magazine to the Transitions page. "Why do I always get the turnip?" Meg asks. "Typecasting," Pearl says. Meg, cleaver in hand, starts toward Pearl, "Do this beauty, Meg," Daisy says, she tosses a huge beefsteak tomato through the air, in a flash Meg's cleaver is on the counter, she catches the tomato triumphantly, holds it up for inspection, "Not a bruise," she says, "That's from handling dynamite." "Wonderful," Pearl mumbles. "What'd you say?" Meg says, her hand draws back to aim the tomato at Pearl, Rita walks in.

Rita smiles vaguely, everyone in the room secretly wills her hands still. As people want to touch Gretchen's legs, people want to touch all parts of Rita, they want to tear her apart. Rita is used to this reaction. Before she became the belly dancer at the Museum, she was a carhop at an A&W root beer stand. There are always about her faint but definite aromas. This very moment, although she has been on leave nearly two months, the kitchen is permeated with incense, clove, and cinnamon. "Might be old root beer," Pearl speculates sotto voce. Daisy cuts her eyes to Pearl. "Those are her *roots*," Pearl persists. Pearl falls silent.

One is Daisy the curator, Two is Pearl the comic, Three is Rita the belly dancer, Four is Meg the cop, Five is Gretchen the cheerleader, Six is Maggie the translator, and the sounds of the absent Seventh, Quasi the surd, fill the room.

"You all hate her," Meg says, "but you're too chickenshit to say so."

Everyone stares at Meg, except Rita who stares at Gretchen's brown shiny thighs.

"Who cares if she's in a coma!" Meg growls.

Now Rita stares at Meg too. "I care," she says.

"You care about anything in underpants," Meg says.

Rita throws her hands up in disgust, turns her back to Meg.

"*Est-ce qu'il y a quelque chose qu'on peut faire?*" Maggie whispers, "Can we do anything?" she translates.

"Either way, they'll call," Daisy says.

Although only Daisy knows she does it, each waits for the call.

Pearl lies on her bed, a hard board covered by a thin piece of foam, and stares out the window at the tree. It is late May, but the tree is just beginning to bud. Pearl has watched this tree, an enormous elm, bud, flower, change, drop, sixteen seasons now. If Pearl were a painter instead of a comic, she would paint a series of this tree seen through this twelve-paned window from this particular angle in Spring, Summer, Autumn, Winter. She'd call the series: Depression. Pearl lies on her board, gives her full attention to the tree, and hardly sees it.

Meg the cop thinks about dispatching a police car to the hospital to arrest Quasi, thinks about calling the station to check the accident report, if Quasi crossed the Canadian border on her joyride Meg can get Interpol in, throw the book at her. The only call she makes is to her insurance agent.

Gretchen thinks about bodies falling apart, about doing her Mark Eden Breast Exercises.

Maggie thinks about getting a drink and gets it.

Rita thinks about polishing her shoes.

Daisy thinks about men. Her thoughts narrow or broaden to various men in her life she has not gone to bed with, their faces flash before her like the Stations of the Cross, she counts them off like beads on a rosary. She sighs. IN THE MUSEUM OF THE REVOLUTION THERE IS A VAST SOUNDPROOFED ROOM FULL OF SIGHS FOR ALL THE BOYS AND ALL THE GIRLS AND ALL THE WOMEN AND ALL THE MEN WHO WERE LEFT UNTOUCHED FOR THE WRONG REASONS. OUTSIDE THIS ROOM, LIKE A RECORDING STUDIO IN SESSION/ AN OPERATING ROOM/ A CHURCH SANCTUARY, THE VIGIL LIGHT PERPETUALLY BURNS, BUT THE ROOM ITSELF IS ALWAYS LOCKED, TUNNELS EVER INWARD TO AN ENDLESS CAVERN, FOR THE SOUND OF THOSE COLLECTED SIGHS OF REGRET UNDILUTED WOULD BE UNBEARABLE. Daisy thinks of death.

Behind a glass wall in Room #7 in the hospital's Intensive Care Unit, a form on a bed swells and heaves and makes unintelligible sounds. Quasi hurts. All the cuffs and kicks and buffets of Quasi's experience are as nothing next to this pain. Quasi is exploding with pain.

"Makes you sick," one of the nurses says. She speaks literally. She barely makes it to the bowl. God, I hope I'm not pregnant, she thinks.

"Those goddam motorcycles," a silver-haired doctor says. "I'm not a goddam mechanic to put something like this together again."

In a skillful balance of boldness and humility, a new RN widens her eyes and says, "All the students say You're a miracle worker, Doctor."

"Is that so?" he says and winks at her across Quasi.

The doorbell at Heartbreak Hotel rings, "I've got it," Meg says to Gretchen who's racing toward the door. She waits until Gretchen goes back into the living room.

She stares coldly at the police reporter inquiring about Quasi.

"Unknown, unrelated," she says.

"Come on Meg, she had this address pinned on her," the reporter says, "Give me a break."

"I'll give you a break," Meg says. "If I ever see you within five hundred yards of this house again, you'll be covering the story in traction."

"Who was it?" Gretchen asks.

"Guy at work selling tickets for the Policeman's Ball," Meg says.

"You going?" Gretchen asks, she pivots in dance circles around the room.

Meg gives her a look that'd chill the dead.

"Pardon *me* for living," Gretchen says and whirls away.

Daisy calls the hospital. We'll call you back, they say. Who are you, they ask.

"Who are you?" Pearl asks.

"I said I was family," Daisy says.

"You said you were family," Pearl says.

Simultaneous translation, Maggie thinks, then feels shallow for getting caught in the sounds and not the meanings, Concentrate, *Dummkopf*, she tells herself.

Pearl feels guilty. She could never claim kinship with Quasi. She has trouble claiming kinship with herself.

Meg is silent. She's already down on record: Unknown, unrelated.

Gretchen pivots and pretends she doesn't hear the conversation.

Each woman has a flash of family:

Gretchen thinks of her Ma.

Pearl thinks of her Daddy.

Maggie thinks of her Gramma.

Meg thinks of her Uncle.

Daisy thinks of her ex-Mother Superior.

Upstairs, Rita thinks about her first cousin a moment too long.

All the lights at Heartbreak Hotel blow, a woman screams: Rita has caught her hair in the shoe polisher. "Law of averages caught up with her," says Pearl who assumes it's pubic hair caught in the vibrator.

But Pearl's wrong this time. Rita sits on her bed with tears in her eyes and an electric shoe polisher flush to her scalp. Daisy has to unwind strand by strand by strand and finally just yank. Everyone winces. Rita has gorgeous hair. Gretchen keeps her eyes fixed on Rita's hair and pretends not to notice the round bed, the Roman red heart-shaped headboard, the mirror on the ceiling, and the lifesize statue of a naked woman that has gorgeous hair. "She can sit on her hair," Gretchen says.

"Pity she doesn't," Pearl says. Last month, Rita got it caught in the Mixmaster. Daisy had to unwind strand by strand by strand and finally just yank. Last week, Rita stood talking animatedly in front of an elaborate candelabra that cast her in inviting light, Your hair is on fire, someone shouted. Excuse me, Rita said, I'm awfully sorry to be so much trouble, Rita said, Please forgive me, Rita said as people beat on her hair. Then there was the time she caught it in the escalator which Pearl doesn't even want to think of. "Why don't you wear it in a ponytail?" Pearl asks.

Meg shakes her head vehemently No. "Get it cut," she says.

"You should wear it in braids," Gretchen says.

The idea of Rita in braids is so absurd everybody thinks Gretchen is making a rare joke.

Everybody laughs except Maggie and Meg who says, "Only whores wear their hair that long."

"Only Army recruits wear their hair like yours," Rita says.

"Go to Hell," Meg says.

"Kiss off," Rita says.

"Girls Girls," Pearl says.

Maggie stares into her drink.

After they all leave her room, Rita examines her hair, assesses the damage, and does a cost/benefit analysis. She decides to get her hair cut, but doesn't tell anyone in case she chickens out.

She props a note by the phone, opens the door. A Western Union boy leans his bike against an elm, saunters up the walk, spots Rita, his eyes pop out of his head, he gets an erection, Rita gives him a dazzling smile, she never could resist a man in uniform, she giggles, and sways down the walk. He races to the porch, bangs on the door, thrusts the telegram into Daisy's hand, leaps on his bike, flails the pedals, Rita smiles lazily as he draws up alongside her, Wanna ride?, he stammers, Why not?, she says, drapes herself on the crossbar, touches the apple fuzz on his cheek and tells him to take her to the Museum's South Gate.

What's this?, Daisy reads the telegram, The City is confiscating Heartbreak Hotel, they can't do that and they know it, she's got an ironclad contract. It'll be one of the City Fathers wanting a little easy media coverage, he'll get his coverage CITY HALL TAKES ON WOMEN'S RIGHTS FANATIC; she'll get a backhanded apology FANATIC IS PERHAPS A LITTLE EXTREME, and it'll cost her a day's work. Then she remembers the cabbie's comment about the Museum closing: is there something going on she doesn't know about? She buzzes her lawyers to go down to City Hall and file an appeal, she notifies her intelligence network. Daisy's habitually prudent but, at this point, she's not overly concerned: in the Museum as in the convent, crises come and go, usually from the same sources. But Daisy has a superstitious streak. First Quasi, now this, she thinks. She folds up the telegram, puts it in her pocket, and thinks, Trouble always comes in threes, What's on the way?

In a one-horse Midwestern town, an old woman starts to board a Bluebird bus, has an altercation with the driver over the amount of luggage she has. She swallows her anger, summons all her charm, and tells him that she's on her way to Buffalo, New York to visit her daughter, the trunk and suitcases are filled with homemade things like his mother used to make. He says his mother never made a goddam thing but TV dinners and Franco-American spaghetti, and she switches tack, That's a shame, she says, A big strong fellow like you deserves better, If you'll give me a hand with my luggage I've got homemade bread, strawberry jam, apple pie, devil's food cake, lemon meringue You win Granny, he laughs, hop on. She doesn't say she hates being called Granny, hates bus travel, is humiliated to stand here and be patronized by this hairy lug whose shoes need polishing when thirty years ago, even twenty, he would have killed for her, she's on reduced income and all she wants right now is to get on that bus, God bless you, son, she says.

2

Every block in the Museum Of The Revolution has a beauty shop, and the last time Daisy checked the nominations, there were 25,008 shops on the waiting list. On the south side of MOTR, Rita decides against Valley Of The Dolls Hair Fashions because all the models' pictures in the window look like Prince Valiant. In MichaelAngelo Salon, Mr. Michael is busy, Mr. Angelo is busy. Mr. Jon does not accept new customers, Mr. Kenneth is busy, Mr. Charles is busy, Mr. Vincent is no longer with us, Mr. Arturo can take Rita, please have a seat. Rita has a lilac seat with gold speckles for an hour and three minutes and thinks about her gorgeous hair. If she is meeting strangers, she can cover her braless breasts with it, spontaneously flinging it back if the right moment comes. She can cloak herself undressing with a new lover, biding her time and revelations, can throw it over old lovers, covering, warming, wrapping, binding. She can do wonderful things with her hair: it is shield, striptease, mystery, ceremony, play, provocation, and protection. It is her power.

Rita thinks of a time she stood in front of a mirror with Maggie who also has long hair: Did you ever think, Rita said, that if you and I had been born in another time, looking like we do, they'd burn us? Burn me, Maggie said, they'd make you a goddess. Then I'd save you, Rita said. You already have, Maggie said. Who will save me?, Rita says to her mirror image.

Rita thinks of people stroking her hair. So many people have stroked Rita's hair that their faces are a collage of sensation. This very minute in a beauty salon chair, Rita feels fingers touch her hair and her pants get wet.

Mr. Arturo holds Rita's hair as if he holds ringworm.

Rita remembers the feeling of bristles driving cordovan shoe polish into her head.

Rita remembers the feeling of chocolate fudge batter beater grinding into her scalp.

Rita remembers the smell of burnt hair.

Rita remembers a man pulling her hair . . . "Oh, I'd say about here," Rita says to Mr. Arturo, indicating a place mid-nipple.

In ICU Room #7 at the hospital, the miracle worker doctor looks up from Quasi's freshly shaven scalp to catch that cute new RN looking at his silver hair. He doesn't know, nor do they, that young women always see their beloved daddies in his silver locks, but he does know, and so do they, that his silver hair turns them on. He has a momentary worry that he needs a haircut, but then her eyes move down and meet his and he is home free on this baby. He glances up at the clock, over at the EEG, way things are going he'll be out of here in time for Dottie to give him a quick trim.

The phone rings at Heartbreak Hotel. It's the hospital, Pearl mouths to Daisy. Meg, on an extension in the next room, listens to Pearl speak monosyllables for five minutes. When Pearl hangs up, Meg joins her and Daisy. "Who was it?" Meg asks. "The hospital wanted the family history," Pearl says.

Q.	Where did she come from?	A.	Don't know.
Q.	Mother's maiden name?	A.	Don't know.
Q.	Father's social security number?	A.	Don't know.
Q.	How old is she?	A.	Don't know.
Q.	General health?	A.	Don't know.
Q.	Previous illnesses?	A.	Don't know.
Q.	Does she smoke?	A.	Yeh.
Q.	Does she have Blue Cross/Blue Shield?	A.	Up yours.

"We don't know a whole lot about her, do we?" Pearl says.
"They asked the wrong questions," Meg says.

If Meg were in charge, the grilling'd go this way:
1. Who wants to see Quasi die?
2. Who wants to see her live?
3. Why?

Meg's not in charge. Her fingers tighten on her gun. For two cents, she'd shoot out the skylight. She considers going outside to do target practice. Four months off work, she probably can't even hit a starling at fifty yards. She reconsiders: if she goes now, she'll have nothing to look forward to the rest of the day. She heads upstairs.

. . .

In the living room, Pearl asks, "Where did she ever come from anyway?"

"She came with the house when the Museum acquired it," Daisy says.

"But where did she come from?" Pearl persists.

No one answers.

No one seems to know her birth name either or what malicious soul christened her Quasi. "Maybe her father wanted a boy," Pearl says.

"Years ago, there was talk of making her an exhibit," Daisy says, "but the Museum isn't for nature's mistakes."

"There should be places for people like that," Gretchen says. She thinks of a Museum exhibit: A GIRL WEARING A WHITE SILK DRESS SITS IN A BLUE FORD WITH A MAN WHO WANTS TO FUCK HER. HE IS ANGRY AND SHE IS SCARED. . . .

"¿Que pasa si ella se muere?" Maggie asks. "What if she dies?" she translates.

Dying's too good for that heel, Gretchen thinks, and is startled when Daisy says, "We'll claim the body."

"¿Que pasa si ella vive?" Maggie asks. "What if she lives?"

"Ditto," Daisy says.

"Seems the least family can do," Pearl cracks, still guilty as hell.

Where did *any* of them ever come from? The City Fathers have asked each other that question a good many times, but at Heartbreak Hotel, the question hangs unasked in the air although it's not against house rules to ask pertinent or impertinent questions. Hardly anything's against house rules:

LAWS OF THE JUNGLE
AT HEARTBREAK HOTEL
1. What anyone does in her own room is her own business.
2. Never go to anyone's room uninvited.

If anyone wants to answer the question, all ears are pricked. One can always find listeners in this house. Girltalk's the main activity on health leave. For entertainment, for education, for passing the time, for prayer and puzzle, the women talk. My how they talk. Biddies clacking over the backyard fence. Like a round-the-clock Tupperware party. "You old hens talk so much you'd think you were all attorneys," Pearl says.

Nobody's talking now.

Pearl the comic who gets all around the Museum knows this much: Daisy the curator comes from some kind of island.

Gretchen the cheerleader comes from a one-horse town in the Midwest.

Meg the cop comes from the Clearasil Kiosk which may indicate Mafia connections.

It's rumored that Maggie the translator comes from an orphanage or broken home.

Rita the belly dancer comes and comes and comes. . . .

Pearl realizes everybody's looking at her. She looks at each woman in turn, then says slowly, "I don't talk about this much. . . ." Almost imperceptibly, Gretchen leans forward, Pearl looks directly at her and says, "I come from a broken body."

Gretchen feels like slapping Pearl. She gets up, does one dozen no-handed cartwheels in a perfect circle without even breathing hard, sits back down.

"I tried to buy a pair of shorts," Pearl says, "but I couldn't find any that covered my legs."

Gretchen starts tapping her foot.

"Actually, I have perfect measurements," Pearl says. "32-33-34."

Tap tap tap, white vinyl is beginning to blur: Gretchen couldn't tell you how, but she knows Pearl's making fun of her.

Truth is Pearl's only making fun of herself. "I consider diarrhea a wonderful opportunity to lose weight. . . ."

Gretchen springs up onto the toes of her shiny white boots, she'll pull her hair out, the doorbell rings, "I'll get it," Pearl says, Gretchen continues on across the room, begins winding the grandfather clock.

On a staircase landing, Meg watches Pearl open the door: A man in a uniform flashes a badge at Pearl. She raises her arms, says, "I'll go quietly."

"Inspector," he says coldly, he moves past her.

"Hey Inspector," Pearl calls.

He turns around and says, "Boy, have you got problems here, Lady. You're talking ten, probably twenty grand to bring it up to code."

"Ten, twenty grand for the vestibule," Pearl says. "God knows what you'll find in the basement."

In the living room, Daisy looks up from the massive oak library table that she uses as a downstairs desk. "Who was it?"

"City Inspector," Pearl says.

Daisy's antennae ping, they were inspected last week, something's definitely going on, is it serious? This is a job for Rita. Rita's very good with men acting in official capacity; two minutes in the basement, Rita'll find out what's up.

Slamming along on the cross-Museum El, Rita searches her pockets three times for a scarf. I'm dying, she thinks.

Daisy reads Rita's note: Gone to the grocery store. "Anybody know where Rita is?" she asks the women in the living room.

Maggie, Pearl, and Gretchen shake their heads.

Meg enters, says "Nope" before Daisy asks her, shoves a few chairs into a corner, sets up her portable simulator next to a wall where she can keep an eye on all entrances and exits, and starts practicing her high-speed driving skills.

Daisy sits at the round oak table. The odd assortment of noises continues in the basement; nobody says anything. Because the Museum is partially funded by government monies and officially classified as a public facility, the women are accustomed to spot checks which vary in orthodoxy. Daisy considers telling them about her uneasy feeling, but why rock the boat: Pearl's fighting depression, Gretchen'd panic, Meg'd break parole, Maggie'd go on a bender. There's really nothing to tell them: a cabbie heard MOTR was closing, Heartbreak Hotel's been socked with a confiscation notice, an inspector's in the basement harassing them. These kinds of things have all happened a hundred times before, Daisy reminds herself, and returns to work.

Pearl stands to the side of the drapes, lifts a corner, and peers out.

In the willow rocking chair, Maggie rocks and sips her drink and watches Pearl. After some time, she says to herself, "My Gramma used to stand like that for hours waiting for company to come." "For her daughter to come," she translates. For my mother to come, she silently translates.

Pearl lets the curtain drop like a shot, "Must be about time for the mail," she mumbles, she starts pacing around the room.

"Not yet," Gretchen says smugly; without breaking the rhythm of her pliés, she draws out her pocket watch, checks it against the grandfather clock, and nods with satisfaction.

Gretchen's the unofficial self-appointed timekeeper at Heartbreak Hotel. Time is different here: with no work to ground it, people go to sleep and get up and eat and drink and fool around when they feel like it; in fact, any pressure to do things at a fixed time is strongly censured.

"Just like the Romans," Gretchen says about that policy. It doesn't matter how many times Daisy explains that one of the purposes of health leave is to let the body find its natural rhythm after the two month assault at the Museum where people cross time zones and the international date line several times a day. Gretchen always knows what time it is.

"Now that is public service," Pearl says. Through a window at the far end of the living room, she watches a man below go through the trash cans. "They're collecting our trash piece by piece."

"What?" Meg says, she slams on the brakes, squeals the car to the curb, jumps up from the simulator.

"Bum going through our trash," Pearl mumbles, "Hey," she says as Meg elbows her aside.

"Bum in a red jogging suit?" Meg says, she throws the window open and yells down, "Hold it right there, Mister, You're under arrest for trespassing, You have the right to remain silent, Should you give up the right to remain silent, Come back here you no-good lily-livered . . ."

"Go Santa," Pearl yells as the jogger with his black Glad bag slung over his back sprints for the woods.

"I could run you in for obstructing justice," Meg says.

Pearl shrugs and walks away, so some guy was going through the trash, Meg'd have him in the electric chair by noon, she looks up and sees Rita in the doorway.

"I'm dying," Rita says.

"You're in better shape than Quasi," Pearl says.

Rita feels like a turd.

Maggie stares at Rita. "Du hast dir die Haare schneiden lassen," Maggie says. "You had your hair cut," she translates.

"Just a trim," Rita says, her lip quivering.

Pearl starts to notice the resemblance to Prince Valiant, but changes her mind. "It'll be a lot easier to take care of," Pearl says.

"Yeh," Rita says and smiles. She doesn't mention that her power is gone.

Maggie stares at Rita's beautiful hair now bouncing instead of billowing, draping, shielding, Maggie feels sick.

"I gotta do my abdominals," Rita says and runs out.

"I won't name any names," Gretchen says, "but there are plenty of people I could name who should go do their abdominals." Eyeballing Pearl the whole time, Gretchen exits.

"She said a mouthful there," Meg says directly to Pearl. "You look like you're p.g."

22

Pearl laughs although she immediately feels like crying. She lies down on the couch, closes her eyes.

Maggie's eyes are welled up. Daisy takes Maggie by the hand and leads her out through the formal dining room past the mahogany table with Bruges lace tablecloth so exquisitely detailed young girls lost their eyesight making it.

3

Up in the master bedroom, Daisy settles Maggie on the kingsize bed, plumps the pillows behind her, "I'll be right back," she says. Maggie lies there, hardly daring to move: why is someone as important as Daisy so nice to someone like me? she wonders.

Daisy returns with a red-eyed Rita and a reluctant Meg. Rita gets on one side of Maggie; Daisy on Maggie's other side pats a place for Meg; Meg sits on the desk chair. By remote control, Daisy turns on the quadraphonic audio coming from the Museum's Hall of Hair:

> From the time I was seven I did my mother's hair,
> What have you *done* to your hair?
> Just because you're liberated doesn't mean you have to let yourself
>   go,
> That style's out,
> Really packs the years on you,
> It's too long,
> Can't believe you're wearing bangs at your age,
> Your split ends have split ends,
> You're going bald.
> I can tell him things I'd never dream of telling my husband,
> Well of course,
> What do you mean Well of course,
> *You know,*
> Giggle giggle,
> That bitch,
> I prefer a male hairdresser too, Oh me too, Definitely, I wouldn't
>   dream of letting a woman, There's something about a man,
> Men know.
> I saw this photo in a magazine, I'd like you to, I know I don't look
>   exactly like her, I'd really like to,
> Well if you want to look like a pinhead, of course I can go ahead
>   and do it,
> You gotta remember he's an artist just as much as Picasso,

24

Would you like me to see if the manicurist can work you in,
Did you have a nice time in Florida, my your skin is dry,
Well Hel-lo. Long time no see. Where have you been keeping
   yourself, In a cave?, Just kidding, dear, Heh Heh, you look
   wonderful, Look who's here everybody, Just in the nick of time,
   eh?, Heh Heh,
What a tease he is,
Leave them under the dryers till their eyes pop, then they're grateful
   for anything,
I just love him,
He's like a doctor,
I would trust him with my life,
He understands.
I'm waiting for Mr. William, He's not here?, You couldn't reach
   me?, But I was there the whole, Of course, I understand, How
   long do you think,
What I really want to do is own my own shop, not work for that
   slut any longer,
I understand,
You got to build a clientele,
He really cares,
You've put on a little weight haven't you, No, No I *like* it, You
   look a lot better than some of the, Really it's refreshing after the
   stringbeans who come in here, Well maybe a *few* pounds, But
   not too many now, When a woman reaches a certain age a little
   weight softens her, you know what I mean, you don't want to
   look too hard. . . .

   "When I was seven," Maggie says, Daisy turns the tape to mute/
record, "Until I was eleven," Maggie continues, "I wore my hair in
braids."

MAGGIE'S BRAIDS:
   Every morning, Maggie sits on the floor next to the bed.
   Gramma sits on the bed.
   Gramma makes the thick tight braids.
   Gramma skins the hair back so tight Maggie's eyes slant.

   Gramma says she's a great believer in toughening kids up early.
   The truth behind that truth is Maggie's the spit of her mother.
   Gramma cannot see the granddaughter's curls for seeing the
      daughter's curls.
   Gramma no longer believes in raising princesses.
   Gramma gives one last yank and ties the grosgrain ribbon.

Maggie hates the braids.

On the way home from school, mothers call Maggie up on their porches to examine the intricate braids.

The next morning, their little girls sport intricate braids.

The next morning, their little girls hate Maggie.

"What happened at eleven?" Daisy asks.

"She died," Maggie says.

"What if you had a daughter?"

"I'd put her hair in braids."

"But not Rita?"

Maggie shakes her head. "Rita shouldn't be restrained."

Rita giggles.

Daisy clicks on the panoramic video, a tic flashes on Meg's cheek. Extreme Close-Up in a movie theatre: fifteen-year-old is entranced: on the screen, face of gorgeous hunk comes closer, his eyes, that blue, I can't stand it, perfect nose, closer, his mouth is open, my god, look his mouth, I'm gonna die, those white teeth, his tongue, his . . . She freezes. Her wide open eyes see nothing. She knows instantly what has happened but she cannot stand it, her stomach continues to drop, she is going to die, what will she ever do, she won't be able to face anyone again in her whole life, thank god in her pocket a scarf, Thank you God Thank you God, she gets up the aisle without anyone seeing her.

News Squib: Filly's Filly Tail Phhhttt. In a darkened movie theatre yesterday afternoon, the elusive Ponytail Pruner struck again. As in the preceding cases, the entire ponytail was shorn just below the rubber band that secures this popular hairdo. . . . In a telephone interview, Assistant Deputy Capicolla said, "We figure this prankster either likes or dislikes ponytails a whole lot. We don't think he's dangerous, but unescorted females should take ordinary precautions. Particularly those with ponytails should avoid the movies or get themselves a new hairdo."

"The Hell you say," Meg says.

"Meg, stay to the end," Daisy calls, the door slams behind Meg. "Poor thing," Daisy says.

"Look at that," Rita says, she points to the screen.

Maggie lets out a whistle of admiration.

Camera lovingly pans over spires, angels, garlands: the Cathedral is a song of joy in a pure blue sky. A woman nips up steps for a quick visit, oh oh nothing on her head, no hat, scarf, mantilla, veil, lace hankie, she's in luck, in her pocket a wadded up Kleenex, looks kinda used Oh Well, she carefully smooths it out, bobby pins it to her head, and enters Church.

Other possibilities: holding the parish bulletin on her head, a glove laid across the hair won't draw attention if you walk tall, in extremis a dollar bill can be used.

"For if a woman be not covered, let her be shorn," the priest reads St. Paul in Latin and Greek, "If it be a shame to a woman to be shorn or made bald, let her cover her head. The man indeed ought not to cover his head because he is the image and glory of God; but the woman is the glory of the man."

Rita holds up her hand to signal she's had enough religion. Daisy holds up one finger.

At an all-girls school, Sister Maureen is teaching the second-graders. "We learn about the saints so that we can imitate them. It is good to choose particular saints as patrons. We should never feel alone, Children, when we have such powerful patrons." Sister Maureen holds up a picture: "Today's saint is Naomi: The Patron Saint of Hair."

THE STORY:
I asked you not to cut my bangs.
You should have told me that in the beginning, sweetheart.
I did.
Now just don't give me this nonsense.
Give you nonsense? Now lookit. I can go into any prole place in the
    boonies and get my hair cut exactly the way I want and I come in
    here and pay five times as much to have you insult my face and
    make it impossible for me to show myself in public? I'll sue you
    for personal damages.
Well you don't have to pay if you don't want to, honey.
That is exactly correct. I'm not going to pay. Fuck you.

"Many people are full of energy," Sister Maureen says, "but they do not use it to help their neighbors the way Naomi did." She pats the picture, "I love those bangs." She pats her own bangs. "Naomi," she says. "The name rings like a battle cry."

Got to get my roots done, Is it true blondes have more fun,
Gentlemen prefer blondes, bleached blonde, dirty blonde, dishwater
blonde, You know you're the first chick with bleached hair I've ever
been able to relate to, only my hairdresser knows for sure, who's
she kidding, pin curls, rollers, wash, set, tint, bleach, spray, cut, trim,
frost, perm, rinse, Please don't backcomb it makes my hair break
off, Come on Rapunzel let down your hair. . . .

"It will be a lot easier to take care of," Daisy says.

Maggie nods.

Rita snuffs and nods, "I still feel terrible," she says.

"Yeh I know," Daisy says, she switches all machines to cassette/ mute/record/store.

Rolling onto a cassette this very moment: in a lilac dryer chair, Mr. Arturo finds a lilac smock, a pile of lilac curlers, a lilac hairnet, and a twenty dollar bill, he pockets the twenty, throws his hands up in the air, and says, "She ruined my set!"

Pearl opens one eye as someone comes into the living room, gets up from the couch, takes half of Daisy's armload of books and papers, and helps her arrange them on the library table, "Don't you ever stop working, Daisy?" she asks.

"Nope," Daisy says, "Work keeps the wolves from my door."

Daisy sometimes leaves the Museum but the Museum never leaves her. In her bedroom at Heartbreak Hotel, a closed circuit TV scanner monitors Museum movement around the clock. Stereophonic tapes piped into her room perpetually record Museum Yak, Musak the women call it. Also whirring and clicking and dinging are ticker tapes, intercoms, computers, and the hot line. When Daisy leaves Heartbreak Hotel, she carries assorted gadgets Meg has brought her, hot goods or payoff, Meg's never said and Daisy doesn't ask; she carries a two-way radio wristwatch, a walkie-talkie, a transistor radio, an emergency beeper, and a portable lie detector: her evening bag bulges.

"What's all that racket?" Daisy asks.

"Two more wolves came on your coffee break," Pearl says. "One inspector from the Engineering Department and one from Sanitation. They're playing tunes on the pipes with hammers." She listens a moment. "Sabre Dance," she calls down the register, "Very nice." A muffled "Thank you" comes back up the register.

"Something going on, Daisy?"

"I'll tell you as much as I know," Daisy says. As she starts to fill Pearl in, the telephone rings. Frankly Pearl's relieved, she's not really up for a crisis on her first week of health leave.

LATEST HOSPITAL BULLETIN: Quasi bleeds from every orifice. As fast as they put blood into one, she dribbles it out another. Quasi is a poor investment, the blood bank may have to close out her account. Even Quasi's hump bleeds.

. . .

"Gross time," Gretchen thinks when Daisy calls the women downstairs to explain the situation. "I'd like to help out, but I'm the wrong blood type," she double lies. The thought of her blood mingling with Quasi's is disgusting.

Rita begs off. "I'm coming down with something," she says. Impotence, she thinks. She is still so wrapped up in her hair she forgets she owes Quasi.

Meg is silent. The sooner Quasi croaks the better if you ask her, but no one does.

Maggie's practically an automatic pass. She hardly ever goes out. She's a scaredy-cat. She's scared of everything, but particularly of being gagged, spread-eagled, raped, killed, and having a broom handle stuck up her vagina before she has a chance to do anything with her life. Her immediate fear is of saying No to her employer. She screws up all her courage and says, "I'll go with you, Daisy."

Pearl is shocked. She has never thought of Quasi as having blood. She tries to conjure a picture of Quasi Drained Of Blood. Quasi is an albino. Pearl is ashamed of herself. "Count me in," she says. "I've got so much blood I get rid of some every month."

All this talk about blood is making Gretchen nauseous, she feels pale. She thinks about getting under the sunlamp.

Rita feels clammy. She pulls her chair closer to the fire.

Meg feels like seeing a good prize fight. She throws an enormous log on the fire, enjoys the flurry of sparks that shoot up, decides to go out and chop wood.

In her room, Maggie finishes her preparations to go into the sun and begins her preparations to go outside. From her suitcase in the middle of the floor, she unpacks a fawn-soft leather shoulder bag and these things to go into it: a whistle, a set of car keys, a can of mace, a sharpened pencil, a corkscrew, a church key, a plastic lemon filled with lemon juice, and a family heirloom, her Gramma's hatpin. She thinks of Pearl who, when she goes out at night, stuffs her clothes to look like a hunchback and drools at any man who looks at her. Maggie could never do that: she'd die before she'd drool in public. She thinks of Gretchen who says, "Anybody bothers you, kick him where it hurts." Maggie can't even imagine herself doing that, that would really anger him. She does not want to think of Meg who has a black belt in karate and says, "Crush his balls like overripe plums." She thinks of Rita who's only afraid of one thing in the whole world: male strippers. Because that's unnatural? Gretchen asks. No, Silly, Rita says, because it's an economic threat. Maggie sticks a purse-size potent chemical spray in her slacks pocket and joins Pearl and Daisy. Without discussion, they start out walking to the hospital. Today is not a day for motorcycle riding.

BACK IN THE SADDLE AGAIN

The sight of Daisy, Meg, Gretchen, Pearl, Rita, and Maggie cycling along an open road, sun blazing, hair flying, motors roaring, leather gleaming, women laughing, such a sight can exult the heart or chill the spine. "Glorious," says one neighbor. "Grotesque," says another.

Even when Meg does her daily wheelies along Quasi's side of the porch, Quasi never says anything.

As they cross the grounds, Daisy notes Meg at the woodpile; the sledgehammer strikes the wedge, the elm log cracks. Pearl sees Meg put down the sledgehammer and lift the ax and thinks, I'd hate to be arrested by her. Maggie's eyes are cast down: she feels the sun is burning her up. She has block-out on, sun protection factor 75, wears prescription sunglasses, a broad-brimmed hat, long sleeves, keeps her hands in her pockets. I'm like a Goddam Scarlett O'Hara, she thinks in seven languages. Maggie has vitiligo, vittleEYEgo, which is unexplained loss of pigment: When men tell Maggie they like her pale pink nipples, she doesn't explain.

Pearl takes in Maggie's exquisite blouse, rakish hat, oversize horn-rims with tinted blue glass, her hands plunged into the pockets of her tweeds as she strides along. Pearl has tweeds on too, new tweed baggies, she stands up tall, sucks her stomach in, looks down at them, they look like clown pants. Pearl is a toad out with a thoroughbred.

Just before Pearl looks down, Maggie catches the sun bouncing off the planes of Pearl's face. Maggie pulls her hat down. Maggie is the underbelly of a frog.

> "MYSTICAL ROSE, PRAY FOR US.
> TOWER OF DAVID, PRAY FOR US.
> TOWER OF IVORY, PRAY FOR US.
> HOUSE OF GOD, PRAY FOR US.
> ARK OF THE COVENANT, PRAY FOR US.
> GATE OF HEAVEN, PRAY FOR US.
> MORNING STAR, PRAY . . ."

Daisy's lips move, she knows the words by heart, she takes off the mini-earphones.

"A poetry reading?" Pearl asks, "A singalong?"

"The Cardinals are chanting the Litany Of Our Lady," Daisy says.

Pearl resists the temptation to tune in for a while, she loves litanies, litanies are better than Hare Krishna or barbiturates for laying her right out.

White Quasi lays out in her white bandages in her white gown on her white sheets in her white room in the white rotunda. The white telephone does not ring.

Four floors down in the hospital lobby, the receptionist says again, "You have to be family."

"We are family," Daisy says again.

"Your name is not on the list," the receptionist says again.

"Who makes out the list?" Pearl asks.

"The *family*," snaps the receptionist, she has never seen anyone as dense as these people, why would anyone wear pants like that in public, they look like clown pants.

In her bedroom at Heartbreak Hotel, Gretchen switches off the sunlamp, and straightens up her bed, it sloshes gently. The only discordant notes among the oiled teak furniture in Gretchen's room are a mother of pearl lustre finish Madonna on a lace doily on a small table, and her waterbed. Gretchen is a little embarrassed having a waterbed which she associates with hippies and drug addicts, but it is a free country for cripes sake, I guess if she wants a waterbed so she can exercise while she sleeps that's nobody's business but her own. It's also her own business that the gentle rocking and sloshing are almost as good as Librium. She takes a Librium now, freshens up the vase of flowers in front of her Madonna shrine, stands in front of a full-length mirror, and examines her body like a technician checking parts. The skin on her knees seems somewhat looser, she checks her buttocks for cellulite. Lately, every time Gretchen looks in the mirror, she sees time running out. She showers quickly, deodorizes every pit and orifice, puts on a clean white skirt, a red sweater with an **MR** logo, goes downstairs. She has a terrible feeling of foreboding, something awful is coming.

On a Bluebird bus, an old woman sitting in the seat directly behind Fred the driver passes up a slab of banana nut cake. "Granny, you're a doll," Fred says, "I'm making progress," she thinks.

At the butler's pantry sink, Rita pours a bottle of beer over her head. "You're wasting Maggie's fancy Irish beer," Gretchen says as she passes, "You should use cream rinse anyway; it'll flatten your cowlick and then your haircut will look fine," she never understands how people can be in this business and not even know the rudiments, she opens the refrigerator, darts a glance to see if Rita can see her, takes a heaping tablespoonful of sweetened condensed milk, shudders slightly as it slides around her mouth into her system, dips the spoon in again, drops it like a flash, steps away from the fridge, the screen door bangs.

"Daisy even said Quasi was her twin sister, Run a blood test, she told them, Look at our names, but it was no go," Pearl says, she tosses the newspaper on the kitchen table. "We do, however, bring you the LATEST HOSPITAL BULLETIN: They have shaved Quasi's head."

Gretchen visualizes a giant mottled egg dropped by some repulsive extinct creature.

She never had any power to begin with, Rita thinks. Suddenly she remembers that she owes Quasi and why.

"Oughta cut down her dandruff problem," Pearl says in the silence, hating herself.

5

Extra Extra Read All About It

At the kitchen table, Daisy drinks a cup of spearmint tea, checks inventory sheets, and thinks about Quasi.

Pearl drinks a cup of black coffee and reads the front page headline:

CHAOS DEEPENS

She turns to the back page which is all photos for folks who have a hard time reading all about it. There are seven photographs of seven men: the President, the Pope, the King, the Statesman, the Terrorist, the Magnate, the Playboy. There is one photograph of seven women: the finalists in the Miss America contest.

Page 2 has **Mother of 7 Axed To Death By Husband,** Pearl gets gooseflesh: Mothers of 1 through 6 are no longer safe.

She starts flipping through:

Educational/Instructional:
ARTIFICIAL NAILS. Short instruction.
Unlimited income potential. Day or night,
ask for Tony

Pearl jots down the number on a paper napkin.

The Classified Services:
Feminist Hypnotherapist
Experienced crisis counselor
Assertiveness, tension control,
breast enlargement

Pearl jots down the number. She is a compulsive number jotter downer ever since the night she finds out the shelter for battered women has an unlisted phone number to keep the harassment down.

PUBLIC NOTICE 30 YEARS AFTER: IF YOU ARE THE MAN READING THIS RIGHT NOW WHO THE INSTANT THE EGG SMASHED ON YOUR WIND-

34

SHIELD SWERVED YOUR CAR TO THE CURB HIT THE PAVEMENT RUNNING POUNDED DOWN THE GRAVEL ALLEY CLOSED THE GAP WHIRLED ME ROUND SHOOK ME TILL MY EYES ROLLED DON'T YOU EVER DO THAT AGAIN, I SAW THE MOMENT OF SURPRISE IN YOUR EYES WHEN YOU SAW I WAS A GIRL.

Rita flops down in a chair next to Pearl. "What's my horoscope?" she asks.

Pearl ignores Rita. In a showdown, Pearl'd pick the comic strip Nancy over Jean Dixon's horoscope. " 'Dear Helpful Hattie,' " she reads aloud, " 'A few months ago I became the mother of a darling baby girl. She is very beautiful and feminine but has almost no hair. I would never want anyone to think she was a boy, so I attach a little ribbon that matches her outfit to the top of her head with a small dab of. corn syrup. The bow looks so cute and complements her pretty clothes. . . .' " Pearl looks up over her bifocals, "There are some side effects," she says. "Scalp decay, brain cavities, plaque on your head. . . ."

"Come on, Pearl," Rita pleads.

"Shh. I'm getting off on the lingerie ads. Check the nymphets. They put that page in a plain brown wrapper, didya see?"

Rita's jumpy, so Pearl relents: " 'Pisces. Put your house in order.' "

"That's all?" Rita asks, "There must be more," she gets up to look over Pearl's shoulder, but Pearl is pointing out Heartbreak Hotel's address listed in a one column squib on page 27 to Daisy who reads silently, **Metro News: City Fathers request neighborhood zoning change for planned mental retardate home,** "Hey," Rita says, and points to the item directly underneath, "Listen to this, everybody," she reads aloud,

" 'Motorcycle Accident Mystery: Unknown, Unrelated. An anonymous hunchback motorcyclist, medium height, white hair, pink eyes, was taken to Our Lady of Victory Hospital after suffering multiple injuries when the vehicle she was riding was struck by a hit and run driver at the intersection of Grand Island Boulevard and Stony Point Road. A witness who disappeared before police could obtain her name said a blue Ford sped away from the scene of the accident. Anyone with information, call Grand Island or Buffalo Police. Reward.' "

"Reward?" Rita says. "Who's gonna pay?"

"We'll all pay," Meg says and drops a carrier of wood so hard on the kitchen hearth chips fly.

6

The new Administration like the old Administration has been making noises from day one about closing down the Museum, but so far there's been no overt move, Is this it?, Daisy wonders. She calls friends at City Hall and at the newspaper, she calls the hospital.

She hangs up the kitchen wall phone, and says to Pearl, "Nobody's heard anything about an attack, but the zoning commission's meeting yesterday was unscheduled. They notified the paper as they sat down, and when the reporter got there, they were finished. We're going to have to wait for it to blow over, or wait for the leak."

"And Quasi?" Pearl asks.

"No change."

In Quasi's room, the staff is busier than a one-armed paper hanger trying to stem the hemorrhaging and counteract the coma.

They give her blood.

They give her a shot to stimulate the heart.

They give her oxygen.

"I'm afraid she's gonna go rigid on us," a doctor says.

They pump her full of muscle relaxant.

In the grand ballroom at Heartbreak Hotel, Pearl plays the Steinway concert grand, Daisy plays the flute. Meg ignores all the racket and builds a pyre-sized fire in the huge marble fireplace. Daisy and Pearl are feeling bad about Quasi so they play Museum songs MY LIFE A WRECK YOU'RE MAKING/ YOU KNOW I'M YOURS JUST FOR THE TAKING/ I'D GLADLY SURRENDER MYSELF TO YOU/ BODY AND SOUL which will first make them cry and then make them laugh. They play the first part doubletime.

The music and laughter get louder, roll into the living room. Gretchen and Rita head toward the ballroom. Maggie goes up the back stairs to the third floor to get her harmonica.

· · ·

36

In front of Maggie's room, a man in a uniform is on his knees looking through her keyhole. Maggie feels vaguely intrusive, tentatively taps him on the shoulder, "Excuse me, please," she says. He glares at her, "You're in violation," he says. "What have I done?" she asks. He makes a notation on a pad, "Do you think you can just do what you want to?" he asks, and walks down the hall. "*Je regrette*," Maggie calls after him, he doesn't turn, "I'm sorry," she translates to herself.

Two flights down, Gretchen dances off the sweetened condensed milk. Brown legs flash and shine, white boots kick high: her own combination of jazz, ballet, and acrobatics: Gretchen is a knockout dancer.

Pearl pounds the keys and watches Meg watch Gretchen twirl past the fireplace around the parquet floor past the red velvet draperies past Meg again who turns and leaves the room.

Rita's a knockout dancer of another stripe, but she languishes on one of the silk straight-back chairs lining the edge of the ballroom, stares blankly at the Bacchanalia fresco on the ceiling, does not even look over when Daisy ends the song with a flourish of trills on her flute and laughs out loud.

"Laughing gives you crow's feet," Gretchen says generously because she's beholden to Daisy.

Daisy and Pearl roar.

Gretchen smooths her pleats and thinks: Comics and curators don't know everything.

"Play Blues in the Night," Rita says.

"Wait for Maggie's harmonica," Pearl says. "She can play train whistles that break your heart. I hear her sometimes in the middle of the night." Pearl noodles on the piano, plays chords, sings softly, "My Momma done told me/ When I was in pigtails/ My Momma . . ."

"Now you can't wear braids," Gretchen says to Rita.

"I don't want to wear braids," Rita snaps.

"Where *is* Maggie?" Pearl asks.

"She *said* she was going to her room to get her harmonica," Gretchen says.

Pearl's pissed, she hates to wait, she closes the piano. "What's she *doing* in her room?"

"What business is that of yours?" Daisy asks sharply.

Right now in her darkened room, Maggie sits on the end of her bed and plays Gregorian chant on her harmonica.

Right now in Meg's room, the door is bolted, a confiscated radio turned to a station that plays beat so primitive, baboons go into estrus.

Meg stands in front of a full length mirror and practices dancing. She can hear the beat, and see that her body bears no relation to it. She waits a moment, breathes deeply, tries again: limbs jerk, gawk, her whole body is off key. Doggedly, her stern face gauging her progress, Meg tries to move her tin soldier body with the music. In the middle of a song, she stops like a shot, her reflection so ugly and graceless she spits on it.

Right now in her room, Quasi lies motionless and bleeds. "God, I hate sick people," one nurse says. "Get the doctor," she tells the new RN, "I'll get more packs." A team of nurses pack and stuff, pack and stuff: Quasi is the TVA dam at flood time. "How can anyone bleed so much and not die?" one nurse says.

In the ballroom, Pearl taps her fingers on the piano top, watches Daisy chamois out her flute, watches Rita stare at the ceiling mural, snaps her fingers at Rita to get her attention, "See my Band-aid," she says, showing Rita her forearm where she gave blood for Quasi, "I had to ask three times for a Snoopy Band-aid," she says, Gretchen rolls her eyes.

"Speaking of blood," Pearl says, "you'll never guess what I did last week." She plays a fanfare.

Everyone is glad to be distracted by a story, Rita brings her chair over, Gretchen gets herself and Daisy one: Pearl tells about subbing for Camellia, the emcee of the Dirty Days Revue on the 7th Block.

The two women have never met so Camellia arranges to wear a red flower, Pearl a white one. "I'm so excited," Pearl says to Camellia. "I've been dying to do straight drama. I love howling cats and full moons. I know this month's number of man-hours lost due to menstruation. I've had PreMenstrual Tension for 29 years: before, during, and after my period. Do you have any Midol?"

SHOWTIME: "It's Count Dracula time, folks. Camellia can't be here this matinee, she's out with the curse." Pearl hands out complimentary boxes of mini-pads: "These pads are so comfortable, folks, I wear them even when it's not my period." She hands out complimentary purses to put the boxes in. Before she even gets to the complimentary Kleenex to lay on top of the boxes, the crowd is hers.

Ceiling to floor, the theatre lobby's plastered with glossies of beautiful women in evening gowns gazing out conspiratorially and giving the password: Modess . . . because. "Because what?" Pearl asks. Her group laughs, but Pearl's not joking, she wants in on the secret. Of all the mysteries entwined with being female, Pearl considers that "because" the ultimate mystery. "Because what?" she persists. Nobody knows. Pearl makes a guess: she screws up her face and intones like a vampire: "Becaussss it beats wearing the raggg!"

She means it too. She's not of that school that thinks the menstrual products industry is a rags to riches story. "I'm happy to have the opportunity to clear up this misconception," she tells her group. "It's not the cost of napkins that bleed us. It's buying the toilet paper to wrap the used napkins in."

She takes them to the stadium stuffed with surprised women. These women remember birthdays, anniversaries, which neighbors take cream in their coffee, what the menu was for a dinner party three years ago, all their relatives' sizes, and that basil has an affinity for tomato, but every month, for 37½ years, menstruation comes upon them like a bolt out of the blue, I must be getting my period.

The women are in the stadium to see the woman who planned her wedding day not to coincide with her period. She sits on a small padded stool on the fifty yard line. She has a thermometer in each orifice and pit but manages a smile at the crowd before she bends back over her graphs.

To miss the stadium traffic, Pearl cuts down an alley Oh Oh, It's the worst traffic jam she has ever seen. Thousands of women are scurrying toward the back entrance of the laundry flying the red flag. They all have sweaters tied around their waists. They keep stopping to look behind them. They keep stopping to turn around their skirts. Thousands of sniffing dogs follow them. The women all carry balled-up panties, balled-up slips, balled-up nightgowns, balled-up pajama bottoms, balled-up sheets, they are all whispering Blood on the Sheets forgive me.

Back in town, The Menstrual Show where all the menstruals perform in red face and tell jokes has been closed down for obscenity, but they're in time for a method acting class upstairs. Today's class is the versatility of a simple line of dialogue:

A thirteen-year-old getting her first period whose friends have all had their periods for a year says, I got it,

A sexually active high school sophomore who's two months late says, I got it,

A high school drop-out who's two months late whose boyfriend has agreed to marry her says, I got it,

A bride on the morning of her wedding says, I got it,

A woman who desperately wants to conceive says, I got it,

An ICU nurse who's the mother of four says, I got it,

A 46-year-old woman who's fearing menopause says, I got it.

Next door in the Choreography class, the blushing bride's doing the Wedding Night Tango, she sneaks it on, she whips it off, three four, all night long, on off, on off, a hand sneaking pad between legs, a hand sneaking pad beneath bed.

Pearl's warming them up for the pharmacist. Nobody should have to encounter the pharmacist cold.

Pubescent girl with toilet paper wadded back and forth back and forth on top of folded-over Kleenex on top of paper towels secured by two pair of cotton underpants walks into the drugstore. She looks in vain for Winnie on each aisle and over by the comic books, but Winnie's not working today. Slowly she walks to the counter where he waits. Her eyes cast down, her lips shape the whisper, "Kotex please."

For an eternity, blood seeps.

She raises her eyes, he is smirking, she lowers her eyes, "Kotex please," WHAT DO YOU WANT LITTLE GIRL YOU'LL HAVE TO SPEAK UP.

Three times, she hangs on the cross. She feels blood running down her leg. Finally he broadcasts to the store OH YOU WANT KOTEX DO YOU WANT REGULAR OR SUPER KOTEX DO YOU WANT THE LARGE ECONOMY SIZE KOTEX HERE IS YOUR KOTEX DO YOU WANT A BAG TO CARRY YOUR KOTEX IN HERE'S THE CHANGE FOR YOUR KOTEX.

This is her fifth period and the third time the pharmacist has done this. She would not dream of telling her mother, she would die of shame. Her friends will not tell their mothers either. When many years pass, they will tell each other and still feel the shame.

Outside the drugstore, Norman Mailer, making a special guest appearance from the first block, does his smash imitation of a feisty Irishman. The crowd now in the palm of his hand, O'Mailer recites a beautiful prose poem about women being superior because they create a monthly masterpiece, lucky dogs. It brings tears to Pearl's eyes but before anyone can applaud, a woman steps out of the group and begins flogging Mailer with a used Kotex. A man pushes his way through, "Step aside, I'm Doctor Berman, Holder of the Leviticus Award, Get out of the way, I'm . . . ," but by now hormonal imbalances are raging and, though Pearl is tempted by the haunting tones of Erik Erikson leading the keen, she gets her group out of there fast.

There are still good seats left at the Hell's Angels Initiation Rite Demo. Free Wheelin' Frank narrates: "Angel mamas are nymphomaniacs who will do anything related to sex. The angel mama at the time is menstruating, on her period, and real bloody. It is considered the nastier she is, the more class is showed by the member who goes down on her in front of everyone—at least six members—and how he goes about it while everyone witnesses. . . . Sometimes a member has been known to barf while being hassled to do this."

The member who is being hassled to do this barfs. A woman in Pearl's group barfs. "If the idea of tasting your menstrual blood makes you sick," Germaine Greer says, "you've got a long way to go, baby." The participating Angel mama, sixteen-year-old Cindy Lou Ann from Browning, Texas, barfs. Free Wheelin' Frank barfs. Everyone in Pearl's group barfs. Down the block, Erik Erikson stops singing and barfs. Edgar Berman barfs. Norman Mailer rises from the dead and barfs. . . .

MENARCHE MENSES MENSTRUATION FLOW ISSUE THAT TIME INDISPOSED OFF DAYS FEMALE VISITOR FALLING OFF THE ROOF BLEEDING GUSHING DOES IT SMELL DOES IT SHOW CAN THEY TELL NOT TONIGHT DEAR NEVER RENT TO GIRLS THEY CLOG UP THE TOILET WITH DISGUSTING CYCLES OF THE MOON RHYTHMS OF THE TIDE SOUR MILK POISONED FOOD FAILED CROPS BLIGHT FILTH STAIN POLLUTION TABOO MENSTRUAL HUTS BLACK MASSES YOU ARE A WOMAN NOW UNCLEAN UNCLEAN UNCLEAN, Pearl shouts in Moslem, Hindu, Judeo-Christian. . . .

"Play the piano, Pearl," Daisy says.

Pearl pounds the keys and sings Red Is the Color of My True Love's Hair.

Gretchen fidgets.

"This place is a tomb," Rita says.

Pearl slams the piano lid down and shouts, "Period!"

7

In one of the rooms in the ICU rotunda, the physical therapist explains to the patient's family, "We use strong smells to try to evoke responses." She opens a brown kit that contains rows of small glass vials, and starts down the line, "Coffee, chocolate, cinnamon, clove, jasmine. . . . Some are unpleasant," she says and mischievously opens one vial a crack, immediately closes it, wrinkles up her nose and laughs as the smell of sulphur, rotten eggs, spreads through the air. "I start out with the pleasant ones," she says. She uncaps a vial and holds it under the comatose patient's nose. A strong cinnamon smell wafts through the room. As one, the family leans forward, their nostrils unconsciously flared. The patient doesn't move. Unhurriedly, the physical therapist moves the vial back and forth under each nostril, alternating cinnamon with clove. "I do this three or four times a day, alternating scents. You never know which one might get through." She smiles reassuringly at the family, but their eyes are glued to the patient's face, searching for the tiniest quiver.

In Rm. #7, without making even the tiniest quiver, Quasi mounts a cloud of clove and cinnamon and rides swiftly away.

Daisy sits at the oak table; in her swivel chair, she only has to move slightly to the right and left to command a view of the entire living room. At a side table next to the wall, Meg's polishing her badge, she switches on a small green Tiffany lamp which matches the green eyeshade she's confiscated from a bookie, she tilts the badge to examine the crevices. Across the room by the fireplace, Gretchen's doing rib isolation exercises. Maggie's down on the far windowseat, staring out the window at the sky. Daisy lifts her eyes and thinks again how much she loves Buffalo skies. One of the reasons she has chosen Heartbreak Hotel for her home office is its scores of leaded glass windows which, 358 days of the year, frame gray, gothic, Dutch Master, Buffalo skies. She savors the view a moment longer, then programs her watch alarm to call the hospital in an hour, bends her head to work. At any time of the day or night, with or without crises, Daisy has hours of Museum business facing her, and she knows how to work. She is efficient, organized, and above all, disciplined. She knows how to concentrate, focus, and direct her energy. "How'd you learn how to work?" Pearl asks Daisy once. "The hardest part was learning I had a right to work," Daisy says.

Maggie scrunches back against the black walnut windowseat and blocks out some of the window with a large tapestry pillow. Another shroud sky, she thinks, and it doesn't have a thing to do with that hunchback's accident. Every single day, a giant shroud wraps over Buffalo and you can't escape it anyplace in this house. This is the first time Maggie has spent leave at Heartbreak Hotel and all the windows frighten her. She feels a thousand eyes are looking at her. She has never seen a house like this before and she hopes she never will again. She came here because Rita who has been to all of MOTR's health leave centers said that as rest homes go, this was a pretty neat place. A *pretty neat place*: Maggie rolls the phrase around in her head. To Maggie, everything Rita does is exotic so it doesn't surprise her that Rita speaks English as a foreign language. She wouldn't have the nerve to tell Rita this, but Heartbreak Hotel seems to her to be more like a sepulcher than *a pretty neat place*. She wishes she were back at the Y where she could pile furniture against the door and feel safe. She looks past Meg who terrifies her, she wouldn't even stay in this room with Meg if Daisy weren't here, and over at Gretchen. Gretchen is foreign to Maggie in a way different from Rita: Gretchen is one of those girls who has everything: a fabulous body, a tan. Maggie never can think of anything to say to one of those girls. She takes a sip of bourbon and listens to someone prowling around in the kitchen.

Pearl stares at the kitchen telephone for a while, it doesn't ring. She picks it up to check if it's out of order, it's fine, she hangs it up quickly and groans, now she's done it, that very moment her agent was calling, got a busy signal, won't call back for a year. She hears clomps on the verandah and, without thinking, calls out her mother's old greeting, "Come in if you're good-looking." The door stays closed. She curses herself and opens the door to a sad-faced man in yellow rubber hip waders. "May I help you?" she asks.

"Thank you." He hands Pearl his butterfly net, glass bottle, and clipboard, fumbles for his I.D., and holds it up.

" 'INSECT INFESTATION INSPECTOR,' " Pearl reads aloud. "Come on."

"You've got marginal infestation all over this place," he says, he takes back all his paraphernalia, briefly holds up the glass jar which has a rubber tarantula in it, and says, "I'll start downstairs first."

"Don't you have anything better to do than go around bugging innocent people?" Pearl asks.

He winces, "Lady," he says sadly. "Probably the hardest part of this job is having people make that dumb joke." He turns and clomp-swishes down the stairs.

"The Bug Squad's on the job," Pearl tells Daisy.

Meg gets up, starts to pin on her badge. Maggie sees Daisy shake her head once, Meg sits back down. Daisy calls her lawyers who say, "All we can do is make them give you advance notice, we can't keep them out. Take it easy and see if you can find out what's up. We're working on this end."

Pearl stretches out flat on the wooden part of the floor that borders the Sarouk rugs, her back is killing her. Every so often she rolls over on her side, checks for marginal infestation.

Rita steps over Pearl's leg, slouches down into one of the velvet armchairs by the fireplace, sighs and slouches deeper. She's not thinking about Quasi. Rita didn't get to be head belly dancer at the Museum by helping the handicapped. Rita's got her own troubles.

Rita is most alive when she is belly dancing. It's not the incense, the golden bells on her arms and ankles, not the rustling veils, the flashing lights, the tassels twirling on her nipples, not the pulses, throbs, thrusts, undulations, not the smell of sweat, of men in heat, not the man in the corner jacking off, it's not even the multiple orgasms: What turns Rita on is the adoration.

The logs crash down, sparks fly, Rita just about jumps out of her skin. I must be getting my period, she thinks.

Daisy glances up from her invoices. The two hard times for most people on leave are when they first come from the Museum and right before they're due to go back. But Rita's a special case.

Rita's got those health leave blues: She misses the Museum.

Rita is one of the few women in the world who understands how the Museum works and Rita works the Museum to her advantage. Rita's the exception that proves the rule.

The only sounds in the room are the rustle of Daisy's papers and the click, click of ice cubes hitting the side of a glass. Maggie has a habit of slowly twirling bourbon in a glass, staring into it as if it were the healing waters at Lourdes, Daisy thinks.

44

Meg stops polishing her badge, looks over at the far windowseat where Maggie's body is almost completely hidden behind throw pillows. Meg speaks without taking the cigarette out of her mouth, "Goddammit, do you have to drink so much?"

Maggie's heart leaps into her throat. She tears her gaze from her bourbon and looks at Meg. Looks at her.

"The Hell with it," Meg says and stubs out her cigarette. Not ten seconds later, she lights up again. She feels the cough coming, tries unsuccessfully to stifle it: the hack comes out like Morningtime on Chippewa Street. Meg is humilated that her perfectly controlled body has produced such a sound. She sits up ramrod straight in her chair, meets Maggie's eyes, drags to her toes and blows a perfect smoke ring.

Meg can't decide whether smoking is the least of her problems or the solution to them.

Pearl props herself up on her elbow, watches Meg drag and remembers the feeling of lungs shrieking SEND IT DOWN SEND IT DOWN. Pearl thinks Meg ought to give up smoking and Maggie ought to go on the wagon, but then Pearl gives up things all the time. In the last decade, not necessarily in this particular order, Pearl has given up smoking, booze, uppers, downers, hash, grass, tranks, aspirin, junk food, and men. Pearl wonders why people call it the ME decade.

"About the only thing left is to give up," Pearl confides to Daisy one night.

"Giving up stuff isn't good in itself," Daisy says, "and it isn't giving in. Always you give up a lesser good for a greater one."

"THE OPPOSITE, CHOOSING A LESSER GOOD OVER A GREATER, IS WHAT SIN IS," says Flannery O'Connor.

Pearl groans. She gave up sin a long time ago.

Pearl is more nun than Daisy, she's a cloistered Carmelite in comic drag, but she never proselytizes. Right this moment, although she hasn't smoked in four years and eight months, although her life span has dramatically improved, although she feels better and smells better, Pearl is one drag away from being a chain smoker. Pearl misses a lot of things about smoking: most of all, she misses the excess.

Meg drags.
Pearl misses.
Daisy checks invoices.
Maggie clicks ice.

Gretchen does lip toners: lip pops, lip puffs.

"I might as well be working the name-calling room," Rita says to the fire.

PIG CUNT BITCH WHORE TRAMP SLUT GASH HOLE ROUNDHEELS HARLOT
NYMPHO TWAT DYKE PIG CUNT BITCH WHORE TRAMP SLUT . . .

Daisy has a hard time staffing the MOTR name-calling room. After the first week, the name-calling room is exactly like the confessional: same old stuff over and over.

Daisy's alarm buzzes, she phones the hospital.
LATEST HOSPITAL BULLETIN: They've stopped the hemorrhaging, Quasi's condition has stabilized, she's in no immediate danger of death. Daisy hangs up the phone, and presents the news as good news. If anybody else notices that in Quasi's case a stabilized condition is still a coma, they don't let on.

If the women don't notice, the ICU staff does. In the rotunda, one crisis down, it's full steam ahead on the coma.

They give Quasi steroids to prevent swelling of the brain.

The physical therapist arrives with her kit of smells.

The blinds are opened and shut at regular intervals to vary light stimulation.

A radio is brought in.

A TV is rented.

The priest stops by frequently to read uplifting text.

The longer Quasi stays in a coma, the less chance she has of coming out of it. Quasi's still in immediate danger of brain death.

"I'm never gonna get through this health leave alive," Rita says. "They'll carry me out of this house in a box."

Daisy waves an invoice at her, "Your new costumes are in," she says.

Daisy's words are transfusion: Rita's face blooms, she jumps up and does a little Irish jig: everyone's face blooms, they all clap the jig's time. Rita's wearing silk pajamas and this moment in heaven Daisy knows that St. Patrick's eyes are smiling and he's praying that Rita'll dance forever.

Rita's always wearing silk pajamas. No one thinks this means that Rita's a slattern or sick, no one thinks anything about it. At Heartbreak Hotel, you can wear what you want.

Gretchen will probably wear her guide outfits throughout her leave because she loves them so. All her life Gretchen wanted white boots and now she has seven pairs of white leather and seven pairs of white vinyl. Gretchen thinks she must be the luckiest woman in the world. She reaches down and spit rubs a microscopic speck off her shiny white boots.

Meg has exchanged her police uniform for a leather jumpsuit because she's tired and wants to sit down. Meg never sits in her uniform. Authority figures don't have wrinkles, she informs Pearl once. What about Ho Chi Minh?, Pearl asks. Go to Hell, Meg says. Her badge, gun, and black belt look right at home on the jumpsuit.

Maggie is still wearing her tweeds.

Daisy is wearing a light blue silk shirt, blue and purple silk suspenders, and purple chinos.

Pearl is wearing baggy pants.

Pearl has taken a vow of pants. She will not wear skirts until the male members of the Psychology Department at the State University of New York at Buffalo wear skirts and the state of their legs is remarked upon. She figures it'll be a lifetime vow. This is what Pearl has given up: twirling in featherlight materials and wind on her thighs and a certain freedom and a certain grace and garter belts with tiny blue flowers on them and nylon stockings and colorless nail polish dabbed on runs and red taffeta crinolines and twirling and a certain safety and a certain vulnerability and lace garters and groomed legs and a certain link with women and pink razors and nicks and blood and bloodstoppers that sting like hell and stubble and pink electric shavers and a certain power and the skin he loves to touch and waxes and creams and depilatories and electrolysis and a certain privilege and little girls holding her train and skirts looped to the arm like empresses and sweeping into rooms and a certain mystery and rustling and organdy and a man screaming at her for using his razor and mini and midi and maxi and micro and a stranger on the subway sliding his hand down and up and pretending it's not happening and slips versus no slips half-slips mini-slips pettipants teddies and a certain link with herself and twirling and static cling and little boys trying to look up her skirts and an appropriate curtsy costume and curtsying and vulgar remarks and crossed legs in public and don't bend over panties showing and ratings on a scale from 1 to 10 and sometimes winning and always losing and goose bumps and chilblains and leg lotions and fear of thick ankles and fear of fat calves and fear of wobbly thighs and fear of bowlegs and fear of knobby knees and fear of scars and fear of warts and fear of birthmarks and blemishes and being imperfect and leg make-up and suntan front and back matching and limbs so shiny and sleek people can hardly keep their hands off them and most of all the twirling.

You make mountains out of molehills, Gretchen tells Pearl about once a week. Pearl herself feels she spends most of her life waiting for people to make the Helen Keller waa-waa connection: that that wet stuff spilling on them is water. But she never answers Gretchen's charge because she doesn't want to overreact.

"Whew," Rita says, she laughs and collapses into the chair, everyone gives her a round of applause, she takes a little bow. She sits there a moment smiling in anticipation of her new costumes. "I swear," she says, "I could never get enough clothes. If my ship ever comes in, I'm going to blow it all on clothes."
"When my ship comes in," Pearl says, "I'm going to buy a jeep."
"You've got the wardrobe for it," Meg says.
Pearl thumbs her nose at Meg, but she remembers

A LOVE STORY: When Pearl goes home to visit, she gets off the plane, looks down, and suddenly registers how she looks, "Gee, I didn't realize how terrible I . . . ," her brother holds up his hand, "No explanations," he says, "You were the sharpest dresser in this town, I know you must have some reason to dress the way you do."

"There's a timing in clothes," Daisy says.
Everyone looks at her, but she doesn't elaborate.
"Must not be the right time to tell us," Pearl mumbles.
Daisy grins at her, "Just some times, clothes are more important than other times," she says.

The women recite The Litany Of The Clothes, it goes on tape, a continuing background audio for the Hall Of Fashion.
It was Easter Sunday, I was twelve, seventh grade, the girls and the boys were going to the 1:00 show at the Gladmer, that year for the first time the boys walked behind us: I wore a gray box jacket suit with a red hat, red shoes, red purse, nylon stockings with the seams straight up the middle of my legs, and strutted down Seymour Avenue feeling my power, feeling my worth.
I wore an organdy dress, I stood by a grape arbor, my mother had woven Spring flowers in my hair. There's a photo of it, I was so pretty, my hair was curly then, I'd say I was about eight, nobody else had flowers in her hair.

48

The fifth grade May procession I got my first garter belt and nylon stockings, Sr. Mary Ambrose gave us the good news: Ma took me to Penney's, the garter belt had a tiny blue flower on it.

The playsuit was basically just a large red kerchief with strategic knots, one tug could undo it, Gramma saw it in a magazine, she could duplicate anything, she was a fantastic seamstress. Why did they send me out in that goddam outfit?, the boys kept sneaking up behind me grabbing the knots, my mother and my grandmother set me up.

One of the boys said, not my date, How do you hold it up?, I was mortified. It was green tulle, my first strapless, and my date kept trying to look down the front all night long.

I leaned forward for the salt shaker and he dropped an ice cube down the front of my black lace cocktail dress. I jumped all around, everybody laughed.

He ripped my new blouse with the peter pan collar, I'd begged my mother for the blouse, then I had to tell her I caught it on the bleachers, she was furious.

I had a brand new dress. When he picked me up I took it off and said Let's do it now so my dress won't get spoiled.

My dad took me to the most expensive store in town and bought me a mint green lamb's wool sweater and a matching two-toned checked skirt. He sat in one of those pink chairs outside the dressing room and when I came out to show him he said You want them?, I can't tell you how excited I was.

Momma had a maroon wool suit with a fur-lined jacket, beaver I think, my grandmother had cut up an old fur coat, the suit was too old for a girl but Momma let me wear the skirt for the Elks' Dance. It was so tight and looked so sharp, I wiggled in Momma's maroon wool skirt all over the room and everybody looked at me, I felt so good.

The very first thing I bought out of my own money was a red chiffon trailing scarf like Isadora Duncan. *Like Isadora Duncan?* Well, not *exactly* like Isadora Duncan.

Did you ever want matching mother-daughter dresses? I did, me too. I don't remember.

I remember a beige suit with covered buttons, the skirt was flared, the jacket waist-length and fitted, it was a Simplicity pattern: I wore it Easter Sunday the year I was thirteen, eighth grade, that's the last year the boys and girls went to movies in big gangs.

I remember a red striped tent dress cinched in with a gold chain, it had a yoke that made you look busty, I walked across a hotel lobby in that dress on my way to a job interview and all the men looked at me, I walked into that interview really feeling my oats. I didn't get the job but the interviewer asked me out.

June Week, Senior year high school, some of us were invited to a dinner dance at a fancy restaurant: I got this black lace cocktail dress, my first sophisticated dress, my sister fixed my hair in a chignon and pinned poppy red flowers around it. I can see myself now, sweeping into that restaurant in that black lace dress, I looked at least 21.

The best dress I ever had cost $45.00, a fortune then, a flowered linen dress, plus $3.00 more for alterations, they put elastic inside the bodice to keep it from gooping out and showing my breasts, it wasn't that kind of dress. When I wore that dress I looked like Mrs. Gottrocks, I got a lot of mileage out of that dress, I got a marriage proposal out of that dress, it was worth every penny.

My favorite prom dress was pink with a white eyelet bodice and I bought the prettiest white leather high heels to go with it, just a couple of spaghetti straps is all they were and I never had a pair of shoes I felt prettier in.

When I was Queen, my sister drove me ninety miles to find the white lace dress, rows and rows of white lace ruffles, no one in my town ever saw a dress like that.

Beige crewneck sweater, beige flannel skirt with two kick pleats, beige suede shoes: my going away to college outfit, I wore it in 85-degree weather, Hot?, No, I'm not hot.

I had a black summer dress with no back, it was very daring. Two days after we graduated from high school this girl got married and I wore my new backless dress to the church with a sweater over it. When I took off my sweater at the reception, the bride might just as well have gone home.

I had a sky-blue felt skirt with a black poodle appliqué with the tiniest gold chain for his collar, everybody who counted had a felt skirt, I almost got mine too late.

There were five of us, the Gillette Gang, Look Sharp, Feel Sharp, Be Sharp, we were always going to carry razor blades in our billfolds and I saw the Day-Glo jackets first. Shocking pink, green, yellow, blue, and mine was orange: the brightest of all. When people saw us coming in those jackets they couldn't ignore you if they wanted to, God, I loved that jacket, Carol's Mom wouldn't let her get one, we were all sick for her.

When I put on my red rain slicker and my red rainhat, I looked just like those girls in Seventeen Magazine.

My sister said my white silk shirtwaist dress looked like a tablecloth but there was a man who always begged me to wear that dress.

After the rehearsal dinner we all went back to the motel and partied some more. One of the groomsmen said Let's go swimming but all the bridesmaids had had their hair done. I was Maid of Honor, but I said

I'll go, I was dying to show off my new bathing suit, it was baby blue seersucker and made like a little girl's playsuit except when you leaned over, the truth was I hated my hairdo but I didn't tell anybody that. I stood down at the end of the pool and all the groomsmen cheered and I dove in. I hit the pool step and when I came up my nose was cut and bleeding, my best friend screamed at me: if you show up with even one mark on you if you spoil my wedding I WILL NEVER FORGIVE YOU.

I had this party dress specially made, it had a scooped neck, a full skirt, and the most gorgeous puffy sleeves. I had jasmine in my hair and those red flowers against that black linen dress, I was all tanned, well it was one of those nights everything worked: every club we walked into, everybody looked at me. I put that dress on two months later, it was limp, ill-made . . . it was a rag. I never wore it again.

Do you remember patent leather shoes and watching your toes wiggle in the X-ray machine and begging please please please let me wear them to school tomorrow?

What about plaid dresses with white collars and black velvet ribbons at the neck?

What about pinafores?

What about fur-collared coats with matching jodhpurs in the finest wool, my Gramma could make anything, and muffs, brown, black, white muffs, beaver, rabbit, all with silk cords and secret zippers.

What about strings of pearls?

Strings of pearls. I'd forgotten about strings of pearls.

Do you remember those damned blouson tops? I swear everything I bought in college had a skin-tight skirt and a blouson top to hide the roll of fat.

I had a pair of tight black velvet pants. My friend had the whole suit, it had a short toreador jacket lined with white satin, I just got the pants. She was a real knockout in that suit.

I knew a girl who had a whole closet of Ship and Shore blouses. I swear to God I'm not lying. She was the most gorgeous girl in town.

I knew a girl who had a whole drawer of cashmere sweaters. One of each color. I used to go to her house after school and sometimes she'd open her drawer and let me look at them.

I remember a longhair red fuzzy coat, mohair, it'd belonged to that girl with the Ship and Shore blouses and it was beautiful. I felt like a million bucks in that coat. One day I went to my father's office and he helped me off with my coat, then he put it back on and said he was too busy I should go home. What's wrong with you, he kept screaming at my mother that night, can't you see she's walking around in rags, the lining's hanging out the sleeves, the hem I was so embarrassed PULL

YOURSELF TOGETHER. The next day I got a new coat, 10% cashmere, teal blue, the latest style, no buttons, rolled collar, it was real pretty and I liked it a lot, but I never loved it as much as I did that red fuzzy longhair coat with the big red pearl buttons.

My first communion dress was borrowed.

My wedding dress was a size too small, it was so elegant, but even with the merry widow there was no way that zipper was going to close. They put a gusset in, I never told anybody, it didn't show or anything, a gusset, doesn't that sound fat?

I remember a yellow dress. . . .

Pearl has tuned the women down low, lower, until they're a murmur she no longer hears. Pearl's the one who had forgotten about strings of pearls and how much she once wanted them. Why she didn't get any or didn't get the right kind or got them too late: she's forgotten that too. She remembers now that she owns a real string of pearls, Thank you, she said to her husband, They're beautiful, and they were, but for some reason she never wore them much and finally put them in a safe deposit box. She can also remember: a dove gray wool tunic maternity dress piped with gray satin, Saks Fifth Avenue, made her look like a model, a gold silk sheath, an eggshell satin evening gown, a Finnish skirt and stole in multicolored mohair, two pairs of Christian Dior stockings bought by a lover on impulse at Bergdorf Goodman on a rainy Saturday afternoon: she can remember scores of items that have passed through her closets and drawers and life in the last fifteen years, but she rarely does. Pearl leaves the room, goes downtown to the fanciest store, ignores the customers' double takes, the elevator operator's smirk, the saleswoman's flared nostrils, and spends two months' salary in the Girls' and Juniors' departments. She has the clothes sent directly to her daughters. Among the items are: bright jackets, cowboy boots, caps in corduroy, leather, and velvet, back-to-school plaid dresses, Ship and Shore blouses, cashmere sweaters, and fifty-five pairs of Bonnie Doon kneesocks.

Upstairs in Daisy's cassette storage, a camera pans the International Women's Year Conference in Houston, Texas, close-ups on a woman who asks Valentina V. Tereshkova Nikolyeva, Soviet Cosmonaut, first woman in space, "Why aren't you wearing your costume?"

8

Pearl doesn't mouth it around Heartbreak Hotel that she has a husband and five daughters, but she doesn't need Maggie to tell her that 7's an infinite number. Daisy, a closet Quaker, is the only one who knows that Pearl's a runaway, although it has crossed Meg's mind more than once—she always dismisses the suspicion because why would anybody walk out on a steady meal ticket? Meg not understanding such a thing is at the end of a long line. When Pearl left home, her husband didn't understand. Her children didn't understand. Her parents didn't understand. Her best friend didn't understand. Her dog didn't understand. Pearl thinks only other runaways could understand and she's not even sure of this.

"How'd you get out?" Daisy asks late one night.

"People helped me," Pearl says, "and I knew my wares."

People didn't help her very much.

Running away was not Pearl's first foray into the world. She had previously tried humanists, feminists, socialists, patriots, Right to Lifers, friends, neighbors, relatives, Welcome Wagon, even Unitarians: Everybody welcomed Pearl aboard but jumped ship over helping with the children.

Time after time she pulled back, pulled back, little by little she pulled back until she was once again standing next to her husband.

She didn't always know her wares either.

The ghost of Pearl Past perpetually puts a 3x5 card in her recipe file box.

Every time she gets a recipe she reads: I HAVE OPTIONS IN MY LIFE. I JUST HAVE TO FIGURE OUT WHAT THEY ARE.

Pearl Past finishes up the dinner dishes, puts the kids to bed, goes into the bathroom, locks the door, runs the water, silently puts the toilet lid down, sits, and writes a vita:

Salaried Employment
    Kool-aid stand
    raking leaves
    babysitter
    salesgirl (3 times, 3 stores)
        a. men's underwear
        b. ladies' budget hats
        c. ladies' better hats
    waitress (3 times, 3 restaurants)
        a. Johnnie's Fat Boy Drive-In
        b. Mrs. Kay's Wee Toll House
        c. The Cock 'n Strut
    file clerk
    door-to-door sales
    elementary schoolteacher

Unsalaried
    housewife ⎫
    mother   ⎬   SEE ATTACHED BOOK
    volunteer ⎭

Pearl feels there's a thread here someplace, but is afraid if she pulls it, everything will unravel.

The 3x5 card yellows with age and you-won't-believe-it's-not-butter fingerprints.

On her thirty-fifth birthday, Pearl says to her husband, Look at me. I got old. I didn't get old with you. I got old because of you.

WHAT EXACTLY IS IT THAT YOU WANT? Pearl's husband asks again.

Pearl sighs.

Pearl's husband says: Pearl, you are sucking the life out of me like a cat with your sighs.

Pearl tries to sigh more shallowly.

One day, in the middle of making a Christmas tree skirt, something strikes Pearl. She says, "All the women I know without college degrees are going to college. All the women I know with college degrees are going into real estate." Everybody laughs although Pearl's making a simple statement. For the ten-thousandth time, somebody says, You're always good for a laugh, Pearl.

Pearl decides to find out if that's true.

· · ·

"Little by little I got me a rep as a funny man," she says.

"That's better than the rep I got," Rita says.

"My one regret in picking comedy over real estate," Pearl says, "is that I don't get to work with doctors."

Meg puffs on her cigarette and blows smoke in Pearl's direction. "You didn't get out," she says. "You didn't even get away."

"I never wanted to be a divorée," Pearl says and starts crying.

In Quasi's room, a nurse points to the ceiling. IN THE ROOM DIRECTLY ABOVE, A THIRTY-NINE-YEAR-OLD WOMAN/WIFE/ MOTHER OF FOUR, DYING OF CANCER, TELLS A VISITOR, I'D RATHER HAVE IT END THIS WAY THAN DIVORCE.

"I was standing right there," the nurse says to the other. "That's why I like working ICU better than terminal."

9

THE WAITING ROOM

There is a vast Waiting Room in the Museum Of The Revolution. There the girls and women wait

for their nails to dry
their make-up to set
their lashes to curl
to be noticed
for the phone to ring
to be asked to the prom
to be let out of the automobile
for the tire to be changed
for sex to be initiated
for their periods
for a proposal
for the man to come home
for the baby to be born
for the baby to fall asleep
for the baby to wake up
for the pediatrician
for school to start
for the children to come home
for the children to leave home
for the children to visit
for Monday to start their diet
for E.R.A. to pass or fail
for the roast to finish
for someone to get over being mad
for the repairman
for the soldier, the sailor, the convict, the miner, the body
for the flag to be folded and presented
for the bread to rise
for it to happen.

Daisy spent a good many years hanging out in the Waiting Room, but she's a rare visitor these days. She passes through briefly waiting for the City Fathers to drop the other shoe, takes off fast when she sees the same old gang.

Rita waits for health leave to be over.

Meg waits for appreciation.

Gretchen fidgets and frets, thinks about a white shirtwaist dress, waits for something awful coming.

Maggie is positively Himalayan in her waiting, her patience knows no bounds: she waits unruffled to see if the booze will take effect before the ax falls.

An old woman on a Bluebird bus waits for rest stop to finish, her trip to continue.

Quasi waits. If death comes, regular or brain, she will be there to greet it.

Pearl is in the Waiting Room waiting for her booking agent to call. She sits next to a woman who's waiting with legs spread, feet in the stirrups, speculum in, for the gynecologist to come back. The woman stares at the acoustical tile ceiling, counts the holes, stares at the Venetian blinds, counts the slats, stares at the sheet covering the part she can't see, stares at her pink painted toenails.

Pearl wants to fidget, twitch, stride, scream, but she sits perfectly still, her hands loosely holding one another, and marvels at the woman who's waiting for a man to drop by. It is Friday noon. "How long do you plan to wait?" the receptionist asks. "He said he'd catch me sometime this weekend," the woman says, "Put me down till Sunday evening," she glances around, notes the room filling up, "No, make that Monday morning."

Across the room, an eighth grade girl is doing the Elks Dance Countdown. "The Elks are having a big dance for teens, Didya hear? A semi-*formal*. People are going in dates!"
Girl talks turkey to herself:

Friday, a week before: A week's notice, they gotta give you a week's notice or they don't really respect you.

Saturday, 6 days: You can't really count Saturday.

Sunday, 5 days: The week really begins on Monday.

Monday, 4 days: This is really the week.

Tuesday, 3 days: A lot of people didn't even hear about it till today.

Wednesday, 2 days: Well it'd have to be somebody pretty doggone special to get *me* to go this late.

Thursday, 1 day: Tonight is absolutely, positively the *last* night I'd accept.

Friday school hours: It's just a dance, if somebody just heard about it and just decided to go I don't mind going along with him it's just a dance.

After school: Five o'clock, that's it.

5:00: Six-thirty.

6:30: A lot of people don't even get up from the table till 7.

7:05: In closet, tears rolling down cheeks, caressing Mother's black taffeta formal that Mother said was much too old for her but Yes I suppose you could wear it if anybody asks: if anybody has the *nerve* to ask this late I would just hang up the phone on him.

7:30: Hello Nance, You wanta go to that dance at the Elks, well of *course* we can go stag, *Everybody's* going stag, oh her, Well I wouldn't *go* to a dance with *him*, I think it's dumb to go in dates anyway, we're really too young for formals don'tya think, I'm wearing my Mom's maroon wool skirt Yeh she just came in and asked me if I'd like to wear it with my pink lamb's wool sweater, eight o' clock I'll meet you on the corner, okay?

The father's open heart surgery, nine hours if no complications, has begun. On the red vinyl couch, the mother waits with the two daughters.

After two hours, the second daughter asks, "Where's our brother?"

"I told him not to come until this afternoon," the first daughter says, "You know how hard it is for him to sit still."

"He's just like his uncle and grandfather," the mother says, "you know how restless they are."

While the second hand crawls around the clock, the mother and first daughter swap stories of turbulent men. The second daughter does not move a muscle outside: inside her stomach churns, her heart pounds, she wants to scream, Fuck this sitting still for men, but she goes and gets a cream-filled donut instead.

Pearl's insides are twisted like a Japanese tree, Pearl is going bonsai. She gets up, stretches, walks across the room as if she has all the time in the world to look at a memorial diorama called:

WAITING FOR THE MAIL:

"Goodbye, honey," the wife says, "Have a good day."

She pours another cup of coffee, she toys with the aluminum coffee cake pan, she wets her finger and collects the crumbs on the bottom of the pan, she licks her finger. Finally she looks. 8:34. Four minutes down, nine hours and twenty-six minutes to go until he returns.

She thinks she will die.

She makes a pact with herself: If the mail is good, she will stay up the whole day.

Mail comes between 10:40 and 11:00. Maybe two hours and three minutes, maybe two hours and twenty-three minutes. Her sinking feeling lifts a bit: anybody can wait two hours and twenty-three minutes. The calculations have already used up some of that.

Pearl is looking at herself: With her first IRS return, Pearl donated this diorama to the Museum in honor of memory. She looks a while longer at Pearl Past dividing the day into hours, the hours into minutes, the minutes into seconds. For a while it was a toss-up whether she'd become a mathematician or a comic, but there were more opportunities for women in comedy.

Did you get your training on the Borscht Belt?, reporters always ask Pearl. That is a joke. Pearl came out of hysterical housewife. Pearl had them double clutching in the carpool. Pearl perfected her split-second timing in the A&P checkout line.

No, Pearl says, I started out on the Sanitary Belt.

Pearl remembers how Quasi always waited for the mail. Quasi prowls the porch. She cannot see the mailman nor hear his step but Quasi knows time. Time approaches. Quasi slavers at the mouth. Time passes. Quasi climbs into her pile of rags and pulls a dusty bag over her head.

Pearl hates herself for thinking this but, even with a dusty bag over her head, men know the difference between Quasi and other women.

Of course! Pearl realizes her agent has so much news, probably contracts too, she's writing a letter. Pearl makes a beeline out of the Waiting Room. She's just in time. The little blue mail truck is putt-putting around the circular driveway of Heartbreak Hotel. The other women are on her heels, but Pearl gets the mail first.

Nothing.

Pearl fights back the fatigue washing over her.

"Were you expecting a letter?" Daisy asks.

"No," Pearl says, "but I am expecting a phone call." She hands Rita her cassette. Rita gets a cassette nearly every day. Rita plays eight bars, Oh Baby What I Would Like To Do To You, and tosses it into the trash.

Daisy gets bids, bills, complaints, crank mail, the daily cartons of mail from the Museum Dead Letter Drop to go into the shredder, a notice that she's been nominated for a D.A.R. award, an invitation to an island that she slides into her rear pocket, and a registered letter with a wax seal that she sets aside while she sorts the rest of her mail. The wax seal of the City Fathers glows like kryptonite, all the women notice it, but they trust Daisy and won't rush her, she won't tell them before she's ready anyway.

Meg claims the letter for Occupant and reads aloud: THIS IS A CHAIN LETTER BUT NOT LIKE ANY YOU HAVE EVER SEEN. DON'T I REPEAT DON'T SHOW THIS LETTER TO ANY GUYS. THIS LETTER IS A PROVEN FACT. THE GIRL WHO BREAKS THIS CHAIN WILL PAY FOR IT WITH HER LIFE. Meg rips the letter in half, Maggie gasps, Gretchen scrambles on the floor for the two pieces and continues reading: YOU MUST GIVE 7 LETTERS TO 7 FRIENDS IN 7 DAYS. IN THE CORNER WRITE THE NAME OF THE GUY YOU LIKE AND SCRATCH IT OUT. IN DAYS TO COME HE WILL TELL YOU HE LIKES YOU VERY MUCH. IN 7 DAYS SOMETHING SPECIAL WILL HAPPEN.

"The Hell you say," Meg says.

"I don't have seven friends," Pearl thinks.

To everyone, the room seems full of shadows.

Daisy thinks of spells, blessed palms, and amulets. Unknowingly, her hand moves up to her neck to finger medals that are long gone.

Maggie thinks of her Gramma reading the tea leaves. She thinks of Tarot cards, Ouija boards, Wicca, the devil.

Meg thinks of Mme. Le Main, the bunko psychic and palm reader who has her sign out on the 6th Block this week.

Gretchen thinks of love potions, aphrodisiacs, chocolate musk lotion, Blessed Maria Goretti, she thinks, Rid my mind of bad thoughts.

Rita thinks of her long-range horoscope forecast: a good year for marrieds and singles. Rita says, "Count seven stars for seven nights, on the seventh night you'll dream whom you're going to marry."

Gretchen says, "The girl who catches the bridal bouquet will be the next bride."

"Put a piece of wedding cake under your pillow," Pearl says, "you'll get ants in your hair."

"You don't respect anything, Pearl, that's what's wrong with you," Gretchen says.

"Here's a letter for you in my pile, Gretchen," Daisy says.

Gretchen opens it slowly, she blanches.

"What is it, Gretchen?"

"My Ma's coming to visit."

HOLY MOTHER, PRAY FOR US, the Cardinals sing.
MOTHER OF DIVINE GRACE, PRAY FOR US
MOTHER MOST PURE, PRAY FOR US
MOTHER MOST CHASTE, PRAY FOR US
MOTHER MOST INVIOLATE, PRAY FOR US
MOTHER MOST AMIABLE, PRAY FOR US
MOTHER MOST ADMIRABLE . . .

THIS IS THE LITANY OF GRETCHEN'S MA
She touches easily
She likes to give presents
She wraps presents beautifully
She remembers occasions
She celebrates occasions
She keeps on
She is a hard worker
She works outside the home
She takes care of her person
She loves to dress up
She has style
She smells of Shalimar
She wears fur coats and smells of fresh snow
She loves the sun
She collects sea shells
She loves to dance
She shares her clothes
She will not sew
She will not iron
She hates presents for the house
She is fun-loving
She has a wonderful laugh
She makes people who drop in feel like a million bucks
She asks people to stay for dinner at the drop of a hat
She has beautiful manners
She has terrific social skills
She likes to spend money
She is passionate
She has sexuality
She shows her daughter how to use a sanitary belt
She does not trivialize the event
She does not take amusement at her daughter's expense
SHE DOES NOT MAKE A BIG DEAL OUT OF IT
She gives her daughter a black negligee for a shower present
She comes to her daughter on her wedding eve
She tries to talk mother/daughter

She is dying of discomfort
She says I suppose there is nothing I can tell you
She does not know her daughter is dying of discomfort
She feels old and foolish when her daughter says Nahhhhhhh
She gives her daughter a douche bag
She is a good cook
She fills the house with flowers
She loves and honors her mother
She keeps her mother's picture on the bedside table thirty years
    after her death
She changes her clothes and fixes her face for her husband's
    homecoming
She weaves May flowers into her daughter's hair
She takes responsibility
She has a sense of community
She holds people's heads when they throw up
She puts the Vicks cloth on
She visits the sick and buries the dead
She visits old ladies
She arrives with presents
She takes her daughter to funeral homes
She lets her daughter kiss her beloved Grampa goodbye in the casket
She puts flowers on graves
She has religious pride
She has ethnic pride
She is lace curtain Irish
She survives cruel teasing
She is physically tough
She comes each time her daughter has a baby
She keeps an orderly environment
She takes the Test Your Horse Sense test every day
She is smart as a whip
She respects books
She calls hardcover books "library books"
She always has her nose in a dime novel
She reads on the toilet
She is bold
She is adventuresome
She is a gambler
She is an expert card player
She prefers ocean swimming to pools
She thumbs her nose at authority
She is filled with rage
She likes to put on the dog
She wants power
She yells

She is a fighter
She wants to better herself
She is superstitious
She kills bats by herself
She hates the country
She hates one-horse towns
She knows she is extraordinary
She knows hicks do not know extraordinary when it punches them
    in the nose
She likes big time and high life
She hates to be called Ma
She likes excitement
She brings her children sacks of New Year's Eve favors
She sings off-key loudly
She refuses to wear matching mother/daughter dresses
She wears skintight clothes
She drinks
She dopes
She is sex-starved
She says vulgar things
She says ignorant things
She lies and lies and lies and lies she will never stop talking she
    will never tell the truth
She favors
She blows smoke into non-smokers' faces
She does not drive
She is manipulative
She is devious
She steals her neighbors' flowers in the dark
She thinks it's her right to steal her neighbors' flowers
She thinks she is a princess
She will not wear her glasses
She lies about her age
She is jealous of her daughter
She does not see that her daughter wears rags
She is scared
She is puzzled
She nags
She is always hurt
She is a hypochondriac
She is a compulsive buyer
She is a compulsive cleaner
She is a compulsive cook
She spoils her husband's chances
She flirts with the butcher, she flirts with the paperboy, she flirts
    with the priest

She would rather look like Bette Davis than herself
She doesn't know it is years since Bette Davis looked like Bette
    Davis
She thinks being rich would solve all problems
She is professional Irish
She is proud of her tolerance of non-Catholics
She quit her job
She will not learn how to balance a checkbook
She is the world's champion rubber check writer
She says That's the way I am when she means That's the way I'm
    going to stay
She never stops complaining about people dropping in
She is demanding
She said about her child That one has no heart
She is crazy
She is dangerous
She knows that everyone is lying to her
She knows she has been set up but doesn't know how
She hates herself.

LAMB OF GOD WHO TAKEST AWAY THE SINS OF THE WORLD, SPARE US O
LORD

LAMB OF GOD WHO TAKEST AWAY THE SINS OF THE WORLD, GRACIOUSLY
HEAR US O LORD

LAMB OF GOD WHO TAKEST AWAY THE SINS OF THE WORLD, HAVE MERCY
ON US.

Sounds just like my Ma, think Pearl, Daisy, and Rita.

Meg washes her hands of the whole business: she knows a frame when she hears one.

Maggie tuned out at She drinks: Maggie knows half the country are alkies, BETTY FORD JOAN KENNEDY JOY BAKER MERCEDES McCAMBRIDGE PRAY FOR US, knows a momma can't drink without the consent of the family, knows a long list of booze crimes will follow, Booze crimes are so predictable they bore her. She stands at the sideboard fixing herself a drink.

"Just when everything's going so well," Gretchen wails, "why does she have to come *now*?"

On the terrazzo in front of the enormous kitchen hearth, Pearl and Rita bow formally to each other and begin the Mother/Daughter Gavotte. Pearl plays the mother, Rita the daughter.

        M. Please visit.
            D. Can't visit.
                    M. Don't visit.
                D. Can visit.
            M. Can't visit.
        D. Please visit.

Every step of Pearl's is out of synch with Rita's. They switch parts and dance faster and faster. It's a funny dance—everybody's laughing except Gretchen—but it's not a joyous one. In the firelight cast, Gretchen looks like an old woman. Pearl stops dancing.

"My Daddy was my mother," Pearl says.

In the silence, Maggie thinks of her Gramma, Meg thinks of her aunt, Daisy thinks of her Mother Superior, Rita leaves the room.

Your mother fought her life, Daisy's Mother Superior points out. That may be what finally gave you the strength to fight yours. Never forget that she permitted you more than domestic goals. Daisy's beeper pierces the silence and the thought.

Pearl and Maggie's eyes meet—Daisy's Bellboy Beeper, signaling her to contact the Museum pronto, always gets a good workout, but four times in a quarter hour is unusual—Maggie glances down.

"Quasi? The attack?" Pearl asks, but Daisy picks up the registered letter with the wax seal and leaves.

"I said What attack?" Meg says.

"The Japanese bombed Pearl Harbor this morning," Pearl says.

Maggie spits out her drink and a laugh, the laugh stops on a dime. Meg looks at Pearl with disgust. "You should be under guard."

Pearl shrugs, "We'll hear about it sooner than we want to."

"How the Hell am I supposed to keep things under control around here when nobody tells me anything?" Meg doesn't wait for an answer; already talking into her walkie-talkie, she exits.

Pearl shuffles for a few seconds.

"Guess I'll go try to work," Pearl says.

"Here's mud in your eye, Gramma," Maggie says to her drink in Serbo-Croatian.

Gretchen's already in The Waiting Room.

10

Maybe Pearl should have gone into music: she not only plays piano, she whistles Dixie. "You've only been off a week," Pearl tells Pearl, "You've got a right to be here, sweetheart, you're recuperating."

The tree outside her bedroom window rebukes Pearl.

She turns over, curls under the afghan her mother gave her when it went into the Hot Wash by mistake. The afghan is shrunk above Pearl, Pearl is shrunk beneath the afghan. "You're obscene," Pearl tells Pearl.

Her eyes are wide open. She doesn't understand how she can lie here, *be* here, yet be outside watching the curled form of her mother every afternoon on the couch beneath this same afghan. What did she think about?, Pearl wonders.

She closes her eyes. She's fully dressed except for her shoes. She's only resting a moment. What she hopes for happens: Time passes.

Pearl doesn't hear the beeper go off again.

Rita hears the beeper, hears the automatic message recorder switch on, hears the ticker tape going like Orville Redenbacker's popcorn, not an old maid in the batch, Rita giggles, hears all systems go in Daisy's room. Rita takes one last toke and stretches out on the blue velvet love-seat in the alcove, kitty-corner from Daisy's room. The sun streaming in, the patter of Daisy's footsteps from machine to machine, the hum of Daisy's voice are soporific and Rita yawns once or twice, but when the door opens she's there like a cat. "What's up, Doc?" she asks.

"The City is confiscating Heartbreak Hotel," Daisy says.

Rita claps her hands, "Nobody's tried that old confiscation trick in years. What else?"

Daisy holds up the letter with the red wax seal, "We have a week to vacate."

"Tell, tell," Rita says.

"This may be the move on MOTR."

Rita shoots off like the Fourth of July. Rita adores politics.

On the spot, Daisy formally appoints Rita Museum/Heartbreak Hotel liaison.

It's the best liaison Rita can remember in a long time.

Taking the steps two at a time on the way to her room, Rita forgets all her power is gone, and remembers

A WEEK TO REMEMBER: In one week's span, Rita makes love with a good old boy, a woman, a priest, and a seventy-year-old man. They're all people Rita loves: It's a week Rita also loves herself.

Rita shucks her silk pajamas, rifles her closet and dressers, shimmies into a gold satin hi-thigh leotard and a lamé T-shirt. For this job, she needs to blend into the crowd.

Daisy buzzes the other women to meet her in the wood-paneled study in five minutes, but before she leaves her room, she takes the letter out of her back pocket. She knows what it says, but rereads it for pure revel: a foundation for people with creative projects invites her to visit their island retreat this fall. She's been there once before for the happiest four weeks of her life and, even though at the moment it seems a world too removed from her present reality to be real, she's ecstatic to be invited back. They'd like her answer right away, but she's not sure what to reply. She's already due to leave next week for a working vacation on Grand Island, plans to hole up in a friend's cottage to prepare a model for the Museum's expansion for the next round of grant proposals. If this eviction business blows over in time for her to go next week, if Quasi gets better, say a miracle happens and blue skies come to Buffalo, will she be able to get away again in the fall? Will I even have a creative project then?, she wonders, and then the thought that's worrying all the others surfaces for the first time: there may not be a Museum in the fall. "Over my dead body," Daisy says aloud, she takes a brown whorled seashell from her bedside table drawer, caresses it a second, slips it into her front pocket. Just for a moment before she has to go downstairs to tell the women about the eviction notice, Daisy stands in the middle of her room: surrounded by clicking machines and flashing lights, she thinks about tropical islands, the scent of jasmine tangible in the air.

Maggie's scared, but she's steady pouring her drink. "What do they want to do to us?" she asks.

On a teak desk that once belonged to a railroad tycoon, Daisy makes a rub-out with her thumb.

"That's what I'm afraid of," Gretchen says.

"Why do they care about us?" Maggie asks.

"They don't care about us," Daisy says. "They'd like to see us get out of town. We're an embarrassment. My hunch is they think if they knock out Heartbreak Hotel we'll be weakened enough they can finally close MOTR down."

Gretchen shivers.

"What's their cover story?" Meg asks.

"They say they need Heartbreak Hotel for a shelter for retarded adolescent boys," Daisy says.

"That's so dumb it's funny," Pearl says.

"It may sound funny to you," Gretchen says.

"Is there anything we can do?" Maggie asks.

"Rita's going to the Museum to pick up her costumes," Daisy says. "It'll depend on what she sees."

"She'll see what she expects to see," Gretchen says. "I never could please her."

GIRL'S STORY #7: THE HARD-TO-PLEASE MOMMA

Momma, I got a B, the daughter said.

Who got an A? Momma answered.

Momma, I showed in the track meet.

Who placed? Momma answered.

Momma, I placed in the track meet.

Who won? Momma answered.

The daughter was chosen Homecoming Queen, the daughter ran all the way home, Momma, Momma, the most wonderful thing happened, I was chosen attendant to the Homecoming Queen.

Who's Queen? Momma answered.

I am, said the daughter.

On the floor in the corner of the study, Gretchen's in the angry cat, fight or flight, position. She alternates humps and hollows so fast they blur. She doesn't notice that Maggie, Daisy, Pearl, and Meg have left the room. If anyone told her she's alone in the room, she'd think they were blind and crazy.

11

"Maggie Magpie, how's it going?" Rita asks Maggie sitting on the back stoop.

Maggie shrugs.

"You spend too much time alone, Maggie," Rita says. "You gotta get out and around more." She opens up Maggie's thermos and sniffs, "Sloe gin fizzes," she says. She rummages around in her carryall, leans close to Maggie and whispers, "I've got some stuff that's even better than sloe gin fizzes. Take this, and this afternoon I'll come to your room and we'll have a tea party." She giggles, and slips a plastic bag into Maggie's pocket.

From behind an elm, Meg watches a drug transaction. She reads the name and place of an assignation on Rita's lips.

Daisy sits at the computer and double checks, she randomly selects a half dozen of the scores of Museum health leave centers and plugs in: nothing untoward is happening at any other center. That's bad. The Museum is accustomed to attacks, but since few people understand its inner workings, they've always been too diffuse to be totally effective. If the new administration has decided to pick us off one by one we've had it, she thinks. We can't withstand them alone. She plugs into her intelligence network: man in red jogging suit seen exiting premises at high speed, public service inspectors working double shifts. . . . There's dribs and drabs of suspicious activity, but not enough hard data to go on high alert yet. But something's up, and until it becomes clear exactly what it is, Daisy's not taking chances. She posts a notice by each exit:

> ### LAWS OF THE JUNGLE
> ### AT HEARTBREAK HOTEL
> 1. What anybody does in her own room is her own business.
> 2. Never go to anyone's room uninvited.
> 3. If leaving the grounds, sign out on blackboard near the door: time of departure, destination, route, and approximate time of return. Be exact with your approximation. After 30 minutes of grace, a search party will start out.

By the kitchen door, Meg reads over Daisy's shoulder. "How serious is this business?"

"We're sort of like Quasi at this point," Daisy says. "No immediate danger of death, but the future looks a little chancy." She frowns: Something nags her about Quasi's accident, but she can't bring it up to consciousness.

In a flash, Meg's switchblade glitters, "Just let those fuckers get in my way."

"Put that thing away," Daisy says, she puts her hand on Meg's arm and speaks quietly, "Don't do anything till I ask, you understand?"

Meg always understands a direct order, the blade retracts and disappears as fast as it appeared. "You're the boss," she says grudgingly, she thinks Daisy's dead wrong not to show force immediately: one eviction server disappear, they'd get the message who they were dealing with. She takes a step back.

"The eviction notice says a week, but that doesn't mean anything," Daisy says. "The Zoning Board of Appeals doesn't meet again for three weeks. Even if they schedule our appeal first on the agenda, it'll take them another week to hear the evidence and come up with a ruling."

Meg takes another step back.

Maggie adjusts the speed on the ice cube maker to produce faster. "What if they rule against us?" she asks the inside of the freezer.

"Our contract runs through December 31st," Daisy says. "They can't sell the house out from underneath us before then unless we agree to financial terms. We won't agree."

"Let's have a hell of a New Year's Eve party," Pearl says.

Meg continues backing up until she is gone.

"Now if our grants aren't renewed, we're in trouble," Daisy says.

"I don't get what's the big deal," Gretchen says, she stands on her head, flush to but not touching the wall. "Ever since I've worked at MOTR, some administration has been trying to close us down."

"Public sentiment has always saved us before," Daisy says. "We can't depend on it this time."

"The people love us," Gretchen says. "I get standing ovations."

"The people aren't sending any of us valentines in the polls," Pearl says. "A year or two ago, closing down MOTR would've been like closing down Disneyland. Now people shake their heads, sheepishly say . . ."

"I've been in the newspaper four times," Gretchen says, "I've sent my Ma every one of those clippings, it won't be enough. . . ."

Pearl takes a banana from the fruit bowl and holds it to her mouth as if speaking into a microphone, " 'I guess if you gotta do it. . . .', 'with the Arabs gouging us for gas . . . ', 'everything's closing, it's in the Bible. . . .' "

"I cannot get all upset about this!" Gretchen shrieks, flips right side up, cuts off Pearl's imitation of the man on the street being interviewed, "My Ma's coming to visit, Do you understand, My Ma's coming to visit," she runs out of the room.

"That's it from your roving banana," Pearl says, she peels it and eats it, looks up Roving Banana in the Pocket Calorie Counter, groans as she wanders toward the living room.

"Why does Rita have to get mixed up in this?" Maggie asks.

"Rita's the most astute pol I know," Daisy says.

12

THE TAMSEN DONNER MEMORIAL LIBRARY DEDICATED TO THE PIONEER HEROINE WHO CACHED HER PRECIOUS BOOKS IN THE NEVADA DESERT IS OFFICIALLY OPEN, DIES IRAE, DAISY SAYS AT THE CEREMONY AND CUTS THE SATIN RIBBON. THE TAMSEN DONNER MEMORIAL LIBRARY HAS THE LARGEST COLLECTION OF GIRLS' STORIES IN THE WORLD. MANY ARE RARE MANUSCRIPTS THAT HAVE NEVER BEEN PUBLISHED OR CIRCULATED. THERE ARE STORIES ON PAPYRUS, VELLUM, PAPER NAPKINS, AND THE INSIDE OF MATCHBOOK COVERS. TWO ARE WRITTEN WITH LIPSTICK ON MIRRORS. ALTHOUGH THERE IS LITTLE TRADITION OF PASSING DOWN GIRLS' STORIES ORALLY, DAISY HAS A PILOT TRAINING PROGRAM RUN BY IROQUOIS GRANDMOTHERS TO RECTIFY THIS. SHE IS STEADILY BUILDING A FINE TAPE COLLECTION WITH THE AID OF ETHNOGRAPHERS WHO TOOK POST GRADUATE TRAINING IN BEAUTY PARLORS. SHE HAS FURTHER BROKEN CONVENTION BY INSTITUTING A STORY READING TIME FOR PRE-SCHOOLERS AT 10 AM DAILY. ALL THE LIBRARIANS ARE WOMEN OVER 60 WITH CLEAR STRONG VOICES.

"Listen closely, children," the librarian says, "Today's GREATEST STORY NEVER TOLD is . . ."

Out of earshot in the stacks, a browser fingers through Girl's Story 77,005: WRITE YOUR SENATOR (Rita Studies Political Science).

Show Rita the intricacies of a leaf, she says, "Nice." She's faking outdoor orgasm.

Rita doesn't know she thinks birds are for the birds. Once a charter member of the Sierra Club who likes boys better than girls and can't understand why he likes Rita at all screams at her, "YOU'RE NOT EVEN AN OUTDOOR PERSON." Rita is profoundly insulted: he might just as well have accused her of not having a sense of humor. "How can you say that?" she yells back, "I'm saving up to go to Mt. Rushmore."

"Never mind," Rita's friend, Pearl, says, "You'll love Mt. Rushmore. It's like a giant coin."

Pearl knows that all the money in the world couldn't make Rita an outdoor person.

Till death do her part, Rita's an indoor person.

Put Rita in a nightclub, a convent, a casino, smoke-filled rooms, bedrooms, an ICU, a party—the party's never over. Rita could take you to school in indoor: in candlelight, in boudoir, in whisper, in nuance. That's why Rita adores politics or more specifically political men, Political men notice nuance. Rita and political men have something in common most men and women don't: their worlds touch.

CAREER COUNSELING FOR GIRLS, the browser speed-reads: being an indoor person is a matter of training and opportunity. It is not a matter of safety. Indoors is not safe either. Indoors you are beaten, your ponytail cut off, your breast excised, your lymph nodes stripped, your womb removed. Practice indoor-on-the-job safety. . . ."

"Obscene," says the browser, furtively rips the page out of the book to send to the Eagle Forum, hides the book at the back of the shelf, and renews *Cherry Ames Student Nurse*.

Outside the Museum gate, Rita's attention is momentarily caught by a bird streaking through the sky. Sometimes memories come to Rita on a flash of wing:

wind on the face,

clouds sailing,

bicycling down a country road just after sunrise, Rita and her best chum Carol,

the two of them the only people awake in a world blazing with life,

heady with rose smell,

a red-winged blackbird throwing its heart out to the sky,

leaves burning,

moss on a stone,

a frog's eye,

legs pumping full speed ahead.

Sometimes Rita glimpses distant memories from a time, nine and ten, when she was still an outdoor person, and has a strong sense of loss. Sometimes anger comes to Rita on a flash of wing, but not today. She flashes her badge and a smile at the East Gate guard who waves her on through. Rita pauses a moment to watch a woman try for the door prize.

Daisy has a door prize game. No one has ever won. Few try. It is easier than reading minds, harder than guessing age or weight. Daisy will give free lifetime admission to any person who can name her or his maternal lineage more than two generations.

The woman says,
"I am Gabrielle,
Daughter of Helen,
Daughter of Ella,
Daughter of . . ."
After two minutes, the doorkeeper says, "Sorry."
"Close but no cigar," says the East Gate comic.

In her dressing room, Rita closes the drapes, adjusts the lights, oohs and aahs over her exquisite new veils, sets six aside, neatly hangs the others on a tie rack. She switches her leotard and lamé T-shirt for the six new veils, throws a satin kimono over them, breathes a sigh of relief. Now she can move at ease anywhere in the Museum and nobody'll notice anything out of the ordinary. She is impeccably made-up, her fingernails are painted chocolate brown, she has a ring on each finger, gold hoop earrings that dangle to her shoulders, two gold barrettes on her streaked hair, bracelets on wrists and ankles, she flings a pink ostrich boa around her neck, and heads down to the room of mirrors to check herself out.

IN THE ROOM OF MIRRORS, GIRLS STAND IN FRONT OF EACH MIRROR AND PRACTICE SMILING, PRACTICE WIDENING THEIR EYES, PRACTICE COCKING AN EYEBROW, PRACTICE WALKING, PRACTICE MOVING. THEY MUST PRACTICE UNTIL THEIR MOVEMENTS ACHIEVE SPONTANEITY. THEY DO NOT SEE RITA NOR DOES SHE SEE THEM. THEY ARE INVISIBLE TO EACH OTHER, INVISIBLE TO THEMSELVES.

Rita makes a minute adjustment to the ostrich boa, fluffs her hair, it doesn't look as bad as she thought, the creme rinse helped, she owes Gretchen one, yes, it has definite possibilities, she twirls.

Gold flashes, her veils are rainbows.

She gives herself a final inspection. No doubt about it: Rita's a looker.

Old-timers claim that Pearl was once a looker before she gave up artifice. Pearl will not wear any make-up, although according to an underground issue of TRUE CONFESSIONS, she was once a mascara junkie: "Had To Have It Before Breakfast."

Because Pearl does not look like a dog without make-up, people naturally assume with make-up she'd be a fox. Gretchen is not alone in

74

feeling that with the world so drab, it is Pearl's duty to walk that extra mile.

But Pearl knows she would only look a tiny bit better. That she lets everyone go right on assuming she is one step removed from gorgeous shows that she hasn't given up all artifice.

YOU CAN'T FOOL ALL THE PEOPLE ALL THE TIME said the hunk in the beard: Story: "On the Campaign Trail."

Pearl goes to a party in blue jeans, a flag shirt, red suspenders. A woman in a low-cut evening gown gets drunk and sobs: "You are natural and beautiful, I look like a tramp."

Pearl touches the woman, looks her straight in the eyes, and denies all three allegations.

"She was two parts right," a man says later, "one part wrong. Your jeans are pressed, your shoes gleam, your suspenders and your socks match. You are artful simplicity."

Pearl salutes the man. She'd like to do more, but he's black and she's white, she doesn't have Rita's touch with pols, and she isn't asked into the kitchen. She sighs. They are two crusaders taking a momentary notice of nuance. This particular cycle will not complete.

Rita leans close to the mirror, and says, "Shit." Her left eyelash is drooping. She pinches the curler on, her brother got the long curly ones what a waste, says a Hail Mary and an Angel of God which Gretchen says scientific experiment has proven take exactly the time needed for curling and distract from the pain, successfully removes the curler without lash or lid, flutters the erect lash from a 90° to a 65° angle, and repeats Daisy's instructions to herself: keep your eyes open, kiddo.

13

Outside Heartbreak Hotel, two men in state uniforms stand on a utility pole and train high-powered spyglasses on the windows. "Aww, they got the drapes pulled," one says, "You getting anything?"

"I caught somebody standing to the side of the curtains there for a minute. Looked like she had clown pants on. I don't think she saw us."

"Let's try the back of the house."

Pearl leaves the living room, passes a man in a county uniform on the landing measuring the storm windows, goes up to her room, takes a hand mirror and flashes SOS in the direction of where the two men were on the utility pole, pulls the shade halfway down so that from a horizontal position she can still see the tree, lies on her board, and tries to make her mind go blank. She's keeping her eyes open but she can't stand to see much more.

In the ICU, Quasi's eyes are closed. The silver-haired doctor lifts one eyelid, then the other: only white shows. Quasi's eyes are rolled back into her head.

"Kinda looks like one of those movie monsters," says an intern. "Wonder what she sees up there," says the silver-haired doctor, he lets the lid drop, washes his hands, and leaves the hospital.

From a turret, Meg sees two men on the front utility poles, on the back utility poles, leave in a state truck. She sees a man in a county uniform put a tape measure in his pocket and adjust his nuts. No one sees her put her uniform in a bag and leave Heartbreak Hotel. She does not sign out.

In her room, Maggie is having an anxiety attack. She is filled with fear that she'll never see Rita alive again. Every time she closes her eyes, she sees a man pulling Rita's beautiful hair out of her head. Maggie has had anxiety attacks before, she knows that this is a bad one, and she knows what to do. She drinks bourbon to steady her hand so she can roll the joint. She keeps her eyes open.

14

Rita bops down the block up up up in the elevator three blocks over to catch the cross-Museum El to Madame Le Main's whom her friend Vivian swears by. Madame Le Main keeps inner and outer eye open on everything that goes on in the Museum. The sky is blue, the sun brilliant: it is one of the seven days of the year the sun shines in Buffalo: Rita's ecstatic.

She passes little girls sliding down lampposts. She smiles at them and knows they will keep on smiling after she passes.

She passes the flower shop, sticks her nose in to give the good word to Vivian who works the wrist corsages, but Viv's out with cramps. Rita spots anthurium and, on an impulse, sends five dozen to Quasi, even when they aren't sick, Rita loves to send flowers to people, especially to men, it brings out their innocence, she says, "Put in a bunch of jasmine too," she says, plucks one sprig out to put in her hair, signs the card, Your secret admirer, talks the florist into immediate delivery, "You're a lamb," she says, blows him a kiss.

She passes the butcher shop, the butcher is screaming I DON'T CARE WHAT HE MIGHT EAT FOR LUNCH LADY YOU WANT THE BEEF YOU WANT THE CHOPS I AIN'T GOT ALL DAY MAKE UP, Rita gives the poor man a smile to make up for the woman's indecision and curlers in her hair.

A tiny arrow points the way to "tinytown." Rita loves "tinytown," and wishes she had a sec to stop in today. Everything is so tiny. There are kittens everyplace, there's the Dolly Madison stamp, a tiny stamp for a tiny lady, a woman says in a tiny voice, it's so cute, it's like a play stamp, there's a tiny coin for Susan B. Anthony, tiny dolls and tiny doll houses with tiny furnishings, tiny lace coverlets, tiny boudoirs, everything you can imagine all in miniature, sometimes you feel like a great big clumsy in "tinytown," but most of the time you feel as delicate as a surgeon doing microsurgery. Rita's favorite "tinytown tale" is: "everyone wants to be tiny." A short-short. Two women share a room in the maternity ward. One is obese, the other tubercular thin. Both give birth to seven-pound babies. The fat woman glares at the thin woman a lot, and rebuffs all attempts at conversation. On the day they're discharged, she says, I have the tiniest cervix, you probably have a great big hole, you probably have a hole that looks like the Grand Canyon, my doctor said he's never seen a tinier hole than mine.

Rita passes a woman wearing a silver-blu mink coat. The woman, jaybird naked underneath the coat, is perspiring. "What a gorgeous coat," Rita says. The woman laughs and says, "I'm worth it." Rita hopes that someday she'll be worth a silver-blu mink coat.

Rita passes the charm school. The director of the charm school is the rudest person in the Museum. You are a rude boor, Jack, Pearl tells her one day. The director roars with amusement, and because Pearl tells her some truth, she tells some back: charm school is not to be charming. Charm school is to know charm. To do charm. To do charm charmingly. Pearl passes this on to Rita who says, I learned that in Brownies. Rita still thinks that if she'd had the opportunity to go to charm school, her life might have taken a different turn. The contacts alone would have been invaluable.

On the El, a man moves his eyes up and down Rita's body the whole ride: his hand in his pocket clinks coins.
When she gets off, she passes a man who says, "Hey Chicka, Wanna fuck?"
She passes a man who says, "Hiya Sweet Momma."
She passes a man who says, "Shake it, Sweetheart."
She knows she must look pretty good.

She passes the drugstore and waves through the glass at Winnie who's reading a comic book and doesn't see her. Winnie's 35 and loves comic books. She's of normal intelligence, is employed at the drugstore, lives with her mother and great-aunt, has never heard of comic book dealers or conventions, and is known among the neighborhood kids as a sharp trader. "Nobody puts anything over on old Winnie," Winnie tells the kids frequently.

. . .

She passes a little boy shuffling along in his sister's red dress. His cheeks are red. His Momma has caught him red-handed wetting his pants. Rita shakes her head, Tsk, Tsk, Shame on you, Rita thinks.

She lingers a moment at the Up Your Ess Room: waves to the authoress, poetess, Jewess, prophetess, actress, Negress, heiress, adventuress, laundress, seamstress, motorcycless, seductress, hostess, mistress, high priestess, ambassadress, proprietress, waitress, ancestress, directress, post mistress, inspectress, janitress, bartendress, chiefess, giantess, abbess, adultress, millionnairess, pawn brokeress, temptress, princess, murderess, manageress, Empress, shepherdess, Goddess . . .

Next to "tinytown," Rita loves the Up Your Ess Room best. Everyone's so small and sibilant.

A parade of little girls, barelegged, bareshouldered, prance by like ponies.

The crowd examines their thin shanks, cheap white boots, wrinkled pantyhose, red sequins on gooseflesh, batons dropping all over the street, and collectively says, Aren't they darling?

Rita sighs. Another one of her regrets is that no one ever invested a thousand dollars so she could learn to throw a shiny stick into the air.

At Dottie's Gentleman's Choice, a gentleman with gorgeous silver hair is getting a trim. Rita debates if she has time to stop in and say hello to her friend, Dottie the Lady Barber, but on a dime, her fingers stop itching to touch that silver hair when she glances through the one-way mirror next door and sees the dentist who gives double pain.

PERVERTS ARE NOT JUST GUYS WHO SNIFF GIRLS' BI-CYCLE SEATS ON HOT DAYS: While the dentist drills the young girl's teeth, his arm and elbow press and rub her breasts. Rita starts a slow burn. She went to this same dentist when she was thirteen. A family friend, she cannot tell. From fourteen until seventeen when Rita leaves home, she stops regular checkups, once a year leaves the house, fools around for two hours, sneaks the money back into her mom's purse. No one ever suspects, the dentist is not about to give her away, her mom has so much trouble managing money she never questions a godsend. When Rita is eighteen, she goes to a public health clinic and gets two impacted wisdom teeth pulled and eleven cavities filled. Rita watches the young girl squirm and suddenly does something out of character.

· · ·

Rita Goes On The Offensive: She nips into an office down the block where her friend Sal's an executive secretary. "Give me a sheet of paper and envelope, Sal," she says, she's really excited, she has a great idea. Sal sips diet soda, Rita types, THE COMMITTEE IS FULLY COGNIZANT OF WHAT YOU'RE DOING IN THAT OFFICE, MISTER, AND FULL SCORE IS BEING KEPT. Rita giggles: she has not known paranoid leftists for nothing. Her great idea turns into a brilliant inspiration: she signs the letter, BUFFALO ROSE. She types the dentist's name and address on the envelope. "When's your next messenger, Sal?"

"On the hour," Sal says. "What's up?"

Rita whispers her great idea and brilliant inspiration in Sal's ear, they both giggle. "Mum's the word," Rita says and sails the letter into the messenger bin.

Sal, who three times has trained male junior executives to be her boss, types 143 words a minute. By the time the messenger arrives, the bin is overflowing with Sal's version of Rita's great idea and brilliant inspiration.

The messenger, Pooh, a 36-year-old who doesn't look her age or like she's a shafted wife supporting three children, is the first woman hired by the delivery service. "This little girl's as good as any of our men," Pooh's boss says in public. In private, he pinches her and asks when she's going to deliver. As Pooh dumps the bin into her sack, Sal whispers a great idea into Pooh's ear. They both giggle.

Pooh covers every building in the West End. Still giggling, she takes off peeling rubber.

Down on the opposite corner from Sal's office, Rita's caught by a freak show convoy. After twenty minutes, she pokes the man next to her: "What's so special about them?" she asks. The man takes off his Bobby Riggs tennis cap and puts it over his heart: "Those are women with balls," he says. Rita's eyebrows shoot up: With the new full cut fashions, you really can't tell.

She wonders if they're in for tomorrow's pageant. Her bum luck to be on health leave: maybe Daisy'll let her come or she can sneak in. Tomorrow is the only day of the year the Museum closes: Memorial Day. Most of the workers sit around trying to forget, but there's an unbelievable pageant: one-half of the world is a spectacle for the other half. Last year, Rita was Chairman of the evening festivities and was mightily rewarded when Paulus Tillich cried out delightedly, "10,000 women's legs," at his first fancy dress ball.

Rita loves holy men. Pearl's blasphemy profoundly shocks her.

Pearl stands in front of the guru school and sings: Show me the way to go Ommmmmmmmmmmmmmmmmmmmmmmmmmmmmmmmmm.

Pearl is never going to be voted Layman of the Year, forget the Brotherhood Award.

"Pearl will burn in Hell, God rest her soul," Gretchen says.

Daisy looks up and says, "Pearl's the most religious person I know."

Gretchen makes the sign of the cross slowly and broadly, but Daisy doesn't seem to notice.

AT THE MUSEUM CONVENT, TWO ROMAN CATHOLIC NOVICES SIT ON THE FLOOR FLAGELLATING THEIR LEGS WITH WHIPS AS THEY'VE BEEN INSTRUCTED. ONE LOOKS AT THE OTHER HORRIFIED. "THIS IS *sick*," SHE WHISPERS. "WHAT DO WE KNOW ABOUT BEING HOLY?" ASKS THE OTHER.

"Today's story in our continuing series, Profiles Of Holiness," says the guest grandma reader over at the library, "is *From Time To Time* by Hannah Tillich." She reads: " 'AH,' SAID THE OLD WOMAN, ENTERING HIS ROOM WITHOUT KNOCKING, 'THE OLD TORTURE GAME.' THE OLD MAN HAD PUSHED THE BUTTONS ON HIS CUSTOM-MADE SCREEN. THERE WAS THE FAMILIAR CROSS SHOOTING UP THE WALL. 'SO FITTING FOR A CHRISTIAN AND A THEOLOGIAN,' SHE SNEERED. A NAKED GIRL HUNG ON IT, HANDS TIED IN FRONT OF HER PRIVATE PARTS. ANOTHER NAKED FIGURE LASHED THE CRUCIFIED ONE WITH A WHIP THAT REACHED FURTHER TO ANOTHER CROSS, ON WHICH A GIRL WAS EXPOSED FROM BEHIND. MORE AND MORE CROSSES APPEARED, ALL WITH WOMEN TIED AND EXPOSED IN VARIOUS POSITIONS. SOME WERE EXPOSED FROM THE FRONT, SOME FROM THE SIDE, SOME FROM BEHIND, SOME CROUCHED IN FETAL POSITION, SOME HEAD DOWN, OR LEGS APART OR LEGS CROSSED—AND ALWAYS WHIPS, CROSSES, WHIPS. . . .' "

Rita glances into the window of a Savings and Loan Company, her antennae flutter: One of the clerks is male. Before she has time to reflect on what that might mean, a white Cadillac with MD license plates speeds by. Rita thinks of Quasi and wonders how she is.

Quasi's lungs are filling with fluid. When Quasi breathes, one nurse thinks of Slurpees. Where the Hell's the Doctor?, she says. Emergency call, says the new RN, Maria Onesti, oldest of nine, scholarship student, summa cum laude, determined to escape her mother's life, she has seen the doctor drive off in his white Caddie and already feels those beige suede seats against her haunches. Emergency, my ass, says the head nurse, he's probably getting a haircut, Get X-ray up here, Onesti, she's gonna check out.

Rita doesn't want Quasi to die. Rita's terrified of dying. She doesn't want anybody to die. She thinks of all the people she doesn't want to die and her eyes fill. She thinks of her Mom, her Dad, her sister, her brother, her cousin, Paul Newman, George McGovern . . . eventually getting back to Quasi, don't die, Quasi. Rita's never told anybody this, but she and Quasi have a secret.

Having a secret with Quasi, Pearl says, is like having a secret with yourself.

15

A ROOM OF HER OWN

At Quasi's christening, an old woman draws the swaddling clothes back, looks at the misshapen bairn, looks around to make sure no men are within hearing distance, lowers her voice into the cracks of centuries of accumulated wisdom, and says "She was conceived by a menstruating woman." The X-ray technician preparing Quasi has one more comment. "P.U. Smells like rotten eggs."

Not only is Quasi a hunchback, an albino, nearly blind, and mute: she has body odor so fierce no one ever gets close enough to tell her that all of these things can be minimized, even totally disguised, if she works on her personality. Quasi is not the personality kid. Forget Miss America, Quasi is not even eligible for the pits prize: Miss Congeniality.

Although Quasi always tries to sit to contain herself, the first thing people see when they look at her is her hump.

Gretchen's back is smooth.

Daisy's back is strong.

Rita's back is dimpled.

Maggie's back is white.

Meg's back is up.

Pearl's back is out.

The technician adjusts the scanner and for an instant Quasi's hump is perfectly reflected in the glass. Like a refugee, Quasi carries her house on her back. She has no friend to tell her that vertical stripes can minimize her full figure.

The second thing people see is her whiteness. Quasi is the fairest of them all. Even though she has attained the essence of whiteness, no one wants her to live on their block. She is whiter than a vestal virgin, Snow White, a borrowed first communion dress, a silk shirtwaist dress a man always begged a girl to wear, a wedding gown with a secret gusset, a nun's habit on a tropical island, and a closet full of vinyl boots, but Coppertone will never ask her to show her bum on a white sand beach. Even Gretchen concedes that Quasi is beyond the help of cheek blusher. Quasi has no shadows. She is all light.

She is blinded by the light. Whenever she takes the bag off her head now, she shields her eyes with her beefy arm, but Pearl says that, years ago, Quasi wore glasses with coke bottle lenses. "Then one lens shattered, and then the other one too, and for the longest time she wore them with radiating cracks like bullets through a windshield. After all the glass fell out, she wore the frames until even the tape wouldn't hold them. She used to crawl along the verandah, groping and squinting with those ridiculous empty tortoise frames. It was the house joke; people'd say, Men don't make passes at girls who wear glasses. . . ," Pearl dwindles off, wondering what was so funny. Only Meg laughs and her laugh is mirthless.

Maggie shudders and pushes her glasses up on her nose. Her greatest fear is that she will wake up in the dark, someone malevolent in her room. Her hand on her glasses on the nightside table, they slide from her grasp, she hears the sickening sound of plastic snapping, glass being ground under a heel. A man will rape her, probably murder and mutilate her, and she will not be able to see his face. She will die not knowing her enemy.

Quasi is spared this fear. No one would touch Quasi if he had a ten foot pole.

At least one person wonders if Quasi might have a ten foot pole stashed away inside her size 22 peacock-blue polyester stretch pants.

After Gretchen sees the movie "Psycho," she asks Rita, "Do you think Quasi's a transvestite?"

Rita screams her off the porch.

Gretchen is shaken, but she tells herself that some people get uptight talking about sex.

"Okay, Peeping Tom, do your stuff," says the technician. The CAT scanner glides over Quasi, offers exquisitely detailed pictures of almost all parts of her body.

No sweat, Gretchen.

Quasi is rehooked to the other machines. Her room sounds like the GM plant. She is being sucked, tapped, filtered, dredged, pumped: Quasi is so out of it she doesn't know she's getting the Helena Rubenstein Special for free.

The nurse who barely made it to the basin says, "They just oughta pull the plug."

This is the first time it's been said, but it won't be the last.

Ugly, bestial, monstrous, menacing, scary Quasi. Who cares if she dies?

16

A Gallup Poll taken this moment shows:
1 for
2 against
1 undecided
2 abstain.

"I'll cut line to be first to pull her plug," Meg says. She doesn't care about the hump, the gimp, the mole eyes, the spots, or the smell: she knows from her stint at the Clearasil Kiosk that everybody's got imperfections. But to Meg, Quasi's the most dangerous breed around: a person out of control. Meg hasn't feared anybody so much since Janis Joplin, she had no control over her abandon, Meg thinks, and Quasi's worse, she can't even sing.

Gretchen will go to bat for Quasi: she's block chairman of the local Right To Life chapter. She puts frogs and lizards in formaldehyde and mails them to her Congressman once a month, This is a war for life, she says, Onward Christian Soldier. But instead of saying Yea Quasi, Gretchen tells the Gallup man, "So much suffering. It would be a mercy if God took her." Gretchen really believes this, but she does not believe for one minute that God will keep her. God's not running a welfare state, she says. Quasi's clearly the punishment for some terrible transgression, conceived in lust by an adulterous woman, a botched abortion, the wages of sin, she has to be paid off, Go Quasi Go.

Pearl knows where she stands on Right To Life groups—she sends lizards and frogs in formaldehyde once a *week* to Gretchen's Congressman who is beginning to be disgusted by these revolting smelling bottles piling up in his office—but she doesn't know yet about Quasi. It takes Pearl two days to figure out her feeling on every serious matter by which time the information she's based her decision on has changed significantly. "Give me a couple days to think on it," she says.

Maggie's mum, but she's only seen Quasi from a distance. From what she's heard, she figures that, around Quasi, she'd come off looking pretty good by comparison.

Daisy's still working on her Heartbreak Hotel/Museum strategy, but she knows her mind about Quasi: Daisy cares. She's getting on and cares about a lot of things she didn't used to, like veggies and her Irish blood and her Momma's endurance. "If Meg pulls the plug, I'll plug it back in," Daisy says. She leaves the pollster, slips into a doctor's uniform borrowed from the Museum Medical Complex, stencils the first name that comes to mind on a badge, pins it on, and M.VALENTINE M.D. enters the hospital through the Physicians' Entrance Only.

Rita thinks the pollster's awful cute, she can hardly keep her fingers off the downy hair on the back of his hands, but she's too good a pol to give away her vote this early in the game. But Rita owes Quasi and, though it may slip her mind temporarily, Rita never permanently forgets a debt.

17

RITA AND QUASI'S SECRET: One night as Rita comes down the path around the hedge, one of her many secret admirers jumps her. He twists her arm behind her back. He throws her to the ground. He holds a knife to her throat. He slaps her face. He tears at her clothes. "I love you," he says. Through her panic and terror, Rita is confused. She tries to say, "This is not a loving thing you're doing. . . ." "Shut up you bitch I love you I love you I love you. . . ," he says, he wraps her hair around his fist and is pulling it out of her head, Rita sees his eyes, sees that he does not see her, knows with every fiber of her being he is going to kill her, there is nothing she can do, she is sick with panic and revelation, there is a flash of white, in the whiteness everything goes slack. Rita faints, comes to, throws up, faints again. When she opens her eyes, Quasi sits watching her. Next to Quasi is Rita's attacker, his neck broken in two, his balls crushed like overripe plums. It is one of the men in the corner who jack off during Rita's act. Rita looks at Quasi. Quasi looks at Rita. In the moonlight, Rita would stake her life that Quasi has 20/20 vision. Soundlessly, Quasi picks up the rag doll body, Rita walks next to her supporting the head that lolls like a limp organ, together they walk to the orchard. Quasi lays the broken form on Rita's lap and begins digging. Silhouetted in the moonlight, Quasi's massive, curved form moving the earth rhythmically looks powerful and graceful, not grotesque. Together, they lay the body in the grave. "Dies Irae," Rita says the Requiem words that Daisy always says at memorial services. Quasi throws the dirt.

At breakfast, Rita tells people she caught her hair in the escalator. "My God," Pearl says, "You're lucky to be alive." "You're telling me," Rita says. She wears a Band-aid where the knife broke skin on her neck. Everyone assumes she has a hickey. Quasi's eyes are opaque, but till death do her part, Rita cares if Quasi dies.

18

Does Quasi care?

If Daisy has anything to say about it. In the ICU, M. VALENTINE M.D. strides into Rm. #7, nods to the physical therapist selecting vials from a kit, nods to the priest reciting ". . . These cities shall be a refuge . . . ," nods to a reporter from the Buffalo News, leans over Quasi's bed, whispers in her ear, "You're going to live."

Two nurses' aides come in with fresh linen. Daisy acts as if they're invisible, taking her sweet time to straighten up and exit, so they won't suspect she's not an M.D. They never suspect. They look at each other and mouth, Dyke.

The aide removing the bloodied sheets looks at Quasi and says, "What do you suppose goes on in their heads when they're like that?"

A jackhammer starts up outside blocking out the other's reply. "I think it's out to lunch time," she shouts, shaking out the new sheet.

It often is out to lunch time in Quasi's head, but this moment in her coma, the fog clears and she is jogging with Lazarus The Dead along a seashore. The trade winds blow Lazarus's burial wraps: the flutter of sheets is deafening—Mary and Martha clap their hands over their ears.

The sky is brilliant blue. The sea is turquoise. The sands are white. The trade winds carry the sickening smell of Lazarus The Dead into Quasi's nostrils. Quasi knows the cheesy, musky, shellfish smell, but she cannot place it. She wills all her orifices shut.

Lazarus says something, but her ears are shut. Lazarus speaks again, more sharply, and Quasi tries to keep her nose and eyes shut, open her ears a crack. She is having difficulty coordinating the various holes, her eyes slip open: dazzling light is everywhere: bouncing off the sea, catching in the sand crystals, bouncing off Lazarus's white hood: the light is killing Quasi. Lazarus turns directly to Quasi and shouts. As people always avert their eyes from her eyes, Quasi tries this same trick on Lazarus, but pushy Lazarus leans closer until Quasi must look directly into his hood. Lazarus's eyes are burnt-out orbs: Quasi recoils. "Will you get a move on?" Lazarus snaps, "You're going to be late for your own funeral." He leans so close his hood falls on Quasi's head like a moldy bag, Quasi thinks she'll be suffocated, but mercifully, it shields her eyes from the dazzling light.

At first all is darkness, gradually darkness turns to shadows. Far off in the shadows, lights flicker in the holes in Lazarus's face. Quasi moves toward them. The holes grow larger. Larger. The holes grow enormous until they envelop Quasi.

She is in Heartbreak Hotel's chapel, but it doesn't look as she has ever seen it: Instead of being deserted as it was for years, or throbbing with a minivac computer as it does now, the chapel is filled with statues, stations of the cross, and women reciting the rosary. One of the women moves toward the bank of flickering candles in front of a beautiful blue and white statue of the Blessed Virgin Mary. Quasi sees that it is a long ago Gretchen. She drops the money into the slot, strikes the taper, and lights a candle. She kneels to pray.

For every day this summer of her twentieth year, Gretchen has alternated being on her knees and being on her back. While Gretchen stays motionless, hands folded, head bowed, Quasi sees time passing as in a stereopticon: sees thousands of Gretchens aging in barely perceptible distinctions, sees thousands of candles flickering into life and snuffing out, sees with the weight of revelation that Gretchen will never be able to pray away this summer of her twentieth year, and sinks back into the fog.

19

Oh-Oh, there's Meg coming down the street, What's she doing here at the Museum?, and in uniform? If Daisy's put her on the case too, she'll just tell Daisy straight out No way, she's not working with anyone, she's not into dogs, children, killer cops, or partners, she does a *solo*, Rita wipes her eyes, ducks her head, and crosses the street to the other side. She especially stays clear of Meg who has already busted her three times this year: for slipping pasties, for sloping G string and, Rita can't forgive her this one, for jumping out of a cake after hours.

Jesus Meg, it's Jaycees, Rita says.

The law's the law, Meg says and runs her in.

Meg swings her stick. It is the only excess she allows herself in uniform. Meg never twitches, stutters, startles, or lets her stomach muscles sag. Meg is always in control. It's not easy to be always in control, but Meg makes it look like a piece of cake. That is part of her control. Meg watches Rita dart between traffic, watches a man in a porkpie hat saunter after her. She's after bigger game right now, but she's pleased that Rita's getting a little respect for the law. She is going to give people respect for the law if she has to bash their heads in to do it.

Rita nips into Frederick's of Hollywood and immediately forgets Meg, forgets Quasi, has an orgasm. If Rita has to die, she wants to go to Frederick's of Hollywood, Main Branch. She lingers, she fingers, she handles. She cannot resist a pair of purple satin panties with a keyhole vag cut-out edged in pink lace. She puts them on layaway.

She gets a block down the street, runs back and gets the matching bra with nip cut-outs. Her extravagance twinges her, but she reminds herself that she can probably take them off her income tax. She'll have to check that out with Lil, the unofficial tax adviser of the 9th Block.

TAKE IT OFF TAKE IT OFF CRIED THE BOYS IN THE BAND: Just like a secretary who brushes up on her typing before applying for a job, Lil, a topless go-go dancer, makes every effort to appear more employable, she gets silicone implants to increase the size of her breasts, deducts the cost of the procedure from her taxable income.

On Lil's advice, Josie, an exotic dancer, deducts her primary stage prop as a casualty loss when her pet viper perishes in a house fire: "You're like a farmer whose tractor burnt up," Lil tells Josie, "Your whole act went up in smoke."

Outside of Frederick's, Rita notes a woman in uniform carrying a box of Chinese takeout, the woman climbs into a messenger truck and takes off, but Meg is nowhere in sight. The sky is still azure. Rita's hips sway, her veils ripple, her high heels tap tap tap on the sidewalk. Shiny red patent leather with four-inch high heels, Pearl's Folly, Rita's Good Fortune, where did you get those gorgeous dancing shoes?, I covet them, Rita says to Pearl, They're fuck-me shoes, Pearl says, You can have them if you want, I'm giving up high heels.

High Stepping Blues: Sometimes Pearl regrets giving up high heels almost as much as giving up men. Power in a size 8 AA. Oh is there anything so sweet as strutting down a sidewalk in a brand new pair of red patent leather high heeled dancing shoes, the height, the frivolity, the balance, the rhythm, the sheer dazzle of it, the vulnerability, the weapon, tap tap tap go Rita's high heels down the sidewalk.

On her board at Heartbreak Hotel, Pearl remembers her Irish Momma born in Michigan who has Chinese feet, looks down at her earth shoes, remembers the power, and sighs.

Rita pauses on the sidewalk, one hip slung out, she flips open a gold compact, wets a fingertip with saliva to smooth down an eyebrow, she arches her neck, moves the mirror around to check out her image, the man is still there, she clicks the compact shut. For some time she's been aware that a man in a porkpie hat is following her. He looks harmless enough but it's been Rita's general experience that men wearing porkpie hats long for adventure, so she's keeping an eye on him.

Rita passes the woman who knows which men to wear sexy underwear for and which men to wear no underwear for.

She passes the woman who knows when to call young men by their full names and old men by their diminutives.

She passes the woman who knows which men are gay and which men aren't.

She winks at the woman.

The woman winks back.

· · ·

A gigantic wooden hand points to Mme. Le Main's. The hand is purple and webbed with black lines, somewhat similar to Rita's new panties: Rita takes this as a good omen. Rita can use a good omen right now because she notes that the purple hand has an unusually short lifeline.

Quasi's not the only one out to lunch. It's doubtful she'll be back in an hour, but a sign says Mme. Le Main will be.

GOTTA EAT: Rita's stomach makes a little rumble. She considers places she can go into unescorted and feel comfortable.

The cafeteria's open around the clock and it's comfortable as Ma's kitchen. It serves all the food girls can't order on dates: anything that drips or slurps or gets caught in the teeth. Every day is spaghetti day at the cafeteria, and Rita loves it, but she has to watch the pasta or nobody'll watch her. She waves to all the girls without boyfriends who sit in the corner and pig out on jelly doughnuts and cheese balls. One girl holds up a plate of homemade Hershey cocoa fudge, "Got your favorite," she calls. Rita moans and moves on. "We'll see how long you last," her friend calls after her, laughs, and opens up the caramel corn.

Rita peeks in the window of Chez Gerald. She knows it's a fancy restaurant even before she sees the waiters RULE OF THUMB: CLASSY = WAITERS/ MODEST TO POOR = WAITRESSES. She sees a romantic tête à tête.

A man and a woman are at a table. Violins play. Waiters hover. Flambés flamb. The woman reads the vellum tasselled menu three times. She is in an agony of indecision. She orders tentatively. The man tries to look like a bon vivant as he follows the woman's order, but he looks sick. His eyes continually slide to the right-hand corner where the prices are listed. The woman's menu has no prices.

Rita sighs, if she's lucky they'll seat her by the kitchen, unlucky the bathroom, and moves on down the street to a restaurant where her friend, Olga, an ex belly dancer, works. Inez, the hostess, tells Rita that Olga's varicose veins are acting up again, Rita slides onto the counter stool, drinks a glass of water, watches two men play Abuse the Waitress JUST STIR MY COFFEE WITH YOUR FINGER SUGAR WHEN I SEE YOU DUMPLING MY APPETITE INCREASES DO YOU WANT TO KNOW WHAT I REALLY WANT TO EAT WHAT'S A NICE GIRL LIKE YOU YOU'RE NOT LIKE THE USUAL WHAT TIME DO YOU GET OFF decides she'll go down the street and get Chinese.

ON VETERANS' DAY DAISY PRESENTS THE GOTTA EAT SURVIVOR MEDAL AND A LIFETIME SUPPLY OF SUPPHOSE AND HASSOCKS TO ALL THE WAITRESSES

As Li Ting, who has been told from birth that she is a girl and dung, hands Rita her takeout order, Wang Hsiu-chen, who has been told exactly the opposite, that she is dung and a girl, comes from the kitchen with fresh fortune cookies, whispers something in Li Ting's ear; they both giggle so delightedly Rita joins in, still has a smile on her face when she pushes open Mme. Le Main's picket gate.

Mme. Le Main holds Rita's right hand. Her finger traces the palm marks for Rita. "See this island," she says, "and see this island over here." Rita nods though she herself would call them simple oval shapes. She squints a little and sees how you might call them islands. "I see a man on this island, there's always a man, dear, but this island is changing shape, that's quite unusual . . ." Mme. Le Main strokes Rita's hand. "Just to be sure, we'll go over it again, and then see what the cards say. . . ."

Mme. Le Main pats Rita's hand with her right hand, turns cards with her left. Pat turn pat turn pat: the hanky-panky stops like a shot. Mme. Le Main sits up straight. She shuffles the cards. Three times she lays them out.

"What is it?" Rita asks.

"Beware of the stranger in your house," Mme. Le Main says.

Rita immediately remembers her horoscope, Put your house in order, and begs Mme. Le Main to elaborate, but she will say no more.

I gotta get home pronto, Rita thinks as she saunters out, hips swaying.

Behind her, Mme. Le Main makes the sign of the cross against the evil eye.

20

At Heartbreak Hotel, the heat is on and Daisy's in the kitchen.

Sometimes when she has a difficult problem to work out, Daisy chops and sneaks up on it. At the butcher block table now, she chops up a storm, chops celery, chops peppers, chops onions WHEN I FEEL BAD I CHOP ONIONS THE WOMAN SAID I GO INTO THE KITCHEN AND GET THE BIGGEST ONIONS I CAN FIND AND I CHOP AND CHOP AND CHOP AND CRY MY EYES OUT but Daisy's not crying, she chops methodically and thinks past a small pleasure at her competence hovering at mind's edge, thinks past Quasi, Gretchen's Ma, Heartbreak Hotel and the Museum to a young woman and a young Englishman standing on a verandah on an island in the tropics. Everything is lush and verdant and rampant, the air seeps jasmine and warmth and sensuousness. The young woman makes a declaration of faith and the Englishman laughs: He thinks she's pulling his leg. "You don't honestly mean to stand here and tell me you believe everybody came from Adam and Eve?" he says. A young Daisy is stunned by revelation: evolution is more than a Mason plot. "Maybe not everybody," she says and laughs and the Englishman laughs and she would like to reach up and touch his face and smell his skin through the smell of jasmine so strong it makes her giddy, light-headed. Daisy chops and thinks, Our sexual nature is at the heart of us: our wounds are coming from the same source as our power.

"Smells like a Thai whorehouse in here," says an orderly wheeling a lung suction machine into Quasi's room.

"It's jasmine," the physical therapist says coolly, "Jasmine," she says to Quasi, continuing to move the small vial back and forth, "Can you smell the jasmine? My mother always wore a perfume called Evening in Paris that was jasmine. I love the smell."

"I do too," says the orderly.

. . .

Upstairs in her room, Pearl tells herself sternly, Take up thy board and walk, she staggers to the typewriter, sets a clock timer for an hour, changes it to forty-five minutes, Just try to get something down besides yourself, she tells herself and starts typing: asdf jkl; It probably won't lead to anything significant, but typing is one of the few things Pearl can't do in bed.

In her room, Gretchen's trying to get something down too.
She writes "Dear Ma," crumples the paper up, takes a fresh sheet.
"Dear Mother," she crumples it up, takes a fresh sheet.
"Dear Momma," she starts to take a fresh sheet, moans, starts scribbling "I have always felt . . ." lickety-split until she gets to the end, scrawls her signature, sticks it into an envelope. It's so terrible I could never send it, What am I going to do, she crams it into her pocket, falls to her knees Please God Don't let her come I'll do anything you ask I swear to God I'll never do anything wrong again Please God Don't. . . . Suddenly her heart plummets, How could she, her oversight staggers her, what else has she forgotten, St. Jude, Patron of Hopeless Causes, intercede for me, she runs to the closet, goes beyond her Lane hope chest to the farthest recess, removes diaries, scrapbooks, stacks of movie star magazines from the top of her college trunk, unlocks the padlock, dumps out the top shelf, digs past pennants, a sky blue felt skirt with a black poodle appliqué, a cracked red rain slicker and matching hat, a rubber douche bag with a hole in it, lifts up the thumbtacks holding the bottom material down and, with trembling fingers, draws out a 9x12 manila envelope containing her greatest shame.

Where can she hide it so her Ma can't ever find it?, her Ma would kill her, can't lock it up, her Ma's got the fingers of Fagin, would hold it to the light, steam it open, dig it out of the trash, find it in the cinders, it's too big to eat, for a second Gretchen completely panics, then a crafty look comes over her face, the *Dead Letter Drop*. She slides the manila envelope down her leotard onto her midriff, puts on a bulky turtleneck sweater, zips a jacket over, puts sunglasses on, signs out for the grocery store, and leaves Heartbreak Hotel by a side door. She doesn't see Rita cutting through the yard, but Rita sees her.

A man in a porkpie hat steps out of the bushes, looks Rita up and down, nods thoughtfully. "Very nice," he says.
"Are you the assessor?" Rita asks.
"I'm CEO of Cherry Films," he says. "I can make you a star."
"I may be looking for a job soon," Rita says.
"Here's my business card," he says. "Don't lose it. The number's unlisted."

. . .

"Stir fry again?" Rita says, she dumps her U-Haul bag on the kitchen counter. "Here's dessert," she plucks out a bag of fortune cookies so fresh they're still warm, lounges on a bar stool, selects a fat carrot out of the veggie bowl, and makes her way around, across, up and down the Museum and the carrot. Daisy nods and chops, every so often asks a question. By the time Rita gets to Mme. Le Main's, the piles of veggies are mounting and the carrot is getting a real work-out. "Hey listen," Rita says lazily, "I'll be back in a sec. . . ." In the doorway, she turns around and says, "I was gonna take the tunnel home but it was jammed with employees all heading this way. They had chicken wings and beef on wek and overnight suitcases, I thought it was a bridal shower, they were so excited, but one of them said they were involved in a telethon."

"I know about that," Daisy says.

A stranger in the house, Daisy thinks. Mme. Le Main is fine-tuned today. Since Rita left, a dozen and more strangers have tromped through Heartbreak Hotel.

The garbage collector walks into Daisy's study, complains that there's not enough trash for him to make a report on, his job's on the line, they're going to have to come up with some more. Pearl donates all the early drafts of her comedy routines, "Jeez Lady," he says, "I'm not running a paper drive."

New storm windows are noted, the property value reassessed: Heartbreak Hotel's taxes are doubled.

A court summons is served for creating a serious parking problem. "We don't have a parking problem," Daisy says. "We don't even have a car." "You can't just think of yourself," the officer chides. "The inspectors have to park."

The phones ring incessantly and can't be heard over the chimes, bells, brass knockers, and banging doors.

Daisy gives up trying to work. She switches the phones on automatic message receiver, leaves the doors unlatched, puts the welcome mat out, and chops.

Things are happening at MOTR too. The 1st City Block get a bomb threat, has to be evacuated. The time comes and goes and so do all the customers who were evacuated. A day's receipts down the tubes.

The Zoning Board's report has arrived, it declares "Heartbreak Hotel out of character with the surrounding residential neighborhood, the city, the state, the country, the world, and the times." Daisy immediately sends by messenger a notarized supplement to her appeal which declares that "the State Mental Hygiene Law allows for such neighborhood centers and takes precedence over all local zoning regulations." The Zoning Board, for the first time in its history, schedules a special meeting to decide the case. Tomorrow night at 8:00, Town Hall, public invited. A motion for demolition of Heartbreak Hotel will also be discussed. Refreshments will be served.

Daisy chops. All the phone calls, the data fed in and spewed out of the computer, the codes zinged over short wave and carried by banded pigeons, the leaves at the bottom of the teacup, and the writing on the wall deliver the same message: the City Fathers mean business this time. "They want this place bad and that ain't good," Pearl sings on one of her numerous passes through the kitchen, she plays a little blues riff on the upright, yawns, leaves again, she's in and out, up and down, fighting the Battle of the Board.

Daisy chops. She's got the message all right, but she doesn't have the answers. How far will they go? If she wins this round, how long can she hold on? Should she fish or cut bait?

Although Daisy hasn't yet decided what to do, and public support is burrowing its head in its armpit sniffing the air in uncertainty, not everyone is hesitant. A federal judge, outraged over the invasion of privacy at Heartbreak Hotel, draws up a TRO, temporary restraining order, which excludes all non-MOTR employees from Heartbreak Hotel and property, and forbids harassment on the premises, house and land, up to and including the wrought-iron gates. "It's signed, sealed, and ready to go, Daisy," says the judge. "Just say the word and you're a fortress."

Daisy's not quite ready to say the word. Nobody's come for almost half an hour, she notes, did they get what they needed? At that moment, she hears someone come up on the porch, wipe his feet on the mat, put his umbrella in the stand, start upstairs. She brings the cleaver dead center bull's-eye through the heart of the onion. It takes a steady hand wielding a sharp cleaver, and a heap of chopping, dicing, pushing over to the side to get each separate part sorted out, but Daisy's knife flies, she's closing in on a comprehensive plan.

Pearl hears the vibrator turn on across the hall in Rita's room and sighs.

Pearl's still trying to work on a new routine. She could use the old routines forever because no one ever visits the 20th Block twice, but she writes the new routines for herself. The routine is coming slowly, Pearl's bleeding it out. The words are tenuous, contentious, they haven't gone into the page. Pearl doesn't know if they will go into the page or if they'll continue to lie on top. It's partly a matter of honesty, partly a matter of craft, partly a matter of waiting it out, it's above all a matter of luck. If Pearl allows herself to think about how unlucky she's feeling today, her heart will pound. Pearl fixes on the buzz of the vibrator. Pearl pictures Rita adjoining the vibrator. Pearl's loins warm. Pearl writes on the page, "Good afternoon, ladies and gentlemen, The loin warms at the rear." Ha Ha, says Pearl getting sadder and lonelier and more anxious. Pearl switches off the typewriter.

Pearl lies on her board and thinks about her father. Pearl's father is a much loved man who makes people laugh often, but not like her, not so often they start expecting it and stop loving him when he stops delivering. Pearl's father never planned any of this out as far as Pearl knows. Pearl's father is a reserved man and she doesn't know very far.

THE BANQUET ROOM AT MOTR IS PERPETUALLY RESERVED FOR THE ANNUAL B.F.O.E. FATHER-DAUGHTER BANQUET. ORGANDY DRESSES AND LINKED ARMS AND OLD SPICE AFTERSHAVE. IN FRONT OF EACH LITTLE GIRL'S PLATE, THE FAVOR IS WRAPPED WITH TRAILING PINK RIBBONS. ONE YEAR IT IS AN ANGORA STUFFED KITTEN. ONE YEAR IT IS A SWISS MUSIC BOX THAT PLAYS

SHE'S THE SPIRIT OF CHRISTMAS/
THE STAR ON THE TREE/
SHE'S EVERYTHING GOOD AND SWEET TO BE/
SHE'S SUGAR/ SHE'S SPICE/ SHE'S EVERYTHING NICE/
AND SHE'S DADDY'S LITTLE GIRL.

Pearl's father bows to her. Pearl curtsies to him. She threads her arm through his. All eyes are on them as they walk to the head banquet table. Pearl's father is the most handsome man in the world. Pearl is the prettiest little girl in the world. Anybody can see that Pearl and her father make a perfect couple.

Pearl's mother can see it.

Pearl is in a boat with her mother and father. If the boat turns over and her father can save only one, Pearl knows who it will be. The certain knowledge of this secret weighs Pearl's heart.

Pearl stares through the pane at the tree and thinks:
I'm a bad daughter.
    A bad mother.
    A bad wife.
    A bad comic.
    A bad friend.

100

In that order.

Surely I'm the unhappiest of men.

She doesn't hear her timer alarm ding or the knock on Maggie's door.

Even if the machines weren't clacking and lungs slurping, even if she were home in peak condition, Quasi wouldn't hear the knock. Opportunity never knocks at Quasi's door. At the hospital, she sinks deeper into a jasmine-scented fog.

21

Maggie opens her door. It is not Rita.

The old man takes off his hat and bows formally. "May I come in?" he asks.

Maggie nods, and closes the door behind him. She has never met her visitor, but recognizes him immediately. Although she has not invited him to come, she understands that his visit is a tremendous compliment to her. Her silence takes on a reverential air.

Ceremoniously, he sits and, after a moment, comments on the gray day. "I always have trouble in Buffalo," he says. "If I bring my umbrella, it snows. If I bring my rubbers, I need my boots." He sighs. "Rainy days and Sundays always get me down."

He begins to arrange things on a card table. "This is the female plant," he says. "This is the male plant." They look the same to Maggie, but she keeps it to herself. Deftly, precisely, the old man scoops a spoonful from each pile, mixes them, and rolls the joint.

Maggie and the old man pass the joint back and forth. The smell of hashish is heavier than jasmine. Maggie has never felt so lucid.

The old man takes in the motel room decor. "Besides your bag, there is nothing of you in this room."

Maggie is silent.

The old man raises his eyebrow.

The raised eyebrow waits.

"One place, another place, they're pretty much the same to me," Maggie says.

The old man stares at her suitcase that sits in the middle of the floor.

"Why don't you unpack your bag?"

"I won't be here long," Maggie says.

For some time, they toke in silence.

"You could at least put your Gramma's doll on the dresser or the side table."

That the old man can see inside her suitcase seems to Maggie wondrous and perfectly natural at the same time.

"She wouldn't like this place," Maggie says.

"The doll or your Gramma?" the old man asks.

"Neither one," Maggie says.

Maggie scoops a spoonful from each pile and makes the next round. The old man inhales so deeply Maggie watches him grow to twice his size.

The old man squints at her suitcase. "Where is your yellow dress?"

"I don't have a yellow dress," Maggie says.

"Last night, I had a dream about you. You were wearing a yellow dress and you were gathering daisies. The sun was shining, your skin was brown and glowing, the daisies were sparkling with dew."

Maggie smiles.

"There's more," the old man says.

"From the center of each daisy, one dewdrop began travelling down the petals, growing larger and shinier and opalescent until it turned into a pearl. You were standing in daisies, your arms were filled with daisies, and all the daisies were spilling pearls."

Maggie flushes with pleasure and wishes she had a yellow dress.

In the Hall of Fashion in the Museum's First Ladies Wing, someone flicks a Bic this very second to the hem of Abigail Adams's yellow dress worn to John's Inaugural. Flames leap up the old material lickety-split. Dolly Madison's wax eyes watch without expression.

On 2nd Block, Meg steams out of the Police Body Shop, she is livid, in a half block, she busts a jaywalking jogger, a drunk, and a Moonie panhandler, she may be prohibited from arresting criminals for seven weeks, two days, and thirteen hours, but they won't find that out till they get to court, she cuts over to Sixth Avenue to throw a scare into Mme. Le Main so the day won't be a total waste.

Fuck. At Sixth Avenue, there is nothing but blowing sand. Mme. Le Main has folded her tents and disappeared into the afternoon.

Meg considers. If she takes the El, she might still catch up with Mme. Le Main Downtown before Daisy misses her.

"What language do you dream in?" the old man asks.

"None." Maggie feels sad saying that.

"Everyone dreams."

Maggie shakes her head.

"Everyone dreams," the old man repeats somewhat petulantly.

"If I dream, I do not remember," Maggie says.

"You must remember," the old man says. He takes her hand and leads her to the bed. The moment Maggie's head touches the pillow, she cannot keep her eyes open. "What is happening? I'm so tired. So . . ."

"Sleep," says the old man. "Dream." He removes her glasses and puts them on the night table. He draws the draperies.

Maggie realizes the old man is next to her on the bed. She is awake and her eyes are wide open. There are shapes on the ceiling. The shapes change like a slide show.

For some time, variations of the same shape come on. Each time Maggie changes the slide, the irregular shape is seen from an infinitesimally different angle.

It is shadowy.

It is clear.

There is an opening in the center of it.

The opening is not a circle nor an oval nor can Maggie see where it leads.

Irregular textures surround it.

The shape appears to be bumpy.

It appears to be smooth.

It is fringed with what look like cilia.

Maggie is fascinated: Is it a soul?

Finally the old man says, "Well. Do you recognize it?"

"No," Maggie says.

"It's a cunt," the old man says.

Maggie does not let on that she is embarrassed by his word. In all the languages Maggie knows there is not one word for female private parts FEMALE PRIVATE PARTS BETWEEN YOUR LEGS DOWN THERE CROTCH THING VAGINA GENITALS PUDENDA PUSSY TAIL BOX MEAT PIECE OF ASS HOLE BEAVER CUNT TWAT SNATCH SLIT SLOT SLASH GASH she feels comfortable with. Maggie is also embarrassed by her naiveté: it is obvious what the shape is. Whatever she says will make her look like a prude or a dummy. She stays silent.

22

Ever since ninth grade when Gretchen starts riding a bus with godless atheists and hoods from the public school every day, she fears being thought a prude, but she's no dummy. She pulls the collar up on her jacket and doesn't talk to anybody. She doesn't know this section of the Museum, never comes Downtown, women who go Downtown get what they deserve.

WHO FUCKED LINA MEDINA? says the graffiti on the fence, Gretchen averts her eyes, she hates vulgar language. She thinks of her Ma saying Mabel Mabel get off the table, is mortified, pushes the face, voice out, thinks of Meg who has a gutter tongue.

Every word of it learned from my Uncle, Meg tells Daisy with family pride. Of course not one goddam motherfucking word of it ever used in front of my Uncle, she adds with a snort. My Uncle had as many definite ideas about ladies and their behavior as Miss Gretchen on her high horse.

Gretchen feels like swearing at Meg, but she restrains herself. Swearing is a sign of low class and poor vocabulary, she says. Everybody knows that.

Does everybody know this? Meg asks, she makes the arm/hand signal for Fuck You.

What I hate most about Health Leave, Gretchen says to Daisy, is having to associate with riffraff. Her head high, she leaves the room.

When Daisy prepares her Broom Closet exhibit, she consults Meg: Do you watch your mouth to protect your Uncle's sensibilities or to protect your place in his affection?

Damned if I know, Meg says.

In truth, Meg thinks she protects both of them.

In fact, Meg deludes two people.

DAISY HAS A BROOM CLOSET THAT CONTAINS SWEAR WORDS WOMEN HAVE SAID IN FRONT OF MEN, AND AN UNDERGROUND MISSILE SILO THAT CONTAINS SWEAR WORDS WOMEN HAVE SAID IN FRONT OF WOMEN. THE SWEAR WORDS WOMEN HAVE SAID TO THEMSELVES ARE CONVERTED INTO FUEL TO POWER THE WESTERN HEMISPHERE.

Gretchen passes a seedy bar, its neon sign on in mid-afternoon offering what a man in a blue Ford once said were all of life's necessities, especially the pool:

Girls	Pool
Beer	Music
Color TV	Food

A woman, reeking of beer and musky cologne, comes out the door, Gretchen averts her nose, she knows her kind.

Gretchen passes another bar, **WILD WOMEN**, the sign says, she's heard about that, they got all these women in cages.

Gretchen passes the Museum and School For Strippers run by Miss Forty-Four and Plenty More who also sculpts and, in her spare time, markets a $10 strip kit, complete with pasties, G string, navel gem, and instructions. Slut, Gretchen thinks. The navel gem looks pretty good through the plate glass, Gretchen thinks of Rita—whom she exempts from all her ordinary standards because a) Rita's extraordinary, and b) unlike some people she could mention, Rita is not a mother so it's all right for her to have a strong sex drive—maybe she'll tell Rita about that, Rita has a knockout navel.

When Rita is an infant, she has an umbilical hernia. Tape a quarter onto her bellybutton, says the doctor. As long as we got Rita, we'll never be broke, says her father. Mabel, Mabel, get off the table, that quarter is for beer, says her mother.

Rita's quarter-sized navel is a marvel:
Rita's navel is a wishing well,
the pools of Bethesda,
an orifice,
an oracle,
Children cannot stop putting their fingers into Rita's navel,
Men dive into its dance.

The man who gives Rita a pigeon blood ruby for her navel is probably the man she'll marry.

The man who brings Meg a pair of dancing shoes is probably the man she'll marry.

The man who brings Maggie the warmth of the sun without burning her up, a yellow dress will suffice, is probably the man she'll marry.

The man who brings Daisy the intensity of an island without its confinement is probably the man she'll marry.

The man who makes Pearl laugh is probably the man she'll marry.

The man who goes down on Gretchen and convinces her that her perfume's better than any on the market is probably the man she'll marry.

In her nightclub act, Pearl always brings down the house when she sings The Girl That I Marry. When Pearl finishes, with that soft sweet-smelling satiny pink lace girl of his dreams, there's not an unlumped throat in the place. The men are sitting still, the flower seller sells out of gardenias, and two women look into their compacts and discover they are crying.

There's a bad smell in Gretchen's nostrils, rotten fish, she's mortified. She breathes shallowly, and sprays wrist and neck pulse spots with a purse vial of French perfume that smells like gardenias. She wishes she had douched before she left the house, what if she gets into an accident?

She passes a teenage runaway poured into a pair of blue jeans, that girl is just asking for it.

She passes a bag woman who rummages a trash can, How could she allow herself to sink so low?

She makes a wide circle around a prostitute, nobody'd dress like that unless she is one, pulls her collar up further, why didn't she put on a head scarf, what if somebody thinks she is one?

A woman in purdah approaches, for the first time Gretchen fully appreciates the advantages of purdah, she nods to the woman who is totally covered except for eye peepholes, the woman hisses at Gretchen, "Wait a minute," Gretchen says, she puts her hand on the woman's shoulder to explain, "I don't belong here," she begins, the look of fury in the woman's pupils stops her, she shakes Gretchen's hand off like vermin, "I'm a Roman Catholic," Gretchen says to her back, "This is America," she stands up tall, but she is shaken by the misunderstanding,

The nerve, she thinks, her hand trembles as she puts on fresh lipstick. She has a rare stitch in her side, and the manila envelope containing the secret is chafing her midriff. There can't be anything worse than carrying a lifelong secret on your midriff, she thinks.

She passes an enormous room with cots for all the women who got physically fucked in encounter groups.

She passes two enormous rooms with cots for all the women who got emotionally fucked in encounter groups.

She wishes she could lie down awhile.

She passes Sexy Rexy, the go-go boy who got his bikini briefs ripped off by an old woman who called him a cunt teaser. He glares at her, I'll never return to Bay City, he says, All the women are animals.

Not me, Gretchen whimpers, but nobody hears her.

Sirens blare, red lights spin: Gretchen jumps as half a dozen fire trucks roar by.

Even though Gretchen is a winner of the Iron Kidney Award, competing against one million girls in peak condition from holding it till the date ends, she feels she's going to wet her pants.

She walks up to the Ladies at a Shell station, the knob doesn't turn, the sign on the door says Locked For Your Protection. That's so guys don't hide in there and jump you, the man in the Blue Ford says as if he's giving the weather report. Over at the gas pump, three men in coveralls watch her, "It's okay, I was just going to comb my hair," she says, though there's no way they could possibly hear her, one of the men makes a long slow wolf whistle, Gretchen tries to acknowledge the compliment by putting a little extra bounce in her step but she can feel that her walk is stiff and unnatural, Snap out of it, she tells herself, you look terrible from behind, the day they stop whistling at you, you're in trouble, girl.

She passes the woman with the secret smile who knows that when a man abuses her he really likes her.

She passes the clever girls who ignore boys' scorn because they know disrespect is really respect.

She passes the little girl who ignored the boy who liked her, "I drove him wild," the little girl says. She is bruised and battered, she limps along, clutches a news clipping in her hand:

DEAR MISS FIXIT: I feel sort of funny writing you, but I don't know who else to ask. There's this really gorgeous guy at school who follows me around, pinches me, and punches me on the arm. He's always trying to kick me, grab my bookbag, or push me up the stairs. Once in gym class he even tripped me and shoved me into the bleachers. Everybody keeps saying he likes me, so why does he treat me like this?

—INTERESTED IN HIM

DEAR INTERESTED: He's trying to get your attention. If you react, he'll probably lose interest. Ignore him and you'll drive him wild.

23

Chains flash, Maggie's eyes dart to the right-hand corner of the slide, to the left, center, bottom, she recoils: they jag through the entire slide. Faster, flashing incessantly, she clamps her eyes shut, they flash on the undersides of her eyelids, they are everywhere, she moans, she rolls on the bed.

"What *is* it?" the old man asks.

"Chains," she screams, but no sound carries over the clang.

FLASH: LOS ANGELES—AT THE SYBIL BRAND INSTITUTE, INMATE FERN DALTON, DAUGHTER OF A NAVAJO CHIEF, LABORS AND GIVES BIRTH TO A HEALTHY BABY GIRL WHILE MANACLED AND HANDCUFFED TO HER BED BECAUSE THE DEPUTY WHO HAS THE KEY TO HER CHAINS CANNOT BE FOUND.

FLASH: VIRGINIA CITY, MONTANA—KARI SWENSON, 24, A MEMBER OF THE U.S. BIATHLON TEAM, IS ABDUCTED WHILE JOGGING AND CHAINED TO A TREE OVERNIGHT. THE NEXT DAY, ALAN GOLDSTEIN, A PASSERBY TRYING TO RESCUE HER, IS KILLED WITH ONE BULLET TO THE HEAD, MS. SWENSON IS SHOT IN THE SHOULDER. AFTER FIVE MONTHS, TWO MOUNTAIN MEN, DON AND DAN NICHOLS, FATHER AND SON, ARE CAPTURED. TWENTY-YEAR-OLD DAN NICHOLS TESTIFIES THAT HIS FATHER HAD LONG PLANNED TO CAPTURE A YOUNG WOMAN TO BE THE SON'S SEXUAL MATE IN THE WILDERNESS.

"Please," Maggie says, "Please."

"Put another picture on, Maggie," the old man says.

FLASH: WILSEYVILLE, CALIFORNIA—SEARCHERS CONTINUE THEIR HUNT FOR MORE BODIES SUNDAY NEAR A BACKWOODS CABIN WHERE THEY FOUND HUNDREDS OF HUMAN BONE FRAGMENTS AND A

"HORROR FILM" VIDEOTAPE DEPICTING A TERRIFIED WOMAN BEING HELD A SEX PRISONER. THE SAN FRANCISCO EXAMINER SAID SEARCHERS COULD UNEARTH AS MANY AS 25 KIDNAP VICTIMS OF KILLERS LIVING OUT FANTASIES OF WAR AND SEXUAL DOMINANCE. LEONARD LAKE, 39, WHO LIVED WITH CHARLES NG, 24, ON THE PROPERTY, HAD SURVIVALIST FANTASIES OF BUILDING UNDERGROUND BUNKERS IN PREPARATION FOR WORLD WAR III AND KEEPING FEMALE "SEX SLAVES" TO SERVE HIM. THE VIDEOTAPE SHOWS THE TWO EX-MARINES TEARING AT THE CLOTHES OF A WOMAN HANDCUFFED TO A CHAIR IN THE CABIN, DEMANDING SHE PERFORM SEXUAL ACTS WHILE THEY THREATEN TO KILL HER. THE WOMAN BEGS THE MEN TO GIVE HER BACK HER BABY. . .

FLASH: ORANGE, CALIFORNIA—THE PARENTS OF A HELPLESS, BRAIN-DAMAGED WOMAN WHO APPARENTLY WAS RAPED WHILE TIED DOWN ON HER HOSPITAL BED SAY THEY ARE RELIEVED HER PREGNANCY HAS BEEN TERMINATED. A LABOR INDUCING PROCEDURE THAT LASTED NEARLY 24 HOURS RESULTED IN THE WOMAN PASSING HER 21 WEEK STILLBORN FETUS. THE 80 POUND WOMAN, WHO LIES IN A FETAL POSITION AND HAS NOT SPOKEN SINCE BRAIN SURGERY THREE YEARS AGO, CANNOT EAT OR EVEN OPEN AND CLOSE HER MOUTH. HER HANDS HAVE BEEN TIED TO HER BED FOR MONTHS TO KEEP HER FROM PULLING INTRAVENOUS FEEDING TUBES FROM HER ARMS. THE PREGNANCY WAS DISCOVERED DURING ROUTINE TESTS. . .

FLASH: OKLAHOMA—3 GIRL SCOUTS ON A CAMPING TRIP ARE BRUTALLY RAPED AND MURDERED

"They're all the same picture!" Maggie screams.
The old man shakes her. "Put another picture on."

A nurse glances at Quasi's EEG tracings and thinks, What's the point? They just oughta pull the plug.

At a hologram exhibit at the Metropolitan Museum of Art, one hologram shows two lesbians whipping each other. "This insults women!" shouts brain scientist Naomi Weisstein, she pulls the plug. Bells clang, whistles shriek, uniformed guards come running from every direction.

Two nurses and an orderly hold Quasi while another plunges a shot of Demerol into her buttocks and starts an IV sedative hook-up.

. . .

Forever it seems they watch the darkness.

In the beginning, it is restful. Maggie feels cool. Maggie feels safe. Maggie could lie here forever watching the darkness.

Slide after slide, repeatedly Maggie flips the slides, it is always the same slide.

Maggie becomes aware of the number of flat black slides that are yet to come.

She is overwhelmed. Maggie becomes aware of the old man. "I'm sorry," she says.

"I'm really very sorry," she says later. She hears the small lilt in her voice, she hears the voice of a good hostess whose party is getting boring through no fault of her own. Her attention goes back to the darkness.

Slide after slide.

Slide after slide after slide.

Maggie cannot bear so much darkness. Please, Maggie whispers, Please.

On the ceiling, the darkness begins to move like smoke, shifting sands, waves, the waves begin to roll, so cool the waves, so dark and cool, "Let that go," the old man says sharply. "You've looked at that long enough."

Maggie does not want to let it go.

"Let that go!"

With an enormous effort of will, Maggie puts on a different slide.

"You're taking all my energy," the old man says.

"I must rest awhile," the old man says.

"I am an old man."

But Maggie cannot keep her eyes off the slides.

"I don't have the energy for this. . . ."

Her eyes on the slides, her ears registering the plaintive voice, a part of Maggie registers something else: The old man is finger-fucking her. "The energy needs every opening," he says. Maggie says nothing for these reasons:

    a. The old man is world famous. She is flattered that he has noticed her.

    b. The old man is very wise. He has not only spent time in the Orient, he has spent time on the West Coast.

    c. The old man is scary. He traffics with the occult.

    d. She is embarrassed that he thinks she's so dumb she'll swallow the energy-opening line.

e. For all she knows, it may be true. See a. and b. and c.
f. She is after all lying on the bed with him. Maybe she asked for it.
g. She does not want the pictures to stop.

It is infinitely simpler to pretend she doesn't notice.

24

Maggie can't hold a candle to Gretchen when it comes to pretending not to notice things. At 10, Gretchen starts out pretending not to notice the boys talking dirty; before she is out of her teens, she is classified legally blind. Right this minute, Gretchen doesn't notice Marabel Morgan wrapped in Saran Wrap signing the surrender papers and accepting a trash compactor as a consolation prize. It's a moving ceremony Gretchen misses: Marabel sings The Impossible Dream backed up by the Mormon Tabernacle Choir.

Gretchen doesn't notice porn shops and massage parlors and Linda Lovelace with a dog at her feet, a knife to her throat, a gun to her head.

Gretchen doesn't notice the Kansas woman, who, in 1946 at age 16, is in her apartment when the lights go out, and a bottle is shoved under her nose. She wakes on the kitchen floor, blood pouring from her legs, branded on both thighs with flatirons.

Gretchen doesn't notice the man who calls himself "Poet," who, in 1977, reads about the branding in old newspapers and begins writing the woman that he is fascinated by the brands, can he come see them?

Gretchen doesn't notice the pharmacist and the dentist going into a seedy hotel together.

Gretchen doesn't notice the flasher.

She cannot ignore 2000 "X" rated theatres with marquees blaring GIRLS USA HOT LEGS CANDY GOES TO HOLLYWOOD LITTLE ORAL ANNIE CEMETERY GIRLS and she remembers her hero, John "Duke" Wayne, "I think any man who makes an 'X' rated picture should be made to take his own daughter to see it."

A car draws alongside, two men in it, Hello HoneyHips, says the driver. Gretchen pretends not to see the car. For half a block it hugs the curb cruising at her pace. "Aren't you afraid?" one of the men drawls. She turns down a one-way street. While the car makes a three point turn to back down the one-way street, a gang of teenage boys comes from the opposite direction. Gretchen ducks into a doorway before they see her, cowers in the shadows as they pass by.

IN THE GOOD OLD SUMMERTIME: Maggie lies awake on her bed listening to gangs of boys roam the street, their shouts and laughs and swaggers and boasts filling the air with threat that winds into her bedroom window, laces around her like an indestructible man-made fiber and corsets her in place. No matter how warm the night, she will never sleep naked. No matter how warm the night, she has yet to hear a gang of roaming laughing boasting shouting swaggering girls.

Ah whooey ta whooey, ah whooey ta whooey, clickety clack, it's echoing back, the blues in the night: One night at 10:00, Pearl waits for a friend at the railroad station. The train is late and she chews the fat with a station cop. He points out two boys, 11 and 13. "Railroad buffs," he says. "Down here every night, if there's any history of the railroads left it'll be due to boys like that, those lads keep the railroads alive." Pearl pictures two girls 11 and 13 hanging around a railroad station at 10 PM, and sighs. Depending on their address and color, they'd be severely reprimanded or taken to Juvenile Hall and booked for soliciting. They will never keep the railroads alive, oh ho ho Toot Toot Tootsie Don't Cry, Toot Toot Tootsie Goodbye.

Although it's the middle of the afternoon and the streets are relatively deserted, it feels like Saturday night at Times Square to Gretchen. She doesn't dare take out her watch to see what time it is, somebody'd snatch it away. She digs into her pocket for Kleenex, a crumpled envelope drops unnoticed to the sidewalk, she wipes the beads of sweat off her face, only the secret burning a hole on her bare midriff drives her on. For all her pretending, Gretchen knows that the world contains menace and danger ONE OF EVERY THREE WOMEN WILL BE RAPED IN HER LIFETIME, THE FBI SAYS, EVERY SIX MINUTES EVERY DAY IN THE UNITED STATES ANOTHER WOMAN IS REPORTED RAPED, EVERY 18 SECONDS A WOMAN IS BATTERED but it's not for women like her. She is terrified because these men do not seem to be able to tell the difference. By the time she sees the outlines of the DEAD LETTER DROP she is hysterical and not seeing clearly. She does not see that there's no identifying skull and crossbones on the DEAD LETTER DROP. She fumbles for the envelope through all her layers, manages to get it out, the box lid open, and her secret deposited forever gone down the drop. Someone touches her from behind, she screams. "What the Hell you doing down here?" Meg barks. Gretchen falls into Meg's arms, she has never been so happy to see anybody in her life, Meg is extremely uncomfortable, pats her clumsily the way they said to at Hysterical Management Seminar, withdraws from the embrace as soon as possible, and is damned curious why Gretchen used this remote Library Drop for Overdue Young Girls' Stories rather than one uptown.

25

ANOTHER RAILROAD BUFF

And what of the old woman bouncing along on the Bluebird bus?
She would be very happy to know that in Buffalo, New York, two lads
are saving the railroads, ta whooey ta whooey.

"I used to travel on trains," she tells Fred, just in case he hasn't
noticed she's not his regular kind of passenger.

"The trains are dead," Fred says.

"What do you mean?" she asks.

"Phtttt," he says.

She never understands remarks like that, people just inform her
that something that was part of her life is over, it makes her mad. "Can't
somebody *do* something?" she asks, but Fred doesn't hear or doesn't
answer. She takes a sip of lukewarm coffee, awful stuff, and wishes she
had a drink. Well maybe later. She hates to think about it, but her
old friend liquor is starting to turn on her. Makes her stomach act up,
it's getting harder and harder to ignore it, does everything turn on you
in the end? She stares at the steel back of Fred's seat, remembers velvet
upholstery with white doilies, and wishes she were on a train. She has
too many manners to tell Fred this, but she hates bus travel. Buses are
for people who are going noplace uncomfortably. Though she must
admit there seems a perfectly nice class of people on this bus. Probably
every one of them would rather be on a train. Well you can't always
have what you want. She takes another sip of coffee out of the styrofoam
cup, nothing but swill, thinks of entering railway dining cars, the doors
whoosh behind her, her eyes taking in white tablecloths, roses in bud
vases, silver coffeepots, all eyes raised taking her in. Once in wartime
she rode a train all the way to San Diego to see her husband before he
shipped out, day and night for five days clickety clack sweet boys in
uniform breaking their necks to give her their seats, buy her Hershey
bars, magazines, sloe gin fizzes, one night she stood in the dining car
doorway in a maroon wool suit with a fur-lined jacket, her mother had
cut up an old beaver coat, and an officer rose from his table and asked

her to do him the great honor of, "I said, How's that coffee?" Fred shouts at her like she's deaf, she smiles, "It really hits the spot," she says, "you're a real gentleman to concern yourself with me." She leans back in her seat and sighs. Even if there had been a train to Buffalo, she couldn't have afforded it. She can't find anyplace to dump the coffee so she drinks it down, it'll come back on her too, breaks the cup up and crams it into the ashtray.

26

"Give me a match," Meg says to the police officer she flags down for a ride. Gretchen hugs the window so her body won't touch Meg's, cups her hand over her forehead so no one will recognize her. The officer flips Meg a pack of matches he just got from Wanda Brown, a Chippewa street chippie. Meg lights her cigarette, pockets the pack. "Keep it," the officer mumbles.

The police car drops Meg and Gretchen a block away from Heartbreak Hotel, they cut through the alley, "in case anybody's tailing us," Meg says, she notes two surveyors with walkie-talkies, a city truck, a county truck, a state truck, and Gretchen sniff her armpit surreptitiously.

Gretchen notes that her twenty-four-hour protection can't tell time, she's mortified, she reeks to high heaven, she clamps her arms to her sides so Meg can't smell, Meg's got a nose like her Ma, Gretchen keeps inching away until she walks almost on a diagonal.

"Don't think of taking off again, Missy," Meg says. "I may not be around to save you next time."

"I didn't ask for your help. . . ," Gretchen begins.

"You want Daisy to know where I found you? Look, Sister, you owe me one and don't forget it."

Gretchen sniffs, but she won't forget it.

Even though Gretchen has signed out for the grocery store and Meg hasn't signed out, Daisy already knows from Rita and her intelligence network that they were at the Museum. She doesn't say anything when they come in because Gretchen looks like a truck hit her, and she already has Meg on as short a leash as Meg can tolerate.

"She's here," Gretchen says.

"Not yet," Daisy says.

Gretchen goes to the corner of the kitchen, gets on the exercycle, sets it for Denver and takes off.

"What's the latest on the fire in the First Ladies Wing?" Meg asks, who already knows the latest from the police car radio.

"It's contained," Daisy says.

"What happened to all those beautiful dresses?" Rita asks.

"About forty of them were lost," Daisy says.

"That's like real history gone," Rita says.

"The dresses can be copied, but you can never get back the history," Daisy says.

"Why didn't the smoke detectors go off?" asks Pearl from the doorway.

"Unwired," Daisy says.

Pearl and Rita kick around whether the fire is connected with the City Fathers or is just an isolated act of vandalism against the Museum, but quickly give it up: in Buffalo, fires rank in popularity with football, hockey, and chicken wings. "The Queen City is in flames tonight," Pearl mimics Channel 7's nightly news, "Police round up 300,000 known arsonists, but have no real leads. . . . " To the tune of "April in Paris," she plays "Arson in Bufflo" on the upright rosewood Knabe. Rita's doing alto harmony, "Come do mezzo, Daisy," Pearl says, she casts an alarmed eye at the Olympian pile of chopped vegetables surrounding Daisy, Pearl's system can take only so much roughage.

While Meg waits for Daisy to give her the high sign, she sharpens the kitchen knives on a whetstone. She figures Daisy's too softhearted to call Rita a screw-up to her face and beg Meg to take over the case right in front of her, but she's hoping. She starts on the last knife.

Daisy's knife stops mid-veggie: she remembers what it is about Quasi's accident that nags her. Quasi has nipped off with Meg's Harley at least half a dozen times before this; the first two times, Daisy tailed her herself all the way to Cheektowaga and back. Daisy has never said anything to anyone about this because Quasi has so little pleasure in her life, Meg would kill her, and this is what Daisy remembers: Quasi knows how to ride. For all her ungainliness on earth, a double Y chromosome comes through when Quasi mounts machine: Quasi on the motorcycle is Baryshnikov. Daisy draws Meg aside, "Run a check on your bike."

"I already did," Meg says. "It was tampered with, Goddammit, it's going to fuck up my insurance." She waits for Daisy to continue her instructions, but Daisy turns away.

So they want it that bad. There it is out in the open, what Daisy feared all along: the City Fathers are talking life and death. It's almost a relief to have the stakes clearly drawn.

The doorbell rings: Gretchen moans, "She's here."

Everyone girds for Gretchen's Ma.

. . .

Rita opens the door to the cutest insurance adjustor she's ever seen and, in her racket with all the whiplashes, she sees plenty. If her luck holds, she'll see more of this one.

"Sorry I'm late," he says, "I had a hard time finding a parking place."

"Mmmmmmm," Rita says, which nobody needs Maggie to translate into: you can park your car in my garage any old time.

Sits there delivering his little report to Daisy just like he doesn't know he has those incredible thighs bursting out of those lovely beige flannel slacks, Rita resists the urge to run her finger slowly up the crease of his slacks, she starts toying with the candle on the table. Finally his speech is done and Rita's ready to start but Meg cuts in, "Are you saying you're not going to pay until you find out who's tampered with my bike?"

That's what he's saying with that gorgeous mouth: Rita's tongue, warming up, darts around her own mouth.

"You will never find out who's responsible," Meg says. Her voice is hard as handcuffs.

The insurance adjustor loses his cool, Rita thrills, "Look," he shouts, "That poor lady never had a chance, it was a setup, someone was laying for her, does she have any enemies?"

Meg jumps up, "Where the Hell do you come from Mister, New York City? These things aren't anything personal in Buffalo."

Meg doesn't believe that for a minute, and neither does the insurance adjustor. "You will hear from us after we conduct our investigation," he says so stiffly his thighs ripple, he leans forward to punctuate his statement, his legs part, he's pressed to the left, Rita notes, what a lovely bulge, what would he do if she just reached over and traced the whorls of his bulge ever so lightly with her fingertips, down girl, she tells herself, Rita has a highly developed sense of timing and she bides it now.

"All I want is what's mine," Meg wraps up, and Rita moves in on cue.

"Before you leave, I wonder if you'd mind advising me on my insurance portfolio. . . . " Rita's voice gets progressively softer until she is whispering.

Rita often whispers.
She has great one-to-one skills.
She's working her way one-to-one around the world.
She has developed an elaborate godfather system.
Her godfathers live in America, Europe, Asia, and Africa, come from all walks of life, and are of every race, color, creed, and age.

Her ultimate goal, much more ambitious than Hilton, is to have every spot in the world covered, so that no matter where she goes, a protector will step out of the crowd and say, Back off, Boys, this here's my little Rita.

Pearl watches Rita whisper, and remembers.

Pearl used to whisper too until she gave up men. All men, *tous ensemble, c'est fini, terminado, kaput,* the end, Amen, with the sole exception of her husband. Seven summers ago, she ticks it off on her fingers now with disbelief: it seems like seventy. She remembers acutely the moment of decision.

In the middle of a new flirtation, the man inclining to her, saying something in his delightful Japanese accent, everything going according to plan, she has only to move one millimeter and the dance will begin, the enormity of Pearl's task strikes. Not even getting into cultural differences, just considering the time to choose appropriate candidates, educate them up to her standards, steep them in a Pearl Appreciation Course. . . . Pearl is suddenly staggered by the amount of work she has carved out for herself.

"Pearlsan," he says again in his delightful accent.

"Please excuse me," Pearl says in an audible tone, "I have to get back to work."

A spur of the moment decision, no one should make a decision like that with only thirty-five years to prepare, there are moments she regrets it, like this moment, sitting on the piano stool watching Rita whisper, the insurance adjuster inclining to her, Pearl mutters: she misses the power.

She misses the glory too. Pearl can never make up her mind whether Rita's constantly detouring or taking a direct route.

". . . adequate coverage," floats back as Rita and the insurance adjustor leave the room. Daisy smiles, Pearl guffaws, Meg smacks her fist into her palm, Gretchen bikes into Toledo, Ohio.

Up in Maggie's room, all that priming of the pump is getting to her. She indicates in several languages that she'd like more. "Are you certain, Maggie?" her visitor asks.

Maggie's certain.

"Look at me, Maggie," he says.

Although the room is dim and shadowy, she can see his face clearly. He has done another trick: his seventy-year-old face is a thirty-year-old's. The latter is a cruel face, Maggie far prefers the former. She shuts her eyes and says, "I see you."

"Ahhhhhhhhhhhhhhhhhhhhhhhhhhhhhhhhhhhhhhhhhhhhhhhhh," the old man whispers, "you deserve better, Maggie."

Maggie's not complaining.

She recalls the old man standing on the stage of the World Translators Conference, telling anecdotes about famous translators he has known. Someday, she muses, maybe she will stand there and tell an anecdote about this night.

"You could do worse," the old man snaps.

But he has a certain fullness and a certain gratitude and a certain sense that he and Maggie owe something to each other now. "This is important, Maggie," he says. "Listen closely. . . ."

He tells Maggie something so strange to her ears, so personal, intimate, exciting, and frightening she has to hide it quickly at the far back of her mind's underwear drawer.

Take it out and look at it, Maggie, God whispers, you'll save us all some trouble.

"It's true," the old man says. "I'm not telling you how it *should* be, Maggie, I'm telling how it *is*, and the sooner you come to terms with it, the better off you'll all be."

Maggie shakes her head.

"If you won't take my word for it, look at this."

He shows Maggie Exhibit 7777777 in the Museum of the Revolution.

Maggie's hand shakes as she writes down what he shows her in seven languages on seven pieces of paper, folds each of them until it won't fold more, and hides them all behind the new bikini heart panties with tiny red bows that Rita gave her for Valentine's Day.

Gretchen's eyes pop when she sees those heart pants.

After Rita's screaming at her for asking a simple question about sex, Gretchen chooses her words carefully. "Do you think Rita's a fruit?" she asks Pearl.

"Rita's gay with Rita," Pearl answers.

"That's perverted," Gretchen says.

"Actually," Pearl says, "Rita has friends of all genders."

Gretchen's mouth purses.

Gretchen has definite ideas about sex. No one will ever call her permissive. Yet, when the Cardinals sing "Men Rise Up and Call Her Blessed," Gretchen winces: The last man who rose up called her a cockteaser.

Gretchen believes in moderation: "We don't have to do anything," she tells him, "We can just lie here next to each other."

Pearl wants to, but she can't fault Gretchen: Pearl's energy level is usually so low she's a slug in lovemaking. Sometimes her energy level is fine, but her body is still unresponsive: she doesn't permit herself to feel pleasure as a punishment for being such a crud.

Maggie's silent too. It's not that she's passive, but sometimes when she ties one on, she says, "You can do anything you want as long as you don't hurt me too bad."

Daisy sublimates sexual energy into work energy, but not by choice. She wishes she had sex three or four times a day. She thinks there's a fair chance that if she actually had it once a day, she wouldn't think about it the other three times.

Meg has sex frequently and her partner is never shortchanged: she jacks off.

Upstairs now, Rita hangs from the chandelier and, as always, practices the Golden Rule: Make love unto others as you would have them make love unto you Aaaaaaaeeeeeeiiiiiiioooooouuuuuu and sometimes y.

In one of the rooms in the ICU, a nurse whispers to a nurse, "She's got her fingers in the pudding again."

"What?"

"She's touching herself. Hey stop that, naughty girl," she whispers to the patient, "she won't stop," she whispers to the nurse, "we can't let her do that in front of this zoo, it's embarrassing."

"EXCUSE ME, WILL YOU ALL PLEASE GO TO THE WAITING ROOM? WE HAVE A PROCEDURE TO DO."

"I didn't know women her age did that too."

"They *all* do it, at nighttime we let them go to it, we don't have the staff, Sorry sweetheart, we gotta put the cuffs on again."

They hold the patient's hands to the bars on the sides of the bed with Velcro restraints.

"Why is my mother in restraints?" asks the patient's daughter.

"Coma patients hurt themselves, hon," says the nurse.

27

Upstairs, Maggie and Rita are spoiling their dinner stuffing on sweet nooky.

Downstairs, Daisy, who's still fasting, preparing herself for whatever will come, dishes out stir fry. She offers Gretchen a special portion without onion or garlic, "I'd throw up," Gretchen says.

Pearl hums "My Old Flame."

Nobody says the obvious: whoever tampered with Meg's bike was laying for Meg. Her whole life, people have been laying for Meg. Ever since she can remember, she walks a tightrope over Niagara Falls. And none of them care, she could wash straight down to the whirlpool and not one of them would give a good goddam, Meg strides back and forth in the kitchen, glares at each in turn and waits for someone to say the obvious.

That somebody was laying for whatever cop happened to be at Heartbreak Hotel seems so obvious to Daisy it never occurs to her to mention it. "You sure you don't want any, Meg?" she asks as she dishes out seconds.

"If I wanted any of that goddam commie crap, I'd move to China," Meg says in a remarkably civil voice given the circumstances. She glares at Pearl, if she were a commie Pearl'd pay attention to her, probably emcee a goddam telethon for her.

Pearl looks deadpan at Meg to needle her, she knows ambiguity drives Meg crazy, slowly she turns to Daisy, holds her plate out, "Those commies sure know how to chow down," she says.

Pearl eats her second helping of stir fry with gusto and watches Gretchen pump. Although Gretchen manages to embody just about everything Pearl dislikes in herself, deep down Pearl feels a certain bond with her because Pearl spent so many years cheerleading her family GO HON YOU CAN DO IT COME ON GANG WE CAN DO IT GO TEAM GO YEAAAAAAAAAAAAAAAAAAAAAAA. With men, Pearl was such a terrific conversational cheerleader, the Dallas Cowgirls recruited her to speak at Spring Training.

"When's your Ma coming?" she asks.

"She hates to be called Ma," Gretchen says.

"Ma has no power," Meg snaps. "No pride, no respect, no class."

"Right," Pearl says sarcastically, "Ma's hose are thick and held up with rubber bands. . . ."

"Ma is country," Rita drawls from the doorway, they turn to look at her, she's wearing a purple silk kimono loosely belted, her color is high, her skin moist, "Ma's old and wrinkled and withered," she says, stretches, preens, and seems to forget her track.

Gretchen's puzzled. "Ma as in MaMa?" she asks.

Ma, Mommy, Mama, Mother, Mom, MaMa, Momma
Pearl says, "My whole life I called my daddy Daddy.

"Starting when I was thirteen, for twenty years, I called my mother Mother."

"Why'd you start when you were thirteen?" Daisy asks.

"I started getting mad."

"Why'd you stop in twenty years?"

"I stopped being so mad."

St. Pearl's Letter To The Buffalonians: For 40 years, people have a sad childhood. Then they start becoming so much like their folks, understanding is imperative.

For the last few years, Pearl only calls her momma Momma. Her Momma's never let on she's noticed, but Pearl feels better about it.

On the Bluebird bus, the old woman sighs, and thinks, I'll have to watch every little thing I say or she'll go, "Oh Muh-ther."

"I couldn't eat another thing," Rita says, she waves away the stir fry, she plucks a banana out of the fruit bowl, peels it thoughtfully, nibbles it slowly, "That insurance adjustor was a real sweetie," she purrs.

"You got the morals of a hamster," Meg says. She lets the screen door bang on her way out.

Rita's in a terrifically good mood after her afternoon pick-me-up. "Gribble Gribble," she says, a first-rate hamster imitation if you ask her, she giggles and cracks open a fortune cookie, her face sobers as she reads the strangest fortune she's ever had in a cookie: "Maintain your self-respect against ridiculous odds. Buffalo Rose." But *I'm* Buffalo Rose, aren't I? she thinks and pops the cookie into her mouth. "He told me to be careful," she says. "He said the City just took out a new fire insurance policy on Heartbreak Hotel."

"This place'd go up like an oxygen tent," Pearl says.

"They've got easier ways to get us out," Daisy says, but she takes the fire extinguisher out of the pantry and sets it on top of the piano.

I hate them all, I hate them all, Goddam them all straight to Hell.
Meg hates so much she hurts with it.
Meg hurts so much she hates with it.
"What am I going to do?" she pounds the ground with her fist, "What am I going to do?"

Nobody understands Meg. Meg is an old-timey citizen, a Fifties Catholic, a Fifties patriot, a Fifties marine: Meg is a black and white dinosaur lumbering through the Eighties to Bethlehem, her one model for survival, her Uncle.

This is the Litany of the Uncle:
Like Hell you say
Like Hell I will
Go to Hell
The Hell with it.

LAMB OF GOD WHO TAKEST AWAY THE SINS OF THE WORLD, SPARE US O LORD
LAMB OF GOD WHO TAKEST AWAY THE SINS OF THE WORLD, GRACIOUSLY HEAR US O LORD
LAMB OF GOD WHO TAKEST AWAY THE SINS OF THE WORLD, HAVE MERCY ON US

"The Hell with it," Meg says, and walks around to the side door to avoid using the kitchen entrance.

28

"Sweet Baby Jesus!" Meg says.

"I found her under a mushroom," she tells the others. "She says her name is Peg O' My Heart."

They all want to touch her. Her skin is velvet, she has a certain fullness. She is rosy-cheeked. She is five.

Daisy claims her. Meg doesn't want to let go the little plump hand but pretends she's relieved.

Peg O' My Heart sits on Daisy's lap. She looks at them all directly with wide trusting eyes, yet there is a seriousness about her, a vigilance. Daisy strokes her hair. Daisy is very good with children, frightened animals, addicts, hunchbacks, and battered women. The Mother Teresa of Western New York, Pearl calls her, not without envy.

"Where do you come from?" Daisy asks.

Peg O' My Heart's eyes are at once mischievous and opaque. "I can stay awhile," she says.

Even Gretchen's attention is momentarily diverted: "Who's *she*?"

Peg O' My Heart doesn't answer.

"Listen kid," Meg says, "tell us the truth or we'll have to send you to Boys Town."

"Boys Town?" Pearl guffaws.

Meg looks at Pearl coldly. "They've got fifty, sixty girls there and more coming every day."

"Are you saying it's, it's . . . Person Town?" Pearl says.

"They keep it out of the brochures," Meg says.

"I'd send money," Rita says.

"They know the odds," Meg says. "Now listen, Peg O' My Heart, tell the truth."

Peg O' My Heart looks straight at Daisy and says dead seriously, "I am a boy."

In most areas, Daisy has a long fuse on her temper, but not all. "*You are a girl*," she says, "*and you are wearing cowgirl clothes, and*

128

when you grow up you will be a woman like me!" Peg O' My Heart's eyes widen, everybody else sits up straighter.

"Where did she come from?" asks Gretchen who's read about mushrooms in Time Magazine's Medicine Section, that's all she needs is a druggy kid around when her Ma comes.

"I found her on the porch staring at Quasi's rug," Meg says, Gretchen immediately loses interest, Meg doesn't say that a crowd is building up out in the street, nor does she say that tears were pouring down the rosy cheeks though not a sound was heard.

Meg gets on her CB and makes inquiries without anyone noticing. Patrol cars are on their way to check out the unauthorized street gathering, and no town minor is reported missing.

"I'm hungry," Peg O' My Heart says. She grins.

Daisy starts to dish up some stir fry, but Meg says, "You can't give a kid that stuff, it stunted a whole nation."

Pearl watches Meg making the little girl a sandwich. Ever since Pearl gave up being an honorary man, she is always looking for ways to bond with women. Meg spreads the peanut butter evenly to the edges, cuts it precisely on the diagonal, arranges it carefully on a plate, Pearl shudders. Meg's rigidity gives her the creeps. She even makes a sandwich into a federal case. Pearl wants to poke her finger into the sandwich, scream at Meg, feels like she's going to explode, she jumps up and starts pacing, "I can't stand this waiting," she says.

The bike ratchets to a stop, all eyes swivel to Daisy.

"Who you kidding?" Daisy says. "You took a PhD in waiting."

"This is an exercise in endurance I've already had, Daisy. This is excessive, this is overkill. . . ." Pearl sighs, sits back down.

Daisy looks at the others. "It's too early to be so glum. The results aren't in yet." She starts feeding peels and scraps down the garbage disposal, finds the racket of the blades comforting. Daisy has nerves of steel, but the waiting is getting to her too. Everything in the house chopped, all her thoughts lead her back to the same place: We are being pushed into a corner. I've got to get out of this house, she thinks. Her strategy is figured out and already being set into motion, friends and allies have been enlisted, the bait is dangling, but the pivotal move still hangs fire. Daisy is standing on the edge of the biggest risk of her life, and one thing she's learned from watching the sports trades in this town is that she's got to let the hunger build. "I have to go out for a while," she says matter-of-factly. "The only stranger left in the house is Maggie's visitor. I don't think anybody else'll come. If they don't have what they want by now, they'll make it up. If anybody does comes, use your own judgment about letting them in."

"Use my own judgment," Gretchen moans, she turns away, starts pedaling again.

"The important thing is not to escalate anything while I'm gone," Daisy says. Like an afterthought, she adds, "Meg, you keep an eye on Peg O' My Heart."

"They're all fruitcakes in this house, kid," Meg whispers. "It's from eating all that foreign food with little sticks." She takes Peg O' My Heart by the hand.

Daisy locks the gates of Heartbreak Hotel, a mounted policewoman is herding a crowd, many neighbors gathered in the street stop talking when Daisy comes near, she nods to them, they are polite and remote, she can't tell anything by their reaction, a Doberman pinscher digs a tunnel at the edge of the property, it strains at the leash as she approaches to tell its trainer that the border shrubs are poisonous, he sullenly calls the dog off, it starts barking, a vendor sets up a steam cart to sell hot dogs, a reporter makes his way through the crowd to Daisy, she waves at all the activity which has a festive air, "Are they for us or against us?" she asks. "I think it could go either way," he says seriously. They laugh, but with an edge, they've both seen crowds turn into mobs. "I'll do an editorial tonight," he says, they split a hot dog and Daisy fills him in on the latest developments.

In front of the fireplace in the green velvet wingback chair, Peg O' My Heart crawls into Meg's lap as Meg once, aeons ago, crawls into her aunt's lap.

This is The Litany Of The Aunt:
She is like her beloved Southwest, all browns, deserts and cactus, mountains, unexpected cool rushing streams, purple bruises, gaudy sunsets, reds and yellows, raucous and tough and enduring. Unlike her beloved Southwest, she dies young. Meg hardly remembers her.

LAMB OF GOD WHO TAKEST AWAY THE SINS OF THE WORLD, SPARE US
O LORD

LAMB OF GOD WHO TAKEST AWAY THE SINS OF THE WORLD, GRACIOUSLY
HEAR US O LORD

LAMB OF GOD WHO TAKEST AWAY THE SINS OF THE WORLD, HAVE MERCY
ON US.

Peg O' My Heart fits right into the cracks and corners of Meg without seeming to notice that Meg is all sharp angles, bony points, abrasive surfaces. Meg is ecstatic. She holds her breath and breathes velvet and fullness and feels worthy and honored. She becomes aware of time passing. Because she thinks she must say something, because she doesn't know what to say, she says, "How's tricks, pal?"

BUBBLEGUM FACT #77: THERE ARE SOME PEOPLE WHO ARE NOT CONSUMED WITH SELF-CONSCIOUSNESS EVERY MOMENT OF THEIR LIVES. THESE PEOPLE ARE CALLED MEN.

"Is that a fact?" Dick Cavett asks.

Peg O' My Heart blows a bubble and asks, "Can you play jacks?" "Can a pig oink?" Meg says.

Peg O' My Heart giggles when the ball drops smack on a cluster of jacks.
Meg makes her face fierce. "A little respect, young lady. "You're looking at the citywide jacks champion of a thriving Midwestern town."
Peg O' My Heart is impressed. In the circles Peg O' My Heart moves in, that is big stuff.

EVERY VARIETY AND EVERY VARIATION OF JACKS, OF HOPSCOTCH, OF SYN-CHRONIZED WALKING, OF GUM CRACKING AND BUBBLEGUM BLOWING, OF ALL THE HIGHLY REFINED LIMITED SKILLS THAT GIRLS EXCEL IN IS IN THE MU-SEUM'S GAME ROOM. IN THE BEGINNING DAISY HIRED MALE BRAIN SURGEONS TO BE THE GUIDES OF THE GAME ROOM, BUT THEIR FINGERS WERE CLUBS, THEIR ATTENTION SPAN SCATTERED, THEIR PRIDE INSUFFICIENT.

Peg O' My Heart wants another peanut butter sandwich. Meg cuts the sandwich on a perfect diagonal. She thinks of a mother slapping sandwiches together so furiously that a child never dares ask that hers be cut on the diagonal like Kitty Flanders's and everybody else's who counts in the lunchroom.
Today it matters, but even when it doesn't matter, Meg cuts sandwiches on the diagonal: make-up or memorial, she doesn't know.
"Tell me a story," Peg O' My Heart says.

A STORY: Jacqueline drips snot down her arm and licks it. Jacqueline's disgusting. Kitty Flanders has a white fur jacket with matching muff. Kitty Flanders's nose never runs. On Kitty's birthday, her mother brings presents for every child in first grade: balls for the boys, jacks for the girls. Kitty's cake stands on a pink pedestal on Sister's desk. Happy Birthday, Dear Kitty, the children sing while the pedestal goes round and round.

. . .

"I don't know any stories," Meg says. She opens the fridge and swigs chocolate milk from the bottle. I was Jacqueline from the start, she thinks.

"We could go to the library," Peg O' My Heart says.

"You ought to have some kids to play with," Meg says.

Peg O' My Heart doesn't say anything.

Peg O' My Heart plays with two other children. The sky is blue. The sun is hot. The children peel off their shirts. Sun flashes on their tan and healthy chests. The kitchen door slams, the mother of the boys comes down the steps. "You are a girl," she says to Peg O' My Heart. "Put your shirt on and go home."

"There's some kids down the block," Meg says.

Peg O' My Heart rubs her eyes.

Meg puts Peg O' My Heart down for a nap on the living room sofa, checks the time, and heads upstairs to check out an illicit assignation. She walks on cat's paws down the second floor corridor, up the back stairs, the smell of hash comes down to greet her, her adrenaline rushes. On the third floor, opposite Maggie's room, Meg slips into the shadows.

The old man gets up, he sighs, his bladder is bursting. He leans over Maggie,

"I have to go for a while," he says. "Will you be all right?"

Maggie will be all right.

The bourbon is on the dresser. Maggie feels her way across the room, feels the dresser's bulk, feels the bourbon, Where are her glasses?, feels a matchbook. Maggie strikes the match: her heart constricts: the face in the mirror is so deformed, so grossly ugly Maggie is frozen in panic.

"Is everything all right out there?" the old man calls from the bathroom.

Maggie trembles: Maggie's flesh crawls: Maggie's eyes are locked with the hag's: Maggie's heart is jumping out of her throat: Maggie is going to die right on the spot.

Something funny's going on in there, Meg thinks, she checks that the hall is clear, by the second stride her hand's on the knob.

A second or an eternity later, Maggie doesn't know how long the hag's face claims hers, she suddenly sees the swath of light in the mirror. Before the bathroom door opens fully, she hisses, "Don't look."

"I can explain that," the old man says.

132

"No," Maggie says in every language she knows. She cannot bear to have anybody ever see this face. She would kill to keep people from seeing this face.

"I can explain that," the old man says crossly, but he averts his eyes, goes to the bed, and turns his back.

Meg shuts the door, What the Hell would I look at? Some drug-crazed loonie making faces at herself in the mirror?

To double check, Meg goes down one flight and silently opens Rita's door: Rita's sleeping. They must have gotten wind of a leak. Meg takes her time shutting the door.

Whistling softly, she heads for the house library to look for some stories for Peg O' My Heart. She selects Anderson from the A's, then randomly moves down the first wall of books. As she passes the H's, her attention is diverted.

Upstairs in Maggie's room, the hag in the mirror begins to withdraw, recede infinitesimally, its hideous features, wens, hanging flesh, twisted humped body do not fade nor dim, its eyes never leave Maggie's, it is just suddenly gone, the match is char in Maggie's fingers. Maggie slowly lets out her breath. But her vision is not complete. A new face appears in the mirror, another, and then another, a constant flashing of faces of different ages and miens, some known to Maggie, some strangers, some more appealing than others, but no face of the enormous horror and power of the first. After a score of faces, Maggie says, "You can look now."

The old man turns over from the wall, has the grace not to be peevish, and comments on various faces.

"I like her, she looks interesting."

"She's so depressed it's depressing to look at her."

A perky one, her hair cut in a gamin cap, winks at Maggie. "She looks like fun," the old man says.

"Do you know her?" he asks about one.

The face in the mirror beckons, she has jasmine in her hair, Maggie inclines forward, she can almost smell the jasmine, she shakes her head. "I thought for a moment I did," she says, "but I can't quite place her."

"Ahhhhhhh," says the old man, and Maggie echoes it as the most beautiful face appears. It is Daisy's face. Maggie sees that immediately although it is Daisy Transfigured, her face shines as the sun, and her blue silk raiment becomes white and glistering as the light. And Maggie sees her full glory, but is not afraid nor does the light hurt her eyes, she is transfixed as Daisy Transfigured radiantly smiles at her. No one can look upon this face without smiling, Maggie feels the smile coming over her, spreading, filling her, her palms flat on the dresser top, Daisy leans closer to Maggie until there is no division, and the smile would light up a blacked-out city, has illuminated the pitch black room, "Ohhh," says Maggie, she is filled with joy.

Daisy's smile never dimming, the mirror fills with light, is dazzling for an instant, and just as quickly clouds. When Maggie looks again, it shows only her smiling face.

29

Between this visit to the hospital and her last, there's fresh graffiti on the fence in red piant, Daisy reads: STOP WAITING FOR THE SLEDGEHAMMER TO FALL. THE SLEDGEHAMMER IS NOT GOING TO FALL. BUFFALO ROSE.

Five minutes later in the ICU, the silver-haired doctor is not around. M. VALENTINE M.D. watches a balding red-haired doctor examine Quasi, his fingers move around Quasi's forehead like a caress, kindness spills out of his cow brown eyes onto Quasi's inert form, he has crinkle laugh lines by his eyes, he shakes his head sadly, her heart plummets. "Isn't there anything you can do?" she asks. T. ROBBINS M.D. looks up, a little surprised, "There are always things you can do," he says. "We're trying to relieve the cranial pressure. It's a small chance, but it's a chance." His eyes cut to the badge, puzzlement flits through them. "Are you related to the patient?" he asks. "I'm the family doctor," Daisy says. "What's the M for?" he asks. "Mattie," Daisy says. "Short for Margaret?" he asks. "Just plain Mattie," she says. "Hardly that," T. ROBBINS M.D. says, his laugh lines crinkle.

On the third floor of Heartbreak Hotel, Maggie and the old man share a glass of bourbon, but he keeps forgetting her turn. While she waits for him to remember his manners, she matches him toke for sip.
"You have a great psychic soul," he says.
Sip.
Toke.
"A great psychic soul."
Maggie knows exactly what he's talking about and he's got it a little mixed up.

Maggie was born with a veil on her face.
"Caul," the midwife whispers with awe, "This is a lucky child. She can foresee the future." Carefully, she removes the veil, "Now it's very

important that the veil be peeled from the forehead down, not the chin up. . . ." Or is it the other way around?, she thinks.

It's the other way around.

Gramma puts the membrane in the family Bible.

"You don't need ESP to see that the Museum's days are numbered," the old man says.

Sip.

"An administration that cuts out funding for polio shots doesn't want a place that remembers heroic cripples," he says.

Sip.

"There are things you can do to improve your life," he says.

Maggie can see his face distinctly in the dimness; it's the young, ruthless face again, she clamps her eyes shut.

Six times in six languages, he says, "There are always things you can do."

Six times, Maggie clamps her hands to her ears.

The old man changes tack. "The Chinese believe that you look backwards toward the future," he says. He pours about five fingers of Maggie's Jack Daniels into the glass, plumps the pillow behind his neck, sips, hands the glass to Maggie every other time, and talks. He talks about seeing The Great March in China. He talks about death. Dying. Rebirth and resurrection. It seems that he talks for hours, using a language Maggie has never heard, and to understand anything she must bring to bear parts of every language she knows. The words roll around the thick brown air and Maggie translates them into pictures of monochromes, ceaseless movement, walls, lumbering, whistling wind, people trudging along silent and shadowy, wizened gnarled trees of a kind Maggie will never see making bas relief to the people trudging trudging until the footsteps swell, pound, the earth pulses, throbs, shudders: Maggie is overwhelmed with possibility.

The seventh time in the seventh language, the old man says, "There are always things you can do." Maggie opens her eyes and her ears.

"I can give you seven perfect years, Maggie."

Maggie is startled, but she keeps her face expressionless. Seven is an infinite number, she knows that from Dead Sea Scroll translations. "How many?" she asks.

"You heard me," the old man says.

"What would I have to do?" Maggie asks.

Maggie never leaves her bed but, towering above, cathedral pines sway, she feels the ground cool and warm beneath, feels the pine needles rustling. Her body is shaped in the form of a cross, the old man enters. The sky is blue, cumulus clouds puff and shift, the pines never stop moving, Maggie is dizzy with the motion and pungency of pine needles.

The old man's eyes narrow. His lips shape the name.

Maggie tiptoes along the second floor hallway, points out the door.

Rita feels the presence one millisecond before the pressure. The wind starts in her head but, empowered by Mme. Le Main's protection against the evil eye, and her own natural abilities, Rita can give the devil as good as she gets, she ferments, she sweats, she drips, she runs with it, the bed moves around the room, the wind whirs, roars, slams, every crack and crevice and crater of her body is filled to bursting, the sulphur smell jams her nostrils, the wind screams: Rita is humping the Alaska pipeline.

It will take three days for her sinuses to clear.

The house reeks of incense, clove, cinnamon, pine Air Wick, and root beer. Pearl's fingers on the typewriter pick up speed, more speed, fly. Pearl types like a madwoman until the sound of the striking keys blocks out all smell and sound.

Gretchen hears no sound. The smell seeps under the kitchen door, wafts across the shiny urethaned floor, gathers strength until full-force it attacks her on the exercycle. In a racing crouch, Gretchen gears down and attacks the exercycle until her limbs are in a fugue of pain that blocks out all.

Meg is on her bed flipping through books. The ears of the cop prick: simultaneously, her hand brakes on the page. She doesn't move a muscle. She hears whispers in Maggie's room. She hears a mattress creak. She hears footsteps go down the stairs and stop at Rita's. Hears the bed move around the room. Hears whispers. Hears the footsteps stop at Pearl's. Hears the typewriter clack crazily. Hears whispers. Hears footsteps stop at the kitchen. Hears limbs straining. Hears whispers. Hears footsteps mount the stairs. Stop. Meg moves a muscle: her heart constricts.

The room is suddenly pitch black and Meg doesn't know who or what is outside her door. Not ten feet away, separated by an inch and seven eighths of black walnut, the presence pounds. Meg's heart pounds. She stares into the pitch and clear as day sees a hitman. She pictures the door opening, the hitman moving through the pitch, the hitman entering her bed, she doesn't know if he's friend or foe, she doesn't know if he'll fuck her or kill her, she doesn't know if she allows him entry if she'll recognize him the next morning, she doesn't know what he wants from her, she shuts down every cell in her body and wills the door shut. The wind starts in her head, her head is exploding, the smell of sulphur blots out incense and clove and cinnamon and root beer and sweat and fear, her head hurts like Hell.

She doesn't hear the footsteps nor the whispers.

The old man is in a heat. "I didn't plan it this way, you little witch. I was supposed to run this show, but at some point you took control. . . ."

Maggie is scared, but also thrilled: she has rarely felt she has any measure of control over anything in her life. The only time she has ever felt tremendous power was once when a man went down on her: she felt he was a dog licking her parts.

Once Maggie, drunk, blabs that a man went down on her. Gretchen gags, Shellfish, the man in the Blue Ford says, all cunt smells like shellfish, she goes upstairs to douche. Rita sends a dozen red long-stemmed roses and a box of firecrackers and sparklers, CONGRATULATIONS, MAGGIE, YOU ARE A WOMAN NOW.

Maggie's victory is short-lived.

"It's time to pay, Maggie."

For the fifth time, Maggie reads the same name on the old man's lips: "Daisy."

Maggie is just about out of ante. She plays Judas to her own Christ. In an accentless voice, she says, "Take Quasi."

In a voice that betrays nothing and everything, she says, "What is Daisy compared to Quasi?"

She says, "God loves Quasi the most because He gave her so much to bear."

She says, "Think how purified Quasi's soul is by all her suffering. Think how God will grind His teeth when you pluck that glistening soul."

In no language has Maggie ever been so eloquent, so convincing. Desperation is giving Maggie cunning, for Maggie does not even think that Quasi has a soul.

Maybe Maggie's visitor thinks differently. Maybe after all the pine trees, the Alaska pipeline, the walking, whispering, ins and outs, walking some more, this flight of back stairs and that, all the pounding and noise and odors, maybe Maggie's visitor has a headache too, maybe he's lost interest, maybe he's flexible, sated, not greedy, maybe he believes in free will, maybe his great powers give him some humility, maybe he's shot his wad, who knows? He shrugs, Okay.

In a darkened hospital room, M. VALENTINE M.D. leans over the comatose figure and says again, "Hold on, Quasi, everyone's pulling for you."

30

Behind Quasi's eyes, she feels someone looking at her, her eyes are crusted shut, someone looking directly at her, *seeing me*, she gets her eyes open and a thousand eyes look at her, a thousand mouths move Her eyes are open can she see can she hear it's me it's me can you hear can you hear. . . . A woman in white leans over her, a man with worried eyes, children of all ages and sizes with big sad eyes, a cheerleader with frantic eyes pushes through the crowd holds a red megaphone to Quasi's ear MY MA'S COMING Quasi pulls away tries to close her eyes, an old man leers at her, a woman in clown pants sticks her face right into hers, there's a belly dancer with rustling veils, a cop, a woman in tweeds signs the room's conversation, look at me me me me me, a Mother Superior, a red-haired doctor, a priest, a reporter, a young nurse lean closer, behind them as far as she can see a thousand more eyes look at her, talk at her, every one of them with a need so naked it is going to swallow her up alive, a cat sits on her chest and sucks the breath out of her, she opens her mouth and screams TAKE THE CAT OFF they lean closer, sucking all the air, a silver-haired doctor tries to turn her over to touch her hump, she can't bear it, she screams so long and high the glass breaks, the last thing Quasi sees before she closes her eyes and runs for her life is cracks radiating through glass like bullets through a windshield.

Glass is breaking all over the ICU. Bells clang, lights flash, "What's going on, Who brought those flowers in here, Why are all these people in here at one time, It's like Grand Central Station in here, Clear this room, This patient is getting too much stimulation, they're her favorite flowers, I thought maybe, Go to the Waiting Room all of you."

In the Waiting Room, a man says, "She was trying to say something."

"She just sighed, Dad," a kid says.

They weep.

. . .

There's the sound of glass being ground underneath a heel. Dr. Robbins reinserts the IV needle pulled out by thrashing. He writes out an order limiting visitors. They sweep up the broken vase, turn off the radio, draw the drapes, close the door.

In the darkened room, the silver-haired doctor holds Quasi's lid open and shines a flashlight on her pupil. It doesn't contract.

"I felt she saw us," a man with worried eyes says again.

"What happens when I do this to you?" the silver-haired doctor asks. He moves the flashlight toward the man's eye.

The man blinks.

The doctor moves his finger toward Quasi's eye. He touches the eyeball. There is no response. "Neurological impulses open and close the eyes," the doctor says. "You must face it. She is not seeing anything."

31

THE LONELINESS OF THE LONG DISTANCE RUNNER:
Whenever the house smells too strongly of clove and cinnamon, Pearl
remembers the Christmas present.

Pearl opens the silver box, peels back the pristine tissue paper, looks
at the penis-shaped vibrator. "Some stocking stuffer," says Pearl. Pearl's
embarrassed. Pearl feels smirky. Pearl feels philosophically bound to try
it. Between Christmas and New Year's, Pearl, a nutrition fanatic, pumps
plastic into her body. Twice, because a first time never tells you anything,
might just be a fit of lust or loneliness. Twice, Pearl gets vaginitis.

Pearl's Vaginitis: The tape recording at the self-help clinic says
yoghurt's good, helps to right the imbalance of organisms, just stuff
yourself with it. You think plain or fruit?, Pearl asks her scientific
husband.
If it's a theory of organisms, fruit has more acids, he says.
In the bathroom, Pearl stuffs herself with blueberry yoghurt.
I'll never do that again, she tells her husband. Blueberries got all
over the bathmat.
Pearl, says her husband, I thought you were going to *eat* it.

Fuck it, Pearl says.
But she doesn't. The Christmas present lies around in her drawer
with an impulse buy, a plastic speculum, can't give it to Goodwill,
probably non-biodegradable.
Pearl stares at the page of gibberish in her typewriter, and thinks
of the Christmas present. Because Pearl disapproves of impersonal sex,
she has named the vibrator Harold after a real-life penis of an ex-lover.
"Look at Harold," her ex-lover used to say, "Up to his old tricks again."
Or "Let's call Harold up, see if he wants to play 'Hide The Weenie.'"
At first Pearl laughs. Her laugh grows nervous. She begins to feel there

142

are three of them in bed. She begins to conjure up pictures of her friend arrested for rape and saying, "It was Harold." Harold eventually comes between them.

Pearl averts her eyes from the drawer where Harold lies. She imagines a day coming: a day after there have been no sounds from her room for a week, when the sweet smell of gangrene has finally traveled down three floors to the breakfast table, when they have masked their mouths and bagged her and are poking through her drawers not knowing trash from treasure, a man holds up the vibrator and says, "Who'da ever thought she'd go for Harolds?" Pearl sighs. She crumbles up the paper, throws it in the trash, gets up, lies down on her board. The only thing worse than an aging body, she thinks, is an unused body. She stares at the ceiling. She notes that her hands are folded in the coffin clasp. "I'm dying," she says. "If only someone would come."

NO VISITORS BUT IMMEDIATE FAMILY. 2 MAX AT A TIME says the sign on Quasi's door. Other than the staff and a private physician, no one has come to visit Quasi.

TEN CORRIDORS NORTH OF QUASI, HEIRESS SUNNY VON BULOW LIES COMATOSE FOR THE SIXTH YEAR IN HER PRIVATE ROOM. A MAID, PRIVATE NURSES, PHYSICAL THERAPISTS, A DENTIST, A HAIRDRESSER, A MAKE-UP ARTIST, AND A MANICURIST ATTEND TO HER. HER DAUGHTER AND SON VISIT REGULARLY AND SOMETIMES BRING HER GRANDDAUGHTER. SECURITY GUARDS AND SCREENS PROTECT HER FROM INTRUDERS.

No one knows better than Pearl that no one will come. Half the town could be passing Heartbreak Hotel and no one will take the stairs two at a time calling her name, Pearl, it's me, I'm coming up. No one is even *allowed* to come to her room uninvited, and she doesn't know anyone to invite. She can't invite her family because they're just starting to learn to do without her, she'd set them all back. You made your board, she thinks, now lie on it. I swear to God, she thinks, I must be the loneliest person in the world. And then, because she is Pearl, she wonders: Is that true?

She doesn't know anyone to ask.

When Pearl feels this bad, she is really up a creek because she no longer drinks, smokes, pigs out, dopes, or fucks around with scary strangers. Years ago, she got temporary relief by going to tony spas and chichi beauty salons and paying people a great deal of money to abuse her. Then she read a wonderful How-To book called *Self-Hate Made Easy* and started going out on the town to see exotic dancers, topless go-gos, and when she was really in the dumps, bottomless waitresses who use their vaginal muscles to pick up tips men put on the edge of the table. "That's a mortal sin," Gretchen says. "The good ones can triple their regular tips," Pearl says, but she agrees with Gretchen who has the right sin but the wrong sinner.

Right now Pearl knows that not even a good kick in the belly will help her through this, she'll just have to wait it out. She gets up, drapes her mother's shrunken afghan around her shoulders like an old woman's shawl, goes downstairs, passes Meg in the alcove playing Solitaire, "Hello, Meg," she says, Meg never looks up. Pearl pads on down the long hallway, hears the whir of wheels, goes into the darkened kitchen, says "You poor thing," disengages Gretchen from the exercycle, and leads her into the living room where she settles her in front of the fire in one of the green velvet wingback chairs across from Peg O' My Heart who's sitting up on the sofa taking everything in. Pearl pulls a hassock over, puts Gretchen's feet up, tucks her afghan around Gretchen's legs, and says, "I know, I know, it hurts."

Gretchen looks up at her, her eyes burnt-out holes, and says, "She spoiled my father's chances."

TWO ENORMOUS PITS ADJOIN IN THE MUSEUM: ONE HAS ALL THE COUNTLESS WIVES WHO CANNOT GROW BEYOND THEIR HUSBANDS' LIMITS, THE OTHER HAS ALL THE COUNTLESS WAYS THE WIVES PAY THEIR HUSBANDS FOR THIS.

"She didn't have her own to spoil," Pearl says. She looks into that bottomless umbra and shudders: If she has to drag her family kicking and screaming along with her, they are all going to go together.

At the sound of Pearl's voice, Meg just about jumps out of her skin. Ordinarily if she was feeling a little tense, she could go out and harass homos, throw pimps into the slammer, what she'd really like to do now is rough up this filth who're giving Daisy such a bad time I READ ABOUT THAT GUY WHO GOT A RIFLE AND STOOD UP ON THE OVERPASS, PICKED OFF NINE PEOPLE BEFORE THEY GOT HIM, I KNOW JUST HOW THAT GUY FELT, MEG'S BROTHER SAYS, YOU'RE LUCKY YOU GOT YOUR WORK. She's been off work too long, that's the trouble, if Daisy doesn't come home pretty soon she's going out there. Like an M1 rifle, Meg lays out the cards again.

Maggie helps the old man on with his coat. "Don't tell anyone what you have seen, heard, or done," he warns. Fat chance of that, Maggie thinks in Sanskrit. She walks him downstairs. "Thank you for

144

coming," she says at the door. "Thank *you*," he says, tips his hat, and is gone. Maggie returns to her room, gets her Jack Daniels, and walks sedately to the living room. She anticipates a long night before the returns are in.

Underneath the red tufted heart-shaped headboard, Rita tosses and turns on her round bed, she has a killer sinus headache. Her eyes shoot open, Omigosh I was supposed to go to Maggie's, she gets up, pops three aspirin, puts on her white silk pajamas, and heads upstairs.

She knocks on Maggie's door, but no one answers. The door is locked.

Daisy comes out of the hospital carrying a mass of tropical flowers, hails a cab, it's the same cabbie she had this morning.

"Glad to see you're okay," he says. "Fare I just took out to your place told me about the chemical leak."

"Who was that?' she asks.

"Guy in a pith helmet. Said he was from Albany, but he looked like a narc to me. It's a real zoo out there. I had to drop him a block away. Not that I'm complaining. I don't wanta breathe too much of that stuff. Holy Geez, looks like Nam. You take care, eh?"

He drops Daisy next to a convoy of parked army trucks, soldiers dig foxholes, put up Porta-Johns, a Major winks at Daisy, she winks back. As she moves around a barricade, a Marine staff sargeant stops her, "You can't go down there, Lady, we're not sure what's happening."

"I'm supposed to deliver these flowers," she says. "They may already have started the funeral."

He consults a clipboard. "The funeral's listed," he says. "Hey. Let this lady through," he bellows. "Numbskulls. I'll clear you a path." He throws his bulk into the crowd, it parts like the Red Sea, Daisy hurries through after him, passes the Doberman pinscher, it lunges at her, a man in a pith helmet pulls it back, "I told you to curb that dog," a mounted policewoman says, her horse steps on the trainer's foot, the policewoman blows her whistle for Red Cross, Daisy thanks her guide, he salutes, "Bury them," he says.

At the gates, Daisy's issued a ticket for having an assembly without a permit. "This isn't our assembly," she says.

"If it weren't for you, they wouldn't be here," the deputy says. "Somebody has to take responsibility."

"I can't argue with that," Daisy says.

Inside the gates, a spooky looking old man walks down the driveway toward her, suddenly jumps into the air, kicks his own behind, and hits the pavement jogging. The phone is ringing before Daisy gets to the porch. She looks over at Quasi's pile of rags and feels a great void.

Pearl hangs up the phone. Quasi has done the impossible: Quasi has taken a turn for the worse. Last seen, Quasi is off the road and heading straight for the swamp.

Daisy hands the flowers to Rita, "No flowers allowed in ICU," she says, goes directly to the telephone, identifies herself as M. VALENTINE M.D., and asks for T. ROBBINS, M.D. While she waits, she flips through her phone messages, sorting them into piles, the various parts of her plan are clicking into place, Is this the trade-off?, she thinks, Quasi's life for the Museum, No, Daisy fights that superstitious fatalistic part of herself.

"Dr. Robbins has an emergency now, Dr. Valentine," a voice says. "I gave him your message. He'll return your call as soon as possible."

Rita arranges flowers in porcelain vases, floats them in cut glass bowls, sails them across silver platters, fills every container in the house beautifully with vivid pungent tropical flowers, keeps dipping her head to smell their fragrance, "I can't smell a thing," she says, "I'm all stuffed up."

Meg hears all the commotion in the living room and comes in to see if she can get up a poker game.

"Quasi's dying," Pearl says.

"Oh for crying out loud," Meg begins, spots Peg O' My Heart giving her the big eye, and says, "Don't worry kid, death for that loser is a step up."

Peg O' My Heart looks scared. Meg wishes she'd kept her trap shut. She looks around for someone to comfort Peg O' My Heart. Daisy's scribbling a mile a minute across a sheet of paper, making phone calls, dictating into a machine, doing everything but whistling Dixie out of her asshole. Gretchen looks like death. Pearl looks like death. Maggie looks like death. What is this, an epidemic? She can't tell what Rita looks like, Rita's feet are on the wall, her torso sprawled across an armchair upside down with her head almost touching the floor: Meg finally figures out that she's putting nose drops in, Christ, that stuff's addictive, she'll try anything, this is no place for a minor, Meg thinks. Without thinking, she walks over to Peg O' My Heart, scoops her up and says, "Long past your bedtime, darlin'." Both Daisy and Maggie glance up, but no one is more surprised than Meg who hears the g drop in the identical inflection that her Uncle used.

Peg O' My Heart looks up at Meg and asks, "You gonna stay down here and hoist a couple?"

"Judas Priest," Meg says. Had Peg O' My Heart let loose with a string of obscenities, Meg could not be more shocked.

"We're going to stay down here and keep a vigil," Daisy says. "You go along with Meg and we'll see you in the morning." Daisy holds out her arms.

Peg O' My Heart goes to each woman in turn and gives her a kiss goodnight. When she hugs Maggie, Maggie withdraws internally so her touch won't sully the child. Maggie gives no external signal, but Peg O' My Heart meets her eye, pulls back, goes on to Pearl. Why that kid's a born translator, Maggie thinks.

When Pearl's kiss goodnight is over, she is filled with such a sense of loss she bites her lip to keep from crying out loud.

THE VIGIL

"A growth of stillness hides in this house,
Is it benign or malignant?"

ANONYMOUS

32

The ticker tape blocks out Pearl's sigh. Daisy reads the latest religious news YORKSHIRE RIPPER TESTIFIES HE IS SELECTED BY GOD TO KILL BAD WOMEN, POPE CALLS ABORTION GRAVE OFFENSE AGAINST THE RIGHTS OF MAN, SHI'ITE MOSLEM CLERGYMEN THROW OUT SHAH'S ANTI-POLYGAMY LAW, REDUCE MINIMUM MARRIAGE AGE FOR IRANIAN GIRLS FROM 16 TO 13. . . .

"Same old Shi'ite," Pearl says.

Daisy continues to read ticker tape. "The Post Office just put an extra shift on," she says.

"What's that mean?" Rita asks.

"I don't know," Daisy says. "There's a tremendous volume of mail. It started with the secretaries in the West End office buildings and it's moving across the Museum." She frowns. Arranging exhibits is only a small part of running MOTR, the real trick is figuring out what things mean.

Gretchen notes Daisy's frown and thinks of her Ma's beautiful skin. Her Ma didn't have a line in her face till she was past fifty. "My skin is getting dry," she says.

"I used to have velvet skin," Pearl says. "My skin was so soft men's hands fell off it. I did nothing to get it, nothing to keep it. Every night for years, I squirted dish detergent into my tub. *Dish detergent*, the store brand. Then one day, last year or the year before, I looked down, I looked up, I used mirrors, I used my hands and looked around. . . ."

"How did you look?" Gretchen asks.

"I told you how I looked, I'll tell you what I saw," Pearl says. "I have dishpan body."

Everybody but Gretchen laughs, but Pearl is telling a story, not a joke. She sighs. Gretchen moves her chair back further from the fire, closes her eyes, and sighs.

Gretchen opens her eyes, opens them wider, jumps up, and screams bloody murder, "In the window, a monster in the window, a monster. . . ."

Meg comes racing down the staircase, one hand on her holster, the other shielding Peg O' My Heart behind her, Daisy waves Meg back, and raises the window: A man wearing a gas mask teeters on a ladder. She puts her hand out to help him, he puts a summons in it. "Just let yourself out," Daisy says, she closes the window and turns away, it catches the tips of his fingers, his eyes bug inside the gas mask, Orf, he says, but who can hear?

IMMEDIATE EVACUATION IS ORDERED FOR ALL OC-CUPANTS OF HEARTBREAK HOTEL FOR HEALTH REA-SONS, Daisy reads.

"Jeezo peezo," Pearl says, she lets the curtain drop, "The whole place is ringed with National Guard wearing gas masks."

"YOU HAVE TWENTY-FIVE MINUTES TO EVACUATE," comes over the bullhorn. "THAT IS TWO-FIVE. . . ."

"I have to get my hope chest," Gretchen says, "I have to. . . ."

"Sit tight," Daisy says, "We're not going anyplace yet." She buzzes for a messenger to come pronto, takes a sheet of stationery from a cabi-net and drafts a letter. Her fountain pen moves swiftly across the paper, she would have preferred to have more time but makes her move, signs her name, affixes the Museum seal, and looks up, "Ahh, you're here. Deliver this immediately," she tells the messenger.

"EIGHT-TEEN MINUTES . . ."

"They're going to shoot us," Gretchen screams, "I don't want to die, Daisy."

"You're not going to die," Daisy says. She telephones Richard A. Dick, the fast talking Chairman of the Board. "This morning, we had a week to vacate, Dick."

"You've got foam insulation, Daisy, we have reason to believe you're sitting on top of a nuclear waste dump, for God's sake, Daisy, mascara was found in your trash can, that stuff crawls with bacteria, it's a public health hazard, we're going to put you up at the Mariott a few days till we figure out what to do with you, you'll feel better when you stop breathing all that asbestos junk, they have a Jacuzzi, you know," Dick says.

"I hear Heartbreak's being re-zoned as a center for retarded adoles-cent boys," Daisy says.

"Where'd you hear that, Daisy?" Dick asks.

"From a cabbie," Daisy says. "Dick, how are you planning to handle the health hazard angle."

"They're hardy boys, Daisy."

"We're going to need a little more time, Dick. You know about Quasi."

"My hands are tied, Daisy."

152

"I just sent a messenger over with a compromise suggestion. I think we can work something out."

"For your sake, I hope we can."

"I've got a TRO ready to go, Dick, and three TV stations standing by."

"There's no need to overreact, Daisy. How much time do you want?"

"8 AM will do us."

"No sweat."

"I appreciate it."

"Anytime."

Daisy hangs up the phone, "Well gang, we got till 8 o'clock."

"Dickadick rises to the occasion again," Pearl says.

"He's a prince of a fellow," Meg says. "And that's spelled P-R-I-C-K. We'd be fools to take his word on anything."

"Eight o'clock!" Gretchen wails. "I can't even get packed by eight o'clock, my whites are drip drying, I have to wash my hair, What am I going to do about my Ma?"

"We won't know anything for a few hours yet," Daisy says. "Why don't you go wash your hair?"

"Are you sure it'll have time to dry?" Gretchen demands.

"I'm not Mother Superior," Daisy says testily. "I don't know everything. You'll have to come up with some answers yourself."

Gretchen bursts into tears. "First my Ma and now this." She looks defiantly at Daisy. "I am not going out there in curlers."

Pearl laughs, but Daisy says seriously, "I have something in mind, Gretchen. If my plan works, no one will have to go out there in curlers."

From the picture window, the women watch the evacuation: trucks, jeeps, national guard platoons slowly make their way out to the street.

For Gretchen, everything is bathed in the blue light of Spanish horror movies, she can't stand to look at it, she asks Rita to come upstairs with her while she washes her hair, Rita's happy to go, she hates war movies.

For Maggie, the sodium spots make everything so distinct as to be surreal, she moves back to blunt the images' sharpness.

"Fools," Meg growls again and takes Peg O' My Heart out.

Daisy is incredulous and exhilarated. "When I started my pioneer women museum on the outskirts of the City, the City Fathers listed me as a tourist attraction," she says. "They used to think I was cute."

"You got too big and outgrew it," Pearl says. She shakes her head. "They're killing our lawn."

Daisy and Pearl can't hear the wrought-iron gates clang shut, but a buzzer on the lock board sounds as the lock slides into place.

"Dr. Robbins is still in emergency, Dr. Valentine."

Daisy hangs up the phone and programs her wrist alarm dinger, If there's no word from Robbins soon, she'll go back to the hospital. The messenger must be just about to Dick's now.

The City Fathers open the door, Well Well, Look what was just delivered to our door, Come on in honey, Aren't you out past your bedtime, Cut it out you guys, you're embarrassing her, Aw she's blushing, Now don't pay any attention to us hon, we're just having a good time, you give your letter to that one up there, he's the big honcho, Mr. *Dick*, Pooh focuses on a spot on Richard A. Dick's forehead, walks the full length of the board table, thinks about nothing but the gauntlet she'll have to walk back, hands him the letter imprinted with the Museum wax seal, turns around, her face is flaming, she feels all eyes on her butt, tries to walk stiffly, block out the grinning faces, All right, boys, you've had your little fun, let's get to work, Dick says, the door closes and locks behind Pooh.

The letter, handwritten in beautiful script with a fine pointed fountain pen on the palest of pink stationery, emanates the merest hint of clove and cinnamon. It passes around the board table, each City Father reading silently, thinking his own FEARS OF THE CITY FATHERS: Every time my wife goes up to that Museum, she comes home and burns the dinner. Daisy Billetdoux is insatiable. What does she want of me? There's no way I can ever satisfy her. If my wife/ mother/mother-in-law/Daisy Billetdoux gets any more power she'll crush me. I'm afraid she'll stop loving me. The letter gets back to Richard A. Dick. The Chairman of the Board resists a wild impulse to bury his nose in the letter and sniff deeply, he raises his bloodshot eyes and says, "Gentlemen, I think we have the little lady corralled this time."

The little lady sits at the round oak table, thinks about walls.

A convent is wall to wall walls. Around the infinite variety of walls, there is a wall. It is the only one you can see. There is a sign posted on it: NO JOSHUAS ALLOWED. Daisy knows walls, she could give lessons in walls: An anthropologist sits on an island surrounded by a wall of water and talks with Daisy about walls; Go tell it on the wall that Jesus Christ is born, sing the nuns in Daisy's convent; I am off the wall, Pearl says, that's not something a Catholic's supposed to fool with.

Daisy thinks about convent walls and okays the final designs for

154

THE SISTER MAUREEN MEMORIAL ROOM in memory of the nun from Rochester who had a baby and killed it. It is a self-contained room with no exits, for only in such containment could such passion flourish.

Quasi moves so deeply into the swamp she can no longer separate herself. It is pitch black, and Spanish moss and jungle vines cover Quasi's body, crawl up her face, creep into her nose, her nostrils are stuffed with vines and moss she cannot breathe the skin is splitting her head is exploding jungle vines drive through the membrane and Spanish moss twines round gray matter.

Daisy's wrist alarm rings simultaneously with the telephone.
LATEST HOSPITAL BULLETIN: Quasi, who has never made one honor roll in her entire life, shoots in one day to the top of the Critical List.
"Everything that is possible is being done," the hospital spokesman says.

Like Doubting Thomas whom, after a bad first impression, she has come to admire, Daisy likes to see things for herself. "I'm going to see Quasi," she tells the women.
"It won't do any good," Maggie says.
"I know a doctor in Intensive Care," Daisy says.
"Every connection helps," Rita says.

33

Upstairs in Meg's room, Peg O' My Heart looks at Meg's bed. "Am I going to sleep with you?" she asks.

Meg's cot is so narrow that if she wants to turn over she has to get out of bed to do it. So far she has never wanted to turn over. She shakes her head. "Always be careful who you sleep with," she says. "Most people hog the covers." She seats Peg O' My Heart at her desk, pushes the chair in. "Sit here and be a good girl. Don't touch anything. I'll be back in a while." Halfway across the room, she turns around and comes back. "Here's a magazine you can look at. Be careful with it." She gives Peg O' My Heart a catalogue of the latest motorcycle parts and accessories.

This is the first time Meg has ever stayed at Heartbreak Hotel, but she can recite its property deeds by heart. Heartbreak Hotel was built at the turn of the century by a tycoon who cleaned up on the railroads ta whooey ta whooey; after a turn of fortune, it became a hideaway for unwed mothers and orphan children; after the Pill emptied it out, Daisy picked it up for a song and payment of back taxes, the song was "Somebody Loves Me I Wonder Who." In the attic, there's still a jumble of cribs and children's beds, Meg knows this because she ran a complete premises check when moving in. She makes her way up a small steep staircase now, down a hall, bends nearly double to go through the Alice in Wonderland door to the attic. Inside, she can stand up, the light's burnt out, she knows that too, she shines her Eveready back into the eaves, makes her way past pink, blue, and iron cribs, high chairs, potties, to a bright yellow children's bed that has a trim teddy bear decal, not one of those soupy kind. She hauls the collapsed sections to the top of the stairs, ready to start down when a peculiar flashing from the other end of the hall attracts her attention. Noiselessly, Meg moves toward the room with its door ajar.

What the Hell?

In a room on the top floor that everybody but Daisy has forgotten or doesn't know exists, many women sit at a table longer than that of the Last Supper. The women man dozens of pink and aqua princess phones that run down both sides of the table: no rings sound, but white lights flash like the Fourth of July. The atmosphere is festive; buckets of chicken wings, plates of beef on wek are scattered around. Either it's the stimulation of the constantly flashing lights or they're all on drugs because everyone in the room is energetic, excited, *high*, Meg can spot enlarged pupils from the doorway. They're all MOTR employees, mostly secretaries, she recognizes every single one of them, except for that dreamy one at the spinning wheel in the corner spinning gold out of flax, Meg hasn't seen a dress like that in years, it's not exactly a hippie dress though there is a resemblance, and flax, where would she get flax?, it probably came up through South America.

Meg is flabbergasted. Forget the trespassers, this *room* was not here when she ran her premises check.

Meg is hurt. She lives right in the same house and still wasn't invited to the party.

She mistakes her surprise and hurt for anger, her first impulse is to throw a tear gas cannister in and shut the door.

Not so smart, she tells herself, you don't have your mask with you.

There is no way these women can be here without Daisy's knowledge: that sickening realization comes to Meg. The women's camaraderie hits her like a blow. She's a childless woman looking at mothers, a single looking at marrieds, a divorcée at a golden wedding anniversary, the whole goddam world is a secret she's not in on, even Daisy has cut her out of the plans, the decisions, the big picture, the *kill*.

She stands motionless in the doorway, nausea and fury warring inside her. Okay, she made one little mistake in her career and Daisy saved her ass: does that mean she has to eat shit forever? Daisy better not push her too far. Noiselessly, Meg moves away.

In the bathroom at the hospital, Maria Onesti, the new RN, has just heard that the silver-haired doctor is cheating on his third wife. She comes out of the stall with a thoughtful look on her face and, out of years of habit of holding public bathroom doors open so the pay locks can't click, holds the door open for Daisy.

Inside the stall where Daisy changes into her uniform, this is written in brown eyebrow pencil: Before you say For Better Or For Worse, Remember Farah Diba, Imelda Marcos, Pat Nixon, and Your Mother. Buffalo Rose RN.

In the corridor, the silver-haired doctor asks the new HEALTH OF THE SICK, COMFORTER OF THE AFFLICTED to step into the darkened X-ray room a moment. The door closes and clicks just before Daisy's connection, M. VALENTINE M.D., passes by. She doesn't hear the scuffle or the doctor say Why you little bitch-in-training.

In the Intensive Care Unit, the good news is that there is so much coming and going no one pays any mind to one more doctor or hears her say, "Live, Quasi, Live."

The bad news is that Quasi doesn't hear her either.

"She's only got one thing going for her now," T. ROBBINS M.D. says. "That's the faith of the family."

The family?, Daisy thinks, He's talking about a miracle.

"Dr. Valentine is the family physician," T. ROBBINS M.D. tells the silver-haired doctor who wears no name badge.

The silver-haired doctor looks straight through Maria Onesti RN standing white-faced next to Daisy, and nods. "Dr. Valentine," he says. Nice boobs, he thinks. He pinches Quasi's leg. "Unresponsive," he says angrily. He pinches again, takes a small scalpel, pricks Quasi. "Totally unresponsive. I'm going to have to write her off." He looks at Daisy. "Tell the family that if she doesn't die, they better plan to build a room on their house to put her in."

"Hmmmmmmm," Daisy says, she'd like to slap him, he's so rude and arrogant she can't tell if he's a neurosurgeon or an orthopedist.

But Daisy has underestimated the silver-haired doctor's sensitivity to slight. He is so accustomed to constant shots of acclaim that Daisy's neutral response on the heels of the new RN's rejection hits like cold turkey, his whole system screams. "You disapprove of my diagnosis, Doctor, or my candor?" he asks, Ball-breaker, he thinks.

Daisy tries to finesse the question with a small shrug, a Mona Lisa smile.

No soap.

"I admire sentimentality in a woman," he says, his voice is ice, "but since you've decided you'd rather be a doctor, face facts, Doctor." Daisy bristles, he raises Quasi's arm, lets it drop: it flops and dangles. "All medical evidence indicates she'll never be more than a vegetable. *She will never recover.* There's no reason for me to waste my time here. I have patients I can heal."

In the silence, T. ROBBINS M.D. says, "Maybe she'll heal herself, Doctor."

"I'm not into snake oil or faith healings, Dr. Robbins. You're not on the West Coast now."

Robbins blanches, his freckles stand out in bas relief, he starts stripping off his gloves.

"Where do you stand on miracles, Doctor?" Daisy asks, she doesn't need the audible gasp from the nurses to know she's made a serious mistake.

"You're a disruptive element, Doctor. I'll have your privileges revoked." His face is florid, he pats his hair and stalks out.

Daisy strokes the place on Quasi's leg where the Doctor pinched and nicked her. "Can he do that? Who is he?"

"He can do that," the head nurse says, "He's Chief of Neurology."

"Oh my God," Daisy says.

"You should have said that when he was here," the head nurse says.

Daisy turns to T. ROBBINS M.D., "You've got to do something."

"I'm sorry," Robbins says, "I'm leaving tonight for Seattle."

"Everybody I've ever needed in my entire life is always leaving that very night for Seattle," Daisy says.

"Anything I can do here you can do," Robbins says.

"You're saying there's nothing anybody can do," Daisy says.

"Listen," he says, "you know the family. Tell them to pray."

"What shall I tell those who don't pray?" she asks.

"Tell them not to give up hope. It's probably the same thing."

Quasi makes gurgling sounds: a nurse suctions mucus from her lungs.

"Can she hear us?" Daisy asks Robbins. "*Can* she hear?"

Robbins shrugs. "When somebody's dying, they say hearing is the last sense to go."

"*Who* says?" Daisy asks.

"People who have come back," Robbins says.

The only sound in the room is a sssssst: a nurse spritzes a plant atomizer on Quasi's tracheotomy hole to keep it moist. "What if she can hear everything and just isn't able to respond?" she whispers, "Wouldn't that be awful?"

"My child," the priest touches Daisy's shoulder.

She turns around, "Yes, Father?"

"We cannot question why this has happened," the priest says.

"Why not?" Daisy asks.

The priest is stuck for an answer, he looks at the floor, mumbles, "Dies Irae."

Maria Onesti RN stands next to the EEG machine and says quietly to a third year student, "There is never *no* hope. Even if the EEG shows part of the brain has been permanently damaged, another part can be taught to take over for the damaged part."

That's true, Daisy thinks, she's seen it time and again, it probably even goes for the silver-haired cretin, she adds grudgingly and, think of the devil, the door opens, the silver-haired doctor enters with a retinue. He says,

"Did I make it clear, Dr. Valentine? Put the decision to the family. If by 8 AM tomorrow morning, this patient shows no improvement, the family has three choices. They can

    1) Move her to a nursing facility.

    2) Take her home.

    3) Disconnect the life support system."

34

Each step of the way home, Daisy racks her brain for a new way to help Quasi. They go back a long way together, she knew Quasi in the old country before she even opened her first Museum, she can't remember not knowing her. Although MOTR is bigger than both of them put together, Daisy can't rid herself of the feeling that Quasi's fate is irretrievably tied up with MOTR's future and her own.

Robbin's words, Tell them not to give up hope, and the priest's Dies Irae drum on her, an idea bursts....

Its audacity stuns Daisy. Scares her.

It'd kill Quasi.

Or save her.

Get off the dime, she tells herself harshly, Put it out of your mind or *do* it, she takes a deep breath, flags down a tour trolley which takes her to MOTR's Electronics Department, "Wait for me," she says, she rummages through the new shipment, and races back to the hospital.

A large family looks up as one as Daisy passes through the ICU Waiting Room, their vigilance so naked her heart goes out to them.

Inside the ICU, some of the nurses in the silver-haired doctor's retinue look at her with disapproval, the head nurse raises an eyebrow, M. VALENTINE M.D. says, "I'd like a few minutes alone with her, please." "Any particular reason everybody's standing around here?" the head nurse asks, "if you don't have any work to do, I can fix that up."

Daisy closes Quasi's door. She takes a stereo transistor earphone the size of a thumbnail out of her pocket and inserts it into Quasi's ear. With Quasi already hooked up to go to the moon, it's not easy for Daisy to connect her to Heartbreak Hotel. Like doing fine needlework, she threads the connecting wire through the ganglia of electrode wires, tubes, and needles until it is indistinguishable from the others: Daisy has put a bug in Quasi's ear, she is wired to hear everything that is said at Heartbreak Hotel. "Quasi," Daisy whispers in her other ear, "Did you ever play Showdown?"

35

THE FAITH OF THE FAMILY OY

At Heartbreak Hotel, Daisy activates the last recorder that will feed into Quasi's ear, she puts it on her table in the living room. And now there remain faith, hope, and charity, she thinks, and of these three, though a famous book disagrees, the greatest is hope. Just before she speaks, she says to herself, I hope this works.

The women look expectantly at her. Ever since she called them over the intercom fifteen minutes ago to come to the living room, she's been moving from room to room with monitors, wires, mikes, and jacks.

"Are we going to make a public appeal on TV?" Rita asks, she checks her cowlick.

"Dies Irae," Daisy says.

Meg groans.

Gretchen fidgets.

They all know what Dies Irae means. Scores of times, Daisy has gathered the Museum employees together for memorial occasions.

DIES IRAE
means the day of wrath,
day of judgment,
must be said at all masses on All Souls' Day,
and in funeral masses,
must be sung by the celebrant,
and sung by the choir,
at all high masses of requiem,
nor must any of the stanzas be omitted.

"Who's the service for?" Pearl asks.

"For the faithful departed," Daisy says.

Maggie knows who *that* is, the one way Westbound Express will be passing through tonight, the rest of them will find out soon. Behind her blue glasses, she waits for the old man's plan to unfold.

"The Hell with it," Meg says. She's itching to use her new light-weight short-barrelled burp gun.

Daisy's eyes flash, but her voice is level. "Trust me, Meg."

Meg glowers daggers at Daisy: She's got some crust hauling out the Trust me bit with those women upstairs, she ought to blow Daisy's cover right now, but Meg owes Daisy and they both know it: There's a body buried in the orchard that's not talking, but there's a wife-beating D.A. who ran off at the mouth, the fink slapped a police brutality suit on Meg, her job and her ass in a permanent sling until Daisy pulled strings.

"Look," Daisy says. "This may be the last night we'll all be to-gether. We can keep each other company. Like a family. If we feel like it, we can talk. Will that kill us?"

"I get it," Rita says. "Sort of like an all night Quaker meeting." She's always been fond of Quakers, they make wonderful lovers, they don't rush things.

Daisy nods. She doesn't mention that the neurologist has laid down the law. If she put the decision to the family now, it'd be curtains for Quasi. Dies Irae is not only memorial, ritual, ceremony, and investiga-tion: It's also a stalling tactic until people are able to make a few con-nections. She also doesn't mention that Quasi will be tuning in.

They lock the doors and split up the preparations. Pearl hooks the telephones to the stereo jack, tapes a special message for the answering machine: "You have reached Heartbreak Hotel, where the women are tough, the men are tender, and all the children are prime. If you wait for the beep, which will come right after the music, and leave your name, number, and nature of business, we'll get back to you pronto. Now hang on. This is a recording." The four-record set of Handel's Messiah follows.

Maggie, Rita, and Gretchen close the shutters, pull the shades, draw the drapes. Snug as a clam in a shell, Maggie closes a thousand eyes.

Daisy sees one eye left open, but keeps it to herself. The images she's getting are: The women marooned on an island. All around them, a hurricane rages. They can't go outside, they must go inside. What appears to be a cocoon or a clamshell is actually the eye of the storm.

"Leave the tunnel door by the back staircase open," Daisy says. "I have Museum work going on upstairs."

Her words are a direct cut to Meg's heart. She hasn't budged from her post at the fireplace. What kind of cockamamie scheme is going on upstairs? Meg thinks of bank deposit stings, pyramid scams, black masses, suddenly narrows her eyes: *call girls*.

HIGH PRICED CALL GIRLS RUN LOVE NEST IN THE SUB-
URBS: Meg's got the wrong game, but she is in the ball park.

In the living room, a memorial service for Heartbreak's past is
commencing; three flights up, in a room connected by tunnel to MOTR,
a telethon for MOTR's future is ongoing.

For years, people have said to Daisy, If I can ever return the favor,
say the word.

Early this morning, Daisy started saying the word to friends and
allies built up over the years, an army major, a Marine sergeant, a
mounted policewoman, Alan Alda. . . .

"Now."

A woman hangs up a pink telephone, "Alan Alda just donated a
helicopter and an ambulance," she says, everybody cheers, "Shhhhhhh,"
the woman puts her fingers to her lips, everybody tries to pipe down,
smother their giggles, they're all higher than Georgia pines, they believe
so wholeheartedly in this cause they'd staff the phones and computers
for free, but it doesn't hurt their spirits one bit that Daisy's paying time
and a half.

"We only have till 8 AM and we need every minute of it," Daisy
says. "We're going on Einstein time." She opens the door of the grandfather clock and stops the pendulum.

Gretchen's lips thin. MOTR runs on Einstein time and Gretchen
hates it. On Einstein time, time speeds up slows down is relative to the
frame of reference of the observer, here today gone tomorrow. She
respects Daisy, but really, sometimes Daisy goes too far. By the time
her Ma gets here she'll think Gretchen's living in Sodom and Gomorrah,
she'll never be able to explain why the clocks aren't working and she's
losing her dream job and the Army's outside, her Ma'll blame her, well
she still has her gold watch, Daisy's not stopping that, she slams a chair
in place, it pulls a wire out, so what?, she sits down sullenly in the chair.

"Gretchen, please fix that connection by your chair," Daisy says.

"What's all the fancy wiring for?" Meg asks.

"I want a good recording for the Archives," Daisy says.

Like everything else Daisy has asked her to do in the preparations,
Gretchen takes her sweet time rehooking the wire. When she finally
finishes, Daisy says, "Now decide if you're going to stay or go."

Gretchen stares incredulously at Daisy: If Daisy thinks she's going
upstairs with the whole house surrounded. . . . In a tone that clearly
implies she's doing everyone a favor, she says, "Oh all right, I'll stay."

Meg starts to walk out.

"Meg?" Daisy says.

"You can pretend to shut the attack out all you want," Meg says, "I'm not having any part of this slumber party, this is what dames always do, this makes me puke, locked up in here like a bunch of females doing nothing about our lives. . . ."

"We are a bunch of females," Daisy says, "and we are doing something about our lives."

"I'm going to see that the kid's settled," Meg says without turning around.

"As opposed to what dames ordinarily do," Pearl mumbles.

Daisy shushes her with her hand. "When will you be back, Meg?"

"When you see me walk in the door."

"We'll be here," Daisy says, she flips the recording button on, leans close to the mike and says, "Testing, Testing."

36

At the hospital, Quasi holds a clamshell to her ear, hears the ocean.

She rasps through a hole cut in her windpipe.

A nurse presses an oxygen mask over her mouth.

Glucose drips through a tube in her nose.

Blood drips through a hole in her arm.

Fluid drains out a hole drilled in her skull.

Pee passes through a catheter in her urethral orifice.

She lies on a bedpan.

Quasi is filled up, tapped, and emptied like a maple tree in Springtime.

If Pearl strains, she can hear murmur, mutter, rumble in the distance outside Heartbreak Hotel but, in the living room, inside the closed drapes, the fire crackles, the lights are dim, the voices muted. She looks around and says, "Put on a Johnny Mathis record, this'd be a night to remember." In truth, Pearl feels like she's in a wildlife refuge, both the hunters and the tourist buses due momentarily. She doesn't want to be here or stay here but can't think of any feasible alternative. Without even knowing she's doing it, she softly whistles her theme song, "Don't Fence Me In," as she makes her way from the windows over to watch Daisy who sits at the round library table surrounded by charts, diagrams, blueprints, flow plans. "Figuring out your cycle?" Pearl asks.

"Relax," Daisy says.

"That's what they told Marie Antoinette."

"You've got to learn to pace yourself, Pearl."

Pearl resumes her whistling and her travels around the room.

Rita sits on a Madame Recamier sofa facing the fireplace, her feet immersed in an antique Buffalo China bowl that's white with yellow roses and filled with warm fragrant water. Periodically, Rita wiggles her toes, takes a little teakettle from a hotplate next to her, and adjusts the water temperature, sometimes she takes a little vial and sprinkles in droplets of oil, they smell like essence of root beer to Pearl.

Just a hint of incense, Maggie thinks over in the corner where she's taken all the pillows off the windowseat and built herself a magic circle. She lies in the middle, her head propped up on Rita's red satin lips pillow, she's tired but she wouldn't miss this night for the world. Rita was right, she has been spending too much time alone. She wonders what Rita would say about her visitor this afternoon. She had better not look at Rita, Rita has a way of getting her talking before she knows it. A cut glass decanter full of bourbon is on a table next to Maggie, she sips bourbon neat from a matching cut glass tumbler.

In the old Sing Sing tradition of executing the most distraught prisoner first, Pearl says Gretchen should go first to the chair. Gretchen, a towel wrapped around her head turban fashion, the afghan cloaked around her shoulders, sits in the red velvet antique barber chair, her hands grip the elaborately carved wooden arms, her feet up on the matching prie-dieu. Pearl takes her place at the Steinway baby grand.

"Dies Irae," Daisy says.

"I never could please her," Gretchen says, and bursts into tears.

Pearl plays softly in the background, "Mam-mee, how I love ya, how I love ya, my dear old Mammy, I'd walk a million miles for one of your smiles. . . ."

In the longest running play in Museum history, the mother has two lines she repeats continuously.

To her son, she says, You're breaking my heart.

To her daughter, she says: I knew you'd let me down.

MOTHER'S PLANS:

Why'd you have to become a drum majorette parading around in public in those sleazy red sequins? asks the feminist mother.

Why'd you have to become a Charismatic? asks the atheist mother.

Why'd you have to get pregnant?, Why'd you have to stay child-less?, Why'd you Why'd you, I had such plans. . . .

Every daughter has one plan: I'LL NEVER BE LIKE HER.

Gretchen thinks it's her Ma's fault she's the way she is, thinks her Ma has *chosen* to be like she is. Gretchen's Ma thought the same thing about her Ma.

GRETCHEN'S CHOICE:

Because her Ma is loose, Gretchen's chaste.

Because her Ma drinks, Gretchen's a teetotaler.

Because her Ma's a spendthrift, Gretchen's frugal.

Because her Ma's compulsive, Gretchen's spontaneous.

Because her Ma's a bigot, Gretchen loves all people.

Because her Ma lies, Gretchen tells the truth.

If you swallow any of the above, Daisy thinks, you'll swallow anything. Gretchen carries her Ma as visibly and irreversibly as Quasi carries her hump.

Pearl is getting so upset by Gretchen she starts forgetting notes, then forgets the melody; she starts crashing out chords. What's upsetting Pearl is she wants to tell Gretchen it's not so easy to be a mother, what she'd really like to do is strangle Gretchen, but then she remembers she is not like her mother either.

Pearl has five children in eight years to show her mother a thing or five about mothering.

Pearl leaves a lot behind when she runs away.

In her old neighborhood, Pearl is Mother Of The Year every year, a woman clothed with the sun, the moon under her feet, on her head a crown of twelve stars, and the coffeepot always on.

MIRROR OF JUSTICE, the Cardinals belt out, SEAT OF WISDOM, CAUSE OF OUR JOY. . . .

"Come on, fellows," Pearl says for the 500th time, "I'm not such a hotshot mother."

Day after day, Pearl throws out the same message in bottles which float out into an endless sea SPIRITUAL VESSEL, VESSEL OF HONOR, VESSEL OF SINGULAR DEVOTION. . . .

Day after day, Pearl gets more and more bottled in until she bangs smack up against the edges of herself and starts realizing a few things. When Pearl realizes

she is resentful of her daughters' friends,

she is violating her daughters' privacy,

she is jealous of her daughters' possibilities,

she is trying to control her daughters' lives,

she is not letting her daughters move toward men,

she is not letting her daughters become women,

she is not letting her daughters be funnier than she is,

When Pearl understands she is using her daughters to fill up the hole inside left by her own preoccupied Momma, she blows her cork and starts packing.

BUT WHO WILL TAKE CARE OF HER KIDS?

My daughters, Pearl hears herself say again.

168

Fifteen years after she gives birth, she leaves home in an attempt to give her husband children.

HOW CAN YOU LEAVE HOME MOMMA BLUES:
Her neighborhood and her dog think Pearl's a monster. She tries to tell them she has needs.
She needs to be honest with her daughters.
> needs to have adventures, then her daughters will have adventures.
> needs to be a sexual creature, then her daughters will be sexual creatures.
> needs to let her daughters go.
> needs to lay off her husband.
> needs to trust herself.
> needs to learn patience.

Her neighborhood and her dog have needs too. A delegation wearing black armbands tramps across Pearl's azaleas, removes the Block Mother sign from her window, her dog pees on her leg.

"How could he pee on my leg, the dog," Pearl mutters.
Rita snuffs and asks, "What are you muttering about over there?"
"I am NOT MUTTERING," Pearl says.

ON THE BRINK OF CRANK: Pearl knows a dissident of one is only a crank, she's terrified that she'll go from a whisperer to a mutterer, end up her days one of those old women who mutter at bus stops. Already she mutters at pianos, in donut shops, theatre lobbies, women's rest rooms. . . .

She notes Gretchen's lips moving, but can't make out the low mutter. Just as Pearl opens her mouth to speak, the old pipes shriek and moan, ratchet through Pearl's nerves, she thinks she's having a cerebral hemorrhage until she realizes somebody's running a tub.

37

Upstairs, Meg confides to Peg O' My Heart, "That was my *favorite* fairy tale." She smiles with past and present pleasure, closes Andersen's "The Red Shoes," the story of the little girl who's so vain about a pair of red dancing shoes she's condemned to dance forever, her feet turn to bloody stumps, a kindly executioner chops them off, she gets wooden feet, repents, and God in His great mercy takes her to Heaven where people know better than to lust for red shoes.

"What's wrong with you?" she asks Peg O' My Heart. "Are you sick?"

Peg O' My Heart is crying. "She died," she says.

"She *had* to die to get to Heaven," Meg says. "Here, wipe your nose. That's better. You play your cards right, young lady, there might be another story tomorrow, maybe even a jacks game, but right now it's your bath and to bed."

"Aren't they going to come and get you tomorrow?" Peg O' My Heart asks.

"Don't you worry about that."

Peg O' My Heart throws her arms around Meg, "I don't want them to get you."

"The only way they'll get me is feet first," Meg barks, but Peg O' My Heart's concern touches her deeply, eases the hurt she feels about those women upstairs and Daisy's lack of confidence in her, somebody cares about her, her heart does a soft shoe. She adjusts the taps so they stop whining, and tests the temperature. She cops some of Rita's bubble-bath and squirts it in. She sprinkles in some of Gretchen's bath oil beads. She tosses in Pearl's rubber duckie. She turns around and gasps. There are welts all over Peg O' My Heart's body. "Who did that to you?"

She realizes her mistake as the words shoot out. Peg O' My Heart's face is ashen, but her body is tensed, she looks Meg right in the eye and says, "I forget."

Meg wants to shake her to make her tell. Meg wants to kill. Her heart and her mind race. "Just one dunk and out," she says, "You don't stink too bad." She is afraid the water will soften the welts which appear about a week old and are starting to heal, but she can't figure out how to eliminate the bath.

She has Peg O' My Heart out of the water in a trice.

It takes every bit of control Meg has to get through the next ten minutes. She thinks her heart is going to knock right out of her body as she gingerly pats around the sickening welts that are on top of healed welts, slips her Buffalo T-shirt over Peg O' My Heart's head. "Buffalo: City Of No Illusions," Peg O' My Heart reads the T-shirt, "What's that mean?" she asks. "It means in Buffalo we know which way is up," Meg says. She tucks Peg O' My Heart into the yellow bed in the small room adjoining hers, and leaves a small table light on.

Around the clock, Meg deals with seam and sleaze and scum. She prides herself on being one tough cookie with balls, but when she turns around at the doorway and sees that little kid's eyes on her, she feels like she's going to puke. She makes a vow: no matter how long it takes, she'll find out who's responsible for this, and she'll kill the fucker.

There's no man on the force who's afraid that at the moment of danger Meg'll panic and fail him as a partner: they all know she shoots to kill. That's why they're afraid.

Meg has a strong sense of retribution; only one exhibit in the whole Museum completely satisfies it:

Down an alley off the waterfront, day and night, even on Memorial Day, honey sounds seep out from the narrow hallway leading to a vast room.

Day and night,
Sweeter than Gregorian chant,
Sweeter than the Vienna Boys' Choir,
Sweeter than an alto sax humping a love song,
Shhhhhhh, Sportin' Life's singing

> "*I'll buy you de swellest mansion,*
> *in de latest Paris styles....*"

Even on Memorial Day,

> "*I'll buy you de swellest mansion,*
> *Up upper Fifth Avenue....*"

Sweet, sweet, sweeter than the voices of courtesans whispering from the grave is the voice of Sportin' Life crooning,

> *"Come wid me,*
> *Dere you can't go wrong,*
> *Sister*

Silenter than the automobile the instant after impact
Silenter than 3 PM on Good Friday,
Silenter than the courtesans' graves, is the vast room filled with jars of pimps' larynx.

Meg strides into the living room, stands flint-eyed at the right of the fireplace, snapping and unsnapping a pair of handcuffs, and humming a thin tuneless version of "Hard Hearted Hannah."

"Speak up, Gretchen," Pearl says again.

"Every afternoon at a quarter to five, no matter what," Gretchen says, "she would get up from her catnap on the couch, go upstairs, change her clothes, comb her hair, and fix her face for my father's homecoming."

Daisy looks up and says, "She had a sense of celebration."

"She understood authority," Meg says.

"She had a feel for ceremony," Daisy says.

"She had a feel for what side her bread was buttered on," Pearl says.

"She saw herself as more than a housewife," Daisy says.

"She liked to dress up," Rita says.

"She had respect," Daisy says.

"She had fear," Maggie says.

"She cared," Daisy says.

"True," the women say.

Daisy remembers what her Mother Superior tells her: "Your greatest strength, Daisy, is that you care. As long as a person cares, there's always hope, always the possibility of change."

38

Rita is so bored by Gretchen's Ma and THE VISIT she thinks she'll die, maybe she is dead, she wiggles her toes, that's a relief, she moves them to the side of the bowl, warms up the water, and snuffs. She tries to catch Maggie's eye again, but Maggie won't look at her. Somebody probably blabbed about the insurance adjustor, Rita thinks. Somebody is always upset with Rita about some insurance adjustor. Rita yawns. Firelight hits the downy hair on her forearm and turns it golden. Little glints jump off her arm. Rita stares at the glints, and all of a sudden, telescopes: sees herself clear as day a pubescent girl waking early in the morning, sun pouring in. She lies on her side and looks at her arm where the sun strikes the golden hair, makes little glints and sparks, is there too much hair? she wonders, do I look like a gorilla? Rita stares at her arm trying to see it the way a boy will, will he find it attractive, is it too thin, bony, oddly shaped, soft enough?, she runs her fingers around her elbow, is my arm beautiful, what will he think? Rita studies the premiere lesson of pubescent girls: not How do I see? but How do I look?

Rita doesn't have to worry a whole lot about her arm. Rita's just about the hottest little number that ever strut her thirteen-year-old stuff down the halls of Our Lady of Perpetual Help High. When Rita thumbs her tight little bottom at the world, half the school has erections. Rita doesn't know it, but others do: Rita's exploding.

Rita's mother is exploding too, but it's not genetic. Everybody tries to keep it hushed up, but Rita's mother is unnatural. Unlike other mothers who are kept going by their daughters' intrigues, Rita's mother wants her own. Rita's mother was once the hottest little number that ever strutted her stuff down the halls of Our Lady of Perpetual Help. Rita's mother is thirty-seven and things have been going downhill for eighteen years. Rita's mother does not think she can bear any more.

Rita's mother has tried everything, religion, Oil of Olay, booze, barbiturates, flirting with the boys who come sniffing after Rita. The boys are afraid of Rita's mother, but Rita's scent is strong.

Rita's mother has a few sloe gin fizzes and kisses one of the boys Hello. The boy is embarrassed, the boy is scared. On the front porch swing, he wipes his mouth again and says to Rita YOUR MOTHER WEARS TOO MUCH LIPSTICK.

SHE DOES NOT SHE DOES NOT GO HOME I HATE YOU, Rita screams the boy off the porch. Even when she is grown up, she hates him.

Rita tries to will Maggie's attention to her. People don't understand about bodies, Rita shouts silently. Bodies are something, but they're not everything. Maggie stares into the fire as if she's possessed. Rita sighs. Her head is blowing off. God punished you, Rita Past whispers, but Rita says, Gotta take the blame for this one myself. That she has cut out the middleman is small solace. She has overindulged, is getting too old for this kind of excess during the week, and is ashamed of herself. Her needs are simpler now.

SIMPLIFYING YOUR LIFE: Rita's Needs. Rita would be perfectly happy doing her work, and every couple days having a little fuck which would take her through the next couple days REPEAT getting her through to a bang-up weekend WHAT DO YOU SAY TO A LITTLE FUCK SAYS THE FAMOUS SCIENCE FICTION WRITER TO A WOMAN HE HAS JUST MET AT A PARTY, GET LOST LITTLE FUCK, SAYS THE WOMAN.

Rita sighs again, snuffs, and just about shoots to the ceiling when Gretchen shouts, "Call it adagio dancer forever, nobody else's Ma dressed as a streetwalker for the Elks' Masquerade Ball!"

"You're going to wake up Peg O' My Heart," Meg snaps.

Gretchen starts to cry.

THE CRYBABY: For all important occasions, Gretchen cries three times: once imagining all the terrible things that are going to happen, once enduring all the terrible things, and once reliving them. Plop, plop, the tears steadily drip.

"Gretchen," Pearl says. "THE MOTHER is an overdetermined figure in your mind."

"The problem is, it's also an overdetermined figure in Gretchen's Ma's mind," Daisy says.

. . .

174

Pearl makes a little peekhole with her fingers and peeks through, she thinks of her mother, thinks of her daughters. It's a triangle and, at each point, she's impaled by guilt and anger.

Rita doesn't have much time to think about her mother. Rita has troubles of her own.

Rita follows the natural road of exploding thirteen-year-olds with exploding mothers.

GREAT ROAD SHOWS #1: On the Road To Wild.

Rita spends a year on the Road to Wild. She hangs around the White Spot Grill. She drinks black coffee. She smokes unfiltered cigarettes. She picks up rides. She French kisses boys in the back seats of cars. None of this causes what happens, but it leaves Rita vulnerable. What happens is that Rita gets a bad rep.

The bad rep is a bum rap.

The Museum librarian sifts past Oldies But Baddies: *Humanae Vitae, The Total Woman, Malleus Maleficarum,* and says, "Today's young girl's story, children, is "Rita's Bad Rep."

"One summer's evening before tenth grade starts, Lem Devereau, who is a pig but a sexy pig, is sitting around with the boys at the gravel pit. The boys are trading masculinity cards, getting their egos up. Lem plays an Ace: 'I went all the way with Rita,' Lem says."

"Bad boy," says the librarian who has already read this book twice. "The truth is, children, he and Rita have French kissed in the back seat of cars, and even as they're kissing, Rita knows he doesn't like her very much, but she likes the kissing, we all know the steps to *that* dance." She turns the page.

"Tim Olds, who takes Rita out every Friday night for a chocolate tastee freeze is stunned because he has never even tried for more than French kissing in back seats. He feels like a fool. He looks Lem right in his squinty bedroom eye and says, 'Big Deal, I done it to Rita a million times. She begs me sometimes.'

"With the score, Lem 1, Tim A Million Times, Rest of the Boys Zero, the rest of the boys feel conned. They are furious at Rita for never giving them any. They fill in Rita's oversight. The old gravel pit fills with sludge that night."

Some rep.
Boys call Rita up on the phone and ask, Can you handle six inches?
Who was that? Rita's folks ask.
Rita thinks she is going to die.

· · ·

Rita gathers all her courage, calls up her old grade-school chum Carol whom she left at the side of the Road to Wild, I'm dying, she says, They've killed me. Carol is the Blessed Virgin Mary The Second, a shoe-in to crown The First on May Procession Day, and she puts out the word that nobody better say that bad rep stuff around her. She sticks like glue to Rita. She glares people down. The stories cool.

POSTSCRIPT:
    Tim Olds begs forgiveness.
    Rita forgives him.
    Wherever he is today, Lem Devereau still oinks.

"Meanwhile, children, in an unrelated development, Sister Rosita throws Rita out of tenth grade Latin class. . . ."

Meg watches Rita run her fingers lightly up her forearm, stare at it as if it's a precious jewel. Tramp, Meg thinks. She is so jealous of Rita she can't stand to look at her. It's the day before Meg's period and she feels murderous and horny. These are two distinct feelings.

39

The sounds in the room are familiar and mundane: fire crackling, Rita snuffing, Gretchen sniveling, Pearl sighing, Maggie clicking ice cubes, Meg snapping handcuffs, Daisy turning pages. But in Quasi's room, blood drips through an IV, on a wall an old man dressed in a fly's suit rubs his hands together in glee, high-pitched animal sounds slide through the jamb, climb over the cracks, ooze through the keyhole. Everyone in the rotunda winces and chills. If Quasi could make distinct sounds, if her sounds played back to Heartbreak Hotel, if Maggie were there to translate the sounds, Please Please, but Maggie's in the Waiting Room, "Who knows what she's saying," says the nurse, "Give her another hypo."

For the first time in her memory, Maggie is not fearful. The worst thing that could possibly happen has: Everything is out of her control. She feels as if her entire life has been building toward this inevitable conclusion, it's a relief to have reached it intact.

She knows Quasi will die. She has sold Quasi down the River Styx. No stranger to sports trades herself, she has traded Quasi's life for hers. The old man will claim Quasi's body tonight and after seven perfect years will claim Maggie's soul, which will be damned to everlasting Hell. She is a pretty shrewd trader if she does say so herself. While waiting for her life to begin, she settles in for a night of serious drinking, one eye kept on the flames.

At the snap of Meg's handcuffs, Maggie checks back in for a second. While she waits for the word of Quasi's death, she has stopped listening to other words, only attends to sounds by conditioned reflex. People say Maggie's a born translator, but in fact, it's a learned skill.

MAGGIE GOES TO TRANSLATOR SCHOOL: Pearl's serious when she says that Maggie speaks tongues without an accent, but she never dreams that this is an advance of the generations. Maggie's folks have a mixed marriage, he's male and she's female, and they speak tongues with an accent so gutteral that early on, Maggie has to rely on other clues to follow the conversation. She's younger than Peg O' My Heart when she learns that the way something is said is as critical as what is said. By the time she's seven, and lives half the time with Gramma, who's the strong, silent type, Maggie is advanced enough to work for the U.N. which would be a snap after her family: She knows the 777 signs of DANGER, verbal signals, undertones, overtones, facial expressions, body movements, and the wavelengths of emotion. By the time she's eight, she can do all this with one ear closed.

Maggie swirls Jack Daniel's around in her mouth and observes Meg bristling by the fireplace, Rita having an LSD trip with her arm, Daisy observing, Gretchen's eyelids puffing, and Pearl making a little triangular peephole with her thumb and first two fingers and peeping through. All's quiet on the Western Front: Maggie checks back out.

Oh God, it's those Thorazine blues, Pearl thinks as she realizes she's staring through her fingers at nothing, feels herself slipping through that tiny hole deeper into depression. Deep down, beneath the sinking feeling, she knows what that hole looks like and she wants out. Move, she tells herself. But there's no way she could ever move: her gaze is caught. With an enormous effort of will, she remembers the magic words: Body, do your stuff. She lifts her seven-hundred-pound body off the piano bench, slowly walks back and forth until she is strong enough to pull herself over the edge of the hole back into the room.

Maggie hears Pearl's shuffle change to trudge to prowl to pace to stride. That seems like something interesting one might comment on, contribute to the conversation so to speak, but by the time she weighs the nuances and decides, the moment has passed and Pearl sits in an armchair going through her billfold. It's not the silences that bother Maggie, it's the words in between. I have to learn to talk, she thinks, it would help me in my life. Then Maggie remembers that her life is fixed up anyway, it really doesn't matter if she talks or not for the next seven years.

Pearl shuffles quickly past a billfold snap of Veronica Lake, her hair over one eye, pictures of her daughters, an old photo of a little girl in an organdy dress standing by a grape arbor, flowers woven into her hair, Who's that?, Tony?, she squints at a napkin with telephone numbers jotted on it, an expired library card, she takes out a little wrinkled white card and reads it, then holds it up in Maggie's direction.

"I carry this card in my billfold," Pearl says, Maggie nods and smiles. "It says if I die, they can have all my organs." She pauses and mutters, "At the rate they're deteriorating, maybe I should tear it up."

She waits in vain for someone to say they're not deteriorating. Finally, she looks back at Maggie who's no longer smiling. "If you ever will your eyes, Maggie, you should will your glasses too. They're the right prescription."

Maggie pushes her hornrims up on her nose and thinks, If a person can only see what I see, it'd be better to be cut out of the will.

40

Rita jumps up, sloshes water on the rug, tracks wet footprints across the floor, "I've got it!" she says. "If all MOTR employees sold their diamonds, we could keep the Museum open indefinitely, we wouldn't need any more grants."

They think *I'm* dumb, Gretchen thinks, but I know that much. You can't get women to band together to do anything.

"It'd glut the diamond market," Pearl says. "They're only worth something because women want them so bad."

"It wouldn't have to be just diamonds," Rita says. "Everybody could pitch in all their treasures."

"Are you nuts?" Gretchen says, she clutches her watch. "This is my pension plan."

Rita sits back down. "It was just an idea."

Meg hooks the handcuffs to her belt, paces back and forth fondling her gun.

Just watching her makes Pearl nervous.

Just watching her makes Rita horny. "I know what your treasure is," Rita says. "You're just like a man. You love that little old gun better than anything in the whole world."

Meg's fingers never stop their toying, but she shakes her head. "Second best," she says.

After a minute, Rita says, "Okay, I'll bite. What do you love best?"

"None of your beeswax," Meg says.

Meg's greatest treasure is a photo she found in the belongings of an old bag lady who froze to death in an alley on her beat. Besides seven layers of clothes, the only personal possessions the woman had were a Bible and the photo. Meg turned the Bible in. The photo is a daguerreotype of a group of old women. They are at some kind of meeting—the printing on the picture says National American Woman Suffrage Association, 1890, First International Council of Women—and their faces are so fierce and angry and ugly and unrelenting and ruthless that Meg swells with admiration for them. Every time Meg looks at that picture, she gets a shot of hope.

Maggie's greatest treasure is a china-head doll that belonged to her Gramma. It's called "The Diphtheria Doll," and it has a story.

STORY: THE DIPHTHERIA DOLL. When Maggie's Gramma, Ella, is three years old, her four-year-old sister, Agnes, gets diphtheria and dies. Agnes's bedding, clothes, and possessions, everything that she has touched, is gathered to be burned, but Ella takes the doll and hides it in her bed. Ella gets diphtheria and is deathly ill. Ella's grieving father finds the doll and, in a rage, throws it into the fire. The body is consumed, but Ella's grieving mother secretly retrieves the china head. Ella recovers and, when she is grown up, her mother makes a body for the doll and gives it to her. When Maggie's Gramma, Ella, dies, Maggie takes the doll and hides it in her bed.

One of the reasons Maggie loves the Diphtheria Doll is that it makes her a person with a past. This seems especially important tonight because she is now a person with a limited future.

Pearl has a treasure from her grandmother too: a bracelet that, with the exception of a plain wedding band to ward off offers, is the only jewelry Pearl wears. The bracelet is almost a hundred years old, but looks surprisingly modern. Her grandmother's name is engraved in script inside it: Mary Baumgras. Every time Pearl reads that, she considers it a formal introduction to the grandmother who died at age 38 before Pearl's Daddy was even married. To this day, Pearl's Daddy loves and honors his mother, so Pearl feels a great responsibility to the bracelet. She never performs without it, and whenever she has anything important to do, she always brings her grandmother along.

Rita's greatest treasure is a small sculpture of two girls skipping rope together given to her by her cherished friend, Faith, who is now far away. When ·Rita looks at that statue, she remembers her adult girlfriend, Faith, her girlhood girlfriend, Carol, she remembers a time when she was an outdoor person.

As a remnant of her convent training, a small knapsack left over from her Catholic baggage, Daisy regularly weans herself from attachment to material possessions. At the moment, her greatest treasure is a simple olive shell found on an island beach. She cups it in her fingers, runs her thumb down its smooth surfaces, around its ridges and rim, smiles, and sets it back on the desk in front of her.

Gretchen's greatest treasure is not her 14K gold ankle bracelet engraved with her name: it's her gold pocket watch. She is forever drawing it out and looking at it. She has special tiny pockets with little snaps sewn into each of her white pleated skirts so that she can wear the watch while she works. It's real gold too, and worth a bundle, but nobody knows that Gretchen won it in a competition. She was such an underdog they didn't even put her name on the program. The watch belonged to her Ma's father, and the competition was with her brother, two uncles, one son-in-law, three male cousins, and two nephews.

In fact, a watch for Gretchen is redundant. She is a living clock. Right this minute, her pocket watch lies in her palm, the hunter's case gleams in the firelight, she stares at it, and feels her eyelids get crepey. She pushes the stem that opens the case, stares at the face in surprise, and starts crying again. "I forgot to wind my watch," she says. She has never in her life forgotten to wind her watch.

Pearl has seen a lot of difficult times at Heartbreak Hotel, but can't remember a night like this: everything is breaking down tonight at Heartbreak Hotel. Maybe it's the end of the world.

"It's all *right*, Gretchen," Rita says, "I'll just call Time." She dials, listens a moment, and hangs up looking puzzled. "It said, 'This is Buffalo Rose telling you it's time to take your life into your own hands.'"

"There's only one life we can take into our hands tonight," Meg says. "Let's pull the goddam plug and go to bed."

There it is out in the open without Daisy even saying a word.

41

This is the line-up.

Team 1, wearing yellow trunks, rooting for Quasi are Rita, Daisy, and Wait for me, says Pearl, I come on slow, but I go out fast.

Rita is unanimously elected Captain of Team 1.

Team 2, wearing white, rooting for the plug are Meg, Gretchen, and Maggie.

Meg appoints herself Captain of Team 2.

Team 1:

Pearl has made up her mind to go for Quasi because
   a) Quasi requires so little from her,
   b) a struggler touches her,
   c) she's a fellow depressive,
   d) and finally, for the same reason she gives quarters to
       beggars: cheap insurance.

Daisy can make a lot of cases for Quasi, take up for her out of conscience, her interest in the extremes of human mutation, because she's part of her rituals and life and she's used to her. But her case is much simpler: Because Daisy is confronted constantly with atrocities THE YORKSHIRE RIPPER THE BOSTON STRANGLER THE L.A. HILLSIDE STRANGLER THE SEATTLE GREEN RIVER KILLER IN NEWARK CALL . . . she sees Quasi in sublime proportion.

Rita owes Quasi her life.

Team 2:

Gretchen can't stand Quasi because
   a) she wears her ugliness so openly, BRAZEN
       HUNCHBACK,
   b) she makes Gretchen guilty having to look at the exposed
       parts,
   c) she's the embodiment of other possibilities.

Meg can't understand what's the big deal over euthanasia. She has pulled the plug on other people. She thinks it's okay for Daisy to be a pacifist, but personally, she prefers a more direct approach to life.

These are the people Meg has pulled the plug on:

An ironing board cover salesman attempting armed robbery and assault & battery.							
A mother	"	"	"	"	"	"	"
A father	"	"	"	"	"	"	"
A husband	"	"	"	"	"	"	"

About the scum who jumped Rita, or the wife-beating D.A., Meg takes the Fifth.

Maggie prefers yellow trunks to white, but has no choice. She has already bought a daisy yellow dress at a discount store that takes no returns.

As across a great distance but with startling clarity, Maggie looks over at Rita. Her eyes fill with the sadness of the suicidal depressive who's stinko. Maggie doesn't want to be against Rita. She loves Rita. She starts snuffling.

Daisy watches the women whomp up to war over Quasi's plug. They're supposed to be fighting their enemies, but they fight themselves. Daisy feels an enduring fatigue.

Upstairs, Peg O' My Heart is terrified.

Something is under her bed.

She cannot let her hand, a finger, a toe dangle over the side. Her only chance is to stay dead center.

Peg O' My Heart is surrounded. She lies death still. She nearly chokes on the held breath.

42

Quasi is put into a Stryker frame.

She is the filling in a canvas sandwich held tightly by straps.

She is turned every fifteen minutes to aid blood circulation.

Flip.

Somebody's listening in.

Meg'll stake her life on it.

Snap, unsnap go the handcuffs again, but Meg's eyes are searching the room.

"If she lives and they boot us out, will they let her come back here and live on the porch?" Pearl asks.

"I didn't ask," Daisy says.

Pearl's eyebrows raise, Daisy meets her gaze, but doesn't elaborate.

Gretchen whimpers, it has finally penetrated to her that this attack on Heartbreak Hotel is as serious as her Ma's visit, she strokes the red velvet upholstery of the antique barber chair, looks at the black walnut woodwork, the brass sconces, the crystal doorknobs, she loves Heartbreak Hotel, feels proud to come down the street and turn into this beautiful house, her Ma always kept their house beautifully, you could bring your friends home day or night and always feel pride, no matter how miserable she was she kept the house up, Gretchen's whimpers turn into a low moan, her fingers dig deeper into the velvet, she gets a sick feeling at the thought of leaving this house, if they close the Museum, where will she go, she can't bear to think about it, "If we get rid of her, maybe they'll let us stay," she says. "Yes, I'm sure they will. You can understand if you think about it. Nobody wants something like that around their neighborhood. I mean think about it."

"We're all in this together," Daisy says.

"But we'll all *sink* together," Gretchen says, "We can save ourselves. . . ."

"Not that way," Daisy shakes her head. "If we know anything, we know that."

"What doth it profit a woman to gain a Museum if she loseth her hunchback?" Pearl mumbles.

"Can you imagine what it's like to be a hunchback?" Daisy asks. Only Pearl nods. "Always on," she says.

The hunchback moves through the crowd. Everybody looks. A few look covertly, some stare, but everybody looks. Even God looks. God is a little confused by the hunchback. He can't quite remember why He created her. More and more it seems to God that the hunchback exists to be looked at LOOK AT THAT DID YOU SEE THAT I'VE NEVER SEEN CAN YOU IMAGINE I WONDER. People push through crowds to get a good look, they pursue the hunchback to touch her, Daisy once followed a hunchback to Cheektowaga to check her out and a dozen people darted up, touched her hump and fled, one gave her a good crack before taking off, Daisy wants a good look herself, but to touch the hump without invitation seems to her like touching breasts and venus mounts without invitation. The hunchback shook her head after the thumping but she wasn't confused, she knows she exists to be looked at and touched and she feeds on this, it's her livelihood IF YOU'VE GOT IT FLAUNT IT and she's got it, poor boobie, but no dumbbell, she turns a bad deal into a good hustle, markets her pain for pity, sells her pain for a few coins, exaggerates her pain for a few more coins, and business makes strange bedfellows, familiarity breeds not contempt but comfort, her initial hatred of her hump gradually turns into a lasting love affair, she is AC and DC with her hump, she is S and M with her hump, her hump brings her goodies, her hump is her visibility and her mystery and her livelihood, and if she survives, becomes her life. Many wonder if she has wit or humor or a certain state of grace, but hardly anyone wonders if hustled hump is enough to carry a person through a lifetime.

Why *should* anyone wonder?

Quasi never wonders. She sees herself as hump in a figurative sense. She never sees herself in a literal sense. Quasi has never once looked in a mirror, a toaster, a plate glass store window, an oil slick or, in a crisis, a piece of Reynolds Wrap.

BEAUTIFUL DREAMER: Only God knows that when Quasi dreams, she sees herself as, get this, a beautiful woman, lots of luck, Quasi.

Quasi needs a little luck. At the hospital, the nurse places a canvas frame on top of her, deftly flips her 180°. Nobody sees the look of horror on Quasi's face: she is the monster under the bed.

43

Meg listens to Pearl and Daisy talk about a day in the life of a hunch-back and is dumbfounded: how can anyone possibly care about this freak who can't even control her bowels?

Meg thinks about all the crimes that go on in the world.

She thinks of rape and pimps and coat-hanger abortions and incest and perverts and porn kings and bigamists and batterers and child support deadbeats.

She thinks of a D.A.'s own divorce transcript that burns in her memory like a litany:

In or about November, 1974 . . .
December 6, 1974 . . .
March 8, 1975
May, 1975
April 15, 1976
May, 1976
August, 1976
October, 1976
December, 1976
March 5, 1977
June 7, 1977
June 18, 1977
August 17, 1977
at the marital home
at the marital home
in the bedroom
at the marital home
at the marital home
at the marital home
in the bedroom
in the den
in the bedroom
in the driveway
in the bedroom

at the marital home
at the marital home
in the automobile
at the marital home
at the marital home
defendant hit and beat the plaintiff about the head with his fist and
    hands, causing plaintiff to fall to the floor while holding young
    child . . .
brutally and violently beat the plaintiff about her head and face
repeatedly hit and beat the plaintiff about the face and body
struck the plaintiff and struck the son of the parties
brutally struck the plaintiff
maliciously directed his automobile toward the plaintiff
repeatedly pushed
repeatedly hit
pushed
hit
struck
punched
dragged
hit

Meg thinks of the welts on Peg O' My Heart's back, thinks of the
man who cut off her ponytail, and all these things merge in her mind into
one form that has a distinctive hump.

Meg feels that if she can just rub out one ugly monstrous being,
it's a start. When she shows Daisy how getting rid of Quasi will fix up
their problems, Daisy will never doubt her judgment again, Daisy will
start caring about people worth caring about. It will feel so good yank-
ing that plug out, power surges through Meg, she grinds her cigarette
into the ashtray and exits so abruptly she nearly knocks over Maggie's
upraised glass.

"*Excusez moi pour vivre,*" Maggie says, "Pardon me for living," she
says to Meg's disappearing back.

As soon as Meg is gone, Gretchen coughs, attacks Meg's smoldering
cigarette, waves her arms in windmills to clear the air of smoke, takes
purple candles from the corner armoire, fills the candelabra on the
mantel and on the piano, lights them with an altar boy's self-importance,
and says, "I'm not going to die from her lack of self-control."

"What are you going to die from?" Pearl asks.

Instantly, Gretchen deflates, collapses on the divan, I'm dying, she
thinks.

.   .   .

For one terrible moment, Meg thinks Peg O' My Heart has stopped breathing. She holds her finger under her nose, her relief enormous when the small warmth of breath comes. She looks at the sleeping child a long moment, turns off the bedside lamp, moves feline-like from the alcove to her cot and picks up the books that distracted her when she went to get Peg O' My Heart a story.

"I've always been terrified of a trivial death," Maggie tells her drink.

"I know just what you mean," Rita says. "A cold turning into pneumonia, a bee sting settling in the larynx, choking on a chicken bone. . . ."

Daisy knows what she means too: when Maggie says she's terrified of a trivial death, Daisy knows she's really afraid of a trivial life.

"Story of my life," Pearl says, "Choking on chicken bones."

The ticker tape has another puzzler. "Western Union has a line around the block," Daisy says.

Gretchen thinks of the most often requested telegram form in Western Union's history MAMA DIED ASKING FOR YOU, and swoons again on the couch.

"What does it mean?" Maggie asks.

"Everybody's writing letters and sending telegrams," Daisy says.

"Memorial Day," Gretchen moans.

"Could be," Daisy says.

A telephone booth also has a line starting around the block. Inside, a man in a raincoat holds the phone to his ear, listens to Handel's Messiah, side 3.

Rita completes Phase 1 of her pedicure, she pats her feet dry, slips on terry booties, and makes her way to the kitchen. She washes out her bowl, fills it with some of the anthurium that are stuffed in a peanut butter jar, sets it on the counter, starts poking through the cabinets. It's the damndest thing: all day long, people in this house go to the grocery store and there's never anything to eat, what she craves is a Girl Scout S'more, a Hershey bar and marshmallows melted on toasted graham crackers, she earned a badge in them, but she has to settle for the bag of fortune cookies. As she arranges them in concentric circles on a silver platter, she turns on the TV, yells, "Hey we're on TV, Hurry Hurry."

A shot of the Guardian Angels doing maneuvers out on the street fades into a pan of the property, Heartbreak Hotel looming gothic in the distance, a voice overlay of Curtis Sliwa says, "We're not sure what they're doing in there, but the people of Buffalo have asked us to get to

the bottom of it." An aerial photo of MOTR comes up behind the newscaster, he reads:
THE EDITORIAL

"The Museum Of The Revolution is under attack again. For the last decade, it's become almost a rite of Spring for the Federal, State, and County governments to declare war on MOTR in election years. Every time, the respective legislators in Washington, Albany, and Erie County discover the same things: that the Museum employs more people than Civil Service, is solely responsible for the revitalization of Western New York, and at least one close relative works there. Every time, they change tack and strike medals which emissaries in new down jackets purchased especially to come to Buffalo present to MOTR's internationally renowned curator, Dr. Daisy Billetdoux.

"City Fathers by their very nature hate to be upstaged, but we're puzzled. Why is the Administration attacking so ferociously in an off-election year? We're even more puzzled over the lack of public response. Except for a small band of neighbors, there has been no outcry against the current no-holds-barred attack.

"Just yesterday it seems that public sentiment was solidly on MOTR's side. Not only was the Museum the darling of the affirmative action set, but it won the hearts and minds of Buffalonians who lined up for blocks to see the best show in town. Many who had resigned themselves to hanging around closed car dealers and kicking automobile tires on Sunday afternoons took to packing picnics and bringing the kiddies for a day's outing at MOTR.

"For our money, the Museum Of The Revolution is still the best show around. Both pleasing and provocative, it has been called 'the Nadia Comaneci of the museum world.' Above all, it stands for the thing that Americans love best: the triumph of the underdog. We cannot figure out the motives of the current Administration, but we counsel our viewers not to forget how dark Sunday afternoons used to be in this town before Daisy Billetdoux came and turned on all those flashing lights."

Richard A. Dick gnashes his teeth. "Who ate all the Fritos?" he snaps at his wife, and changes the channel.

"Did you hear that?" Gretchen says, " 'a band of neighbors,' he said, I told you public support will save us the same way we saved this town, my Ma will be *proud*!", she leaps into the air, comes down into splits, Pearl winces, "There goes my hymen," Pearl says, "Nobody'll believe me."

190

Gretchen stops in mid-cartwheel, flips upright, "What did that mean, the Nadia Comaneci of the museum world?"

"A cute Commie," Pearl says.

Gretchen goes upstairs, pins her flag pin on her sweater, takes a Librium, and joins the others in the living room.

A little breeze of hope blows through the room. "We should be having champagne," Rita says, she offers the silver platter of fortune cookies to Daisy at her table, "You can have mine," Daisy says, "Your fortune too? Neat," Rita says, she offers them to Pearl, "I'm on a diet," Pearl says, her whole life she's been on a diet, when she was born she weighed 7 lbs. 4 ozs. and immediately went on a diet aiming for an even 7. Maggie shakes her head, she no longer eats sweets, alcohol broke that bad habit, besides she already knows her fortune, Gretchen takes two, she is cursed with a sweet tooth that no sugar ever satisfies, she takes one more, Rita sets the platter on the coffee table and after much deliberation chooses, "This one's got your name on it, Daisy," she says and reads the fortune, " 'Buffalo Rose say,' " she stops and giggles, Buffalo Rose say, my eye, What is this? What wonderful thing is going on here? In all kinds of intercourse, Rita always keeps her eyes open but she's never one to hurry a mystery. She loves mystery even more than intrigue, and you can hardly find it anymore. She continues, " 'The time is right for new beginnings.' New beginnings, hey that's nice, you sure you don't want it, Daisy?"

"It's yours now," Daisy says. She is at that stage of fasting where she feels not light-headed but light-bodied, as if she's shedding all the things that weigh her down. She won't know about her gamble for some hours yet, but things are looking good, she's checking the computer every quarter hour and all indications are go, her friends are coming through.

"How'd you ever get so many important friends?" Gretchen asks Daisy once.

"I was friends with them before they got important," Daisy says.

If it weren't for Quasi, Daisy might rise right off her chair and ascend through the ceiling. Quasi is a rock grounding her.

These voices go through Daisy's mind: The rock which the builder rejects becomes the cornerstone, Upon this rock I build my church, Jesus says, You have got rocks in your head, Pearl says.

At the hospital, Maria Onesti RN tells a student nurse, "Dr. Robbins is alternating silence and stimuli in a carefully controlled sequence.

He's now playing the radio to try to stimulate her brain. Nobody knows if coma patients are aware of what's going on around them, but it's probably best not to talk about anything you don't want her to hear. Talk about pleasant things. Make encouraging remarks."

Onesti leaves the room and the extern changes the good music station to 97 Rock.

Meg brings in a slew of books, "We were on TV, Meg," Gretchen says.

"Maybe we'll get an offer from Phil Donahue," Meg says, she saw the editorial on the upstairs TV, big deal, PBS, four people saw it while waiting for Wall Street Week to come on. That Sliwa guy, there's something fishy about him, he never takes the red hat off, either he wants to be a Cardinal or he's bald. She starts to set her books on top of the baby grand to the left of the fireplace, its whole top is covered with flowers, "This place looks like a goddam funeral home," she says. She starts moving the vases and bowls off, she sets a cut glass crystal bowl onto the table next to Maggie's decanter and glass, "Might as well complete your place setting," she says.

Maggie looks at the exotic pink and red flowers with the long peculiar stamen, touches one, it feels waxy, "What kind of flower is that?" she asks.

"Anthurium," Daisy says, "They grow on tropical islands."

"Looks just like a baboon's ass to me," Meg says. One by one, she sets the books on the cleared piano top. She puts another log on the fire. Everyone sits up straight. Meg lights a cigarette, throws the match in the ashtray, spots the cigarette shreds, looks around the room, Gretchen pretends to be engrossed in Phyllis Diller's operation pictures in People Magazine, Dear God, she prays, Don't let her find me out.

Gretchen always feels that at any moment she's one moment away from getting into trouble. She thinks people know her in devastatingly accurate ways that she'll never know herself.

Pearl remembers the feeling, but now she knows the truth: she knows herself to such an extent no one else could possibly be interested beyond it.

But Gretchen and Pearl still have something in common: they both live in glass houses.

Gretchen believes that people can see inside her. Pearl believes that people can see through her.

In a dim room, Quasi's eyes are open and stare at a glass wall. If she could move, she would press her nose against the glass and say Let me in.

192

Meg feels publicly chastised, if they'd just leave me alone I wouldn't *have* to smoke, she dumps the ashtray mess into the fireplace, probably was that little priss Gretchen, she takes a deep drag, feels the catch in her throat, if I don't quit smoking, I'll have to arrest them all for murder, she glares at them, they'll be sorry, she aims a half dozen perfect smoke rings all in Gretchen's direction, stink up her brand new clean hair, the big buttinsky.

When Meg is sure everybody in the room has the message that this babe is running her own show, she clears her throat and presents the expert witnesses for the prosecution.

"This is what the novelist says about hunchbacks." Meg reads with a scam artist's feeling and sense of timing: " 'A *hunchback was a lucky man. If you touched a hunchback, he brought you good fortune and health and freedom from bad dreams. Therefore, come in file and each shall touch the hunchback and peace be to him.'* " Meg snorts and closes the book.

"The hunchback does it for you, dig?" Pearl says. "Stores all the nightmares in the hump."

"Carries them like Christ carrying the cross," Daisy says.

Lucky for everybody but her, Maggie thinks.

"This is what the poet says about hunchbacks." Meg reads slowly, lingeringly, like a Sunday afternoon flasher:

> " '*If a hunchback is in the elevator with you*
> *don't turn away,*
> *immediately touch his hump*
> *for his child will be born from his back tomorrow*
> *and if he promptly bites the baby's nails off*
> *(so it won't become a thief)*
> *that child will be holy*
> *and you, simple bird that you are,*
> *may go on flying.'*

Jesus!" Meg says, and closes the book.

Daisy nods. "That's why you touch the hunchback," she says.

"Why?" Pearl asks.

"To acknowledge the gift she gives."

Gretchen wants to scream, Anybody with sense knows you don't get into an elevator alone with *any* man let alone a male pregnant hunchback, what does this porn have to do with her life, what is she going to do, Gretchen wants to cry but they'll all yell at her if she does, she's got to be brave.

Rita hears a lot of weird things about motherhood in her business and this ranks right up there with them. That part about biting the baby's nails was pretty weird too. Maybe she should give herself a manicure as long as she's got all the stuff out. "I liked the part about the bird," she says. "Read some more, Meg."

"This is what the visionary says about hunchbacks." Meg reads like target practice at the Police Academy:

" 'The Multiple Man, also called The Hunchback.
The True Mask—self realization.
The False Mask—self abandonment.
The Body Of Fate—The Hunchback is his own Body of Fate.' "

"Not this time," Maggie murmurs.
"What the Hell are you talking about now?" Meg says.
" /分度 (ı´ʌˑʃ/ı ," Maggie translates.
"I don't buy that Eastern stuff," Gretchen says. "I tried to read one of those books one time and it kept going off into haikus."
Pearl is watching Daisy.
Meg glowers.
Maggie stares into the fire and thinks Nothing personal, Quasi.
Daisy's in a brown study. Daisy's had visions, but never one like that. Daisy looks inside, remembers a vision: some catastrophe has split her into countless pieces, limbs joints bone sinew in a hopeless jumble, as a detached eye watches horrified and helpless each piece of her begins traveling like broken bone fragments moving to join the original part moving infinitesimally but inexorably until miraculously Daisy is whole.
Gretchen tightens her sphincter muscles.
Pearl taps her fingers on the piano top.
Tap, tap, tap, tap.
Rita debates which is worse: hearing more about hunchbacks or sitting in this mausoleum applying cuticle remover. "You got anything a little more upbeat?" she asks cheerfully.

Meg plucks a book from the pile. "There's one more," she says threateningly. She reads like the D.A. closing in for the kill on his wife: " '. . . his whole person was a grimace. An enormous head covered with red bristles; between the shoulders a great hump balanced by one in front: a system of thighs and legs so curiously misplaced that they touched only at the knees . . . huge splay feet, monstrous hands. . . .' " Maggie hiccups, Meg is describing the person in the mirror, Meg flips pages. " 'Quasimodo took up his position in . . . ,' " "Hey," Rita says,

Meg silences her with a look, says, " '*Quasimodo took up his position in the rear . . . facing the crowd, thick-set, snarling, hideous, shaggy, ready for a spring, gnashing his tusks, growling like a wild beast. . . .*' "

Maggie realizes who the person in the mirror is.

"That's ridiculous. Quasi doesn't have tusks," Rita protests.

Pearl rolls her eyes.

Rita persists: "Why would anyone say those things about our Quasi?"

"*Our* Quasi?" Meg shouts. "*Our* . . ." Meg is in a fury. How stupid can people be? The evidence is staring them right in the face and they refuse to look at it. "I hope you all get exactly what you deserve," she says, balling her hand into a fist and shaking it at them.

In the ICU, Elvis twitches, throbs, convulses,

Well since my baby left me/
Well I find a new place to dwell/
It's down at the end of Lonely Street/
That Heartbreak Hotel
Where I'll be
I'll be so lonely baby/
Well I'm so lonely/
I'll be so lonely I could die . . .

Quasi has violent body tremors.

A nurse turns the radio off, but she continues to thrash.

Those are gross body movements that mean nothing, the silver-haired doctor tells his medical students.

The nurse tightens the straps that keep Quasi on the straight and narrow.

44

Pearl takes three calming breaths and watches Meg bring her fist down on the coffee table, the fortune cookies jump. Pearl winces: she knows Meg's hand hurts like hell, Poor Meg, she thinks.

A lot of people, including Meg, think Pearl and Meg will always be like whiskey flavored toothpaste, oatmeal and tomato juice, chocolate covered raisins: natural enemies. But a lot of people are wrong. Pearl's perfect attendance at the weekly meetings of Manaholics Anonymous has paid off, ta da. Pearl feels a certain bond with Meg because she knows temper. Temper is one of the few things Pearl hasn't given up, but she is learning how to direct it more efficiently, effectively, cheaper.

Although people often confuse Pearl with Mahatma Gandhi now, she remembers.

PEARL'S TEMPER:
　　Pearl is mad with rage,
　　Pearl spills with spleen,
　　Pearl bubbles with choler,
　　Pearl loathes, detests, abhors, abominates,
　　Pearl hates men.

"I would not hate my worst enemy," Gretchen says. She smiles piously, "I love all mankind, I am a son of God The Father, brothers with all men . . ."
Pearl froths at the mouth.

Daisy says to Pearl, "You tell me you loved your Grampa. You tell me you love your Daddy. You tell me you love your husband. Why do you think you hate men?"
Pearl is stunned with confusion. Pearl gives the only possible re-

sponse. Pearl hates her Daddy. Pearl hates her husband. Luckily Grampa's long gone or he'd get it right between the eyes too.

I don't understand, says her Daddy.
I don't understand, says her husband.
I hate you, says Pearl.
The truth is, Pearl doesn't understand either. The truth is, Pearl is trying to love her mother. The truth is, Pearl is trying to love herself.
Grampa squirms in the grave.

GREAT ROAD SHOWS #2: On The Road To Understanding. "When people hit the North 40," Pearl says, "they start understanding what their folks' lives were like in the South 40."

Pearl's Daddy used to play practical jokes that broke everybody up. Once he pushes Pearl off a picnic bench and breaks her finger. Once Pearl, crazy with depression, pushes her daughter off a picnic bench and breaks through to her Daddy.

This is The Litany Of Pearl's Daddy:

He holds her on his lap
He sticks up for her. . . .

"Titter ahem," say the shrinks archly which so enrages the head Cardinal he castrates them on the spot for making one truth the whole truth. The Cardinals straighten their birettas and begin again:

He holds her on his lap
He sticks up for her
He whispers in her ear
He tells her that a fountain with changing colors is flavors of soda
   pop
He promises next time they'll bring a straw
He's as disappointed as she when they keep forgetting the straw
He has silver hair
He has broad shoulders
He has hair on his chest
He dresses as an adagio dancer for a masquerade ball
He fixes breakfast
He drives his children to out-of-town games
He sees that his daughter wears rags
He keeps his mother's picture on his dresser
He keeps his daughter's picture on his dresser
He's the proudest father at the father/daughter banquet

He's the proudest father at the Homecoming game
He's affectionate
The lady next door calls Pearl and her Daddy The Smoochers
She bellows THE SMOOCHERS ARE AT IT AGAIN
He's a private man
He's a modest man
He's lonely
He shampoos Pearl's hair in the kitchen sink
He puts her hair in fantastic designs
He carries her to the mirror so she can see them
He teaches her a poem about pelicans
He takes her to see pelicans
He works hard
He quit school at sixth grade
He's a white collar worker
He teaches college graduates
College graduates love him
He's a much loved man
He can move in any circle
He jokes
He bursts balloons
He pricks pricks
He loves to laugh
His comic timing is perfect
He keeps secrets
He never takes the easy way out
He keeps on
He earns respect
He goes deer hunting once, kills a deer, never goes hunting again
He's a good driver
He drives hundreds of miles nonstop
He never has an accident
He can fix his own car, but won't
He gets a new car every year
He takes little kids to root beer stands
He lets little kids drink root beer in his new car
He prefers pool swimming to ocean
He's strong
He keeps busy
He keeps interested
He keeps up
He gives advice to younger men
He makes flowers grow
He wants to be happy
He honors his word
He honors his wife at his retirement dinner
He carries deadweight

He refuses to drown
He parks in front of the movie theatre when the 7 o'clock show
    lets out
He says funny things about the people coming out
He buys children ice cream cones
He brings his wife flowers
He spends money like he's got it
He's a sharp dresser
He's orderly
He's an early riser
He doesn't complain
When he's sick he disappears like an old dog till he's well
He's tough
He mops floors
He cleans toilets
He cooks dinner
He writes a little girl postcards
He tries to control the quality of his life
He tries not to live on the lowest emotional denominator
He keeps his dignity
He feels family bonds deeply
He plucks off Pearl's nose
He brings it back
He throws her so high her stomach drops
He never drops her
He buzzes like a bee, spiraling his finger in ever decreasing circles
    closer closer to Pearl's heart ZAP
He won't look at other women
His right arm was Pearl's seat belt.

"This Daddy of yours," Daisy says. "He's a regular Archangel."

That's exactly what people always say about Pearl's husband, so she says, "Why is it when a man acts human, we make him an archangel?" But she's already at the piano playing softly, so as not to wake up Peg O' My Heart, "My Heart Belongs To Daddy."

Peg O' My Heart dreams:
YOU THINK YOUR FATHER IS SO GREAT I HAVE HIDDEN A LETTER IN THIS HOUSE AND WHEN THEY FIND IT THEY WILL KNOW WHAT I'VE HAD TO PUT UP WITH.

Peg O' My Heart tosses and turns, her lips move, it has to be in Gramma's teapot, we're never supposed to touch that
YOU THINK YOU ARE SO SMART WELL MISS SMARTY PANTS THE LETTER IS NOT THERE

.   .   .

"He's a quiet man," Pearl says.
He won't talk
He won't listen
He jokes
He doesn't know how to talk or listen or stop making jokes
He teases mercilessly
He makes fun of presents
He makes fun of his wife
He uses his baby for his straightman
He's terrified his baby will be hurt
He favors
He won't let her ride her brother's motorbike
He won't let her drive her brother's car
He wraps her in cotton batting and calls her princess
He puts her on a pedestal so he doesn't have to meet her gaze
He whispers in her ear so he doesn't have to listen to her
He's secretive
He's aloof
He's distant
He's afraid
He tries to protect his wife
He tries to protect his children
He tries to protect himself
He's angry
He doesn't know how to get angry
He doesn't know how to set limits
He doesn't know how to ask for help
He takes revenge
He sleeps alone for thirty years
He is always depressed
He shouts in silence
He knows things are terribly wrong
He pretends things don't happen
He pretends people are invisible
He's a rotten pretender
He does the best he knows how to do.

LAMB OF GOD WHO TAKEST AWAY THE SINS OF THE WORLD, SPARE US
    O LORD
LAMB OF GOD WHO TAKEST AWAY THE SINS OF THE WORLD, GRACIOUSLY
    HEAR US O LORD
LAMB OF GOD WHO TAKEST AWAY THE SINS OF THE WORLD, HAVE
    MERCY ON US.

The last time Pearl goes home she is almost forty and she sits on
her Daddy's lap. She is too big and too old, but she sits there anyway to

tell him that whatever the angers of the last ten years she has forgiven him, Please forgive me, Daddy.

The wizened lady next door who has cancer of the larynx and wears a little lace doily on her neck comes over and beeps, The Smoochers Are At It Again.

Daisy starts to point something out, but Pearl looks as if she might cry. Daisy bides her time and ponders THE DOUBLE STANDARD: Gretchen's Ma is to blame for everything she does wrong, but Pearl's Daddy does the best he knows how to do.

Oy, these Daddies' girls give Daisy a lot of trouble.

Well, at least Pearl knows where her Daddy is.

LOOKING FOR DADDIES: Daisy has a terrible time finding space for them, they're on every block of the Museum, every size, shape, and age, little girls dressed up in women's bodies looking for Daddies in

religious cults
political cults
bars
old men
silver-haired doctors
lawyers
priests
bosses
rock stars
husbands
lovers
brothers
uncles
professors
prizefighters
Jim Jones
Reverend Moon
John Paul II
God The Father
any kid Maharishi zooming by on his motorcycle
The Godfather
Ike
Walter Cronkite
Ronald Reagan
Charlie Manson

sugar daddies big daddies o daddyo i'm scared of bugs snakes lighting the barbecue driving in a new town the stock market ordering my own meal in a restaurant giving myself communion forgiving my own sins taking charge of myself taking care of myself being an adult if you'll be my daddy i'll be your baby

> *Oh you must have been a beautiful baby/*
> *You must have been a wonderful child/*
> *I can see the judges' eyes/*
> *When they handed you the prize/*
> *I bet you drove the little boys wild/*
> *Oh you must have been a beautiful baby/*
> *'Cause, Baby, look at you now.*

"So with my writing talent," a Daddy junkie tells Daisy, "I'm asking Jesus to use it any way He wants to, to give me the desire back again if He wants me to write that book."

SOME DADDIES ARE MORE PERMISSIVE THAN OTHERS: Jayne Kennedy sees no conflict between her appearance in Playboy and her born-again Christian beliefs. As far as her fans objecting, she says, "I've learned to live with criticism. When I did 'NFL Today,' I wore a black evening gown open to the navel and got nailed for that. But I don't see anything wrong with clothes like that. I like being a woman. God continues to bless me, and if He didn't want me to wear them, He wouldn't be allowing me to."

"Tell me the Italian again, Maggie," Pearl asks.
It's music when Maggie rolls it out: *"Facie le croce."*
Pearl tells the story.
IT IS MEAT AND JUST: The family is gathered around the table. One piece of meat is left on the platter. The daughter reaches for it.
"*FACIE LE CROCE!*" shouts the father, "Make the sign of the cross!"
The daughter says, "In the name of the Father. . . ."
"You hear that?" says the father, "The Father comes first," he spears the meat.

202

45

Meg checks the living room baseboards again: all the jacks and monitors in use are regulation Archive equipment, she works her way back to the transistorized recorder on Daisy's table, checks its MOTR serial number, everything's in order, but her antennae are screaming that someone's listening in. Suddenly she throws herself down on the wooden border between the wall and the oriental rug and does push-ups, up down, she snaps her body like a pile driver, 23, 24, 25, she starts knuckle push-ups.

Rita is working a crossword puzzle. "What's a seven-letter word for feminine of macho?" she asks.

"Machete," Pearl says.

Rita nods "Thanks," fills in the squares, makes plans. She is just about up to here with her co-workers, Meg, and Gretchen. I can always get my job back curling doll wigs at Mme. Alexander's, she thinks. Okay, I make better money now, but there's something to be said for 9 to 5 steady, walk out the door at 5 o'clock and leave the job behind you. These health leaves are killing me. Then she remembers there won't be any health leaves if the Museum closes.

For all her grousing, Rita'll be plenty sorry to have to go out and hustle up a new job, but she has options. Her show business skills are transferable. Not that she's unrealistic, she's too old to be an aquabelle, can no longer be a sexy weatherwoman either because all the TV stations bought radar machines which require mechanical aptitude, but what the heck, she can:

star in Mr. Cherry's skin flicks

perform for private stag parties

be a ring girl at Buffalo prizefights, with luck end up out in
  Vegas . . .

RITA'S BIG NUMBER:

She climbs in the ring between rounds, the crowd roars,

promenades in spike heels between droplets of blood, sweat, and tears, the crowd roars,

holds a placard with a big number on it telling which round is coming up, the crowd roars,

Never doubt it, Rita knows the ropes

GET HER OUT OF THERE GET THE MEN BACK screams a woman SHADDUP scream the men around her They shouldn't let dames in here they say to each other COME ON HONEY HOLD YOUR NUMBER UP HIGHER ATTAGIRL they call to Rita.

If all else fails, she can always freelance plots for Harlequin Romance.

Unemployment will not be Rita's problem.

What about the others? If the Museum closes, what will they do?

The question has crossed some minds tonight.

Meg can be an undercover bodyguard for celebrities. Maybe she'll lie her age and join the Secret Service.

Daisy can always play a nun on soaps.

Maggie can work for any McDonald's in the world.

Pearl can be a school crossing guard. Maybe it's time for her to go back to school, get into the big bucks. She remembers the morning classified: **Educational/Instructional: ARTIFICIAL NAILS. Unlimited income potential.**

Electrolysis is where the big bucks are, Gretchen says every time she waxes her bikini line, so Pearl figures Gretchen'll head, not unhappily, in that direction.

Gretchen may head in that direction, it's better pay than an aerobics teacher and higher status than a supermarket checker, but she won't go happily. Being a Museum cheerleader was beyond Gretchen's wildest aspirations, and she owes it all to Daisy. Daisy believed in her when there was absolutely no reason to; as far as Gretchen's concerned, Daisy saved her life. If Meg's curse comes true and she gets what she deserves, she won't be able to stand it. Gretchen sits perfectly still in the chair, her distress so acute she thinks she'll die if somebody doesn't notice it and do something about it.

· · ·

EVERYBODY GRETCHEN KNOWS NEEDS SENSITIVITY TRAINING: A SHORT-SHORT.

Throughout her childhood, Gretchen wants her Ma to wear matching mother/daughter dresses in the same way that years later she wants her beaus to bring her French perfume. She wants them not only to do it, but to think of doing it without even a hint. Gretchen's beaus are not blessed with Gretchen's special female intuition which makes mind-reading a breeze, but there's no excuse for her Ma.

"She refused to wear matching mother/daughter dresses," Gretchen says, her chin juts out over the rejection.

Pearl makes sympathetic sounds. Pearl has known rejection. She remembers a New Year's Eve when her date drops her off at a quarter to 12.

Rita looks up from the crossword puzzle. "I remember begging my Mom to wear mother/daughter dresses, and she said, 'Now look, honey, you can dress up in my clothes, but I'm not going to dress up in yours.' "

"You don't understand," Gretchen wails.

"I don't understand how you can keep carrying on about your Ma when Quasi's dying and we're out on our tush tomorrow morning. . . ."

A moan from the magic circle drowns Rita out. Maggie is weepy and maudlin. "I cried when I had no shoes," she blubbers, "And then I met a man who had no feet. . . ."

"And I laughed and laughed," says Pearl, who gets sick of one man's feet being another's poison, she glares at Maggie in exasperation.

Gretchen is shocked dry-eyed. "You're degenerate, Pearl. No wonder they're throwing us out. They think we're all degenerates."

"Don't worry, Gretchen," Pearl says, "It's always darkest just before it gets totally black."

"Is that all you can do is make stupid wisecracks?" Gretchen screams.

The words slap Pearl.

"A 'smartcracker' they called me," says Pearl's heroine, Dorothy Parker, "and that makes me sick and unhappy. There's a helluva difference between wisecracking and wit. Wit has truth in it, wisecracking is simply calisthenics with words." Parker pours herself another drink.

"I beg your pardon," Pearl says with elaborate sarcasm. "We didn't all have your advantages. . . ."

"Spare me the working class crap, Pearl," Meg says. "I get that up to here with the rookies."

But Pearl is into her Poor Me routine now: she plays Chopin and says, "My Daddy only went to sixth grade. . . ."

"Not me, sister," Gretchen says, she marches over to the piano, "My Ma pulled us into middle class, My Ma knew things, she knew how a table should be set, she put flowers in a silver bowl, My Ma was *lace curtain Irish and don't you forget it!*"

Gretchen has no idea where her anger came from, but for once she feels triumphant over Pearl.

Pearl feels so far behind the 8 ball she's got to recoup her losses.

Daisy feels the weight of Quasi's impending death and the fate of Heartbreak Hotel pull at the whole house. She knows her books are threads, Pearl's wisecracks are threads, Rita's vibrator, Gretchen's exercises, Meg's anger, Maggie's booze, all are threads, tenuous and fragile, and they are breaking. Will the center hold?

Pearl jumps up from the piano bench, does her imitation of Woman Carrying Her Hand.

Does her imitation of Woman Mincing.

Does her imitation of Woman Batting Her Eyes: Pearl's eyes widen, get wider, lashes flutter like a hummingbird in heat, great tears roll down her cheeks:

Daisy jumps up, settles Pearl in a chair, "I've got a sweet story," she says. "I may put it in GREAT ROAD SHOWS: On The Road To Saint, but it'll probably go to the Library. It's called . . ."

"Hold it, Daisy," Meg says. "I have to use the toilet."

Meg uses the toilet.

Maggie goes to Mesdames, Fräuleins, Señoritas, Mademoiselles, Gals, Squaws, Wenches, Mares, Does.

Rita goes to the Powder Room.

Gretchen tinkles.

Pearl pees.

Daisy used to go to the Ladies Room, but Pearl says she's now reached such a high spiritual plane she no longer eliminates.

Meg uses one of the upstairs toilets.

Peg O' My Heart's sound asleep. Sweet dreams, darlin'.

Peg O' My Heart dreams of Bonny Loessing, perpetually five. The man in the blue Ford goes down the same roads to the country her Daddy takes on Sunday, Bonny looks out the window at the red barns, cows graze, horses skitter, there's a pig. The brown paper sack with five pounds of orange slice candy is on her lap, she gobbles, stuffs her mouth full, swallows down half-chewed chunks, *You're* a little piggy, the man laughs. This little piggy went to market, he says, This little piggy . . . , he recites the rhyme just like her Daddy, it dawns on her five pounds of candy is an infinite amount, sugar juices ooze, she looks at green hills while candy sogs slowly in her mouth, coats all the corners sticky sweet. She is just starting to get sweet sick when he raises the hammer. . . . Bonny Loessing doesn't know the next part, but Peg O' My Heart does, and always tells herself in the dream and out of it, She's dead when he takes the axe and chops her to pieces doesn't feel anything, doesn't feel anything when he stuffs her in the bag and throws her down the sewer. But these things will forever remain mysteries to Peg O' My Heart: Do her folks open up the sack and put her together like a puzzle, or just bury the whole thing?, Is the sack disgusting?, Does it stink from the sewer?, And the only question that really matters, Why did the man want to hurt her?, He didn't even know her, A sick man, she hears them say, It could have been any little girl: Peg O' My Heart never eats orange slices again.

"Shoot, Daisy," Meg says.

"It's called The Iron Maiden," Daisy says. Just as she turns the cover page, the doorbell rings.

Everybody but Meg tenses. The City Fathers.

Meg stands to the side of the door, her gun drawn, the rope ready. Daisy looks through the peephole. "It's okay," she says.

Who could possibly have slipped through the cordon of friends and enemies ringing this place?

"Avon Lady."

Angie Lopez, who has four kids, an unemployed alcoholic husband, and a full-time job selling hosiery at a discount store, works overtime selling cosmetics. Daisy gives Angie an appointment with the Museum personnel director at 8 AM sharp, "Bring the whole family," she says, and Angie gives Daisy a free sample of face moisturizer and a brochure.

Underneath the regular sales pitch on the cosmetics brochure, a handwritten addition says, BECOME ALL THAT IS IN YOU TO BECOME. BUFFALO ROSY.

Daisy flips the tube of moisturizer to Gretchen, "Thanks, Daisy," and beckons Rita to come to her desk. "You know everybody in the Museum," she says, "Who's Buffalo Rose?"

Rita's caught in the act: she looks down and giggles. But Rita has no idea what she has started: In less than 24 hours, Buffalo Rose has more persona and more surprise packages than Santa Claus.

The Post Office puts on an extra shift .
Western Union has a line around the block.
UPS puts on an extra fleet.
Gretchen's guess is right: everybody's sending messages for Memorial Day. What Daisy's information is revealing is that every single one of them is signed Buffalo Rose.

Several file clerks who have been screwed literally or figuratively by Richard A. Dick take up an office collection and send him a Dump-O-Gram: a dozen dead roses and a card that says, "A little symbol of our affection for you. Buffalo Roses."

Dick feels like a fool. He's not only embarrassed, he's also struck off-balance. He's not accustomed to either feeling. He goes bananas. Automatically assuming it's Daisy Billetdoux up to another one of her dirty female tricks, he tells his wife, "That little lady is gonna get her big tits caught in a wringer this time."

His wife winces and wonders.

"Mmm, what's that smell?" Gretchen asks as she smooths the moisturizer on her face.

It smells a little bit like Rita, Maggie thinks, but she says, "Cloves."

A slight fragrance of clove, maybe a touch of cinnamon, wafts through the room.

"It reminds me of French perfume," Gretchen says.

Daisy sits up straight and reads:

THE IRON MAIDEN: A Story For Girls
When Daisy is sixteen, she spends a year in bed wearing a chin-to-thigh brace that weighs fifty pounds and makes her look like a Martian.

Daisy has scoliosis: the curve of her spine is shaped like a question mark.

Daisy has a question: Why me?

Daisy's question is never answered, but her prayers are: Daisy is cured.

She will always have scoliosis, one shoulder will always be askew, one shoulder blade will always protrude, trace her spine and your fingertips will always find a question, she will always have back exercises, she will always have pain, but Hallelujah, Daisy says, she will no longer look like a Martian.

. . .

All the time Daisy is in her brace her breasts are growing, but she doesn't know because she's lying down.

When Daisy goes in, she's a 32 A.

When Daisy comes out, she's a 36 C.

Dutch Schultz sees Daisy the first night and his eyes just about fall out of his head.

Daisy is pleased though she never lets on.

Everyone thinks Daisy is a martyr, Daisy is a saint, STAR OF THE SEA/ ROSE OF SHARON/ LILY OF THE VALLEY/ QUEEN OF ANGELS ALLELUIA ALLELUIA ALLELU-OOO-YAH. The truth is, Daisy will have a lot more worse years in her life than that one. Nevertheless, Daisy still lets them make her Homecoming Queen.

Daisy wears a white lace dress and rides around the field at half-time. The weather is perfect, the breeze plays on Daisy's bare shoulders and arms but never disturbs her hair, the dress is perfect, the city dress her sister drove ninety miles for, never has anyone in the town seen such a dress, Daisy lives that brief shifting moment in time when the girl and the woman use the same body simultaneously. Three times they circle the field, round and round and round: the people will not let them go. Dutch Schultz, the captain of the football team, waits with the flowers. Home team is behind 12 points. Dutch Schultz's face, his blue and white uniform, are streaked with mud, his eyes are serious. Daisy leans down from the haunch of the silver convertible to receive the roses. Daisy is so close to Dutch Schultz she smells his sweat rising sweet sweeter than the burning leaves and the blood red roses. The applause grows so loud only Daisy hears Dutch say, "I'll win it for you."

He wins it for her.

"Ohhh," says Rita, she creams her pants.

"Told you it was sweet," Daisy says, she closes the book.

Three floors down from Quasi over in the Burn Ward, the winner of the Countess Pulaski Pageant is moaning too. She lies on her stomach with second degree burns on her buttocks and the backs of her legs from riding on the front of a convertible in a bathing suit in 95° weather. "I knew it was getting uncomfortable," she tells a nurse, "but I wouldn't have given up being Countess for anything." Her crown is on the side table next to the bedpan.

·   ·   ·

"Read some more," Rita says.

"Another time," Daisy says.

"I'll read it," Meg says.

"I read the best part," Daisy says.

Meg opens the book: " 'Pictures shot from the bleachers reveal two inches of cleavage. Daisy buys up all the photos and tears them into microscopic pieces. The rest of Senior year, Daisy wears blouses buttoned all the way up. . . .' "

Meg's voice muzzles the room. " 'Dutch Schultz sells prints off the negative. Daisy never lets on she knows. "How's tricks?" Dutch Schultz asks Daisy every time he passes her in the hall. . . .' The Hell you say," Meg says and tosses the book down.

46

In the ICU, Quasi pulls her arms up against her chest. The nurses wrap her arms in gauze to keep them down at her sides, but she pulls them out and back up with tremendous force.

"Use more gauze," says one nurse, "Don't let her go into a fetal position."

"We use much more gauze," says the other, "she's not gonna look like a fetus, she's gonna look like a mummy."

"You're sick," says the first nurse.

There must be something going around. At Heartbreak Hotel, everybody's feeling a little sick too.

Daisy looks down at her breasts and sighs.
Daisy's breasts are full moons in the tides of time.
People look at Daisy's breasts and want to paint them.
I know a lot about art and I know I'm not an art object, Daisy thinks.

Pearl looks down at her breasts and sighs.
Pearl's breasts are round and full.
People look at Pearl's breasts and want to cup them.
Pearl raises her cup in a toast and wonders: who'll drink a cup o' kindness yet for auld lang syne?

Maggie looks down at her breasts and sighs.
Maggie's breasts are soft and sweet-smelling.
People look at Maggie's breasts and want to suck them.
Maggie gives a raspberry and thinks of cows.

Gretchen looks down at her breasts and sighs.
Gretchen's pecs are at peak.
People look at Gretchen's sassy breasts and want to see them jiggle.

211

"What if I get Cooper's Droop?" Gretchen asks.
"Cooper sucks," Pearl says.
Another one, Maggie thinks.

Meg looks down at her breasts and sighs.
Meg's breasts are trim and compact and stand at attention.
People look at Meg's breasts and want to salute them.
Meg remembers Heil Hitler.

Rita looks down at her breasts and sighs.
Rita's breasts are curve and shadow and veiled women passing through bazaars.
People look at Rita's breasts and want to mutilate them.
Rita shivers.

What are these things called love that people want to paint, touch, stroke, suck, kiss, pinch, feel, taste, measure, knead, nuzzle, tickle, mouth, play with, rest the head upon, look at, lick, handle, hurt, have?

Breasts, tits, boobs, knockers, bosoms, bust, bazooms, paps, puppy dogs with pink noses &/or *substitute any cute animal of your choice,* cupcakes with cherries on top &/or *substitute any sweet or bland or dairy food of your choice,* if you unhooked her brassiere she'd fall over, jugs, dugs.

Collectively, the women look down and sigh.
Daisy wishes her breasts were less important.
Pearl wishes her breasts were more assertive.
Maggie wishes her breasts were less maternal.
Meg wishes her breasts were softer.
Gretchen wishes her breasts were guaranteed.
Rita wishes her breasts were insured.

IN THE MUSEUM OF THE REVOLUTION THERE IS A TIT MEASURER. IT HAS MEASURED EVERY TIT THAT HAS EVER BEEN. EVERY ONE IS THE WRONG SIZE.

On the waterfront, a woman goes into the tattoo shop, has her breasts tattooed HOT-COLD.
HOT-COLD goes over so well she returns for SWEET-SOUR which has equal success.
This same woman has an arrow tattooed on her inner thigh to guide men with poor sense of direction.

· · ·

212

Gretchen has a breast story.

STORY: ON THE BREAST BEAT

When Gretchen is 22, she goes to Washington, D.C., to seek her fortune. She fills out forms at an employment agency. A pleasant looking man smiles at her. He may be her fortune. He leaves when she does. They talk in the hallway, they talk in the elevator. Whether or not he's her fortune, he may be her luck: he's a medical doctor running a large research project at Georgetown University and he's looking for girls like Gretchen. He invites her for a cup of coffee. Gretchen is beside herself: she has never been vertical with a medical doctor.

The doctor is researching breast cancer: does Gretchen know, does Gretchen have any idea . . . ? Gretchen doesn't. The doctor educates Gretchen. Gretchen is close to being bowled over: she has never been educated by a medical doctor. She has never even met anyone who has been educated by a medical doctor.

The doctor telephones Gretchen nightly and talks about his work. Each time, he asks Gretchen questions. His team has the scientific tools, but Gretchen has the raw data. He is particularly interested in breasts Gretchen has seen close up: maternal breasts, sib breasts, friends' breasts, locker room breasts. Talking about breasts embarrasses Gretchen but she doesn't want to sound like a prude. Catholics often sound like prudes, Gretchen has been told often. *Small-town* Catholics, Gretchen corrects, for breasts are everyday stuff to the big-town doctor and the big-town Catholic hospital.

Gretchen is hopelessly small-town. She begins to wonder if he's *really* a doctor. She telephones the Catholic hospital, disguises her voice, asks for the doctor by name. The call is put through, a secretary answers with the doctor's name, Gretchen hangs up ashamed of herself.

It is 11:00 PM. Gretchen's ear burns from the phone and the questions. Were your college roommate's nipples pink, red, or brown?, the doctor asks. I don't want to talk about this anymore, Gretchen says. This is very important, the doctor says, Large, medium, or small? This makes me feel funny, Gretchen says, Pointy, flat, or inverted?, the doctor screams, Gretchen hangs up the phone.

It does not occur to Gretchen for some years that people borrow other people's names. Some years after that, she wonders why a medical doctor would be hanging around an employment agency in mid-morning. You boob, Gretchen says to Gretchen, you got what you deserved.

Every morning, religiously, Gretchen takes the pencil test taught her by a Gyn known for his understanding of women's problems: place a pencil under your breast. Stand up. If the pencil falls, you don't need a bra.

To this day, Gretchen is haphazard about monthly breast self-examinations, which she suspects are a form of masturbation.

"Did I ever tell you about the pathological pathologist?" Pearl asks.

"Is this story fit for mixed company?" Gretchen asks.

"You could tell your mother this story," Pearl says.

PEARL'S STORY: THE CURSE

Pearl has a lump in her breast.

She is scheduled for biopsy.

Pearl tells the surgeon: Do unto my breast as you would have done unto your balls.

The surgeon's assistants put one hand on their mouths, one on their balls, and titter.

The surgeon explains procedure: Pearl will lie under anesthetic while the biopsied tissue is examined; if the report comes up malignant, the surgeon will immediately perform a mastectomy.

Tell me all my options, Pearl says.

I always do radical mastectomies, the surgeon says.

Are you saying I don't have any options?, Pearl says.

Don't you trust me, Pearl?, the surgeon says, Didn't I take your daughter's tonsils out?, Go home and sleep on it.

Pearl goes home and sleeps on it.

She decides she doesn't want to go to sleep with two and wake up with one.

She calls up a summa cum laude pathologist who used to work in the basement of the hospital but now works out of her own basement.

The pathologist gives Pearl a few tips.

Pearl fills out the surgical permit.

She gives permission to perform a biopsy only. She underlines the *only*.

She inks out the line giving the surgeon permission to perform any additional procedures he deems necessary.

In the borders, she writes 3 addresses, one of which is a basement, where the biopsied specimen is to be sent.

The surgeon is upset.

I would do a radical mastectomy on my wife, he says.

The surgeon's assistants are upset.

This man has an international reputation for doing radical mastectomies, they say.

The interns are upset.

Are you a Christian Scientist?, they ask.

The hospital pathologist is upset.

214

We diagnose more breast cancers here than any hospital in the city, he says.

The nurses are upset.

You are upsetting the doctors, they say.

A red-haired intern comes back late at night and asks, What are you trying to prove?

Pearl explains.

Why, I'd do the same thing myself, he says. Good luck. He turns around in the door, and says, Whatever happens, don't give up hope.

And the biopsy's done and looks benign and everybody's relieved though nothing'll be definite for 3 days and Pearl feels maybe now she can get a little sleep.

On rounds, the surgeon wakes her up.

You are really a character, he says.

For a while there we thought we'd have to get a lawyer up here to deal with you, he says.

I told the pathologist, Well it has nothing to do with me, it's you guys she doesn't trust, he says.

He chuckles again and tweaks Pearl's nose.

Three days later, the hospital pathologist calls Pearl at home. His voice is venom. The specimen is benign, he says.

I don't know what you were trying to prove, he says.

Why did you make all that trouble?, he asks.

When Pearl explains, he says, A little knowledge is a dangerous thing.

He mails Pearl the slides and a curse: the note says: May all your future biopsies be benign.

Fran Norris, pray for us

Vera Peters, pray for us

Marvella Bayh, Rose Kushner, Betty Ford, Happy Rockefeller, Betty Rollins, Audre Lorde, Ingrid Bergman, Tish Sommers, Paula Armel, *start your names here*, pray for us.

"Wasn't that terrible about Miss New York State wearing falsies in the Miss USA pageant?" Gretchen says. "That's why men don't trust us." She stands sideways, sticks her chest out, examines her profile in the full-length antique mirror.

47

SURSUM CORDA: LIFT UP YOUR SPIRIT

Daisy's fighting despair, but every half hour on the hour, she delivers these Get Well Cards directly to Quasi's ear:

The family all send their best.

When you get better, let's go to Barbados and lie in the warm sun and get a nice tan.

I never want to hear you say you can't do it because I know you can.

You've got to try harder.

You're stronger than you think.

Do you understand the gravity of the situation?

Abide, Quasi, until we figure out a plan.

Choose life.

FIGURE OUT A PLAN HAH:

Pearl lies on the floor listening to her heartbeat. She has those kamikaze blues. "I remake my life every twelve minutes," she says.

"Don't despair," Daisy says. "The world's changing."

"If it doesn't change faster," Pearl says, "I'm going to be a loss leader."

"Face it," Daisy says, "You have to risk enormous pain if you take your life in your own hands."

"You can say that again," Sonia Johnson says.

"Face it," Daisy says. "You have to risk enormous pain if you take your life in your own hands."

"You can say that again," Billie Jean King says.

"Give me a break," Daisy says.

Meg's down too. She can't find a bug anywhere in the house, she can't go after Peg O' My Heart's abuser, and Quasi won't die: She drags deeply on her cigarette, starts hacking, leaves the room, goes into her closet, coughs into her clothes so no one can hear her, comes back,

216

finishes the fag. If I don't quit smoking, she thinks, I'll have to write Self-Inflicted Wound on the Accident Report.

In the doorway, Gretchen hangs on the exercise bar, it might as well be a cross, she tries to concentrate on the pain in her shoulder joints, pain in her forearms, pain rippling her thighs, none of it touches her suffering, I'm dying, she thinks.

It's all over, Rita thinks, and I'm painting my toenails.

It won't be long now, Maggie thinks.

Silently, the women recite the Litany Of The Dying.

> When I said I'm just a housewife and she said But what do you *do*, Pearl says.
>
> When he took me to see The Moon Is Blue, Gretchen says.
>
> When they called me on the phone and asked if I could handle six inches, Rita says.
>
> When I didn't have one friend, Daisy says.
>
> When I couldn't get a job, Maggie says.
>
> When the judge said I was worse than a man, Meg says.
>
> When he said You want to keep this job you better come through, Maggie says.
>
> When they attacked the Museum the first time, Daisy says.
>
> When I knew I was pregnant again, Pearl says.
>
> When he said I just want to fuck her, Gretchen says.
>
> When he cut off my ponytail, Meg says.
>
> When he kept saying I love you I love you I love you, Rita says.
>
> When she said I was a puke and a scum I always had been and there's nothing I could ever do about it, Quasi says

A nurse places the canvas frame on top of Quasi, "Oopsy Daisy," she says and flips her 180° Squawk bleep nonny nonny nonny nonny nonny: a small wire connected to nonny hangs unnoticed: Quasi's on her own again.

Daisy gets up from her desk, Meg sees she is visibly upset, "I'll be back as soon as possible," Daisy says. She switches the phone bell on, reaches beyond a white uniform in the closet for one behind it: at this hour, she shouldn't have any trouble sneaking in, but she's not going to press her luck. She takes the tunnel cart which travels a direct underground route between Heartbreak Hotel, MOTR, and the hospital.

Meg sniffs the doctor's uniform in the closet, jasmine, What the Hell's going on? She follows the trail of jasmine through the tunnel

217

door, just has time to step behind a bush as an airport bus roars up, the driver jumps out, wimple flying, Meg counts her stripes, it's a Mother Superior, the nun flips around a fist of keys to one marked TUNNEL DOOR, looks surprised when the door is unlocked, Mother Superior takes the steps two at a time to the fourth floor.

In the ICU, a silver-haired doctor thinks in a tiny corner of his pea brain, if it's inevitable, might as well lie back and enjoy it, he increases Quasi's morphine and goes out to tell the desk to tell the family.

Not five minutes after Daisy leaves, the LATEST HOSPITAL BULLETIN is: Quasi's condition is critical and worsening. Her injuries are so massive they are not compatible with life. Pearl hangs up and says, "Goddammit, she's gonna pull her own plug." She throws on her evening clothes, checks her profile, stuffs one more pillow into her trench coat to make the hump larger, and starts jogging to the hospital.

In the silence and gloom, the eerie blue light from the monitors, Quasi looks like she's already laid out. A cleaning woman with a cheap wig moves a mop around the comatose form, she bends over stiffly to mop under the bed and, before you can say Josephine Hulett, fixes Quasi's broken connection. "Sursum Corda, Lift up your spirit," she says into Quasi's ear. Drip drip goes sweet morphine into Quasi's veins.

Even at peak alertness, Quasi has so much time missing from her memory that strange visions often come back to haunt her. Right now she feels that someone familiar is looking at her. She slips away. She feels herself slipping away more and more distantly. It is not an unpleasant feeling. Not unlike riding the Harley into the countryside on a sunny day and seeing a beautiful woman in her rear-view mirror. Not unlike digging a grave in moonlight while a beautiful woman watches. "Come back," a voice whispers so lightly it may just be the rustle of a leaf on the elm tree near the watching woman. The leaf continues to rustle. It is a bother to attend to it. If she looks up out of the hole, if she squints, Quasi can see a woman dressed in white standing on the edge. The woman cups her hand to her mouth and shouts. Sounds float down to Quasi, but she is floating away.

Two nurses come in, "Help me flip her," one says. "Why don't we just leave her be? What could it possibly matter now?" says the other. "The chart says every fifteen minutes," the first says, "I'm not getting my ass kicked by that old battle-axe." The cleaning woman pushes her mop out the door.

·   ·   ·

218

At Heartbreak Hotel, the phone rings incessantly. "Can't somebody besides me ever answer the phone?" Gretchen says.

I'm not expecting a call till 8 AM, Maggie thinks over in the corner.

Gretchen drops off the bar, it's a good thing she took another trank, she'd never get through this night, she clears her throat, pitches her voice low, "Hel-loo," she says.

"She's not here," she says. "Whom shall I tell her called?

"She's not here either. Whom shall I tell her called?

"Is there any message, Mr. Gonoff?

"Just your name, sir.

"Yes, I have it, Mr. Gonoff."

Meg hangs up the basement extension with disgust.

Gretchen gets back on the bar and the doorbell rings, she opens her mouth to scream; "I've got it," Rita calls from the landing. Rita opens the door to a uniformed chauffeur who thrusts an envelope into her hands and speeds away in a waiting limo before she even has time to say Well Hello There.

Meg checks behind the furnace, under the hot water heater, whips around to look behind her: the presence of someone listening is almost palpable. Meg has had strong feelings like this many times before and every single time she has found Quasi lurking in the corridor, hiding behind the door, pressing her snout against a windowpane. Meg doesn't believe in ghosts, but she's starting to feel spooked. Her hand on her billy club, she cautiously opens the door to the fruit cellar.

At the hospital, Pearl moves down the corridor in the shadows, passes a cleaning woman who does a double take and quickly looks away, passes two nurses making a notation on a chart, one glances at Pearl and thinks, Finally one of her family shows up, high time, looks back at the chart, Pearl hotfoots it into Room #7, passes a large rumpled group that look like the Trapp Family Singers on tour without their seeing her, talks impassionedly to Quasi for some time until she realizes that even Quasi isn't this deadpan, Oh for cripes sake, she crawls underneath the Stryker frame, lies on her hump, looks up at Quasi face to face, and says, "Look you dumb fucker, stop feeling sorry for yourself, get up and come home, there's a place for you, things are looking up. . . ."

Quasi makes gross body movements. "That's the spirit," Pearl says.

48

Sursum Corda, Daisy says to herself the whole way home. But things don't look good for Quasi. And leaving her dangling can't have helped. That wire pulling out has shaken Daisy badly.

She leaves the tunnel an exit early to check out front, stands in the shadows behind the wrought-iron fence and feels sick. The street is a zoo. Her people are here and there, but most of the crowd are ambulance chasers. But Gretchen was right: public support wouldn't let them down. The faces of their neighbors are fierce and determined, they scream LEAVE THEM ALONE, THIS IS A FREE COUNTRY, they wave enormous banners that say SAVE HEARTBREAK HOTEL: BETTER DYKES THAN DODOS.

Daisy sits down heavily behind the oak table, goes through her messages, holds up one in Gretchen's handwriting, "Mr. Jack Gonoff? Tell me exactly what he said, Gretchen."

"He asked for Rita first," Gretchen says, "then for you, and when I asked if there were any message he just kept saying 'I'm Jack Gonoff. . . .'" Gretchen blushes, she buries her face in her hands. Daisy sighs.

"This one came by limo," Rita says, she hands Daisy a tan envelope bordered with dark brown.

Daisy scans the matching stationery which has a light smell of Brut aftershave; the message, in broad-tipped felt pen, is impeccably polite: a bad sign. "The City Fathers request a meeting in two hours," she says. Suddenly she feels overwhelmed, she's not going to be able to do it, it's too much, too deep.

"What are you going to wear?" Gretchen asks.

When Daisy doesn't answer, Gretchen feels like a fool, and then mad, she knows as much anyone in the world about dressing for success, she'd be able to help Daisy in lots of ways if Daisy would just let her. She pretends she hasn't asked a question.

Pearl watches Daisy pick up one thing, put it down, stare at another. Pearl saw that sorry mess out on the street too, half of them took off after her, one guy even gave her a good crack, "Hey, it's soft," he yelled. Pearl puts her arm around Daisy, "What's wrong, old pal?"

"I'm scared the exhibits will seem trivial."

Pearl knows that Daisy's really scared that *she's* trivial WOMEN CANNOT PAINT GREAT PAINTINGS WOMEN CANNOT WRITE GREAT LITERATURE WOMEN CANNOT COMPOSE GREAT MUSIC WOMEN CANNOT BE GREAT SURGEONS WOMEN CANNOT BE GREAT DIRECTORS WOMEN CANNOT BE GREAT CHEFS WOMEN CANNOT BE GREAT THEOLOGIANS WOMEN CANNOT BUILD WONDERFUL BUILDINGS WOMEN CANNOT FORMULATE SOCIAL THEORY WOMEN CANNOT

Pearl remembers days she is so uncertain and indecisive she makes drafts of the grocery list. "Deep down, I'm really shallow," she says. "There's less to me than meets the eye."

Daisy can hear Pearl's words, tries to attend to them, feels panic rising, we're going to be buried, she thinks, suddenly the air in the room is close and cloyingly sweet, she seems surrounded by rotting flowers, can't get her breath, feels lids closing, dirt filling the hole up and, down in utter darkness, out of eyesight, earshot, fingernails clawing pink tufted satin to shreds, *"Daisy,"* Pearl says, shaking her, "Open your eyes." Daisy shakes her head to clear it, opens here eyes, rests her head on Pearl's shoulder, takes a deep breath, lets it out. So leave a mark that you were here, she tells herself, that's all you can do, the work stays, continues, you've got to believe in connection. "The problem is, Pearl, if I fail, I set back every woman who wants to be a curator."

"The problem is, Daisy, the Museum can contain everything in the world."

There are one thousand indexed boards in the foyer of the Museum, but every day, people ask for exhibits the Museum hasn't yet acquired. Daisy receives one hundred letters daily asking for exhibits the Museum hasn't even heard of. The suggestion boxes are emptied on the half hour. Around the clock, a large revolving stage auditions acts for possible inclusion in MOTR. Museum agents drop by regularly to size up the talent. Right this minute, Howard Bellin, the socially prominent plastic surgeon, who allegedly misplaced a woman's bellybutton, placing it two inches off center when he tried to tighten her tummy to give her "a nice, flat, sexy belly," climbs up on the stage. Two agents exchange pained glances. The Museum already has more doctors than the A.M.A. In fact, it has the A.M.A.

"Take five, Daisy," Pearl says. "Rita's just finishing her toenails."

· · ·

221

With the two-color coats and one-sealer coat interspersed with the various dryings, Rita's toenail painting is a full hour procedure. Rita knows rushing it botches the job. She is a pro. She never slops over the cuticles, no brush marks ever show in any light, her strokes are exquisitely precise. She arches her foot and asks, "Like this shade?"

"Nice," Daisy says, and thinks of Renoir, Titian, Fragonard, Matisse.

" 'We call him Leonardo da Toenail,' says Sgt. George Farina of the University of Southern California's campus police, referring to a man who reportedly crawls underneath library tables and paints the exposed toenails of coeds. The case breaks when one of the alleged victims notices she has a fresh coat of polish on her toenails after leaving Doheny Library. The nails are pink when she walks in; green when she walks out. Campus police quickly find a man, neither student nor library employee, carrying a bag containing fifteen bottles of nail polish. L.A. police question the man, in his mid-twenties. However, painting someone's toenails without permission is only a misdemeanor, and since officials must witness a misdemeanor to make an arrest, the man is set free."

Meg thinks of the man who cut her ponytail off and says, "Set free? I'd cut his balls off."

Rita giggles. "I'd just paint 'em green," she says.

Pearl looks at Rita's pretty foot with rosebud toenails: it looks like a garden party. Pearl arches her own foot: it looks flat. Where her pants are pulled up, her leg is hairy. Pearl sighs. It's not easy giving up looking like a garden party.

STORY: IT'S A LONG ROAD TO TIPPERARY: Every so often Pearl can't stand it and she locks the bathroom door and shaves one leg. The reason she shaves one leg is that the picture of sleek female skin is still too strong in her. But Pearl's working on another picture. Take my picture on this side, she tells the photographer, this is my good leg. Pearl's unshaven left leg is a role model for her right leg.

Daisy picks up the nail polish box and reads it. Reading is Daisy's bottom-line drug. When work doesn't work for her and there's nothing left in the house to chop, she reads. Even at sixteen, lying flat on her back in a brace, Daisy reads: the library brings a machine that projects book page images onto the ceiling. For a long time, Daisy reads for downer, so she won't have to feel, is so good at blanking out between the covers of a book she is Barbara Cartland's dream: she can reread the same book again and again and find it fresh. Now she knows better, knows any feeling is better than no feeling, knows downers are the pits, now she reads for upper.

UP UP AND AWAY: Daisy reads history, reads novels, reads poetry, art books, magazines, TV ads, librettos, wills, cave walls, diaries, almanacs, department store windows, graffiti, minutes, letters to the editor, textbooks, obituaries, fairy tales, song lyrics, doctoral dissertations, and the sides of buses. Generally, she reads women's abuses and women's humiliations, now and then she reads women's triumphs. Either way, adrenaline starts. Daisy swears that reading works better for her than amphetamines and its side effects are more desirable. She sets the nail polish box down A LOVELIER YOU IN MINUTES gives Pearl a kiss, "You're a lifesaver," she says, and returns to her desk to block out strategy for the meeting.

Pearl's a reader too. She used to keep copies of the same note in her bedside table, recipe box, and liquor cabinet: THE IMPORTANT THING IS NOT TO TAKE TO YOUR BED/OVEREAT/DRINK. IF ALL ELSE FAILS, GO TO THE LIBRARY. Pearl reads every self-help book and every disaster book she can get her hands on. She especially likes books that tell how to cope with a life-threatening disease. The more dire the disease, the better: Pearl reads to find out how bad things can get.

But Pearl and Daisy combined couldn't convince Rita that reading's better than amphetamines. To Rita, uppers are taking the corner of Princeton Street and Daleford at age thirteen in Al Dubrinski's stick shift: speed, rush, power, and touch, squealing tires, bodies falling into each other.

Pearl's a reformed junkie. Her pusher was her OB who turned her on to both speed and tranks. For a while it was touch and go whether she'd kick them or have another baby.

Meg divides druggies into scum and bum. Scum are big dealers, bum are peons. In her room she has a box of joints confiscated from bum. She puffs her Winston and thinks about bum.

Once Maggie loves the library too because there is NO TALKING ALLOWED. The library is Maggie's grade school sport and high school hangout, no one fights in the library. People come and go but books are steadfast friends. Maggie considers it one of the great breakdowns of civilization that people are now permitted to chitchat in the library.

223

As far as drugs go, she has never had any yearning for them. She is perfectly content with booze.

One time in her life, Gretchen downed nineteen aspirin and was in a life-threatening situation, but now except for calcium and Vitamin D to prevent osteoporosis, massive doses of Vitamin C at the first sign of sniffles, her tranks, and happy hour white wine spritzers, Gretchen's clean.

Drip drip drip. Any time Quasi wants to, she can look up and see that face. That face is her lifeline. She can always come back to it. Daisy will keep watch, but Quasi does not want to look up.

The torch singer on the third Block blows the microphone, weeps and wails:
"Caaaaaaaaaaant
      help
                  mannnnnnnnnnnnn. . ."
                that
            ving
         loooooo
"TRY!" Pearl shouts from the audience one night, is still shouting when they throw her out.

On the side of Quasi's oxygen tent, a small brass plate says:

DO YOU USE LIFE SUPPORT EQUIPMENT?
Call us immediately
Give your name, address, type of equipment used and whether you have an emergency generator at home.
We can provide emergency aid in the event of a power failure.

The Chicago & New Haven
Women's Liberation Rock Bands

49

Downtown, outside the Bluebird bus station, an old woman asks another taxi driver, "Do you have a special fare for Senior Citizens, Son?"

"You kidding, Lady? With all that luggage, you're gonna have to pay extra."

If my luck doesn't pick up, I'm going to pay through the nose for this trip, she thinks, and moves on to the next cabdriver in line.

In the living room, Rita switches on the radio, runs up and down the dial a half dozen times, finds a station she likes. She glides around the room, hums, sways, switches off all the lights, starts dancing in earnest on the slate in front of the fireplace.

Maggie's grateful that Rita's turned off the lights: the light is starting to hurt her eyes.

Daisy gets up and turns back on the lights closest to the table.

"If you'd put pink bulbs in those, we'd all look a lot better," Gretchen says.

Maggie switches her hornrims for her sunglasses.

Without missing a beat, Rita turns the radio up, starts singing "Sentimental Journey" along with a crooner.

Maggie snuffs. She loves that song. She thinks of home and snuffs again. Maggie's getting sentimental.

MAGGIE TAKES A SENTIMENTAL JOURNEY: Maggie takes a swig and feels the tears start. After all her practice, she still can't handle the stuff. Any more than her uncle, or her grandfather, or her brother, or her mother can. Snuff. It makes them too sad, Snuff, Swig, sets the fury free, they want to kick things in and frequently do. One minute her uncle's saying I think I'll go hoist a couple, the next minute he's kicking things in. What a temper, everybody says about the uncle, the grandfather, the brother. About the mother, they go silent. They pretend the angry mother does not exist, Snuff, which makes her so sad and so mad she opens a fresh bottle Swig. Behind her shades, Maggie the orphan

225

wipes a tear away. "The Hell with it," she mumbles, and leaves to get more ice.

On her way back, Maggie passes Rita who, in one fluid motion, takes the glass and silver ice bucket out of Maggie's hand, sets them on the table, and pulls her into the dance.

"I don't know that dance," Maggie says.

"Dance whatever dance you know," Rita says, her smile, her whole body an irresistible beckon. She draws up Maggie's arms, fingertips on fingertips, bodies swaying slightly.

"I'll lose the beat," Maggie says.

Pearl empathizes.

LOSING THE BEAT:

Pearl is afraid that in the middle of fucking Sid she'll call him Sammy.

Pearl is afraid that in the middle of fucking Sammy she'll call him Sid.

Instead of thinking about fucking, Pearl is thinking about fucking up. It throws her timing off and she loses the beat.

"The beat is in you," Rita says. "You can move you can dance."

"My grandfather danced on a wooden leg," Gretchen says.

"That's a metaphor for my life," Pearl says, snapping her fingers on the afterbeat.

"It's just a form of fucking," Rita says, giggling, she sways and thrusts; Maggie melts, maybe this is the beginning of her new life, Her feet start moving, the movement travels up her calves, thighs, hips; "It's a way people learn each other's steps," Rita says. "It changes with every partner. People dance themselves."

Pearl's never thought of it that way, but Maggie's doing League of Nations: Slavic spirit/ inner city funky/ British class, just looking at Maggie makes Pearl happy, just looking at Rita makes Pearl damp, Rita's doing belly dancer pol, sliding back and forth from nuance to no-holds-barred without a seam.

Public fornication, that's all it is, they ought to be ashamed to do that in public, Gretchen thinks. She realizes her toe is tapping and stops it.

Daisy hears the radio announcer say in the middle of her patter, "This is Buffalo Rose telling you you're an original, an edition of one . . ." but nobody else seems to notice.

On the small balcony that overlooks the living room where the railroad tycoon used to survey his guests, a figure stands stock still, surveys the two dancers, everybody in the goddam world dances but her, and is consumed by an envy so strong she thinks it's righteous rage. They ought to lock Rita up, throw away the key, and now Maggie down there acting like some kind of Ginger Rogers, goddam lush, goddam them all to Hell. Meg doesn't need tramps to tell *her* that dancing's a form of fucking. That's why it was beaten out of her.

SOMETHING IN THE WAY SHE MOVES:
What is it tonight
just a school dance
Your skirt is too tight
Change your clothes
You'll get in trouble
Nice girls don't
You come straight home
Don't dance close
Leave room for the Holy Ghost
Early you hear me
Will they be playing that kind of music
Are you listening to me
I can't stand that music
Don't ever bring that kind of music in my house
Stand up straight
Who'll be there
I don't want you hanging around with those girls
Those girls are cheap
When I was young we did waltzes
Beautiful dances
Those kids just stand on the floor and dry run
Their skirts are too tight
They'll get in trouble
Nice boys won't
Early you hear me
AND KEEP THE LIGHTS ON.

Meg wants to dance so bad she doesn't allow herself to feel it. She clicks the safety on her gun. Maggie hears the sound and identifies it correctly but is having too good a time to bother looking up. Meg's arm raises, Daisy gets up, snaps on the overhead light, locks eyes with Meg who puts the gun back into her holster and leaves the balcony. She was just going to shoot out the floor lamp, make them dance a little.

"This is Buffalo Rose signing off, telling you to listen to the sounds of your own life. . . ."

"Who turned the radio off?" Rita says.

No one has turned the radio off, but that particular station has momentarily gone off the air during a slight scuffle between the regular deejay, Dave O' Leahy, who has a wife, five kids, and a groupie collection, and Deena Lansing, a former groupie who not only learned about older men from O'Leahy but also how to make smooth audio cut-ins on the automatic equipment he uses when he wants a little time to mess around.

Maggie heard the voice, it seemed to be speaking directly to her and it made her happy, but she's not about to mention it, she knew a woman once who said she received a personal message broadcast from a radio and they locked her up for observation.

50

Rita sits on the sofa, her knees clasping Maggie who sits on the floor in front of her: Rita brushes Maggie's hair. Maggie stares into the fire and remembers her Gramma brushing her hair, she sinks back against the couch, feels the legs holding her, the rhythmic strokes of the brush, the tingly feeling on her scalp, Your hair's full of rats' nests from the playing, Gramma says, Your hair's wild from the dancing, Rita says, Maggie feels the fingers working out the snarls, the slow even strokes begin again, stroke stroke, stroke: even with the snarls, Maggie revels in such exclusive attention.

Daisy watches Maggie and figures out a riddle:
RIDDLE: Why do women endure hairdressers' abuse?
ANSWER: Better a mean Momma or Gramma in drag than none.

"You have a lot of naturally curly hair," Rita says.
Maggie smiles.
"I conked out this afternoon," Rita says. "I went to your room when I woke up, but you were gone. I'm sorry."
"It's okay," Maggie says. She bites her tongue to keep from telling Rita about the old man.
"Talk to me, Maggie," Rita says.
Maggie has crossed her heart hope to die. She reaches for her glass on the coffee table.
Rita leans over and casually moves the glass out of reach.
Maggie's cheeks flame, she fills with a welter of feelings: she hopes no one saw Rita do that, she's confused as to why Rita did that, she wonders if people think she drinks too much, she wants her drink.
"I like you a whole lot, Maggie," Rita says.
From her position, Rita can't see that Maggie's nonplussed, but Pearl notes the disbelief cross Maggie's face. Pearl wouldn't say that Maggie thinks poorly of herself, but once at a football game between

229

the Buffalo Bills and the Pittsburgh Steelers, someone in the packed stadium yells, "Hey Shithead," and Maggie turns around.

Maggie finally remembers the English word for why. "Why?" she asks.

"I like your way with words," Rita says. "I know a lot of languages, but none of them have any words."

She's giving praise, but Maggie takes it as a mock. "I know I can talk," she says stiffly.

"That's a silly thing to say," Rita says.

"I used to talk once," Maggie says formally. "I'm not making that up." She strains for memory: it seems to her sometimes that her verbal precocity as a child was much admired, bits and pieces of an impassioned past sometimes come back to her too clearly to only be imagined or wished for, who's she kidding?, she's always been a dummy.

Rita ruffles Maggie's hair, "Maggie Magpie," she says with admiration, and resumes brushing. Pearl sees the tear roll down Maggie's cheek.

"Well sure you can talk," Pearl says, "but I'll tell you something, Maggie, if you find it leaving you, don't worry, silence never hurts you."

"*Je ne comprends pas*," Maggie whispers, "I don't understand," she whispers.

"When I'm silent, I look stuck for an answer," Pearl says. "When you're silent, you look profound. You look so profound it unnerves people."

"There was a swami on the TV," Gretchen says. "He speaks sixteen languages, but he's taken a vow of silence."

"How do you know he speaks sixteen languages?" Pearl asks.

"He still communicates with people from all over through his translator," Gretchen says.

"I wonder how many languages his translator speaks," Pearl says.

"You'll all talk out of the other side of your mouth when the vote on Quasi's taken," Meg says from the doorway.

Then Maggie remembers that if Rita ever finds out what she has done she will never forgive her, she is forever on the other side from Rita, and she has brought this on herself; the strokes of the hairbrush begin to sear her scalp. "I'm tired," she says abruptly, gets up, and moves to the windowseat on the other side of the room.

Rita stares momentarily at the hairbrush before she sets it down, shrugs; she doesn't have a clue as to what altered the mood, so she doesn't pursue it. She slides down onto the rug, does a few stretches, gets into lotus position, bends her head to her knees, and starts her mantra, One One One One One. . . .

.   .   .

In a room full of people, Maggie feels completely isolated. She looks out at the women through blurry eyes and sees how they're split. She remembers what the old man told her and knows that unity is impossible.

In the back of Maggie's underwear drawer, seven pieces of paper record the old man's words:

You have a whole family of selves, Maggie, not one self acting many different ways.

You feel schizophrenic and scared because you don't understand this.

You deny and kill parts of yourself.

In a just and joyous world, all the parts would integrate.

The best you can hope for right now is recognition and naming, for someone once named can never again be a stranger to be feared blindly.

You must find out who your family of selves are.

Name as many as you can, learn their strengths and weaknesses, call on them when you need them.

And when Maggie still doubts, the old man shows her:

Exhibit 7777777 in the Museum Of The Revolution

MARGARET: "A pearl" (Greek). The original Persian word might be translated "born of moonlight" from the fancy that pearls were created from dewdrops which pearl oysters rising from the sea received on moon-lit nights.
Diminutives and Variants: Maggie, Meg, Peg, Rita, Gretchen, Daisy, Mattie.

QUASI: As if, as though, as it were . . . , having some resemblance to, seemingly. . . .

QUASIMODO: So called from the first words of the Latin Introit "*Quasi modo geniti infantes.*" "As newborn babes, desire the rational milk without guile, that thereby you may grow unto salvation."

Maggie remembers all the faces in the mirror and is filled with a great despair. If she can't even get herself together, there is no possible chance for all women to unite. MOTR is dead and so is she. She makes a last desperate try.

"Come on, Rita, let's have a little party." She holds up the decanter.

Rita doesn't look up.

"Pearl. How about a drink?"

"I gave it up, Maggie," Pearl says and turns away. The sadness on Pearl's face drives Maggie on.

"Daisy?"

"The City Fathers, Maggie."

"Gretchen?"

"I don't drink," Gretchen says. With drunks, she adds in her mind.

"Don't ask," Meg says.

There isn't going to be any miracle, Maggie thinks. The old man duped me. I went to bed with him on top of it. I must be the stupidest woman since Eve. There is no hope, she tells herself, she crosses the room, her eyes brimming with tears, she reaches over Rita to get the ice bucket on the table, and doesn't even see her.

Rita doesn't feel Maggie brush her, One One One One One One One

51

On the top floor, Daisy checks pledges: it'll be tight, but if this rate of contribution keeps up, they'll make their goal. Mother Superior's on the horn explaining to the bishop why MOTR qualifies for a cut of the Special Collection For The Missions. She catches Daisy's eye and makes a circle of her thumb and first finger.

At her desk, Daisy reads over her strategy one last time, That's the best I can do, she thinks. She puts a contract, a deed, and her fountain pen into her briefcase, and files everything else. The table top is clear except for the micro-recorder and the seashell which she pockets.

Pearl lies on the couch watching Daisy. "How'd you ever get into this racket?" she asks.

"That's a *long* story," Daisy says.

"I got all night," Pearl says.

"Count your blessings," Daisy says, "I got an hour."

"Let's do the vote," Meg says.

"I'd have to start with the islands," Daisy says.

Daisy brings her swivel chair around to the front of the library table, switches off the desk lamp, and takes her seat. The vote'll keep, Meg thinks, Quasi's not going anywhere, she makes herself comfortable in a wooden straightback chair. The only light in the room is from the fireplace, and the candles Gretchen has lit, they flicker, illuminate Daisy's face, make Gretchen think of a long ago time when she spent half a summer on her knees.

"A lot of people go to the desert to pray," Daisy says, "but I'm partial to islands."

Rita thinks of the islands Mme. Le Main saw on the palm of her hand.

Maggie thinks of the islands in the ocean of her mind, the size of each island determined by the time she spends on it.

Gretchen thinks of Fantasy Island.

Pearl thinks of Coney Island.

Meg thinks of Alcatraz.

"Two islands have been important in my life," Daisy says, the women listen closely, there is excitement in the air, Daisy so rarely speaks about her past people rarely think about her having one, and now, Gretchen thinks, she's just like us. "I went to the first when I was twenty-one. . . ."

PEOPLE DON'T KNOW THEIR LINES: A SHORT-SHORT

In the beginning of her senior year at college when everyone announces her engagement or vocation to the convent, Daisy says, "I have an apostolate to the bars. I will go where the people are." Everybody laughs, though Daisy's not joking.

At the end of her senior year, Daisy says, "I'm going to an island in the British West Indies as a lay apostle." She pauses, then adds, "That's somebody who lays apostles." Nobody laughs, though Daisy's joking.

The women in the room wonder the same thing everybody in Daisy's town wonders: Why would a twenty-one-year-old girl go to a remote island like that?

To do penance, Gretchen thinks, she immediately dismisses the thought.

To train, Pearl thinks.

To see what exotic looks like, sounds like, tastes, smells, feels. . . , Rita thinks, she exudes a little root beer scent.

To beat the rap, Meg thinks.

To escape, Maggie thinks.

Daisy tells everybody the half-truth: "To share the wealth," she says.

Hallelujah Hallelujah GloryGloryGlory, Everybody thinks Daisy is a saint.

Gretchen, Meg, and Maggie are closest to the other half of the truth: Daisy escapes to the island to do penance for losing her virginity, not to beat the rap but to beat herself.

"Almost all islands tend to be shaped like an organ," Daisy says, "a part of the human body. The trick is to figure out what organ it is. . . ." She closes her eyes. Sometimes when Daisy has a problem, she closes her eyes and lets a series of images unfold like a movie in her head. Sometimes ideas she can't express in words unfold on the screen. The women don't interrupt her, they see she is looking inside: the shape Daisy sees is sometimes shadowy and sometimes clear. Every time she looks at it, she sees it from an infinitesimally different angle. It is not a circle nor an oval. . . .

Maggie knows what shape it is, cuntcuntcuntcunt, the slide show on her ceiling reruns in the swirls of her bourbon, Maggie stares into her drink, sees darkness, recesses that hide shellfish, a bottomless ocean, no islands in sight, everlasting damnation.

"I never told anyone this," Daisy says, "not even myself, but for a long time, I thought the island was shaped like a vagina."

After Maggie's sharp intake of breath, there's no sound in the room.

Gretchen sits rigidly. If anyone else said that, Gretchen would think they were talking dirty, Not Daisy.

Daisy opens her eyes and says matter-of-factly, "After many years of studying, I became convinced it was shaped like a brain."

Gretchen relaxes a little.

"Maybe it changed shape," Meg says.

"That's very unusual," Rita says, remembering what Mme. Le Main told her.

"Maybe it had a sex change operation," Pearl says.

Daisy shakes her head. "When I went to the second island, it became absolutely clear that all the time *both* islands were shaped like the human heart."

Not even Maggie's sure what language Daisy is speaking in, but Daisy is so visionary people rarely question her obscurities for fear of revealing denseness. This hesitancy and deference sometimes allow Daisy to get away with wonderful scams, but they're always in the service of truth. Right now no one would question her because she's radiant, she's Buddha in Benetton, Rita thinks, Whatever she's found I want it, Pearl thinks, Can she possibly be pregnant, Gretchen wonders, Maggie remembers the Daisy in the mirror.

"Why did you go to the second island?" Meg asks.

"I went to the first island to bury myself, the second to dig myself up," Daisy says.

"How old were you?" Meg asks.

"Forty," Daisy says. "After all the years of serving the needs of others, I was living in the City of One, running a small truck-stop museum on the outskirts. I had won some recognition. . . ."

Daisy wins the DAR Award.

The Daughters Of The American Revolution are ferocious in preserving history, terrified of making history: along the whole California/Oregon Trail, the DAR will not allow the graves of white pioneer women to go unmarked, in Constitution Hall in Washington, D.C., they will not allow a black pioneer woman to sing praises to the Lord MARIAN ANDERSON PRAY FOR US. Daisy wins the DAR Mixed Media Award for courage and fear.

". . . but I was unsure of my direction, depressed, popping pills, drinking heavily. . . ."

"YOU?" the women say collectively.

"Why should I be different from any of you?" Daisy asks.

Everybody laughs, except Gretchen who's insulted but not brave enough to say so, she's glad the dim light hides her disapproval.

"Instead of helping, the booze made me mean, it made the pain too acute," Daisy says. "I could sometimes stand my life without alcohol, but drinking made it intolerable. I knew that so well by then, that to keep on that track was the essence of despair. Right about that time, I was invited to an island retreat for people with creative projects. It was supposed to be a quiet place."

The island is the quietest place Daisy has ever been. She can hear her heart beat, her blood flow, her thoughts run from one another.

When she eats on the patio, people sit behind her and listen to her chew a banana.

One day, an anthropologist, Gus, joins her at the table. Together they chew bananas so loudly no one can hear.

Gus's project is writing down the songs of people who have no written language. At one time in his life, he lived in the Land of the Dead.

Daisy's been thinking about going there for some years. "How is it?" she asks.

"Lonely," Gus says. "Tell me about the City of One. What's it like living there?"

"Lonely," Daisy says for the first time out loud.

"Go on," Gus says.

Once Daisy gets to talking, there's no stopping her. In the City of One as in the Land of the Dead, one of the pleasures people miss most is a real conversation.

Daisy tells Gus every truth that comes into her mind. Gus will not stop being her friend, no matter how hard the truths. Gus knows that Daisy is telling herself the truths. Everybody else thinks they are getting it on, but the truth is Daisy is getting it on with herself. That is Gus's gift to Daisy.

One day there's only one question left to ask and Gus asks it: "You going back to the City of One?"

236

"I haven't decided," Daisy says. "Got any advice?"

Gus comes up with another question. "Is it a city if the population's one?"

Daisy meets each woman's eyes in turn. "In the City of One," she asks, "Who will call out the surgeon's name for malpractice?"

"I will shoot the surgeon right between the eyes," Meg says.

"The surgeon will die laughing," Pearl says.

"I will freeze out the surgeon with my silence," Maggie says.

"I will race him until he drops," Gretchen says.

"I will tickle him to death," Rita says.

"Hmm," Daisy says.

The next morning at breakfast, Gus tells Daisy, "You have been living on a mirror disguised as an island. And I'll tell you something else, kiddo. You're passionately connected, you feel responsibility to others, you *care*, and yet you think you're a loner. You're not a loner at all, you've just got lousy social skills."

Daisy reaches into her pocket and gives Gus the key to the City of One.

Once the walls come tumbling down, it's only a matter of time before the City of One becomes Levittown. Levittown's an attempt at community, but Daisy wants more. One day, she reads the Bible and gets a great idea. She applies for a grant to enlarge her pioneer museum.

The times are propitious, God's in His Heaven, and Daisy is the grant committee's dream token. Because she's an ex-nun, they understand why she's not a wife or mother, she's a spiritual mother, a priest explains. They understand why she's good at museums, she is Woman The Conserver, a philosopher explains. She's got great legs too, says a psychologist who's not going to let rabid feminists intimidate him from stating biological facts. Only a silver-haired medical doctor who can sniff a bitch a mile away abstains, but he doesn't dare speak up for fear the psychiatrist will peg him a mother hater. A quarter million dollars renewable in two years drops out of the sky on Daisy like a perfectly shaped blue speckled egg.

AND THUS LEVITTOWN NÉE THE CITY OF ONE
BECOMES THE CITY OF REFUGE:

"And the Lord spoke to Moses,
You shall appoint cities
To be cities of refuge for you
that the slayer

who kills any person unawares
may flee thither.

They shall be cities of refuge
from the avenger,
that the manslayer does not die
until he stands before the congregation in judgment.

These cities shall be a refuge
both for you
and for the stranger
and the sojourner among you
that every one
who kills any person unawares
may flee thither
until judgment is made by the congregation."

"Sanctuary," Pearl whispers, so awed she has to restrain herself from genuflecting.

"I don't get it," Gretchen says crossly, she's always being left out, pretty soon they'll start talking Yiddish.

"The Museum is sanctuary until the trial," Pearl says.

"It's evidence *for* the trial," Meg says.

"You're both right," Daisy says. Although she always calls the Museum Of The Revolution by its secular name so as not to violate the rights of atheist taxpayers including her own, in her heart, MOTR's real name is always the City of Refuge.

"But they're going to close it down," Gretchen says.

"Yes and No," Daisy says. She closes her eyes. When she opens them, she says, "All right, we'll take the vote now."

With tremendous force, Quasi breaks the gauze bonds, the canvas straps, and goes into fetal position. Luckily, her Stryker frame's right side up, or down would come baby, cradle and all.

238

52

Daisy counts the ballots.

Both Meg and Rita smile in anticipation.

"It's gonna be a tie," Pearl says.

"What's the point of going through this?" Gretchen asks, which is exactly what the doorkeeper asks a woman with a mass of luggage at the main entrance of the Museum.

"Because the sign says I can try," says the woman.

"Nobody ever wins," says the doorkeeper, "I'm just about to go off my shift, Please Lady."

"I feel lucky tonight," says the woman, she's just had a great cabbie who brought her here for free, she doesn't want to break her string of luck, "If you don't have a bingo game, I can at least try this." She is a small woman, but she stands up straight, puts her hands at her side, meets the doorkeeper's eyes, clears her throat. Her voice hits the rafters:

"I am Bridget,
Daughter of Helen Marie Dailey Baker,
Daughter of Ella Campbell Dailey,
Daughter of Sarah Paul Campbell,
Daughter of Meghan Donahue Paul. . . ."

Bridget is only just beginning her begats, but whistles blow, bells clang, flags fly, Gretchen's Ma has arrived, she is so touched by the welcome, Gretchen shouldn't have gone to all this trouble, she thinks, "Well I'll be damned," says the doorkeeper, "You are the first person in the history of the Museum to win Daisy's game," he reaches over and pulls the red handle.

The ballots are in two neat piles on the table, Daisy's face is jubilant. She says, "The winner is . . ." when all the buzzers at Heartbreak Hotel including the one on her wrist go off. She jumps up, "Somebody's won the door prize," she yells, takes the stairs two at a time to the video.

The minute Meg sees Daisy's face she knows something has gone wrong, she has lost, how could this happen, who sold her out? Meg scans the faces, Maggie, it has to be Maggie, she charges over to the windowseat, "Well?" she says to Maggie's back.

Maggie rolls over, surprises Meg by turning a mean face to her, "If it isn't our illustrious Cap'n," she slurs. She belches in Meg's face. "Pardon *me*," she says to her drink.

Meg wants to slug her but she needs her right now. "I know how to deal with this," she says. "You come along with me, I'll get this straightened out."

"Yes *Sir*", Maggie says, she lurches after Meg.

Where she can help it, Meg doesn't leave things to chance or democracy. MEG'S BACK-UP PLAN: To wire a timer to blow up the warehouse of Memorial Day Fireworks while, a mile away, she pulls Quasi's plug.

"You going out?" Rita asks Maggie.

"Going out for a little action," Maggie says. "You know all about that." She has forgotten she doesn't want to be against Rita, she has killed the whole bottle, and underneath her seeming carelessness she drowns in despair: Maggie the lush is getting mean. She scrawls across the sign-out board: DESTINATION: A LITTLE ACTION.

Rita shrugs. Rita's got nothing against a little action. She's been around the block and intends to go around again. But Maggie's keeping bad company and heading for trouble.

What a great looking old woman, Daisy thinks as she sees the winner on the video, I hope that's how I turn out, she radios her congratulations and her apologies that she can't set up an immediate meeting, but they'll get together as soon as she finishes her next appointment. At the thought of what's waiting at her next appointment, Daisy's heart plummets, but before the feeling can take her over, she takes three deep breaths and says to herself, That woman beat the odds, Give it your best shot.

"Wish me luck," she says to Rita on her way through the hall.

"Don't shoot till you see the pinks of their eyes," Rita calls.

When she comes out of the tunnel, Daisy sees a lethal combo ahead of her on the street: booze and violence walking with linked arms, but she can't stop to deal with Drunken Maggie and Murderous Meg now. She does make one stop.

. . .

A nurse's aide in a blue striped uniform, her ponytails bobbing, nods to the family keeping sentry in the ICU, carries a tray of syringes over to a side cabinet, tiptoes over to look at Quasi, "Oh my," she says and touches her. When she takes her hand away, a miraculous medal, its blue ribbon Velcroed to Quasi's white gown, has this inscription on the back: I AM A CATHOLIC. IN CASE OF EMERGENCY, CALL FR. VALENTINE. Daisy's beeper number is engraved on the medal.

The formal ceremony to present the prize of lifetime free admission to the Museum will take place after Daisy's appointment with the City Fathers, but the doorkeeper pins an interim blue ribbon on Bridget when a man appears with a clipboard and says, "Move on, please."

"I just got here," Bridget says.

The man puts the clipboard into a briefcase and takes a padlock out. "Sorry, sister, you got here too late, this joint's being closed down by order of the City, power of attorney, injunction 77, violations 4073 1st Block alone . . ."

"What did you say?" Bridget asks, "My daughter, Gretchen, works the 1st Block, Where's my daughter, Gretchen?"

"Order of the City, Lady, power of attorney, injunction 77, violations four thousand. . ."

Bridget draws herself up to her full 5'1", and says, "I didn't come here to argue with you, young man, so *please be quiet.*"

The man in uniform turns to the ticket taker and says in a long-suffering voice, "I haven't been home for my supper yet, all I need is a hysterical woman on my hands. . . ."

"Hysterical? You wanna see hysterical I'll show you hysterical," Bridget screams, she grabs his padlock, wings it over the wall, grabs an enormous suitcase, and makes her getaway into the Museum interior as he turns incredulously to follow the flight of the lock.

Bridget sees a police officer holding up a drunk woman, "Pardon me, Officer, I'm looking for my daughter, Gretchen." The drunk woman makes a little sound, and just for an instant under the streetlight, she meets Bridget's gaze, Bridget's face puzzles, "Do I know you?" she begins, but the woman bends over and begins to throw up. Poor thing, Bridget thinks, she reaches out to help, but the cop turns on her with a look so cold Bridget backs up a step. "What kind of mother are you you don't know where your own daughter is?" the cop says, and moves on, half dragging the drunk woman with her.

. . .

There's nothing in the world that Maggie'd rather do than go out brawling, but her body's got other ideas. She tries to stay vertical against the wall of the warehouse while Meg sorts her keys, tries to focus on signs Meg has had the foresight to post: NO ENTRANCE BETWEEN THE HOURS OF 12 AND 12, TEMPORARY RESTRAINING ORDER 1234 PERMANENTLY IN EFFECT, ATTACK DOGS ON PREMISES, TRESPASSERS WILL BE PERSECUTED. . . ." Maggie blinks, "*Prosecuted?*" she asks.

"It's time to stop coddling criminals," Meg says, and swings open the heavy door.

"Where can I find my daughter, Gretchen?" Bridget asks each woman she passes.

Each woman shakes her head, moves quickly away.

"She's about this height, her eyes are the same color as mine. . . ."

Finally, one woman directs Bridget to Daisy's office.

"Goddammit, Maggie, hold the flashlight steady," Meg says again.

Inside a vast warehouse, Maggie reads the words stamped on crate after crate FIREWORKS EXPLOSIVES DANGER she senses the danger but can't bring meaning to her feeling, Meg works with wires, dials, clocks, timers, Maggie tries to hold on to the light and concentrate, she's going to be sick again Oh God, "You good for nothing lush," Meg says, "you aren't even any good to yourself."

Daisy is almost to her Museum office when she spots Meg pushing Maggie along the street. Maggie reeks of vomit, Meg reeks of trouble. When Daisy calls, Meg stops on a dime and says, "Everything's under control."

"You need less control and more discipline," Daisy says sharply. "Control and discipline are not the same thing. Go home and stay there till I come."

CONTROL AND DISCIPLINE ARE NOT THE SAME THING: A SHORT-SHORT

Sometimes it works the other way.

A famous writer writes 173 books.

He has discipline.

At a writer's conference, he goes up to a stranger, puts his hands on her breasts, smiles, and says, "No bra."

He does not have control.

. . .

242

If Meg messed up this deal, I'll put her back in the Clearasil Kiosk, Daisy thinks. She pushes open the door to her office where three men in three-piece suits put down their attaché cases and stand up when she enters. "Good evening, Gentlemen," she says. "Please be seated and we'll begin."

Meg is struck to her core by Daisy's rebuff. Since her Uncle died, Daisy is the only person in the world Meg cares about. Now she's lost Daisy too. She pulls Maggie along roughly, "This is all your fault," she says. "You're a puke and a scum, you always have been and there's nothing you can ever do about it." She doesn't feel Maggie stumble along. Her legs are wobbly. She feels her supports are gone. She is on the outside again.

DAISY PLAYS HIGH STAKES POKER: During the negotiations, one man sweats so much his white on white shirt is soaked. Lucky for Daisy that women don't sweat. It's about her only advantage this evening. The sweating man thinks, If we don't stop her she's going to bury us, he leans forward, says, "Now we're not unreasonable. If you help us out, maybe we can help you out. What exactly is it that you want?"

Daisy looks at the red arteries criss-crossing his eyeballs and shoots.

53

Bridget waits in the outer room when Daisy comes out of her office, head bowed. Behind Daisy, an elated man with bloodshot eyes claps two other men on their shoulders. Daisy thinks Bridget is there for the formal ceremony, but Bridget asks, "Can you help me find my daughter?"

Daisy looks Bridget in the eye, sees her own image reflected in Bridget's pupil, sees strength and passion and determination.

Bridget sees a woman like and unlike herself, a younger woman accustomed to being in charge in a way she will never know, yet not unapproachable nor a stranger to trouble. "I know you have your own problems," Bridget says. "I wouldn't ask you this if it weren't terribly important. I don't know who else to ask."

Daisy has taken every other chance she knows this evening, she decides to take the final one: She clasps Bridget's hands and says, "Look on the 20th City Block."

Outside, even as Daisy points toward the 20th City Block, the streetlights in that section go out. "It's a gamble," she calls after the small figure lugging a big suitcase toward the darkened street. "Be bold, but be careful." Already Daisy's having second thoughts.

At the border, a uniformed man beckons Bridget into a small booth. "Name?"

"I am Bridget," she intends to begin her begats, but he cuts her off, "Are you mother or daughter?"

"Both," she says.

He is clearly exasperated, "Business?"

"Self-employed. . . ," she begins.

"Business on the 20th City Block," he snaps.

"I'm looking for my daughter, Gretchen," Bridget says.

GRETCHEN'S MA, he stencils on a badge, "Don't take it off," he says.

244

She winces, "I hate to be called Ma," she begins, but he shoves papers at her, "Sign here." When she hesitates, he says, "You're not setting one foot down there without signing the release." His finger jabs the line.

She signs: "*Gretchen's Ma* releases the Museum from any harm, damage, grief incurred while visiting the 20th City Block." "Just what is this place?" she asks, but the man snaps out the light, collapses his pre-fab booth, and leaves without answering.

THE 20TH CITY BLOCK IS ALL THE LIES MOTHERS TELL THEIR DAUGHTERS AND ALL THE LIES DAUGHTERS TELL THEIR MOTHERS. IT IS SO HEINOUS FEW EVER SEEK IT OUT, NO ONE CAN BEAR TO VISIT IT TWICE.

A sign says ENTER AT YOUR OWN RISK, but all Gretchen's Ma is aware of are her own edges and the darkness down there. She stands stock-still, tries to gather courage. When her eyes become accustomed to the moonlight, she recoils from the desolate terrain. The whole area looks like it's bombed out. The land is pitted and pocked with craters. Buildings are shells or rubble. The street is deserted. She's not going down there. "Gretchen?" she calls, her voice comes back to her ears strange, eerie, it frightens her into silence. She doesn't know what to do. If Gretchen is down there, she's got to go down there. Would Gretchen go down there for her, she wonders, fills with guilt for wondering such a thing. She is paralyzed.

Down the block, an enormous red arrow flashes on: THIS WAY. I'm too old for this, too tired, she thinks. Gretchen's Ma picks up her suitcase, takes a deep breath, and starts toward the arrow.

She hears rats and rustlings, she's not afraid of small creatures, used to kill bats by herself, stun them with a towel, beat them with a broom, Did she ever tell Gretchen that, but she doesn't *like* them, moves further out from the boarded up storefronts until she hugs the curb. Her eyes on the flashing arrow, a truck roars around the corner, headlights blind her, for a moment Gretchen's Ma is caught like a rabbit frozen in the headlights' glare, then instinctively she jumps away from the truck barreling down on her. What the, her heart pounds, she presses against the taped plate glass window, signs flapping **Lady Madonna Stork Styles We Make Pregnant Prettier Sale Drastically Reduced Everything Must Go BANKRUPT,** watches the truck, a sound system on its roof, careen down the street, jump the curb, ride the sidewalk, crash over cans, burn rubber, Judas Priest U-turn and head right back toward her, Gretchen's Ma flattens herself into the glass wall, the truck misses her by an inch, as it passes, the loudspeaker blares: NOW THAT I'VE GOT YOUR ATTENTION, HOWDY HOWDY AND A WARM WELCOME TO THE HEARTLAND

OF AMERICA, THIS IS PEARL'S SELF-GUIDE TAPE TO THE 20TH CITY BLOCK, I'VE STEPPED OUT FOR A MOMENT TO ADMINISTER MOUTH-TO-MOUTH RE-SUSCITATION, THIS TRUCK IS ON AUTOMATIC PILOT, YOU'RE ON YOUR OWN, JUST LIKE OLD TIMES, SEEMS LIKE OLD TIMES, HAVING YOU AROUND. . . .

More money is poured into Pearl's show than the rest of the Museum's combined budget. Pearl changes the show every twelve minutes. She feels she has to be a super comic to make up for wanting to do something besides be a mother. She hopes everyone will say, See her talent is so great it justifies her demands that her husband share child-care.

So far all anyone's said is, I wonder who's taking care of her kids.

BEFORE I WAS A COMIC I WAS A MOTHER, Pearl's taped voice blares, ENCOURAGE ME A LITTLE AND I'LL COMPLETELY DESTROY MYSELF. The truck peels off around the corner, siren wailing, in mid-wail cuts off. The silence is chilling. I'm getting out of here, Gretchen's Ma picks up her suitcase, suddenly all the streetlights flash on off on off on, the shouts start:

It's eleven o'clock, do you know where your children are

They never come to visit me

What did I do to end up in this place

You expect that from a son

Gretchen's Ma runs back in the direction she came from, but the street has changed DEAD END ONE WAY NO EXIT DO NOT ENTER, she must have gotten turned around, she shifts the suitcase into her other hand, considers dumping it, but what if she finds Gretchen and has nothing to give her, starts in the other direction, hears footsteps behind her, runs, runs faster until she outdistances them, breathes a little easier, even as an old woman with varicose veins she's fleet footed, did she ever tell Gretchen she was the only girl to have boys' black hockey skates, gave them a run for their money you better believe, a hand grabs her hem

"Get your hands off me," Gretchen's Ma says.

"Take some free samples," whines an old woman so bent over Gretchen's Ma at first thinks she's a hunchback, but it's the woman carrying a pack of lies, she's disgusting, smells of shellfish, I will never be reduced to that, Gretchen's Ma thinks. "Come on now, dearie," she says, "I'm looking for my daughter, let go my dress."

The old woman cackles, "So you got dumped too," she says, and for an instant Gretchen's Ma feels like thrashing her, it seems her whole life people never understand plain English, but the old woman is such a mess she just wants to put distance between them.

246

The old woman glances at Gretchen's photo, shakes her head.

"You hardly looked at it," Gretchen's Ma says.

"I'd remember another cheerleader," the bent woman says. "There aren't many of us down here. Listen, take some more free samples. No, no, take more, I never get rid of them, they manufacture them faster than I can hand them out." She tilts her wrinkled face at a coquettish angle, and speaks in a little girl's voice: "Do you have anything for *me* in your bag?"

Gretchen's Ma feels she's been manipulated, but can't quite put her finger on it; she dismisses the feeling, opens her bag and somewhat reluctantly, because Gretchen's quite fond of them, gives the woman a jar of bread and butter pickles.

"I don't like bread and butter pickles," says the bent woman, pops a half dozen in her mouth, "That's a lie, Heh Heh," she says with her mouth full and limps away.

Gretchen's Ma glances at a couple of the samples, some religious tract, turns around to make sure the woman's not looking, tosses them down. The wind picks them up and blows them down the street:

You've never looked more beautiful

Don't worry about a thing

It'll all come natural to you

DOING WHAT COMES NATURALLY #1

Six hours after the young woman has her first baby, the nurse comes in and says, Put the soiled napkins in the can, do you understand?

She doesn't understand, she doesn't even care, she's just had a baby, but she doesn't want to be trouble, she nods.

Comes time to dispose of a soaked napkin, she wishes she'd understood. There's only one can in the room: a stainless steel cannister that's full of *new* napkins.

She doesn't dare ask. Mothers know.

She drags her wound across the bed, starts wrapping. Around and around and around: she wraps the used napkin in twenty coats. Stuffs it in the bag the new napkin came in. Folds the bag over once and once again. Puts the bag in the stainless steel can.

The nurse enters, Change your pad yet?

She nods.

Where's the soiled one?

In the can.

THERE'S NOTHING IN THE CAN.

Her heart sinks: she knows she's done something very wrong.

I SAID WHAT CAN?

She points.

YOU WHAT? YOU PUT THAT DIRTY THING IN THE, THAT IS DISGUSTING, SOILED NAPKINS GO IN THE CAN, THE TRASHCAN, WHAT KIND OF PERSON, YOU CONTAMINATED ALL THE CLEAN NAPKINS, I DON'T BELIEVE THIS, WAIT'LL THEY HEAR THIS, SHE PUTS IT IN THE. . . .

The landscape changes dramatically. A shaft of golden light illuminates rolling green hills. Young couples race hand-in-hand through meadows. The women all wear white dresses and have flowers woven in their hair, The men all have sea-green eyes and perfect teeth.

"How does it change so fast; Momma?" Cornelia Wallace asks Ruby Folsom Ellis Austin.

"I believe it's done with mirrors," Miz Ruby says.

"Oh Momma, you are a stitch," Cornelia says, "What would I ever do without you?"

Holding hands, they stop in front of a magnificent cathedral to watch the light pour through the stained glass windows. "Listen to the Cardinals swing," Cornelia says, she and her mother do a little jitterbug on the sidewalk.

"I think I'll nip in for a visit," Gretchen's Ma says. She finds a wadded up Kleenex in her pocket, looks kinda used, Oh Well, she carefully smooths it out, bobby pins it to her head, and enters Church walking tall.

The Cardinals wail:

MOTHER MOST PURE
MOTHER MOST CHASTE
MOTHER INVIOLATE
MOTHER UNDEFILED. . .

"Tell it," Pearl's voice shouts from the pulpit.

A spotlight hits the new mother who kneels at the railing in front of Mary's statue. Head bowed, she receives the purification after childbirth. Cleansed, she leaves the Cathedral lighter than air and heads downtown. All along the street, people smile at her. She's different now, everyone can tell.

DOING WHAT COMES NATURALLY #2

She glides into the department store, floats over to the Infants and Toddlers' Department.

The saleswoman leans over the counter and says to her, "You've just had a baby."

Young woman preens, beams, glows. The saleswoman confirms what everyone says: MOTHERHOOD SHOWS.

The saleswoman leans closer, "There's a huge milk stain on the front of your dress."

248

DOING WHAT COMES NATURALLY #3

Upstairs in Juniors, a somewhat crazed looking woman in clown pants is buying 55 pairs of Bonnie Doon knee socks when a young woman holding a sack in front of her dress comes in and says to the clerk, "I'm looking for something very special to wear to my baby's christening party."

"I could show you the perfect thing," says the woman in clown pants, she leads the new mother to a rack, and points out:

A silk blouse with these exquisite details

*** White as snow for purity and majesty, for it's not just a christening, dear, it's a coronation, SALVE REGINA SALVE SALVE . . .

"Please lower your voice," says the saleswoman, "Sorry," says the woman in clown pants, she whispers

*** Tiny silk covered buttons down the front, Momma's nursing, What a woman.

*** Strategically cut neckline, cleavage every time you offer an hors d'oeuvre, Remember, before you were a mother you were a woman, Whew Momma, "May I?" asks the saleswoman, she leans close

*** As a bonus fillip, my dear, may I suggest you fix your hair in a chignon, two tendrils erupting spontaneously, a very special blend of regal and bawd for your very special new role.

DOING WHAT COMES NATURALLY #4

New mother is invited to a fancy cocktail party.

She thinks about it for days, she wears a beautiful white silk blouse, her hair is in a chignon, her cheeks flush with the excitement of being back out in public.

The hostess introduces her to a famous psychiatrist, "This tiny little thing just had a baby," she says, and leaves.

Famous psychiatrist says, "You're nursing, aren't you?"

New mother is both shy and proud.

"I could tell by your pendulous breasts," famous psychiatrist says.

New mother bursts into tears.

"I'm sorry, Sorry," new father makes the apologies as they leave, but it's not necessary, everyone understands postpartum depression.

Gretchen's Ma understands it too.

"Why that blankety blank," she says, she plucks a Bloody Mary off a passing waiter's tray, moves over next to the psychiatrist, stumbles, and spills the drink into his lap, "Oh, I'm terribly sorry," she says.

54

"What's up?" Pearl asks as Meg stomps in, dumps Maggie in a heap on the floor, turns on her heel and heads upstairs. "Not Maggie," Pearl says to herself.

Maggie opens her eyes, "Gonna be sick. . . ."

Pearl holds Maggie's head while she throws up, helps her rinse her mouth, splashes cold water on her face.

Maggie looks into the mirror and recoils.

"You've looked worse," Pearl says.

But Maggie isn't seeing what Pearl sees. Maggie sees Quasi. She tries to say, "The face in the mirror. . . ."

"You can't see a clear image in these old mirrors," Pearl says. "The silver backing's all gone, they're all cloudy. . .", but Maggie continues to stare at the mirror, fixed, anguished. "Whatever you're seeing, Maggie, it doesn't show on the outside, I swear," Pearl says. She's not sure Maggie hears her, but Maggie allows Pearl to turn her from the mirror, Pearl gets her to the couch, "I could stand a little help in here," she yells.

Rita makes a pot of espresso, and holds the cup for Maggie to sip. "Let her hit bottom," Gretchen says, "That's the only way she'll change." But Rita believes in intervention, and she persuades Gretchen, pretty please Gretchen, to contribute her aspirins and vitamins to the cause.

"Need air," Maggie says, she feels like she's suffocating. She stumbles across the living room, strikes her knee a sharp crack on the coffee table, a bruise tomorrow on Maggie's pretty leg, Rita thinks—Maggie falls often, and if she's not careful, someday the purple contusions, rather than be a place for a lover's detour, poor baby, will stop the eye and hand cold. "We'll take you to the steam room," Rita says.

"Come on, Rita," Pearl says, "This is our last night at Heartbreak Hotel, Would it kill us to ask her?"

Rita rolls her eyes.

"HeyMegYouwannagotothesteamroomwithus?" Pearl calls from the bottom of the stairs.

Meg's door slams so hard plaster sifts down from the ceiling.

"So we got a freebie," Pearl says.

250

. . .

"This is our last night at Heartbreak Hotel Would it kill us to ask her?" Meg mimics, what do they think, she's deaf and dumb like Quasi?, The Hell with them, she tosses things out of her dresser drawers, let the whole Museum fall apart, not a minute too soon for her, she's getting out, they don't need her she sure as Hell doesn't need them, spend your life being a good cop, what's it get you, everybody turns on you sooner or later, Miss Goody Goody Daisy telling her where to get off, Meg is so crushed by Daisy's rebuff her heart pounds, her throat lumps, her stomach pits, Go to Hell, she says, she heaves the contents of the dresser drawer across the room, blackjacks, brass knuckles, aliases fly and scatter across the braided rug, frighten Meg, acting like that's not like her at all, she hates people who act like that, Get a hold of yourself, she says, you go to pieces they'll bury you, she forces herself to walk in measured step to her cot, Sit down, Close your eyes, she tells herself, If you sit very still with your arms crossed, you will not fall apart.

Peg O' My Heart's eyes are wide open. They are turned inside out. They look at terrors. Her body inches away from the center. Her foot is pulled over the side of the yellow bed first, her leg, her other leg, she starts across the alcove. She passes Meg without a sound. She does not stumble, she does not bump into things. Her foot is steady on the stairs. She stands in the living room doorway. She stands in the kitchen. Her eyes sweep the room. She moves on to the next room. She opens and closes doors. She tries different floors. Some nights she stands for hours at the side of a bed waiting. When she cannot stand it any longer, she makes a little noise.

Meg's eyes bolt open. Peg O' My Heart stands flush to her cot. Her eyes are wide open. They are turned inside out. Meg's heart constricts. She stands up, takes hold of the cold plump hand, leads Peg O' My Heart back to bed. Peg O' My Heart's eyes close, she will remember none of it, and Meg won't tell her secret.

In the center of the large oval rug, a small brass pipe glitters. Bum, Meg picks it up, toys with it, her eyes narrow, on her hands and knees she looks around, finds the plastic bag under the bed. Too much control, huh, she mimics harshly.

Goddam hippie weirdos, Meg says, she fills and taps the pipe expertly as she's seen a dozen times in goddam hippie weirdo drug identification films. She flips open the book of matches given to her by the officer who drove her and Gretchen home. The officer got the matches, a back rub, and an I.O.U. from Wanda Brown, a frequently harassed prostitute on the 13th Block. Written on the inside cover is: STOP TRYING TO CONTROL EVERYONE ELSE'S LIFE. CONTROL YOUR OWN GODDAM LIFE. BUFFALO ROSE.

55

Gretchen's Ma's greatest treasure is her Grandma's bracelet, one charm for each of her grandchildren. The charms are to ward off Gretchen's Ma being tossed out on the heap. She knows for a fact that some women wear Wellington Grandma bracelets, the nerve, hers is the real goods, every one of those grandchildren authentic and earned. She picks her way across a mined field, her arm raised to shield her eyes from the constant explosions, the charms going before her.

Many Indian women cluster around a tree in a courtyard. As she approaches to ask their help in finding Gretchen, a gulf opens in the earth. Across the chasm, she sees their tormented faces PLEASE PLEASE PLEASE PLEASE PLEASE let me be a mother, they scrabble over each other to tie petitions on the tree for barren women.

At some signal Gretchen's Ma doesn't see, everyone turns around and begins pelting her with gardenia corsages. She runs down the block.

Legions of lost little girls wander and wail Ma-Ma, Where are you, Ma-Ma, the noise is deafening, they all grab at her, she shakes them off, a woman about Gretchen's age comes straight to her, looks beseechingly at her, but when Gretchen's Ma asks for help, the woman weeps and moves on, it's the woman who feels unmothered, she searches all her life for surrogates, on Mother's Day she buys out the Hallmark section that says You're like a Mother to me.

At least she sent a card, says the red-faced woman who posts a letter:

DEAR MISS FIX IT,

I did it again this year and I'm so ashamed. I sent myself a dozen red roses on Mother's Day, and signed my daughter's name on the card. She's alive and very successful, but she's always too busy to give me a second thought. Am I the only mother who has ever done this?

—HEARTSICK IN HARTFORD

The streets are jammed with women now, but they all avert their eyes, clap hands over their ears. No one will respond to Gretchen's Ma's question. It's as if she's invisible.

Every other step, Gretchen's Ma steps over abandoned girl babies, It's beginning to get aggravating, This is hopeless, she thinks NEWS-FLASH SCIENTIFIC BREAKTHROUGH: USING A NEW METHOD, CHINESE DOCTORS HAVE BEEN ABLE TO IDEN-TIFY AND ABORT FEMALE FETUSES, she's never going to find Gretchen.

She passes three little girls who plead Have you seen our mother?, shakes her head, ducks into the small Pioneer Women Museum Daisy used to run on the outskirts of the City of One, and asks the doyenne who says, No, I haven't seen your daughter, but I'll show you a noble mother.

In the Sierra Nevada mountains, Tamsen Donner bites the bullet and chooses her dying husband over her living daughters. She sends her daughters out with the rescue party and says, "I may never see you again, but God will take care of you."

God Falls Behind In His Child Support Payments: IF GOD TAKES CARE OF THOSE WHO TAKE CARE OF THEM-SELVES, GOD TAKES JIMDANDY CARE OF ELITHA, LEANNA, FRANCES, GEORGIA, AND ELIZA DONNER grates Pearl's voice from a rusted wagon wheel with a broken axle. At SUT-TER'S FORT, THE WOMEN FIND ELITHA A HUSBAND BE-FORE THREE MONTHS PASS. AND A LOVELY STORY IT IS TOO. NEXT CASE PLEASE.

ROMANCE AT SUTTER'S FORT, says the display blurb, it lists all the marriages performed at the fort. In flowery script, fourteen-year-old Elitha is listed first.

Outside the museum, little Frances, Georgia, and Eliza Donner keep their eyes perpetually turned to the mountains, all day long say, "If only Mother would come."

Up in the mountains, after she has wrapped her husband for burial, Tamsen Donner tells Lewis Keseberg, "I am bound to go to my chil-dren." Even if the doyenne were not switching off all the machines, these are the last words anyone will ever hear Tamsen Donner say.

Gretchen's Ma pulls her sweater closer around her, quickens her step and starts whistling as she passes the Museum Cemetery, blood seeps out onto the sidewalk onto her shoes, she screams and starts run-ning, she passes all the graves of the women who hemorrhaged to death in childbirth, all the graves of the women who died in botched illegal abortions, there are more graves than every military cemetery in the world combined, all the graves seep blood, Gretchen's Ma crosses herself, "Hail Mary full of grace . . . ," she prays.

"Here's Ave Maria in the tropics," Pearl says, she and Luciano Pavorotti sing "Guava Maria," the duet brings tears to John Paul II's eyes, he listens to Pearl's sermon: Making Religion A Part Of You: "In El Salvador, when the girls are leetle, their mothers take a razor blade and make the sign of the cross on their clitorises. They say it makes them better workers and they don't get ideas. . . ."

"Suffer the little children to come to me," John Paul II says, "I have the greatest respect for womankind, my mother was one, I'm off to Poland now to support the workers."

"You think he jets around, you should have seen me on my carpool day," Pearl says, "Vroom Vroom." Her voice comes from inside the golden chariot that carries the holy book to the golden temple.

Surrounded by a pool of water, the Golden Temple rises out of the mist right before Gretchen's Ma's eyes, "That is beautiful," she says, she's always been an admirer of churches. Inside is even more impressive. Priestesses sit on satin pillows and take turns reading from a huge book with gilt edges. When they get to the end of the book, the next volume is brought in. They read The Litany Of The Lies Mothers Tell Their Daughters And Daughters Tell Their Mothers, and are clearly the center ring act, but all around them in concentric circles are colorful sideshows:

Mothers in purdah putting their daughters in purdah

Mothers binding their daughters' feet

Mothers performing clitoridectomies

Mothers performing infibulation

Japanese mothers talking behind their hands to their daughters in tiny voices

Moslem mothers leading their daughters into the mosques LADIES ENTRANCE THIS WAY

Eskimo mothers averting their eyes from their aged mothers and baby daughters set out in the snow to die in periods of famine

Mothers feeding their families in this order, husbands, sons, daughters, themselves

Mothers who don't believe their daughters' story of incest

Mothers averting their eyes from their married daughters' bruises

Mothers reading their daughters' diaries

Mothers opening their daughters' mail

Mothers who won't let their daughters be sexual creatures

254

Mothers who don't tell their daughters why they're abusing Daddy
Mothers who won't tell their daughters why they're acting crazy
Mothers telling daughters, TELL IT MOTHER, Pearl shouts,
> Telling daughters virginity's the greatest gift you can give
> Telling daughters a mother's the most wonderful thing a woman can be
> Telling daughters that when labor's over they won't remember it
> Telling daughters they'll love babies
> Telling daughters This is the way it is always was always will be

CHANGE PARTNERS EVERYBODY, From the director's chair, Pearl speaks through a megaphone. In a dazzling kaleidoscopic choreography, the daughters step upstage. ON STAGE I WANT THE
Daughters staying in purdah
Daughters who don't make trouble
Daughters who pity their mothers
Daughters who say their mothers are too old to change
Daughters who let their mothers do everything for them
Daughters who don't say anything about their mothers' drinking
Daughters who stay silent about their mothers' lives
Daughters who say the truth would kill their mothers
Daughters who don't let their mothers be sexual creatures then or now . . .

"Those things aren't problems here," Gretchen's Ma says. "We treat our children the same."

YEH YEH shout thousands of mothers dressed in Uncle Sam suits, they march down the streets, their banners high THIS IS AMERICA AFTER ALL, behind them as far as Gretchen's Ma can see rows of corn-fed apple-cheeked All American daughters, each one bent over carrying a corn-fed apple-cheeked All American son, step smartly to the tune of:

He Ain't Heavy He's Your Brother

Do the dishes
Because that's your job
Why that's not true
Your brother does the yardwork
Why just last week
Because he's a boy
He needs to be outside
He's stronger

What a thing to say
Of course you can't beat him up
Even if it's true that would make him feel bad
You're a girl
That's not proper
That's not fitting
That's not allowed
And put your legs together
I don't know what to do with her
Girls are so much more trouble than boys
A son's a son till he takes a wife
A daughter's a daughter all her life
I asked her Does he bother your record player
She doesn't understand
I *know* she'd better start understanding
Do we have to go over this again
Because it's more important for a boy
He has places to go
All right, he *likes* to be outside
We can't all have what we like
He *needs* more allowance
He can't go out without money in his pocket
That's the way it is
With that attitude you're headed for trouble
Nobody will ever want to marry you
You'll end up an old maid
Don't even joke about not getting married
That's bad luck
What do you mean you're not joking
Are you making fun of me
That's what a woman does
It'll be the happiest day of my life
What do you mean What about your life
That goes without saying
It's time you learned to cook
Don't start that again
Well you better find yourself a rich man
They say it's just as easy to love a rich man
Sometimes I wish
Never mind
Come out into the kitchen
Just to please me
I hardly ever see you anymore
You're growing so big
You're so pretty
You want to lick the bowl

Guess who I ran into at the store
Isn't it a shame she never got married
She would have made some man a wonderful wife
They say she's a very good doctor
It's a pity she never had children
Someday you'll understand
You children are my whole life
I don't expect gratitude
That's what a mother's for
I'd do it over again in a minute
I'm worried about your sister
She's been married two and a half years
What do you mean Leave her alone
After all I did for her I'm supposed to leave her alone
I'm the only one without grandchildren
Because that's what a woman's for
You're what
Oh My God
Don't tell your father
This would kill your father
That Was Not Funny
I thought you were serious
Don't say you'll never have children
You'll change your mind
I'm telling you the truth: You'll love babies
I *know* school's important to you
Do you think I'm stupid
Don't you think I know what's going on
I had dreams too when I was your age
Sometimes I wish
Never mind
I understand that's all
I'm on your side
Now don't cry, it is *not* hopeless
This is what we'll do
I'll cook his favorite meal and after dinner you ask him
From the time you were born you could wrap your father around your
little finger
Shh, not now, he's in a bad mood
Occasion?, There's no occasion, I just felt like making kuchen tonight
She's just fooling around, don't pay any attention to her
You should never have asked him then
I never dreamed he'd get so upset
I'm so upset
You understand your brother has to come first
There's only so much money

Grades have nothing to do with it
He has to make a living
You can always get married
I don't know why you have to say such ugly things
I only hope you have a daughter and she causes you as much grief as
you've caused me
Is that so much to ask
Suit yourself then
Do whatever you want to do
Go off and leave me
When did you ever take my feelings into consideration
I expect that from them
I expect more from you
What am I but the floor mat around here
Between you and them my life is a misery
Sometimes I wish, *Never mind, who cares what I wish*
Someday you'll understand what I've had to put up with
Someday you'll be a mother too
ARE YOU LISTENING TO ME

"I wouldn't have dared to do the things she wanted to do," Gretchen's Ma begins.

Grace Kelly on the other side sees this BUBBLEGUM FACT clearly: JUST BECAUSE THERE WASN'T ADOLESCENCE WHEN YOU WERE AN ADOLESCENT HAS NOTHING TO DO WITH YOUR DAUGHTER'S ADOLESCENCE.

"I only wanted to protect her," Gretchen's Ma says.

An image of a mother lioness shoots up five hundred feet on the side of the Empire State Building, "Ooooooooooooooooooooooohhhh," says the crowd. As Gretchen's Ma watches, it continues to grow monstrous, another shape advances, "Sssssssssssssst," says the crowd as an image of Pearl The Explorer in a pith helmet fourteen stories high clubs off the lioness, "Hear me out," pants Pearl.

PEARL THE EXPLORER'S DISCOVERIES:
When Pearl discovers that she can't control what happens to her
daughters
that they'll hear, learn, know a great deal more than she
can tell them
that her problems and secrets won't be their problems and
secrets . . .

"Jump," yells the crowd.

"One more," Pearl yells.

ONE MORE: When Pearl discovers that she fears her daughters discovering sex because then they'd leave her, she leaves them.

PEARL MAKES HER DEATHBED CONFESSION: The worst thing she ever said to a daughter on a Tuesday was, A girl as passive as you *deserves* a husband.

Pearl holds her nose and jumps.

The firefighter directing the net holders into position to catch her broadcasts over a megaphone YOU'RE SUCH A HOTSHOT CONTROLLER, CONTROL YOUR DIRECTION.

Pearl misses the net by a mile.

"Why doesn't her husband do something with her?" asks St. Paul.

"Aw Shaddup," says Pierre Trudeau.

On the outskirts of town, Pearl's husband looks down the hole in the pavement and says, "I don't think you have a clear sense of what you want, Pearl. You dig your own grave. You even hand out shovels. You say Come on everybody, help me dig. Everybody digs and digs and digs and at the last possible moment you jump out, grab all the shovels, and run away."

Pearl climbs out of the hole, collects his shovel, shakes his hand, "It hasn't been easy without you," she says, and walks on, a little dazed.

Her head is fuzzy with blurred images, she walks slowly, bent over, mirroring exactly the army of hunchbacks who trudge silent and shadowy around the rim of the earth, they're the women who carry the burden of the human race, packs of lies, their brothers, Eve's curse. . . . Pearl shakes her head, "I know what I *don't* want," she says, she straightens up so tall her clothes look like they still have the coat hanger in them.

She approaches a young woman who steadily, patiently, smashes a Matterhorn of mother figures: icons, idols, molds, graven images, fetishes, effigies, imagos ee-Ma-jos. The young woman methodically smashes a pedestal, looks up at Pearl watching, says, "Nothing personal, Ma."

"You think that would make me feel bad?" Pearl asks. "Aren't I the one who taught you: 'Thou shalt not have false gods before your mother.' " Her eyes well up, she stumbles on.

"But where is Gretchen?" Gretchen's Ma calls after her, but Pearl disappears into an apartment building. In moments, the saddest voice Gretchen's Ma has ever heard sings:

Sometimes I feel like a motherless child,
Sometimes I feel like a motherless child,
Sometimes I feel like a motherless child,
A long, long way from home . . .

Tears stream down Gretchen's Ma's face, she thinks her heart will break, she rushes to comfort this child, the door is locked, she pounds Let me in, Let me in, but honky tonk piano blasts over her knocks and pleas, at top volume Pearl's wailing HITLER IS HIS MOTHER'S SON BLUES.

"Now just a minute," Gretchen's Ma says, her Irish up, "There's plenty of times *I* felt like a motherless child *and* a childless mother."

"The thing about *my* mother," Pearl's voice says from the intercom, "is that she never took the short end of the stick and said Thank you, she jabbed and poked and stuck every chance she got."

Gretchen's Ma rips off her badge, I AM BRIDGET, she says. Her voice carries all the way to Alberta, Canada.

I NEVER KNEW
I NEVER MEANT
IT WASN'T LIKE THAT
IT SEEMED
WHAT DID I KNOW ABOUT BABIES
YOU JUST TRY TO DO WHAT YOU CAN
I PAID. . . .

She sets the bag down, rends her clothes, her body in the moonlight a mass of scar tissue, LOOK AT MY SCARS, she yells . . .

"She's been on an awful long time," says Rose, Gypsy Rose Lee's mother, from the wings, "When do I get my turn?"

Gretchen stops in mid-step and looks over the dark canal bordering the 20th City Block, "I could have sworn I heard my Ma," she says.

"Oh God there she goes again," Pearl says.

Maggie tries to tell them again that the face in the mirror was Quasi, but though her spirit is willing, her flesh keeps giving out on her, one minute she's walking along, the next she's looking at the moon. An extraordinary moon. From far off, she hears Rita say, "Maggie, get up. You're too heavy, we can't carry you the whole way, you gotta help."

Gretchen both inclines toward the sound and draws back, but all she hears is a dog baying at the full moon, an eerie strange sound that spooks her, makes her think simultaneously of attack and pursuit.

"I DID WHAT MY MOTHER DID, SOME OF IT WAS GOOD AND SHE KNOWS IT. AND PUT THIS IN YOUR PIPE AND SMOKE IT: THE BIBLE SAYS HONOR YOUR

FATHER AND YOUR MOTHER, YOUR MOTHER YOU HEAR THAT, THAT IT MAY GO WELL WITH YOU, AND YOU MAY BE LONG-LIVED UPON EARTH. IN OTHER WORDS, HONORING YOUR MOTHER IS GOOD FOR YOUR HEALTH."

And here we go again, folks, Pearl's voice calls from the carousel, just before somebody's mother or daughter reaches out and catches the brass ring.

56

"I could use a drink," Bridget says. She looks like she's already had a few: she staggers off the 20th City Block, weaves through the Demilitarized Zone. A crumpled letter lies in her path, she debates a moment. She's not expecting a letter, on the other hand it's not addressed to anybody. A long time ago, Gretchen's Ma broke her bad habit of reading other people's mail, but she likes to keep her hand in. She picks it up and speedreads:

> Dear Momma,
>
> I have always felt that I've disappointed you.
> I have always tried not to disappoint you.
> Ever since I can remember, I've spent a great deal of energy trying to keep things from you that I thought would disappoint you.
> I will probably keep on trying not to disappoint you, but it's time for me to move on down the road.
>
> Love,
> Signature Smudged

"Fair enough," Bridget says, addresses the envelope To Whom It May Concern, and drops the letter in the postal box.

She heads across the street to the first bar she sees, The Steam Room, she needs to let off a little steam all right, about ready to blow her cork, just getting across the street exhausts her, she can barely push the heavy glass door open: What the?, a blast of steam hits her, is this one of those kinky bars, well one drink and she'll move on, she collapses on the lowest hardest barstool she's ever seen, it's like a wooden bench, she's never cared for rustic decor.

"This your first time here, honey?" a woman asks. "Oh you'll love it, there's cubbies for your clothes in that little room."

The Hell you say, Bridget thinks, she's keeping her clothes on, her legs closed, and her eyes open: she smiles sweetly.

"You've got the place to yourself, see ya," the woman says and leaves.

Bridget investigates. As far as she can tell, The Steam Room *is* a steam room. The only illumination is a hazy red light in the ceiling; in the wisps of moving steam, it reminds her of a siren turning in fog. She holds her hand six inches in front of her and sees only blurry outline which continually changes in the swirls of rolling steam. "Hello?" she says. No one answers. Cautiously, one hand feeling along the warm rock wall, Bridget edges her way along the bench.

At Heartbreak Hotel, in her room on her cot, Meg turns on the MOTR radio and takes another drag. She's puzzled by the pot, let down, thinks the same thing she thinks the first time she has intercourse: stuff's a bunko.

Bridget leans back on the bench. From someplace in the wall, music is piped in, Bridget hums, taps her foot. The wet steam feels good, penetrates to her joints, loosens her, she rolls her shoulders, This place isn't bad, "My, it's hot in here," she says, and removes her clothes.

All of a sudden, Meg realizes that she hears every single note of the music: Something's happening, she thinks, and intends to follow it closely, but the guitar strikes and holds the most wonderful note.

THE TRUTH TELLER: "We're gonna get you there, dearheart, in spite of yourself," Rita says: Rita, Pearl, and Gretchen half carry, half drag Maggie across the Museum to the Steam Room. Maggie tries to tell them again about the face in the mirror, she *wants* to tell them: Give Maggie five fingers of bourbon she'll tap-dance on the frontiers of truth, but nobody can understand Jack Daniels' dummy, Maggie won't even understand what she's saying for three days and then she'll say Oh My God did I really say that?

"She's babbling about Quasi again," Pearl says. "Poor Quasi. No matter what the vote is, I think she's a goner."

Gretchen starts to retort Good Riddance, but at the moment can't quite remember what it is about Quasi that bothers her so, compared to the eviction and the uncertain fate of the Museum, everything else pales. She wishes her Ma would get here, get it over with.

Quasi wants to get it over with too. The needle on her EEG is playing a record that is not hitting the charts.

"Maybe we should call the priest," one nurse says.

"Have Onesti do that when she gets back from dinner," says the other, "She's Catholic, she'll know all the mumbo jumbo."

"Tan-tum er-go makes your hair grow," giggles the first.

MEG DOES A LITTLE PRIVATE EYE WORK: Meg goes into each musical note, moves around inside it, it moves back into her, back and forth, Meg's body is the concert hall.

Daisy sees the women up ahead as they start to cross the canal bridge. "Wait up," she calls.

"Listen," she says.

All over the Museum there's the tap tap tap of hammers. Daisy tells them the news. Right this moment at every Museum gate, a uniformed man posts a sign: CLOSED NO FORWARDING ADDRESS.

"Say it isn't so," Gretchen says.

Before Gretchen can wail, Maggie moans, "Mea culpa mea culpa mea maxima culpa, my fault, my fault, my most grievous fault. . . ."

Daisy turns and shakes her, "It's *enough* we bear the shame, we don't take the blame too, you hear me?"

Maggie's head bobs. "I hear you."

"It's not the end of the world," Daisy says. "You'll see. Now I am ready for that steam bath. Who's coming?"

"What will I tell my Ma?" Gretchen asks.

"Tell her there are some things you want to talk about with her."

Gretchen looks aghast, "I couldn't. I can't talk to her. She won't listen. I just couldn't, not in a million years."

"You must aim higher, Gretchen," Daisy says.

"That's easy for you to say," Gretchen says.

"Only after a lot of practice," Daisy says.

The five link arms: Rita, Maggie, Daisy, Gretchen, Pearl. Now that the verdict is final, the relief almost makes them giddy except for Gretchen, her lip quivers. "Look around, Gretchen," Pearl says, "Surely you've been thrown out of better joints than this." Gretchen manages a wan smile, Pearl does a little ball step change so they're all walking in precision, "This looks real neat if anybody's watching from across the street," Pearl says.

Meg dances. She remembers looking down, seeing her feet moving, her feet are the Pied Piper, she has to follow them, she giggles, springs her feet from her shoes and socks, sees herself move in the mirror with the music, cannot stop herself, does not want to ever stop herself from dancing, she watches her body meld with the music, laughs out loud with pleasure without missing a beat.

264

57

Maggie's head is clearing a little, but her body's still wasted. "Remember how you took turns carrying each other when you were a girl?" Rita says; she and Daisy clasp each other's wrists to make a chair to carry Maggie the final one hundred yards.

"Hallelujah, you've crossed the River Jordan," Pearl shouts, she holds open the door to the steam bath anteroom, "Whew, feel that heat," while the others pull off Maggie's shoes and pants and shirt and get her in on a bench. Maggie is sober enough to be grateful for the steam: in these hazy swirls, her body looks good.

"I'm gonna strip down," Rita says, already shucked to her Tampax string.

"Me too," Gretchen says.

Pearl unlaces her shoes. "You guys are flashers. You flash your bodies all the time."

"Come on, Pearl," Rita says. "We've all got the same thing."

Pearl pulls off her sock. "That's like saying a Rolls Royce and a dune buggy got the same thing," she mumbles.

Rita stretches. "People got it wrong about bodies. These are just wonderful tools. I really don't understand about you, Pearl, you've got a real nice shape."

Pearl is tremendously pleased, but says, "If I put on any more weight around my hips, I'm going to look like a bottle of Mateus."

"You have to remember you're an older woman," Gretchen says.

"Older than whom?" Pearl snaps and strips down so fast her clothes blur.

Pearl is forever after her husband about aging.
One day he says to her, "Do you want me to die young, Pearl?"

Rita reaches up behind Gretchen, twirls the radio dial, OF THE 800 MILLION ILLITERATE ADULTS IN THE WORLD, TWO-THIRDS ARE FEMALE. UNESCO REPORTS THAT THE

NUMBER OF WOMEN WHO CANNOT READ OR WRITE HAS RISEN STEADILY IN THE PAST 10 YEARS, "That just makes me sick," Pearl says, "I get an actual visceral feeling. . . ."

"It's not as important for women," Gretchen says, "because most of them don't work, they just raise kids."

"AWWWWKKKKKKKKKKKGGGGGGGGGGGGGGGGGG," Pearl gags, manages to get out, "That's just plain ig."

"Ig?" Maggie asks.

"Ignorant, that's an ignorant thing for her to say," she turns toward Gretchen, "I know you're feeling bad, but you've got to learn to think before you speak."

"You think you're so smart," Gretchen says. "You don't have enough brains to take care of your body, you look ten years older than I do . . ."

"Hey, hold on there," Daisy says.

"She started it," Gretchen says.

After a noticeable silence, Pearl says, "For years, I looked younger than my age. Day in, day out, people would say You look like one of your daughters. Now if I looked like one of my daughters, one of us was doing something wrong. I never knew how to respond. If I said 'Thank you,' as if they'd given me a compliment, that'd feed into the youth cult. If I protested, that'd sound dumb or falsely demure. Then one day, I found the perfect response: I got old looking."

"I'm growing old gracefully," says a voice from the corner. "At my age, what other choice do I have? It's when you're thirty-five and fighting it that the illusion's still possible."

"Who's *that*?" Gretchen thinks. "Let's just forget it, okay? It's totally inconsequential. It's just that my Ma always said such ignorant things."

"Was she smart?" Daisy asks.

"Like a whip," Gretchen says.

"What did she say that was ignorant?" Daisy asks.

"Only about a million things. Like she always said, 'Two things are never discussed in this house: religion and politics.' For crying out loud, is it any wonder I have trouble thinking?" Gretchen whimpers.

I HAVE TO LEARN TO THINK AGAIN, THE WOMAN SAID TO DAISY, I KNOW THIS SOUNDS DUMB BUT I USED TO BE ABLE TO THINK, I'M QUITE SURE THERE WAS A TIME I COULD THINK. It doesn't sound dumb to Daisy. She knows most women haven't been trained to think, not even about their own situations.

"Religion and politics make people so ugly," says the voice in the corner, Is it that Ferraro woman on the 11th Block?, Gretchen can't see. The voice continues, "Brawling and shouting like a lot of immigrants. Nice people didn't behave that way."

"You don't understand," Gretchen says. "Even when she was dead wrong on something, she'd hold onto it, even if she looked ridiculous."

"Some people say dumb things because they feel backed into a corner," says the voice. "They have so little ground they have to hold onto every scrap."

"I'm talking about *rigid*," Gretchen says through clenched teeth.

"If you admit one thing," Pearl says, "you're sucked into the whole damn thing."

"I didn't give an inch," the voice says.

Well Bully for you, Gretchen thinks, she wishes this busybody would bug out of the conversation.

"She could have been Simone de Beauvoir, it wouldn't have mattered," Pearl says. "They never appreciate what you do anyway. No matter what I did, it was never enough. Even if I did it all, there was always something I hadn't done. I felt guilty all the time. That made me furious."

"I thought I was the only one who felt that way," the voice says thoughtfully.

I have been cut out of this conversation, Gretchen thinks, They're having a Mothers Convention and I'm ending up wrong again. "You want to hear about furious mothers. . . ," she begins, suddenly she realizes the time. "Oh my gosh," she says, "Get the library, Rita, it's time for the Gothic."

"I love Gothics," says the disembodied voice in the corner.

"Tonight's Gothic, children, is 'The Man In The Blue Ford. . . .' " There's the crackle of an antediluvian manila envelope being opened, fusty pages being drawn out.

Shock roars through Gretchen's body, she jumps up, "Turn that off, that's an evil story, That story degrades women. . . ." She reaches to turn the Museum radio off, a dripping arm locks with hers in an Indian wrestle over who'll control the dial, it's the stranger in the corner, "Who do you think you are," Gretchen says, "Barging into a private party, butting into my affairs," sweat drips down her face and body as she focuses on the blur, the stranger is surprisingly strong, the two women are nearly evenly matched, their hands slip and slide in the steam, piped-in organ music swells through the room, Daisy thinks of Jacob wrestling with the angel, I will not let thee go until thou bless me, the stone cuts into Gretchen's elbow but she is in top physical condition and has ire on her side, she feels the stranger's arm lose slight ground, Gretchen has the advantage, she can take her now, but suddenly the organ music fades, the announcer's voice begins, Gretchen just lets go, the stranger's arm practically breaks falling over on top. Gretchen sits down and folds her legs into lotus position. She is fatalistically resigned. Everything else in her life is crumbling, clearly it's the will of God, Kismet, cosmic fate that her greatest shame in the 9x12 manila envelope be broadcast publicly over the radio tonight, it's meant to happen, has to happen, it won't be the only punishment she gets for being sinful and/or ignoring the chain letter.

"Doggonit, Gretchen, why'd you just give up?" Pearl says.

"Que será será," Gretchen says, perspiration or tears rolling down her face.

" 'The Man In The Blue Ford' will be run without commercial interruption thanks to a grant from Roman Polanski."

HOLY VIRGIN OF VIRGINS
VIRGIN MOST PRUDENT
VIRGIN MOST VENERABLE
VIRGIN MOST RENOWNED
VIRGIN MOST POWERFUL
VIRGIN MOST MERCIFUL
VIRGIN MOST FAITHFUL. . . .
croon the Cardinals.

"Love that tenor," Rita says.

The Man In The Blue Ford

When Gretchen was nineteen-and-a-half, she lost her virginity. She lost it to a man who was thirty-four, an ex-con, had an ex-wife, had a common law wife, had a legal wife. It never occurred to Gretchen that anyone but she was responsible for her great shame.

The first day the man met Gretchen, he told her he could have her in bed before the summer was out. Gretchen was shocked. He brought her in nine days ahead of schedule.

August 21st.
Chicago, Illinois.

"When I get married, what will I tell my husband?" Gretchen asked. "If he doubts enough to ask, he'll never believe the answer," the man said. It was the only kind thing the man ever did for her.

·   ·   ·

268

Every evening for two months and twenty-one days, the man pursued, cajoled, teased, bullied, begged. Every morning, Gretchen went to Confession. "You were here yesterday," one priest said. "You're not taking this seriously." Gretchen would never again in her life take anything so seriously. "I'm not going to absolve you," the priest said. Gretchen's soul harrowed. Gretchen wept. Gretchen pleaded. Gretchen promised. The priest relented.

The next morning, Gretchen went into a different box.

"Why?" said the man every night. "I must save myself," Gretchen said every night. Gretchen spoke truth, but not the truth she meant. Gretchen was also going to save the man. Gretchen thought the man was St. Augustine and she was St. Monica. Gretchen had always had a vivid imagination.

The first time the man touched Gretchen's breast, she went into orbit. Gretchen had never been touched anyplace. She did not know that the man could have touched her nostril with about the same results.

After the breast, it was only a matter of time before the man was getting everything but.

Gretchen could not stop seeing the man. Gretchen stopped going to Confession.

Gretchen stopped praying to the Blessed Virgin and started praying to Mary Magdalene.

Gretchen stopped being a functioning part of a nationwide publicity tour for a new fiberglass discovery. What that boiled down to is that Gretchen stopped selling ironing board covers door-to-door.

Every morning, Gretchen's crew chief dropped her off. Every evening, Gretchen's crew chief picked her up. In-between, Gretchen hated herself.

One afternoon, Gretchen's crew chief saw her sitting on a park bench. Gretchen's crew chief had eyes in his head. "Cheer up, kid," he said, "it'll all work out." Gretchen took hope. Gretchen took comfort. Gretchen put her head on her crew chief's shoulder and sobbed.

Gretchen's crew chief put his hand on Gretchen's breast. "Sorry, kid," Gretchen's crew chief said, "it's just you got such a nice set." Gretchen knew she had reached the bottom.

Gretchen had mortal sins an inch thick on her soul. Gretchen was one truck hit away from Hell. Gretchen stood outside a long time gathering her courage to ring the bell. When the priest opened the door, Gretchen blurted out everything. The priest cleansed Gretchen. In that town, instead of sitting on park benches, Gretchen sat in the rectory. For three days, the priest asked Gretchen questions about the evenings. Often, Gretchen's cheeks flamed. On the fourth day, the priest blessed Gretchen and walked her to the door. At the door, he began rubbing up against her and making little moans. Gretchen learned that bottoms don't quit.

Gretchen had a white silk dress.
"Wear your white dress," the man said often.
Gretchen thought it was because of her dark hair and tan.

Gretchen began thinking of the relationship as a contest between good and evil. Gretchen had always had a gambling streak.

Gretchen found a packet of contraceptives in the man's pocket. Gretchen had never seen rubbers. Gretchen examined them closely before the anger hit her. In the bathroom, the man was singing in the shower: Gretchen was insulted, Gretchen was indignant: Fear of pregnancy was not a consideration in Gretchen's saving herself. Gretchen took all the rubbers and blew them up into long, pallid, obscene-looking balloons. Gretchen worked like a madwoman blowing, tying, hanging them all over the room: how dare he! The room began looking like a party. Gretchen began humming. Gretchen strung balloons across the mirror, the windows, they were waving from the bedstead. Gretchen was just hanging the last one from the ceiling light when the man came out. He stood deathly still. Gretchen stopped humming. Her heart turned over. "What are you doing?" the man said so softly it was menacing. "Those cost a buck apiece," he shouted. "Baby killer," Gretchen screamed and ran out the door.

Gretchen and the man and six others were in the restaurant. Gretchen was carrying on a fake, animated conversation with the others. The man flicked water at Gretchen with his spoon. Gretchen continued to ignore the man. The man flicked more water. "Really, isn't he childish?" Gretchen said to the others. The man flushed and flicked again. Everybody laughed. Gretchen picked up her water glass and threw it across the table. Everybody stopped laughing. The man blanched. Water ran down his face. He picked up his chocolate malted, reached across the table and slowly, deliberately, poured it over Gretchen's head. Everyone in Howard Johnson's stared. Gretchen's eyes never left the man while she mopped malted milk off her face, her hair, her clothes. Gretchen reached a new dimension of hate.

Gretchen and the man are parked in a blue Ford in the middle of a field at 3 AM. The man is angry and Gretchen is scared. She explains again, I wanta do it too, oh so bad I wanta do it, but I can't, can't you understand that, I can't. The man pins Gretchen's arms behind her, he forces her down on the seat WHAT MAKES YOU THINK YOU'RE SO GODDAM SPECIAL, IT'S JUST A HOLE, JUST A GODDAM HOLE. In a voice she has never used before but will use again, Gretchen says You can do anything you want as long as you don't hurt me too bad, Gretchen is afraid he is going to kill her. A red light swirls through the car, Jesus Christ, the man says. He pulls up his pants and walks back to the police car. Gretchen thinks about jumping out, but she is afraid of two men in an open field. The police car honks and drives away. The man chuckles, "I told him I was having a hard time getting my girl to come through," he says.

The man is a master salesman. He knows when to switch pitches. Albany, Rome, Utica, Troy, Rochester, Syracuse, Buffalo PLEASE PLEASE PLEASE PLEASE PLEASE

Gretchen runs away. Three days later, she comes back. Home is not the same once your breast has been touched.

Gretchen craved a present. Some little thing, some little tangible thing that'd be proof: Gretchen hinted even. "If I bought you anything," the man said, "it would cheapen you." That was an incremental impossibility.

Gretchen said there were ways to get his marriages straightened out so they could get married in the Church. Gretchen and the man sat in a rectory in his hometown. The priest looked up from the forms. "What about your common law wife?" The man laughed. "Oh yeh, I forgot about her." The man had also forgotten to mention her to Gretchen. The priest looked up again. "This says you're thirty-one.

271

How'd we go to school together and I'm thirty-four?" The man laughed again. "I forget these things, Padre." The priest's voice has an edge, "Don't you think this girl's a little young for you? Do you really think you'd be suited with a college girl who's obviously had a more conventional upbringing . . . ?" My God, Gretchen thought, Here it comes. It comes. "This is just some crazy idea of Gretchen's, I don't care if we ever get married, I JUST WANT TO FUCK HER."

At this time in history, children, the word fuck was not even allowed in books.

The priest throws the man out. The priest tells Gretchen, "He's a bum, he always was a bum." When Gretchen stops sobbing, she tells the priest, "Real love is sacrifice." The priest sighs.

Across the whole state of Indiana, one or two days in every fair-sized town, PLEASE PLEASE PLEASE PLEASE PLEASE PLEASE PLEASE PLEASE PLEASE PLEASE GRETCHEN.

It happened in Chicago. Gretchen has never been so tired, PLEASE GRETCHEN PLEASE Gretchen lets him put it in. Gretchen stares at the beige hotel wall and waits for the man to finish.

Gretchen counted all the aspirins she had. She called a physician from the Yellow Pages. "My friend just took nineteen aspirin," Gretchen says, "What should I do?" "She'll sleep a long time," the nurse says, "but it won't kill her." Gretchen hung up the phone, took the nineteen aspirin, and went to sleep for two days.

When Gretchen wakes up, the man says, "You'll get a real kick out of this movie." It is the first time the man has spent money on her. Gretchen feels she's earned it. "It'll cheer you up, honey," the man says. He is warm and gentle. Gretchen is already cheered up. The movie is "The Moon Is Blue." It's the story of an older man trying to seduce a younger girl. The man has seen the movie before. When the protagonist calls the ingenue "a professional virgin," the man chuckles and pokes Gretchen. Gretchen squirms. In the end, the ingenue saves herself.

Gretchen went home the next week. The first thing she did was put her white silk dress in the poor box. The second thing she did was take a nap.

.   .   .

In the next four years, Gretchen does everything but, but nobody else ever gets in. She marries the first man who does not beg. She is almost a virgin on her wedding night. Her husband does not ask.

The week before the wedding, the man calls. "Who knows?" he says. "Someday I may come knocking at your door and I'll come in and you and your doctor husband and I can all sit around talking about old times." "You do that," Gretchen says, "you just do that."

For the first two years of her marriage, Gretchen has nightmares, Please Please, she wakes up crying. Every time the doorbell rings, her heart constricts. By the fifth year, the nightmares are infrequent.

And there, my children, is another story of a time forever gone and always there. *Move on, please.*

    Rita wipes her eyes: she has laughed so hard she has cried.
    "It was sad," Pearl says.
    "It was funny too," Rita says.
    Rita's not the only one who laughed and each time Pearl was shocked. This often happens to Pearl: she earns her living by making people laugh and yet people continually shock her by laughing at unexpected places.

    You never laugh, a man says to Pearl.
    Say something funny, Pearl says.
    The man tells jokes. He tells wife jokes, mother-in-law jokes, nurse jokes, stewardess jokes, dumb blonde jokes, big tit jokes, ski bunny jokes, farmer's daughter jokes, secretary jokes, woman driver jokes, waitress jokes, chorus girl jokes, fat lady jokes, club lady jokes, old maid jokes, nymphomaniac jokes, Listen Pearl you think you got it bad I am so unlucky that if they sawed a woman in half I would get the part that eats. . . .
    Laugh? Pearl nearly died.
    Pearl the cat nearly dies twice.
    That night in her nightclub act she says, Listen you think you got it bad I am so unlucky that if they sawed a man in half I would get the part that eats. . . .
    The audience throws shot glasses, beer bottles, wine carafes, Pearl only escapes with her life because Patti the bartender hustles her out the kitchen exit.

. . .

"Most women can't keep a secret," Gretchen says, "but I kept that secret twenty-one years."

"You were so innocent," says the voice in the corner.

"I didn't know that until I heard the story aloud just now," Gretchen says.

Pearl braces for Gretchen to burst into tears, tries to think of a joke to lighten the tension, but Gretchen jumps up and yells, "Goddammit to Hell!"

"*Gretchen!*" all the women jump up.

"It wasn't *worth* keeping twenty-one years!" she says, she's in a fury, she begins doing deep knee bends.

"You sure do have a temper," says the voice in the corner. "You remind me a little of my daughter, her name is Gretchen too, I'm on my way to see her now, you might be able to help me find her, I've got some pictures of her in my suitcase, she's been in the newspaper four times, I'll show you when we go outside. She is so clever. I know I could have been interested in something if I'd thought about it. But *she* is the most beautiful, cleverest, brightest, most talented girl to ever come out of this one-horse town I live in, and I'm not just saying that because I'm her mother either, she always could run rings around any other girl ever lived. When she was growing up, I never could understand how any other girl ever beat her in anything. It didn't happen very often, but whenever she'd come home and say she won second or third place in something, I could barely ask the question without anger, half the time these things are fixed, and never ask it without surprise, to my core surprised, that *any* of those other girls who were just *girls* could be chosen over *my* daughter. . . ."

STORY: Angry And To Her Core Surprised Momma:
   Momma, I got a B, the daughter says.
   Who got A, Momma barely asks.
   Momma, I showed in the track meet.
   Who placed, Momma barely asks.
   Momma, I placed in the track meet.
   Who won, Momma barely asks.

The knee bends have stopped, someone has turned the Museum radio off, a tentative, puzzled "Ma?" has formed on lips, not making enough sound to get over the ssssstt of steam on rocks, the voice in the corner goes on, "She was just about perfect, I always say they gave me the wrong baby in the hospital. . . ."

"Don't say that," Gretchen snaps, "That's a terrible thing to say." Her Ma always says that, and Gretchen thinks her Ma is hating her; in

274

fact, Pearl, who's said that same thing herself a few times, could tell her that her Ma's hating herself.

"You're touchy, just like my Gretchen the cheerleader," the voice says. "Ask the simplest question you might get your head snapped off." In the stillness, the voice continues, "She did the strangest thing once. . . ."

Angry And To Her Core Surprised Momma Continued

The daughter was chosen Homecoming Queen, the daughter ran all the way home, Momma, Momma, the most wonderful thing happened, Momma, I was chosen attendant to the Homecoming Queen.

Who's Queen? Momma barely asks.

I am, the daughter said.

Over the sssstt comes a sigh. "I'm no dummy, I could see she was furious. She was telling me something, but to this day I don't know what." She sighs again. "Half the time you don't even know what you did wrong. The other half you know, but it's too late."

"Well I'll tell you what I was trying to tell you," Gretchen shouts, "That even a wonderful thing like my being attendant wouldn't please you!"

"Gretchen, is that you, that *is* you, Well what's the matter with you, Why should your being an attendant please either one of us?" Bridget shouts back. "In case you don't know it, you're a queen to your bones, and the only reason they wouldn't give it to you is because some mealy-mouthed girl who's got a face like a pan of milk has also got a big wheel father who belongs to the Country Club."

"Oh Ma, I'm only a queen to you," Gretchen says with disgust.

"I thought you said You never could please her," Pearl whispers in Gretchen's ear.

Gretchen's eyes puzzle, widen, puzzle again: she needs some time to think this all out, if her Ma sees her only as a queen, she's still got a problem, but it's a *different* problem from the one she thought she had. "Ma?" she says, her voice breaks, "Why didn't you ever tell me all this before?"

"One of us was always so mad, Gretchen," Bridget's voice breaks, "I didn't know how to begin."

"Oh Ma," Gretchen says, she gathers her courage and aims higher for both her Ma and herself and blurts, "Let's begin now."

Gretchen and her Ma embrace, tears stream down both their faces, simultaneously both say, "I love you," and just for the length of two heartbeats in their chambers, the sound reverberates in the steam room, crashes off the walls like waves in an ocean, rebounds off the rocks sssstt like flames in a furnace, rays in a mirror, echoes until it sounds like tens of thousands of mothers and tens of thousands of daughters all weeping and saying simultaneously, "I love you, let's begin now."

Gretchen's Ma opens her suitcase, the most wonderful aromas of chocolate cake and Shalimar and fresh snow come out, her face falls, "I've got hardly anything left, I thought Fred was bad but they really cleaned me out on the 20th City Block, those people were desperate." She has managed to hold onto Gretchen's favorites: peanut butter cookies, lemon meringue pie, chocolate fudge cake, butterscotch brownies, and a bag of Hershey's with almonds.

Everybody except Gretchen squeals with delight as Gretchen's Ma hands around goodies, "Uuuuuuhhhhhh," says Rita as Hershey cocoa fudge, bittersweet and gritty with sugar, melts in her mouth.

The smells draw Maggie closer to the bag, she peeks in. "My Gramma used to make chocolate cake," she says, "and she'd make me a little one in a pan that was all my own. I'd eat it hot right out of the oven without frosting."

"I got one of those in here someplace," Bridget says, she rummages around and produces a small steaming chocolate cake.

Maggie beams. "I don't want to be greedy, but I think I'll have one of those orange slices too."

"Eat, Eat," Bridget says.

"I'm giving up diets," Pearl says. "From now on, I'm going to eat anything I want in moderation." She takes a single chocolate carmel Blowout, and enjoys every one of its thousand calories, "Oof," she says, talking with her mouth full.

Gretchen takes one butterscotch brownie, one piece of chocolate cake, one peanut butter cookie, a day's workout worth, she puts a Hershey bar in her pocket for later.

"You don't like lemon meringue pie anymore, Gretchen?" her Ma asks.

"Ma," Gretchen bristles, then bites her tongue, and aims higher again. "Maybe tomorrow, Ma," she says.

"It's certainly lucky I left the trunk at the front gate," Gretchen's Ma says.

"Last one in is Phyllis Schlafly," Pearl yells, spreads her arms with nary a thought about her armpit hair, and does a perfect swan dive off the high board. When she surfaces, everyone cavorts in the water.

Maggie cheers herself along in dolphin, *feels* sleek as a dolphin as she backstroke races Rita the length of the pool.

276

Daisy dives for obscure objects at the bottom of the pool.

Down toward the shallow end, Gretchen and her Ma Bridget play a water game that Bridget said Gretchen used to love when she was a little girl, Gretchen pretends she remembers, they take turns burbling lyrics underneath the water, trying to guess the other's song, Gretchen's glad they don't have to talk. She can't bear to look at her mother's naked body, she knows it's collapsed and withered, scabby, purulent, rotting, Bridget bounces around in the water like Flipper the seal, she doesn't look anything like Gretchen thought she would, for one thing she's a foot shorter, isn't that odd, and Gretchen notes with a certain puzzlement and relief the way her Ma casually carries her wrinkles and stretch marks and broken capillaries and Caesarian scar like an old war-horse or, Gretchen thinks the queerest thing, like an old war hero, Bridget starts a bawdy song, "Oh Motherrr," Gretchen says, but she's half embarrassed, one sixteenth amused, and seven sixteenths feeling grown up.

Pearl laughs out loud with pleasure. She feels like a girl again in this respect: she is filled with a sense of possibility. She remembers a girl wondering countless times: What will I be doing next year, in two years, five? She remembers never wondering that again after she married; she knew what she'd be doing in two, five, fifteen years, the house might change, but the life wouldn't: she'd be doing time. Pearl dives again from the high board, and at the bottom stands on her head to see how long she can stand under.

When all the cavorting calms down, the women move next door to the room that adjoins the showers and Daisy tells them something about themselves that she's known a long time:

Gretchen carries her Ma
Pearl carries her Daddy
Meg carries her Uncle
Maggie carries her Gramma
Rita carries her cousin
Daisy carries her entire family
Quasi carries the whole kit and kaboodle.

"You've caught these people at times of their lives that are past," Daisy says, "and if you stop them there, you also stop yourself. Bury them or let them move on."

Daisy the atheist leads the prayer: "On this night of dyings and endings, let us lay the family to rest."

Daisy holds out her hand to Bridget, "If you would give us all your blessing. . . ."

Bridget starts with Gretchen, goes to each woman in turn, "If you would give me yours. . . ."

Everybody weeps and laughs and hugs and kisses.

Daisy hasn't seen so much spontaneous affection since the 60's peace marches.

"I want to go to Confession," Maggie says.

"Shoot," Rita says.

Gretchen's shocked, "You can't have women priests because men would never go to Confession to them," she says.

Bridget chuckles, Rita starts laughing and can't stop. Even though it's forbidden in Deuteronomy, Rita often takes men twice by the secrets. Rita has personally heard 17,438 men's confessions I'M SCARED I'M LONELY I DON'T FEEL ANYTHING I WANT TO BE LOVED I WANT TO BE LOOKED UP TO I'VE DONE TERRIBLE THINGS TO WOMEN "Shh, Shh," Rita says, forgiving men things they cannot forgive themselves. Rita laughs so hard tears roll down her cheeks, but she can't say anything because she's bound to secrecy.

"I'm a horrible person," Maggie blubbers.

"You have no idea."

"You'll all hate me."

"You'll think I'm the most dis-gusting. . . ."

"Condense, Maggie," Pearl says.

"The face in the mirror was Quasi!" Maggie blurts.

This confession produces the greatest dud since mini-pads for daily wear.

"YOU DON'T UNDERSTAND," Maggie shouts, "I SOLD MY SOUL TO THE DEVIL."

Everyone tries to rise to the occasion, but there's a distinct half-heartedness to the little clicks and murmurs: there's not a woman present who hasn't done her share of business with the devil.

Pearl is agog. "That's the *worst* thing you ever did? *Forgive* yourself, Maggie, forgive yourself."

Daisy leads the absolution and everyone takes a line:

Forgive yourself

    for sucking Anna Guarnaschelli's buds when you were eleven
    for losing your virginity at nineteen
    for deceiving your husband
    for hating your mother
    for abusing your daughter

for you were innocent in 1 and 2,
you saw no alternative in 3,
you have done penance thrice over for 4 and 5.

Forgive yourself for not being perfect, Daisy says.

AMEN, the women say.

Then they all have a good cry to wash away the guilts, shames, regrets, remorses dumped in interior Love Canals to lay in wait, toxic and radioactive, to waste the land for generations untold.

Go in peace, Daisy says.

Only Rita notices the dove in the rafters, she thinks it's a pigeon and hopes it doesn't get nifty on her. Only Daisy sees the small tongues of flame that appear over each of their heads as they race out for the showers.

Daisy stops off at Kimiko's for a quick massage, but she's not around and a small sign on the door says in elegant calligraphy:

MOUNTAIN MOVING DAY IS COMING/
ALL SLEEPING WOMEN NOW AWAKE AND MOVE.
                    Yosano Akiko, 1911, & Buffalo Ro-san

As Daisy comes in to tell them about Kimiko's sign, her beeper goes off. She dresses in a flash, grabs a piece of pineapple upside down cake from Bridget's suitcase, and says, "I'll see you all back at the hotel. Pack up everything we need, and check to see how Meg's doing."

279

58

Meg wears earphones confiscated with the tape deck, sings along with the tape, and dances barefoot. "I think I like the tango best," she says in an Argentinian accent to her mirror image who snaps her fingers and says, "Olé," she punches the tape deck button at random again, her hips start to undulate, "Boogie's kinda nice," she winks at herself, "Here I come, lean and mean, Watch out Rita," she giggles, undulates some more.

She takes the earphones off, but still hears the music, over and over and over again as she sambas next door to check on Peg O' My Heart. With exquisite care, she brushes a lock of hair back off the sleeping child's forehead, heat of soft flesh goes into her fingertips flows back out, her fingers move in slow motion across velvet soft skin and hair, if she died this minute she'd die happy.

Suddenly Meg remembers Quasi. Her face puzzles, "She's not the enemy. Why would I want to pull her plug? No wonder Daisy was mad at me." She shakes her finger at her mirror image, "Naughty girl," and giggles. Well, she'll fix it up, first thing tomorrow she'll talk with Daisy. "I'll tell her, there'll be some changes made today." Meg snaps her fingers and breaks into a husky whiskey torch,
" 'I'm goin' to change my way of livin'/ if that ain't enough/
Then I'll even change the way that I strut my stuff/
My walk will be different, my talk, and my name. . . .
But first," Meg puts her finger to her lips and says "Shhh" to her mirror image, "I've got something to do."

Meg has not forgotten about the explosives set on a timer, "You think this stuff rots your brain," she giggles, things are crystal clear inside the haze, but she is being super cautious anyway. She goes over the list mentally to prove this: I remembered to use the tape deck instead of the radio or the stereo so I wouldn't wake up Peg O' My Heart, I remembered to check Peg O' My Heart, I made sure I blew out the matches, I have not forgotten about the explosives set on a timer. . . . Plenty of time to dismantle the explosives, that's the wonderful thing about this stuff, all the time in the world and time enough for every-thing, "First things first," she whispers to herself.

The Shadow tiptoes down the stairs, moves through the hall, across the living room to Daisy's table, and giggles. She writes Yes on a slip of paper, admires the remarkable Art Deco curlicues contained in her script, she opens the ballot box, what an interesting cigar box this is, takes out all the votes and counts them. The tally is:

Daisy—Yes
Rita—Yes
Pearl—Yes
Gretchen—No
Maggie—No
Meg—No

"Meg—*Yes*," Meg says slowly and precisely as she tears up her old vote and puts her new vote in.

"That's odd." There are still two votes left. She opens the first: Maude Gonne—Yes.

"That devil," Meg says. Rita, acclaiming her Irish heritage, has stuffed the ballot box. "But what's this?"

The final vote is:
Buffalo Rose—Yes.

Quasi wins by a landslide.

But justice doesn't always triumph, and Meg's timing is off, her mischief and Maggie's already done.

59

Father Valentine enters Quasi's room. She worries for a moment that the silver-haired doctor will recognize her but he merely looks at the roman collar with distaste and thinks, Episcopalians have just gotten tacky with this equal crap. Two male nurses look at each other and mouth, Lezz. Fr. Valentine swings the incense censer in the doctor's direction, "I've come to administer Extreme Unction."

"You're too late, Father. She's dead."

Daisy is riveted with shock.

"She can't be dead," Fr. Valentine gets out.

The doctor shrugs. "See for yourself."

Above her head, the EEG needle traces flat, Quasi lies on her side in a fetal position, she does not look at peace. There is no breath, no evidence of spirit, she is, by any measure that counts, dead. Daisy will not accept this obvious fact; a fury fills her. You cannot die, she thinks, *I will not let you give up,* Daisy is furious at the injustice of Quasi's life being so terrible she seeks relief by ending it. She sets the censer down, bends over her and hisses, "Quasi, wake up." High above the bed, Quasi floats at ceiling level, looks down at Daisy and at her lifeless body. Only an umbilical cord connects her to the inert body and it is gradually resorbing, she feels the most wonderful sense of release, but Daisy begins pulling the cord, Quasi resists, Daisy pulls harder, they play tug of war, Quasi's amused and, in a detached way, momentarily touched by Daisy's concern. Daisy senses movement, that somewhere deep inside Quasi, something stirs, yearns, reaches to life, she strains with Quasi, reaches deep deeper to touch the pulse, the connection between them, "You *will* get better," she says. All the outward signs stay the same, but she senses Quasi can hear her, "You *will* get better," she repeats, "Don't give up hope," she's getting through to Quasi, she's certain now: she puts her hands on Quasi's hump, and says, "Live Live Live Live Live Live," "Now listen here," the silver-haired doctor starts over to restrain her, kicks over the censer, burns a hole in his new fawn wool slacks, "Shit," the room fills with incense, he coughs, a fly buzzes, throbs like a 747, an ancient voice whines, "I'm an old man, I don't have the energy for this," "Live Live Live," Daisy's voice rivets the room, a tremendous explosion rends the air.

Artillery, cannons, bombs, shells, pinwheels shoot simultaneously, the earth shakes, temples crash, rocks split, tombs open, saints walk, the explosions are nonstop thunder, streaks of flashing light fill the hospital room, illuminate an old man stamping his feet through the floor like Rumpelstiltskin, a magnificent avenging angel, her face is fierce, her arms raise, the silver-haired doctor, his hair yellow in the blazing light, cowers from her force, Maria Onesti RN inclines toward Daisy with awe, "QUASI COME FORTH," Daisy cries in a loud voice.

"And she that was dead came forth," recites Maria Onesti, "bound hand and foot with graveclothes, her face bound with linen, and Jesus saith unto them. . . ."

"LOOSE HER AND LET HER GO," commands Daisy.

The cord snaps, Quasi hits the bed like a ton of bricks, the room is suffused with the smell of cinnamon and clove, a tear rolls down Quasi's cheek, the riot of light is dazzling, Quasi opens her eyes.

A mile away, Pearl, Maggie, Rita, Gretchen, and Bridget ooh and ahh the spectacular fireworks display.

"It's a laser artist's rendition of multiple orgasm," Rita says, "Ooooh I like the pinwheels best."

"It's an early bird Memorial Day celebration," Gretchen says to her Ma Bridget, "Ahh, this is the best year ever."

Meg looks out her window, places her hand over her heart, and sings:
"In the rocket's red glare/
The bombs bursting in air/
Gave proof. . . .
Mother of God," she says, "This is *really* good stuff."

ITE MISSA EST

60

Pearl opens her eyes, instantly alert, excited. I have come out of a twelve-year purification, she thinks. Whatever's coming, she knows she has the strength and energy to deal with it. She takes her diary from the side table, makes an entry, "5 minutes to 6 AM, So far so good," jumps out of bed, eager to see what the day will bring.

Gretchen wakes up feeling she has just swum the English Channel. Her first thought is, My Ma has changed a lot, her second thought is, What will become of us all? She is scared but tells herself to trust Daisy who won't abandon them. She begins her morning limbers, but as she touches her head to her knees, the sadness hits: today she leaves behind the most rewarding work she will ever have. She does ten extra minutes of vigorous exercise and takes a cold shower. From her hope chest, she draws out a blue tissue paper parcel, sets it carefully on the bed. She dresses in a red, white, and blue striped miniskirt and a red skimpy T-shirt speckled with tiny white stars: her Memorial Day uniform. Slowly she unwraps the tissue paper, uncovers a pair of white kid boots, runs her fingers over the leather imported from Italy. The handmade boots have been worn only once for the Museum Visit of Bonny Prince Charles who gave Gretchen the greatest thrill of her life by kissing her on the cheek, she didn't wash the spot for a day and a half and then only to prevent clogged pores. With tears in her eyes, Gretchen sits on the bed, it sloshes gently, comforting her, she draws on the kid leather boots. In front of the mirror, she examines herself as relentlessly as a Navy Captain doing a white gloved inspection of his wife's housework, takes a deep breath, stands erect, and says to herself, Whatever happens, Remember, you are a queen.

A rock singer on Meg's clock radio wails, "Man, I really feel like a woman today." Meg bops her way into the shower.

· · ·

Mon Dieu, Maggie says, there are two on her bed: Maggie and her head.

She lies perfectly motionless: she thinks the rest of her is okay, but she can't get past her head to check around.

Ohhhhhhhhhhhhhhhhhhhhhhhh, she moans in Hebrew, she groans in Italian, she curses in Arabic.

In Gaelic, she vows, I am going on the wagon.

Except for special occasions, *da, nyet,* she hedges in Russian.

She carries her body like a broken bird to the shower and, in slow motion, squints her eyes, sets the Carnal, Inc. showerhead on the red arrow marked GO FOR BROKE, raises her face so she's directly under the tap, and goes for broke.

Rita yawns   s t r e t c h e s
What a wonderful morning
                        eases out of bed
                                    glides over to the window
                        lifts her face to the sun.

Quasi awakens, the radio is playing You made me love you/ I didn't wanna do it/ I didn't wanna do it/ You made me want you/ And all the time you knew it. . . "Ya dog ya always knew it," Quasi sings, Maria Onesti smiles, she has sat with Quasi all night long, "Welcome back," she says.

Quasi asks her to write something down for her.

"Did your life pass before your eyes?" she asks.

"You might say that," Quasi says.

"What language is she speaking?" another nurse asks, but Maria Onesti's pencil is already flying across the page.

Quasi tells a tale that is a wondrous thing indeed.

Only a minuscule cord, a thread really, connects her to her body. She has climbed up that cord hand over hand moving through a dark tunnel toward the most radiant light. It is the most beautiful instant in the world when she comes out of that body and floats above. She has a sense of timelessness, an awareness of her own death, and a strong sense of reality. She knows everything that is going on, she can see everything, she reads her EEG, it doesn't look good, a silver-haired doctor talks to another doctor about the price of gold, it doesn't look good, she feels no physical or psychic pain, she is suffused with a feeling of tranquility, even delight. Then Daisy comes in, suddenly Daisy grabs hold of her cord and begins pulling her down, she resists Daisy's pull, No, No, this is so beautiful, let me go, but Daisy pulls harder, hand over hand Daisy pulls and she pulls the other way but all of a sudden she feels a tremen-

288

dous weight, a stillness at the soul's center anchoring her, she sees Daisy is not going to give up, she values her, she is of worth to her, yes, she loves her, with all her strength Daisy gives one last humongous pull: a pull infinitely more powerful than just wanting respite and Quasi returns to the land of the living.

Daisy hasn't gone to bed yet. In the kitchen, she whips up a little breakfast.

"Eggs Benedict and rum punch?" Pearl asks.

"You never know when you'll find a place to stop for lunch," Daisy says, she turns around, "Well, look at you."

Pearl's hair is washed squeaky clean, her buff-puffed face glows with color, but it's her clothes that are special this morning. "Like my new duds?", she pirouettes so Daisy can admire all sides, "I bought them that day I went shopping for my daughters, I've been saving them for something special, I tell you, Daisy, something's coming, I can feel it, we have turned a corner, I can come out of the cloister and put my hairshirts in mothballs, whatever I've been honing myself for is ready to be tested. The boots I got on sale at Bergers," she holds up one foot, "Aren't they the most beautiful cowgirl boots you've ever seen, one hundred sixty-nine buckerinos and I got them on third markdown, sixty-nine dollars, that's how I knew they were supposed to be mine, 69's my lucky number," she strikes a stance in her yellow silk blouse, Daisy's laugh eggs her on, "Cast your peepers at my dee-signer pants," she puts her hands on her hips and wiggles, "I'm not going to tell you how much I paid for them, I paid a bundle but I took the name off, What do I want somebody else's name on my clothes for, What if I lose them and they return them to that person, all I want is that fit around my butt, look pretty good, huh?" she wiggles again.

"You look gorgeous," Daisy says and hugs her.

Meg comes in humming, " 'I could have danced all night, I could have. . . .' Wheet whio," she wolf whistles at Pearl.

"You don't look so bad yourself, Officer," Pearl says and salutes Meg, who has on her dress uniform, her diamond studded holster, her silver filigree gun, her hat tilted cockily over one eye.

Rita enters. She wears a gas station attendant coverall and makes it look like haute couture. Anyone with senses can figure out she has nothing on underneath, but she leaves no button undone, no zipper plunges.

"One thing I admire about you, Rita," Pearl says, "is that when you wear clothes, you leave them on."

"Why bother otherwise?" Rita says.

Maggie walks in slowly, carrying her head on the afterbeat of her body. "Is this okay?" she asks clearly in English so she won't have to translate. She wears a daisy yellow mid-calf length skirt, and a matching angora sweater with a tiny MOTR logo embroidered in seed pearls.

"You look beautiful," Gretchen says.

"You both look beautiful," Daisy says, who doesn't look like any slouch herself in a midnight blue tux made of sweatshirt material, a tiny enamel butterfly stickpin on her lapel.

"What a beautiful pin," Rita says, and Daisy hears her pal on an island say, You are a butterfly, Daisy, when he gives it to her.

Gretchen's Ma Bridget comes in, dips her head and takes a satisfying sniff of the flowers in the center of the table. The kitchen is a riot of fresh flowers: Bridget has been out for an early morning walk and stopped at a few gardens along the way. Gretchen looks at the flowers and at her Ma suspiciously; Bridget's face is bland, "Morning, darlin'."

"Morning, Ma. Did you sleep well?"

"Like a top."

"Where's Peg O' My Heart?" Daisy asks.

"Sleeping in," Meg says. She doesn't say anything about the sleepwalking.

"You've done a good job with her, Meg," Daisy says.

Meg feels like she's just won the lottery.

"The news will keep till we eat," Daisy says. "We give thanks that we are all well, and together, and have good food. Happy are they who are called to this table."

"*Bon Appetit*," Maggie says.

"I'll try some of that funny looking jam," Gretchen's Ma Bridget says, "How about you, Gretchen?"

"No sugar, Gretch," Daisy says quickly, "hi-pro, the newest thing at the co-op."

"You're like me, Gretchen," Gretchen's Ma Bridget says as she spreads her muffin. "Gretchen and I are never afraid to try new things," she explains to the others, "we kinda like things that are a little off the beaten path. Of course," she turns to Gretchen again, "you and I have always been different from most of the people we know. . . ."

"Wha. . . ?" Gretchen begins, but then it dawns on her that her Ma is claiming her.

"Of course, Gretchen has to watch what she eats because of being an athlete," Gretchen's Ma Bridget says. "I'm glad that part of my life is over. But I do have to tell you that Gretchen comes by a little of her ability naturally. Of course I was never a *trained* athlete like she is, the

290

opportunities were not the same then, but I *was* the only girl to ever have black hockey skates, I gave the boys a run for their money, I can tell you."

"I guess one spoonful won't hurt," Gretchen says, her Ma Bridget beams.

"It's strange, but not unpleasant," Gretchen says as she tastes the jam.

Pearl reads the jam label: 'Consciousness III Chutney,' You've gone too far this time, Daisy."

After the table is cleared and everyone has her second cup of coffee, Daisy says, "I have two announcements. You all know what they are, but I want to make it formal."

One of the things the women love about Daisy is that she makes ritual and ceremony at the drop of a hat. Daisy knows that one of the greatest deprivations women suffer is:

Exclusion From Ceremonies

> Men on the altar
> wearing gowns
> sprinkling the incense
> consecrating the bread
> giving the blessing
> saying the words
>
> Men in the courts
> wearing gowns
> pounding the gavel
> pronouncing the verdicts
> saying the words
>
> Men around the tribal fire
> wearing make-up
> chanting the chant
> dancing the dance
> saying the words
>
> Men in the huts
> making the cut
> Men in the hoods
> passing the flame
> Men in the huddle
> calling the plays
> Men at the head
> carving the meat

Men at the corner
telling the jokes

Men wherever women are not allowed
saying the words
Men wherever women make up the audience
saying the words.

Every woman alive knows exclusion from ceremonies. Meg knows.

EXCLUSION FROM CEREMONIES: When Meg's Uncle dies, she wants to be a pallbearer, she wants to accompany her Uncle on that last walk, to bear guard, witness, and respect. We know you mean well, they say, but a woman pallbearer does not show respect for women: they mean it does not show respect for men, dead or alive. Meg's place is taken by decrepit old men whose social outings are limited to funerals. They dig them out of tombs, stuff them into bedraggled Knights of Columbus uniforms, prop them against the casket with young men to bolster them: Who's in the box?, one young man says before they start down the aisle, Some old geezer, says the other. Tears roll down Meg's cheeks as her beloved Uncle is borne down the aisle by male strangers. Her eyes dry when she remembers that if her Uncle were alive, the odds'd run 60-40 he'd feel a woman pallbearer was a final insult instead of tribute.

Daisy says: "The first and most important announcement is: Quasi will live."

After a slight pause, Pearl asks the question everybody thinks: "Will she be a veggie?"

"After a great deal of remedial work, she'll regain her powers," Daisy says. "She will have a genuine life," she says with such intensity the words ring inside each of the listening women, *a genuine life* resonates like a whisper a beckon in every corner of their being, gooseflesh rises on their skin, the edges of old forgotten dreams yearnings surface, the excitement builds until all speak at once, "That's wonderful, I'm so happy," and each, former friend or foe of Quasi it matters no more, *is* genuinely happy, feels that Quasi's recovery in some way not understood enhances them, increases their chances, "Lucky duck," Gretchen says, cartwheels around the table, feels to her toes she celebrates her own good luck.

When everybody settles back down, Daisy says: "The Museum Of The Revolution in Buffalo, New York, has closed its doors."

Everybody knows it, but hearing the death read aloud is painful.

"Did they just take it?" Maggie asks.

"Not exactly," Daisy says.

"Did you sell it?" Gretchen asks.

"Not exactly," Daisy says.

"My gosh, you didn't just give it away?" Rita says.

"This sounds like a Chippewa Street bust," Meg says.

"Hey, that's a great joke, Meg. I'm going to steal that," Pearl says.

Meg, who hadn't been making a joke, is pleased as punch. "I authorize you to do that," she says.

"I traded it," Daisy says.

The women are speechless: What could she possibly trade the Museum for?

"We're not passive victims," Daisy says. "We have power. We can deal. We had something the City Fathers wanted very much: our absence. I wanted something too, so we struck a bargain. I traded the Museum for something better."

Gretchen looks sadly at her white kid boots: "What could possibly be better than the Museum and this wonderful house?"

Daisy glances around at the elaborate furnishings. "Heartbreak Hotel has served its purpose," she says, "but I've been thinking of moving for some time." She waves her hand, "We don't need it anymore."

"What will we do?" Gretchen asks. "Where will we go?"

"It's kind of a surprise," Daisy says. "Gather up your stuff, there's not much time." She gathers up the linen napkins hand embroidered by nuns in Spain and sticks them in a carton by the door.

"Should we do the dishes?" Maggie asks.

"Leave them for the City Fathers," Daisy says.

Meg's scream stops everybody in her tracks. No one has ever heard Meg scream.

"She's gone." Meg's face is ashen.

The yellow bed is made up without a mark.

The women fan out: search the basement, first, second, third floors, attic wings, a large room on the top floor empty except for a disconnected pink telephone, cubbies, nooks, crannies, trunks, abandoned refrigerators, their hearts are in their mouths as they look around and under and into, call her sweet name.

The cream curdles, the fire refuses to light, there are no birds: Peg O' My Heart is gone.

"I was going to introduce her to my Ma," Gretchen says.

"I was going to ask her to visit me," Maggie says. "I wanted to show her my doll and tell her about my Gramma."

"I was going to tell her that nowadays a good family is hard to find, and if she has one or gets one, hang onto it," Pearl says.

"I was going to tell her that work is important because it has meaning or it searches for meaning, but it never takes the place of people," Daisy says.

"I wanted to tell her to love her body love herself," Rita says.

"I was going to teach her champion jacks, in the basket, and around the world. . . ." Meg stands looking at the jacks in her hand, and tears roll down her cheeks. Meg is crying for her own loss.

"We must have faith that she'll figure out all these things and more," Daisy says. She touches Meg's hand. "It's time to go."

The women gather in the large hall. Maggie, who only had to unpack her diphtheria doll, arrives first. She stands looking up at the *quasi modo* tapestry, Bridget touches her on the shoulder, she jumps nearly to the wooden beam.

"My dear," Bridget says, "I hope you don't mind if I speak frankly, but I think you're hitting the sauce too much. I saw you on the street last night and you were sicker than a dog, poor thing, and in the Steam Room you were not exactly in A-1 condition. This morning, your head is coming along after your body. I have been where your head is, and I can tell you, darlin', it's not worth the trip."

"It occurred to me in the shower this morning," Maggie says, "that if I want seven good years, or *any* good years, I better start thinking along those same lines myself. I appreciate your words."

Rita arrives with her small sculpture of two girls jumping rope, Meg her tintype of the old women, Pearl her grandmother's bracelet, Daisy chooses her butterfly pin over her shell, Meg cops the shell and sticks it into her pocket, she might check out an island sometime, maybe one of those Club Med places, Gretchen has her watch, Bridget shows them all her Gramma charm bracelet.

"We take our treasures," Daisy says. "We'll leave our regrets and sadnesses behind. They'll only slow us down where we're going."

"I've got one I'm glad to get rid of," Pearl says. She tosses into the brass spittoon

"The sadness of wearing countless sailors' caps at a sassy angle, but never being a sailor at sea."

"Never being Captain of the police force," Meg says.

"Never being an acolyte," Gretchen says.

"A stowaway on a frigate," Rita says.

"Playing for the Sabres," Gretchen's Ma Bridget says.

294

They all begin speaking at once:
"Not
getting the motorbike
hitchhiking cross country
roaming the streets on a summer's eve
staying out all night with the girls
saving the trains
being a cowboy
working on the Alaskan pipeline
climbing Mt. Everest
having the joy of battle
IF THERE ARE ANY MEN WHO ARE FIGHTERS IN THIS HALL, I TELL YOU,
GENTLEMEN, SAYS EMMALINE PANKHURST TO A PACKED HOUSE AT MADISON
SQUARE GARDEN IN 1913, THAT AMONGST THE OTHER GOOD THINGS THAT
YOU, CONSCIOUSLY OR UNCONSCIOUSLY, HAVE KEPT FROM WOMEN, YOU
HAVE KEPT THE JOY OF BATTLE.
"Ahem," Daisy says. "About that last one. . ."
She opens the door.

Primary colors blast the eye: the color renders them speechless. The
caravan stretches as far as the eye can see, the mind imagine, the designs
are fantastic, the music the trumpets blare, trombones slide, the big bass
drums TA RA TA BOOMDEAY, Gretchen is the first to understand,
her eyes light up, "It's the Big Time!", she says, she high-steps down the
front porch, flips to the street, stretches out her hands, catches the two
flaming batons tossed from the top of the supply wagon, and to the
music of the Women's Drum and Fife Band, twirls her way to take her
place in front.
    "There's no going back for us," Daisy says. She locks the door of
Heartbreak Hotel with exquisite finality, tosses the key into the bushes,
"Oops," she says, turns around, waves to Angie Lopez and her family,
grins at Pearl, "You like it?"
    "It's gorgeous," Pearl says. "What is it?"
    "We're taking the show on the road."
    Every Museum exhibit has been carefully packed: there are camp-
ers, semis, railroad cars, army convoys, six Sherman tanks, helicopters,
a carillon, a red, white, and blue ambulance with Quasi and Maria
Onesti RN, a Ticketron, a carousel, clowns, stilt walkers, trapeze artists,
color guards of every color, a full-size replica of the Statue of Liberty,
precision units, gas balloons, streamers, loudspeakers, ponies, elephants,
tigers, "I want to be the lion tamer," Gretchen's Ma Bridget says, One

of the guides throws Daisy a top hat, she snaps it open, puts it on, Everybody cheers, flags fly from every nation, the cannon shoots off non-stop, confetti and ticker tape rain, rainbows form above, Daisy blows her whistle for silence, the angels bend toward earth to hear.

The priest blesses the caravan, rolls the r's with one of her favorite Irish blessings: "Shor and may there be a road before you, darlin's, and it bordered with Buffalo Roses, the likes of which have n'er been smelt nor seen before, for the warm fine color and the great sweetness that is on them." Rita breathes to her toes, clove and cinnamon, Mmmmmmmmmmmm, Maggie stares in wonderment at the dazzle, all of a sudden realizes the light is brilliant, she's not wearing her shades, the light is not hurting her eyes, I'm through with the darkness, she thinks, "Lux perpetua luceat eis," she says, translates, "Let perpetual light shine upon them."

A spot hits Daisy, "Ladies and Gentlemen," she says, "Welcome to the Museum Of The Revolution!"

A shower of pamphlets falls from one of the helicopters, everybody cheers again, Daisy picks one up, "Here's the brochure," she says and reads aloud: THE MUSEUM OF THE REVOLUTION IS WHERE YOU TAKE THE LITTLE CHILDREN AND SHOW THEM GIRDLES AND MINISKIRTS AND GARTER BELTS AND SILICONED BREASTS AND FALSE FINGERNAILS AND RUBBER ASSES AND FOOTBINDING SHOES AND SEXIST REMARKS AND STEREOTYPED TEXTBOOKS AND PORNOGRAPHY AND ALL THE WOMEN WHO DIED IN PREGNANCY AND ABORTION AND CHILDBIRTH AND THE MONSTER SIDESHOW FEATURING CONTRACEPTIVE RESEARCHERS AND BATTERED BABIES AND THE VIRGIN BIRTH AND ALL THE NUNS WHO MAKE THE VESTMENTS ONLY MEN WEAR AND GANGSTERS' MOLLS AND KEWPIE DOLLS AND LAUNCELOT AND GUINEVERE AND JOAN CRAWFORD AND CAN CAN GIRLS AND SUFFRAGETTES AND SUF-FRAGISTS AND TOMBOYS AND SISSIES AND GYPSY ROSE LEE AND JACQUELINE KENNEDY AND MAIDEN NAMES AND MARRIED NAMES AND THE SIN OF IN-CURIOSITY ABOUT FEMALE PHYSIOLOGY AND TONI HOME PERMANENTS AND WOLF WHISTLES AND SWEET SIXTEEN PARTIES AND ALL THE PEOPLE WHO SWEAR MAN MEANS WOMAN AND PATRICIA "PATTY" HEARST AND KITTY GENOVESE AND HELEN HAGNES MINTIKS AND BELLYGRAMS AND STAG SHOWS AND SLAVE TRADE AND BROTHELS AND BOXING AND FOOTBALL WIDOWS AND ROSEMARY WOODS AND ELIZABETH RAY AND ALL THE WOMEN WHO DO SIDESHOW ACTS FOR THE POWERS IN CENTER RING AND DATES AND BLIND DATES AND COMPUTER MATCHMAKERS AND MIXERS AND SORORITIES AND FRATERNITIES AND WICCA AND THE GREAT GODDESS AND SUTTEES AND HAREMS AND BRIDAL VEILS AND BARBIE DOLLS AND MOTHER'S DAY AND FATHER'S DAY AND THE FAT LADY IN THE CIRCUS AND ALL FAT PEOPLE AND LADY DI'S TRAIN AND ILLITERATE GIRLS WHO MAKE DESIGNER CLOTHES IN HONG KONG AND YOUNG GIRLS BLUSHING AND FEMALE PRONOUNS ADDED IN

PARENTHESES AND IRISH SONS GIVEN TO THE PRIESTHOOD AT BIRTH AND
FEMALE INFANTICIDE AND GANG BANGS AND DATE RAPES AND ANOREXIA
NERVOSA AND VAGINAL SPRAY AND ALL THE WOMEN WHO'VE BEEN LIVING
ALTARS FOR BLACK MASSES AND ANKLE BRACELETS AND PAIN AND WASTE
AND TRAGEDY AND SAY, LOOK CLOSELY AND CAREFULLY, CHILDREN, THIS IS
HOW IT USED TO BE.

"You forgot mother and daughter dresses," Gretchen says.

"And Martha Mitchell," Maggie says.

"And all the men who debased Marilyn Monroe," Rita says.

"And all the children who think they're the cause of their mother's unhappiness," Pearl says.

"And the whole island of Sicily," Meg says.

"Oh Shoot, I forgot to leave the spaces for people to fill in all the things I forgot," Daisy says. "I, I. . . ."

"She's coming to, Doctor, She's coming to, It's a miracle, Margaret can you hear me, you're going to be okay, Margaret."

"I hear you," Margaret says.

THE BLESSING

Gather Ye Buffalo Rosebuds While Ye May

61

Sun streams into the hospital room. It's an extraordinary day: one of the seven days the sun shines in Buffalo. Outside the window, the blue sky is filled with colors: the Eggert Road School Balloon Launch has just released seven thousand balloons, each carrying a message. The children's cheers still reverberate in the atmosphere. In the distance, band music is playing. Inside the room, everything is bathed in sunlight, yet startlingly clear: the group around the bed, the woman in the bed, the white gown, white bandages, white plaster, white linens and, on the bedside table, a splotch of freshly picked garden flowers.

The tableau breaks, sun motes scatter as Margaret Valentine, her arms and legs in full casts, wiggles the tips of her fingers. "I've never felt so whole," she says.

Her family roars.

Clustered around her are her husband, daughters, mother, they're holding onto fingers, toes, stroking her cropped hair, one kid has a hold of her earlobe with two fingers and holds the morning paper in her other hand. "You made the front page, Ma," she says, she reads aloud.

Woman's Recovery Called 'Miracle'

Margaret Valentine was taken out of Intensive Care at Our Lady of Victory Hospital yesterday, and reunited with her family. "A miracle recovery, I've never seen anything like it," said a silver-haired doctor who declined to give his name.

The curator, well-known to history buffs for the quality of her small Pioneer Women Museum on the outskirts of Buffalo, was on Grand Island preparing a model for the Museum's enlargement when she suffered grave injuries in a hit and run accident. . . .

The girl stops reading. For a moment, the tableau freezes again, the only sound in the room the band music coming in through the open window.

"Memorial Day," Margaret Valentine says thoughtfully.

"Oh Ma we were so scared," a kid says.

And just for a second, the shadow of what easily might have been passes over the room, making what is more sharply sweet.

"Go on," Margaret says.

> The accident continues under investigation. A jubilant Margaret Valentine spoke briefly with reporters about her plans for the Museum's expansion. "It'll be a traveling museum with revolving exhibits," she said. "Life-size dioramas. Sideshows. Video games. Lots of audience participation. It'll go from town to town. Special shows for schoolkids."

"I saw exactly the direction the Museum must go in," Margaret says. "A place large enough for all that's in storage."

"Was it like a dream, Ma? A vision?"

"No," Margaret says. "It was like a preview. I looked back and saw the future."

The daughter continues to read.

The Museum has assembled a distinguished honorary and advisory board including, among others:

Naomi Weisstein
Tamsen Donner
Esther Broner
Mary Magdalene
Faith Gabelnick
Nancy Wilson Ross
Charlotte Perkins Gilman
Lillian Hellman
Jane Fonda
Tillie Olsen
Jessie Bernard
Elizabeth Janeway
Jo March
Emmaline, Christabel, and
    Sylvia Pankhurst
Dorothy Parker
Emily Dickinson
Judy Chicago
Sonia Johnson
Dorothy Day
Sadie Coats
Flo Kennedy
Celia Gilbert

Sandra Elkin
Diana O'Hehir
Marvella Bayh
Shirley Chisholm
Jane Hart
Emma Kay Harrod
Midge Costanza
Pauli Murray
Elizabeth Blackwell
Colette
Ethel Waters
Peg Bracken
Julia Cooley Altrocchi
Carolyn Heilbrun
Diane Christian
Adrienne Rich
Nancy Tonachel Gabriel
Sacajawea
Gloria Steinem
Marge Piercy
Fran Norris
Karen Horney
Ellen Goodman

302

Helen De Rosis
Victoria Y. Pellegrino
Alice Walker
Mary Kay Blakely
Maxine Hong Kingston
Vivian Gornick
Alix Kates Shulman
Sister Theresa Kane
Ann Petrie
Liv Ullmann
Michele Murray
Betty Friedan
JoAnn Gardner
Alta
Ruth Herschberger
Frances Parkinson Keyes
Billie Jean King
Martha Mitchell
Anne Bradstreet
Margaret Sanger
Abigail Adams
Lucy Stone
Lucretia Mott
Eve Merriam
Elizabeth Cady Stanton
Katharine Hepburn

Bella Abzug
Babi Burke
Doris Betts
Rachel Carson
Barbara Copley
Inez Steadman
Dorothy Urschalitz
Rosie Jiminez
Ellen Frankfort
Frances Kelsey
Inez Garcia
Patricia Roberts Harris
Calamity Jane
Sojourner Truth Consciousness
    Raising Group, Bethesda, MD
Patty Baker Boyd
Helen Marie Dailey Baker
Maria Christina Burton
Jennifer Susan Burton
Ursula Catherine Burton
Gabrielle Cecilia Burton
Charity Heather Burton

& the men who tried to let
    them be.

"The Museum will generate countless new jobs," Margaret Valentine said. Those interested in applying, contact B. Rose.

ABOUT THE AUTHOR

Gabrielle Burton lives in upstate New York with her husband.
She is the mother of five daughters.